W

AMELIA RULES!™

SUPERHEROES

Atheneum Books for Young Readers
New York   London   Toronto   Sydney

MEET THE GANG

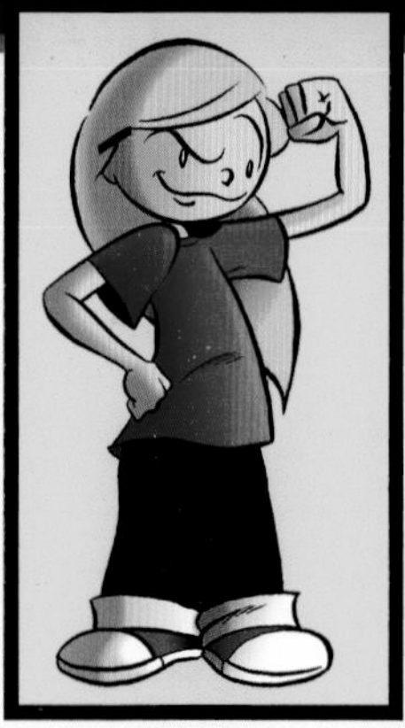

Amelia Louise McBride:
Our heroine. Wise cracking, yet sweet. She spends her time hanging out with friends and her aunt Tanner.

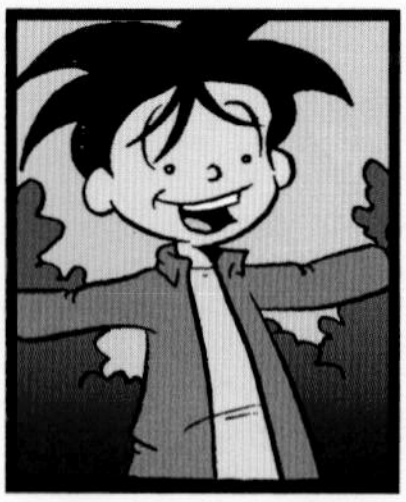

Reggie Grabinsky:
A.k.a. Captain Amazing. Founder of G.A.S.P., which he forces . . . er, encourages, his friends to join.

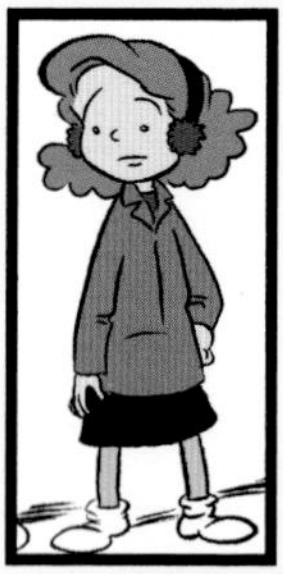

Rhonda Bleenie:
Smart, stubborn, and loud. She wears her heart on her sleeve and it's filled with love for Reggie.

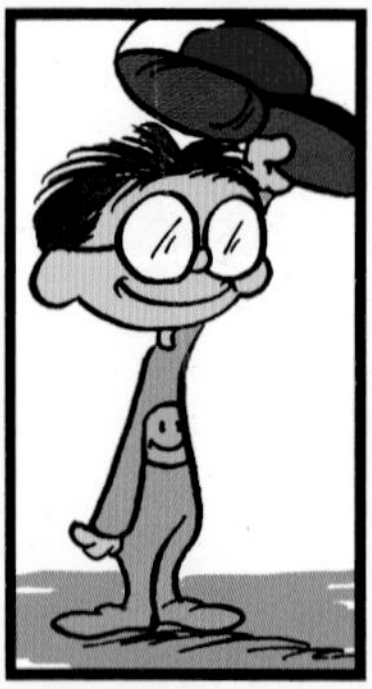

Pajamaman:
Never speaks. Always cool. His feetie jammies tell you what's on his mind.

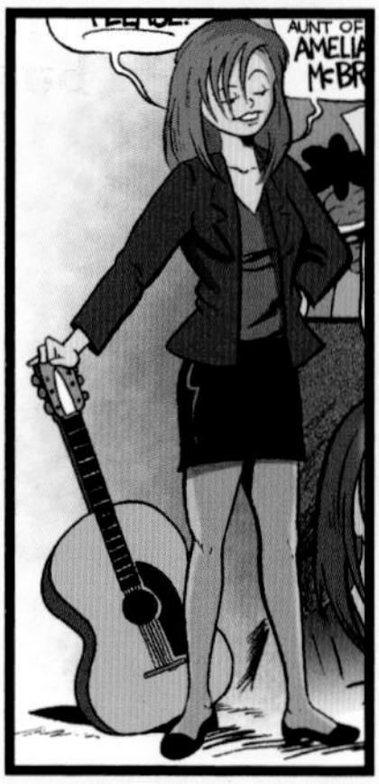
AUNT OF
AMELIA

Tanner:
Amelia's aunt and a former rock 'n' roll superstar.

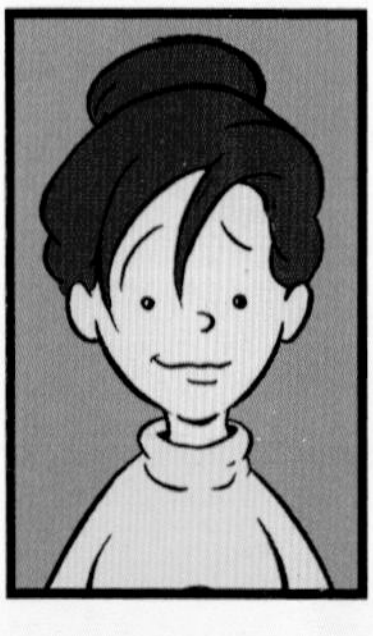

Amelia's Mom (Mary):
Starting a new life in Pennsylvania with Amelia after the divorce.

Amelia's Dad:
Still lives in New York, and misses Amelia terribly.

G.A.S.P.
Gathering Of Awesome Super Pals. The superhero club Reggie founded.

Park View Terrace Ninjas:
Club across town and nemesis to G.A.S.P.

Kyle:
The main ninja. Kind of a jerk but not without charm.

Joan:
Former Park View Terrace Ninja (nemesis of G.A.S.P.), now friends with Amelia and company.

Tweenie Zeenie:
A local kid-run magazine and Web site.

ATHENEUM BOOKS FOR YOUNG READERS
An imprint of Simon & Schuster Children's Publishing Division
1230 Avenue of the Americas, New York, New York 10020
This book is a work of fiction. Any references to historical events, real people,
or real locales are used fictitiously. Other names, characters, places, and incidents
are products of the author's imagination, and any resemblance to actual events
or locales or persons, living or dead, is entirely coincidental.
Copyright © 2006, 2010 by Jimmy Gownley
All rights reserved, including the right of reproduction in whole or in part in any form.
ATHENEUM BOOKS FOR YOUNG READERS is a registered trademark of Simon & Schuster, Inc.
For information about special discounts for bulk purchases, please contact Simon
& Schuster Special Sales at 1-866-506-1949 or business@simonandschuster.com.
The Simon & Schuster Speakers Bureau can bring authors to your live event. For more
information or to book an event, contact the Simon & Schuster Speakers Bureau at
1-866-248-3049 or visit our website at www.simonspeakers.com.
Book design by Jimmy Gownley and Sonia Chaghatzbanian
The text for this book is hand-lettered.
The illustrations for this book are digitally rendered.
Manufactured in China
0212 GFC
First Atheneum Books for Young Readers hardcover edition October 2011
2 4 6 8 10 9 7 5 3
The Library of Congress has cataloged the paperback edition as follows:
Jimmy Gownley.
Superheroes / [Jimmy Gownley].—1st ed.
p. cm.—(Jimmy Gownley's Amelia rules! ; 3)
Summary: Amelia McBride faces more changes as her aunt Tanner prepares to
move away, new friend Trish hides a terrible secret, and super-hero-wannabe
Reggie vows to destroy the evil Legion of Steves.
ISBN 978-1-4169-8606-5 (pbk)
1. Graphic novels. [1. Graphic novels. 2. Moving, Household—Fiction. 3. Secrets—Fiction.
4. Divorce—Fiction] I. Title.
PZ7.7.G69 Sup 2010
[Fic]—dc23   2010286762
ISBN 978-1-4424-4540-6 (hc)
These comics were originally published individually by Renaissance Press.

To Major Stephen M. Murphy.
This book is for you, with thanks
for your service to our country,
and for your friendship.

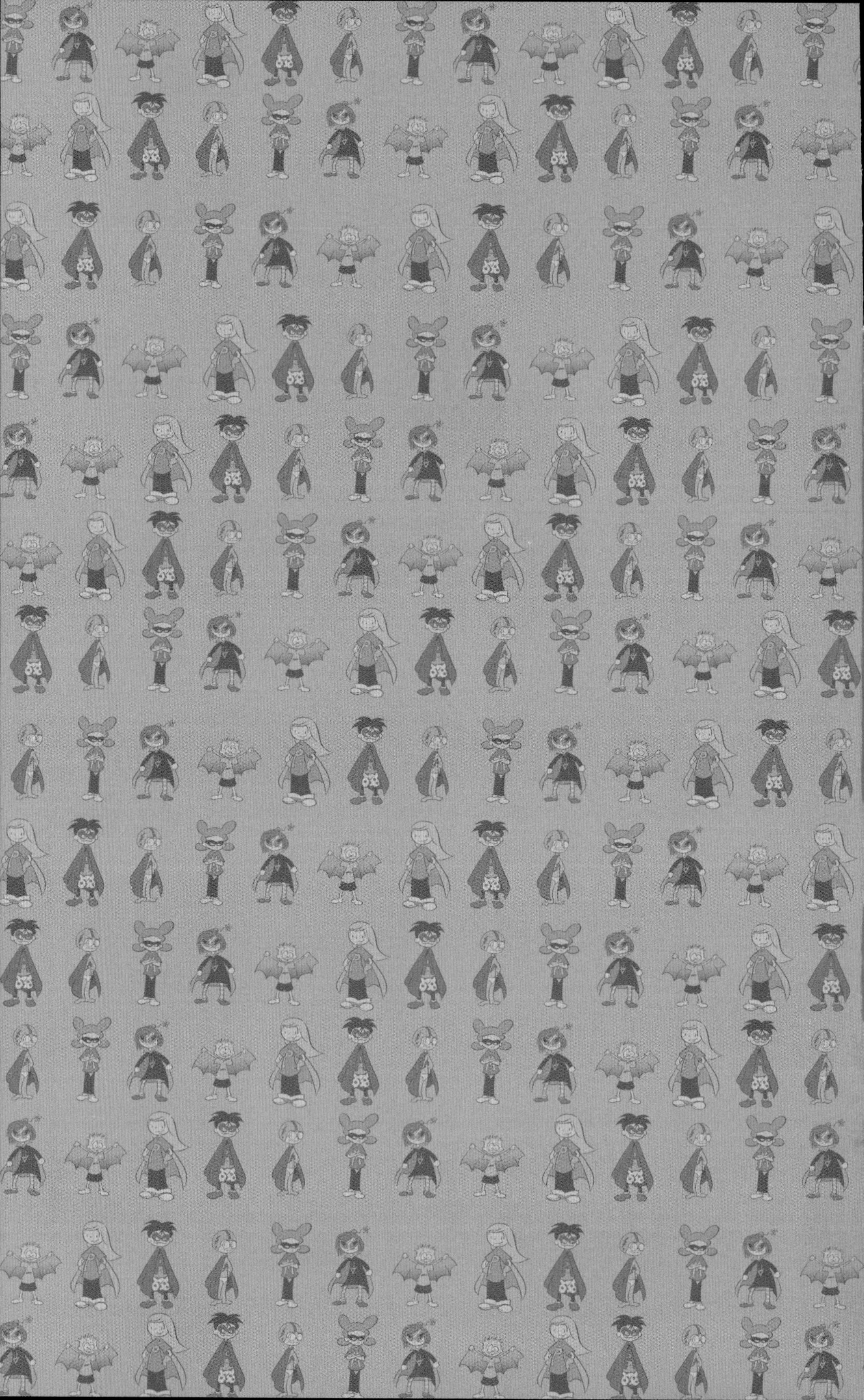

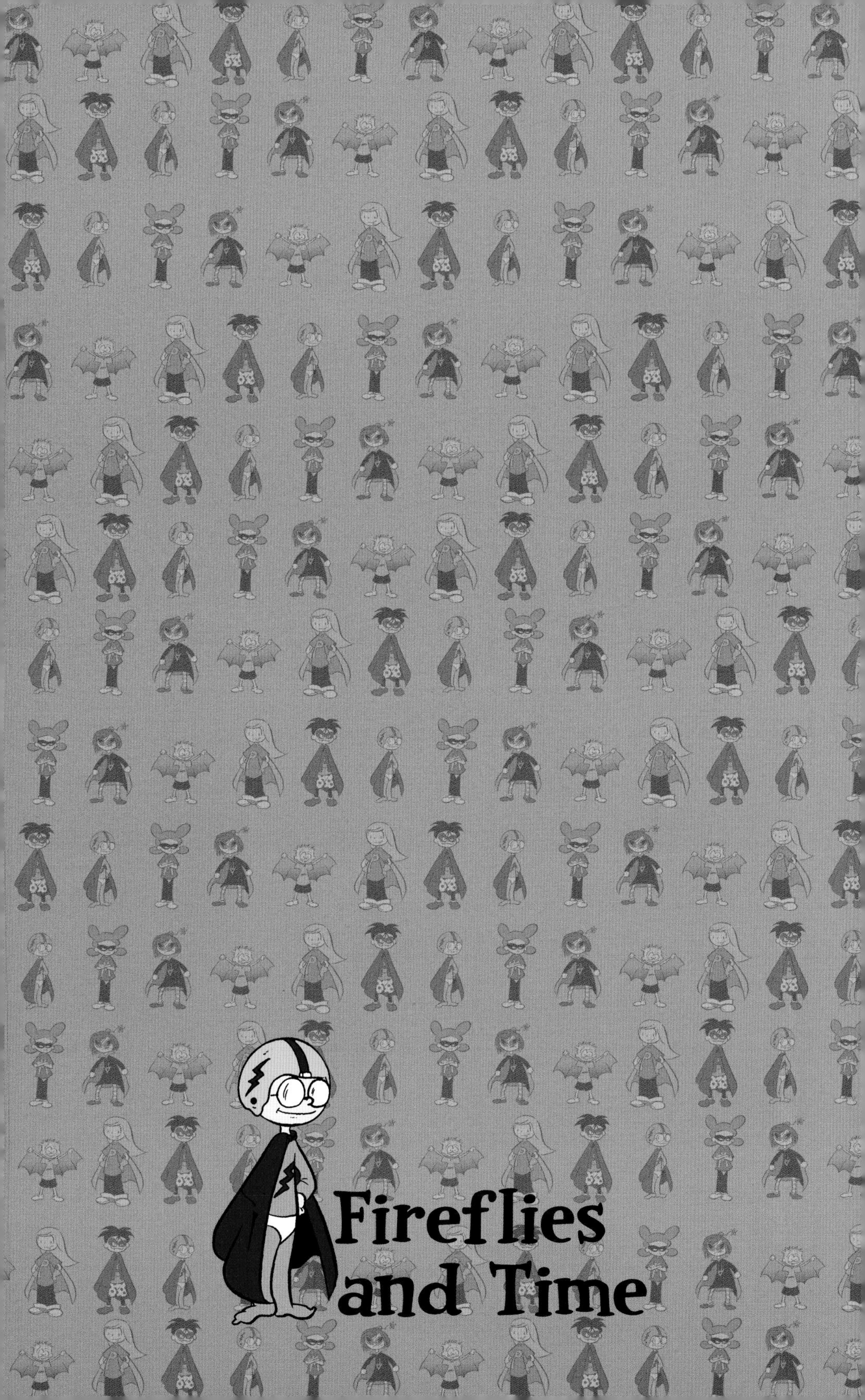
Fireflies
and Time

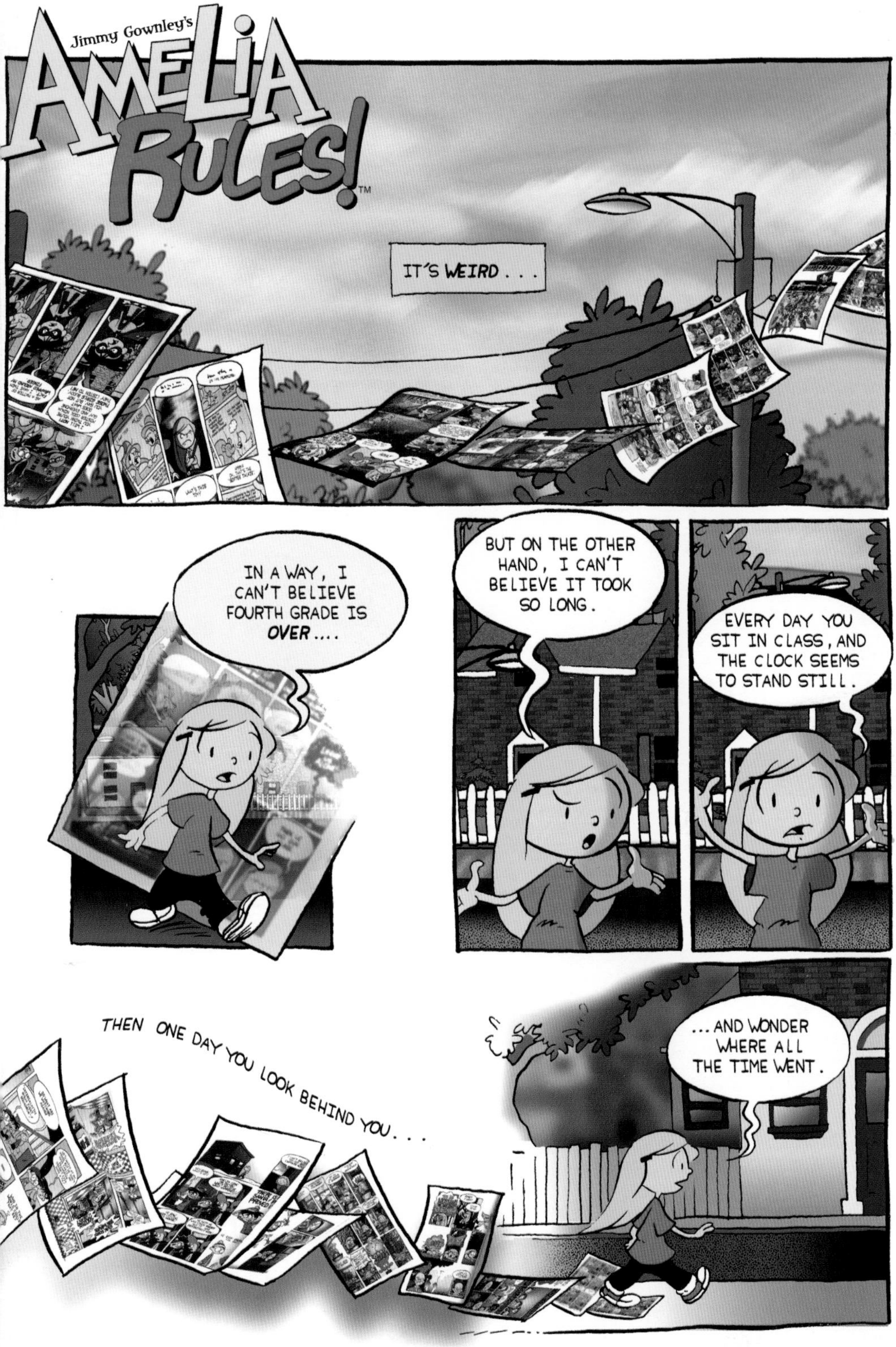
Jimmy Gownley's
AMELIA RULES!™
IT'S WEIRD . . .
IN A WAY, I CAN'T BELIEVE FOURTH GRADE IS OVER....
BUT ON THE OTHER HAND, I CAN'T BELIEVE IT TOOK SO LONG.
EVERY DAY YOU SIT IN CLASS, AND THE CLOCK SEEMS TO STAND STILL.
THEN ONE DAY YOU LOOK BEHIND YOU . . .
. . . AND WONDER WHERE ALL THE TIME WENT.

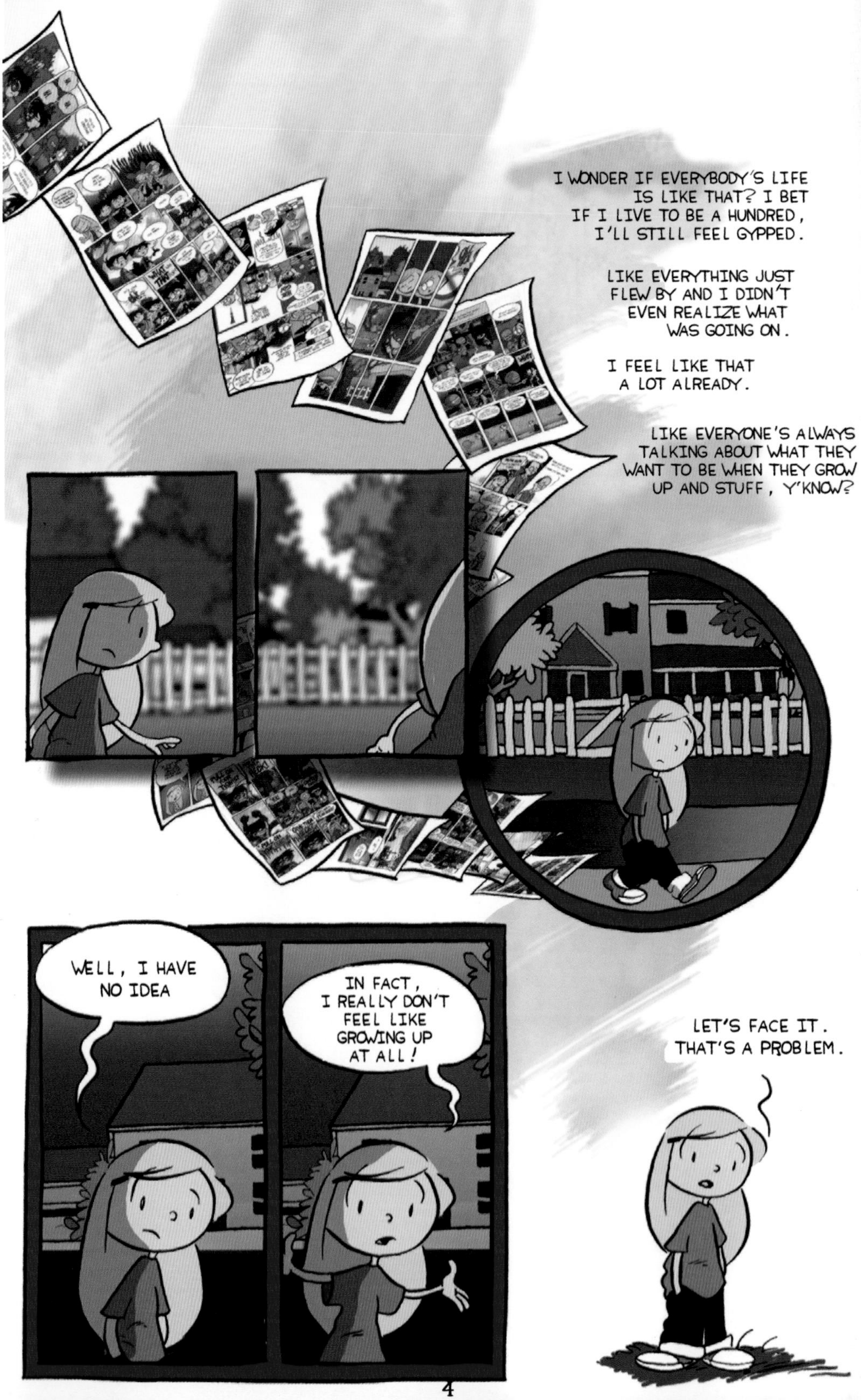
I WONDER IF EVERYBODY'S LIFE IS LIKE THAT? I BET IF I LIVE TO BE A HUNDRED, I'LL STILL FEEL GYPPED.
LIKE EVERYTHING JUST FLEW BY AND I DIDN'T EVEN REALIZE WHAT WAS GOING ON.
I FEEL LIKE THAT A LOT ALREADY.
LIKE EVERYONE'S ALWAYS TALKING ABOUT WHAT THEY WANT TO BE WHEN THEY GROW UP AND STUFF, Y'KNOW?
WELL, I HAVE NO IDEA
IN FACT, I REALLY DON'T FEEL LIKE GROWING UP AT ALL!
LET'S FACE IT. THAT'S A PROBLEM.

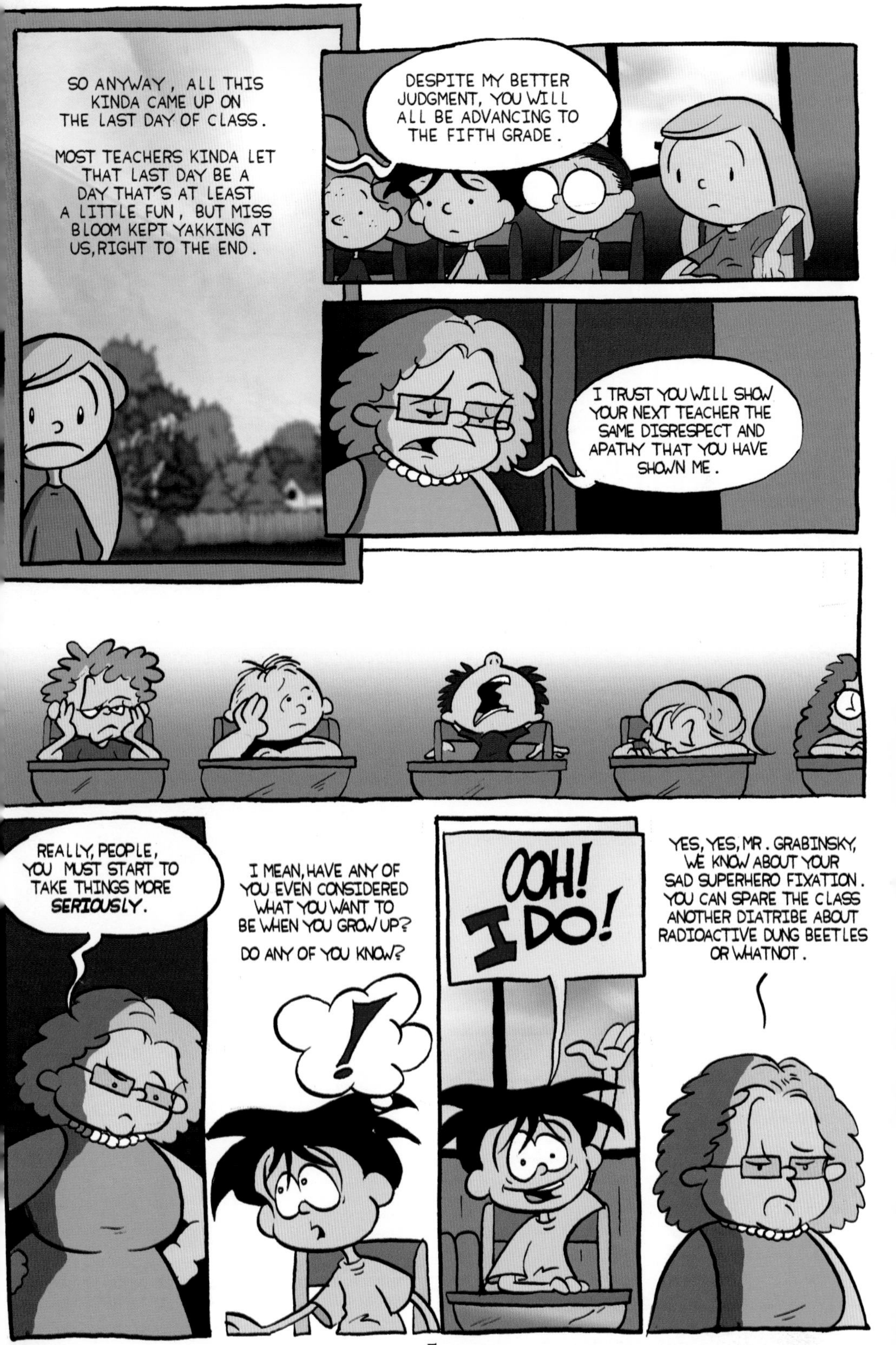
SO ANYWAY, ALL THIS KINDA CAME UP ON THE LAST DAY OF CLASS.
MOST TEACHERS KINDA LET THAT LAST DAY BE A DAY THAT'S AT LEAST A LITTLE FUN, BUT MISS BLOOM KEPT YAKKING AT US, RIGHT TO THE END.
DESPITE MY BETTER JUDGMENT, YOU WILL ALL BE ADVANCING TO THE FIFTH GRADE.
I TRUST YOU WILL SHOW YOUR NEXT TEACHER THE SAME DISRESPECT AND APATHY THAT YOU HAVE SHOWN ME.
REALLY, PEOPLE, YOU MUST START TO TAKE THINGS MORE SERIOUSLY.
I MEAN, HAVE ANY OF YOU EVEN CONSIDERED WHAT YOU WANT TO BE WHEN YOU GROW UP?
DO ANY OF YOU KNOW?
!
OOH! I DO!
YES, YES, MR. GRABINSKY, WE KNOW ABOUT YOUR SAD SUPERHERO FIXATION. YOU CAN SPARE THE CLASS ANOTHER DIATRIBE ABOUT RADIOACTIVE DUNG BEETLES OR WHATNOT.

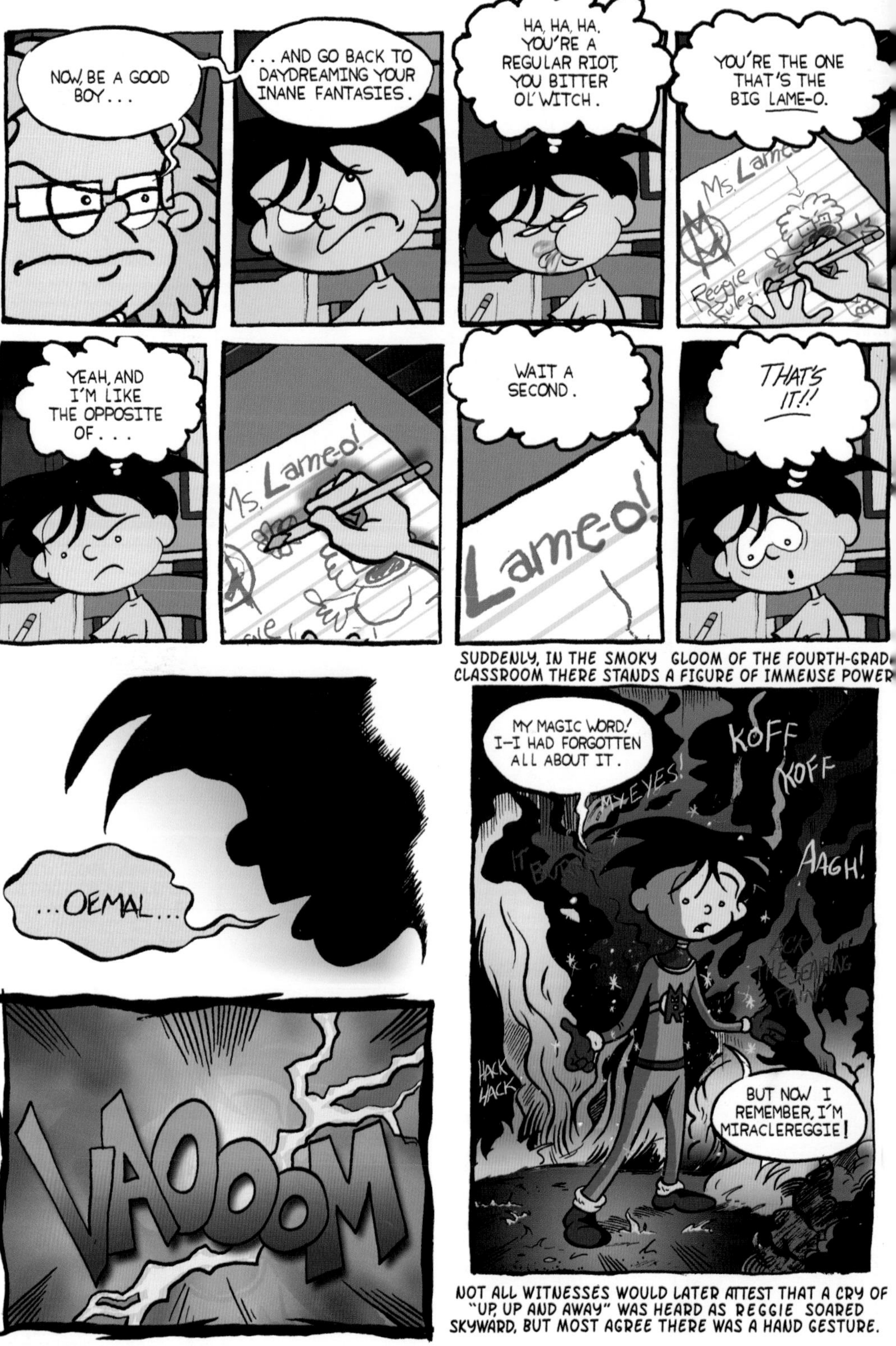
NOW, BE A GOOD BOY . . .
. . . AND GO BACK TO DAYDREAMING YOUR INANE FANTASIES.
HA, HA, HA. YOU'RE A REGULAR RIOT, YOU BITTER OL' WITCH.
YOU'RE THE ONE THAT'S THE BIG LAME-O.
Ms. Lame-o
Reggie Rules!
YEAH, AND I'M LIKE THE OPPOSITE OF . . .
Ms. Lame-o!
WAIT A SECOND.
Lame-o!
THAT'S IT!!
. . . OEMAL . . .
VAOOOM
SUDDENLY, IN THE SMOKY GLOOM OF THE FOURTH-GRADE CLASSROOM THERE STANDS A FIGURE OF IMMENSE POWER
MY MAGIC WORD! I—I HAD FORGOTTEN ALL ABOUT IT.
KOFF
KOFF
MY EYES!
AAGH!
HACK HACK
BUT NOW I REMEMBER, I'M MIRACLEREGGIE!
NOT ALL WITNESSES WOULD LATER ATTEST THAT A CRY OF "UP, UP AND AWAY" WAS HEARD AS REGGIE SOARED SKYWARD, BUT MOST AGREE THERE WAS A HAND GESTURE.

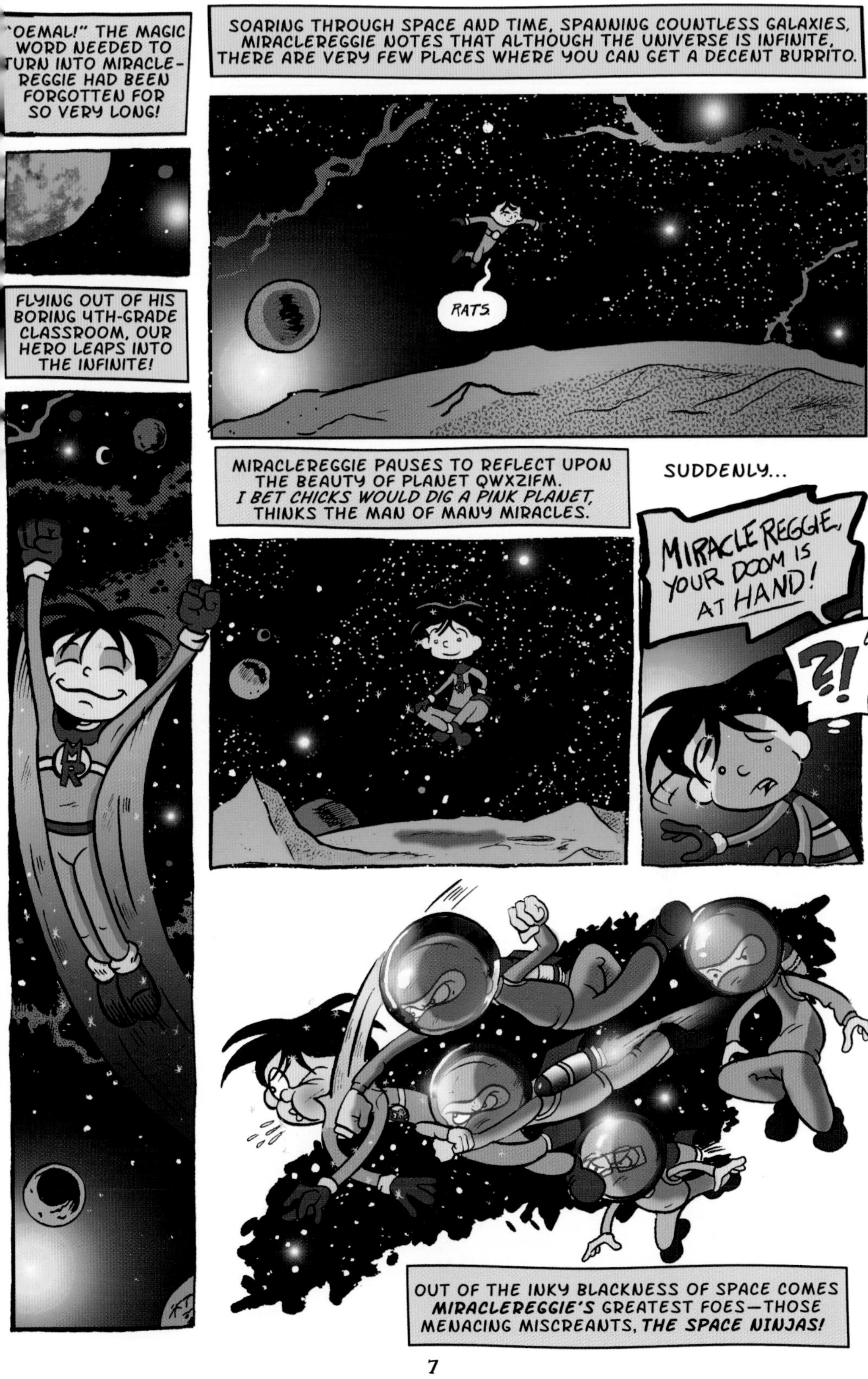
"OEMAL!" THE MAGIC WORD NEEDED TO TURN INTO MIRACLE-REGGIE HAD BEEN FORGOTTEN FOR SO VERY LONG!
FLYING OUT OF HIS BORING 4TH-GRADE CLASSROOM, OUR HERO LEAPS INTO THE INFINITE!
SOARING THROUGH SPACE AND TIME, SPANNING COUNTLESS GALAXIES, MIRACLEREGGIE NOTES THAT ALTHOUGH THE UNIVERSE IS INFINITE, THERE ARE VERY FEW PLACES WHERE YOU CAN GET A DECENT BURRITO.
RATS.
MIRACLEREGGIE PAUSES TO REFLECT UPON THE BEAUTY OF PLANET QWXZIFM. *I BET CHICKS WOULD DIG A PINK PLANET,* THINKS THE MAN OF MANY MIRACLES.
SUDDENLY...
MIRACLE REGGIE, YOUR DOOM IS AT HAND!
?!
OUT OF THE INKY BLACKNESS OF SPACE COMES *MIRACLEREGGIE'S* GREATEST FOES—THOSE MENACING MISCREANTS, *THE SPACE NINJAS!*

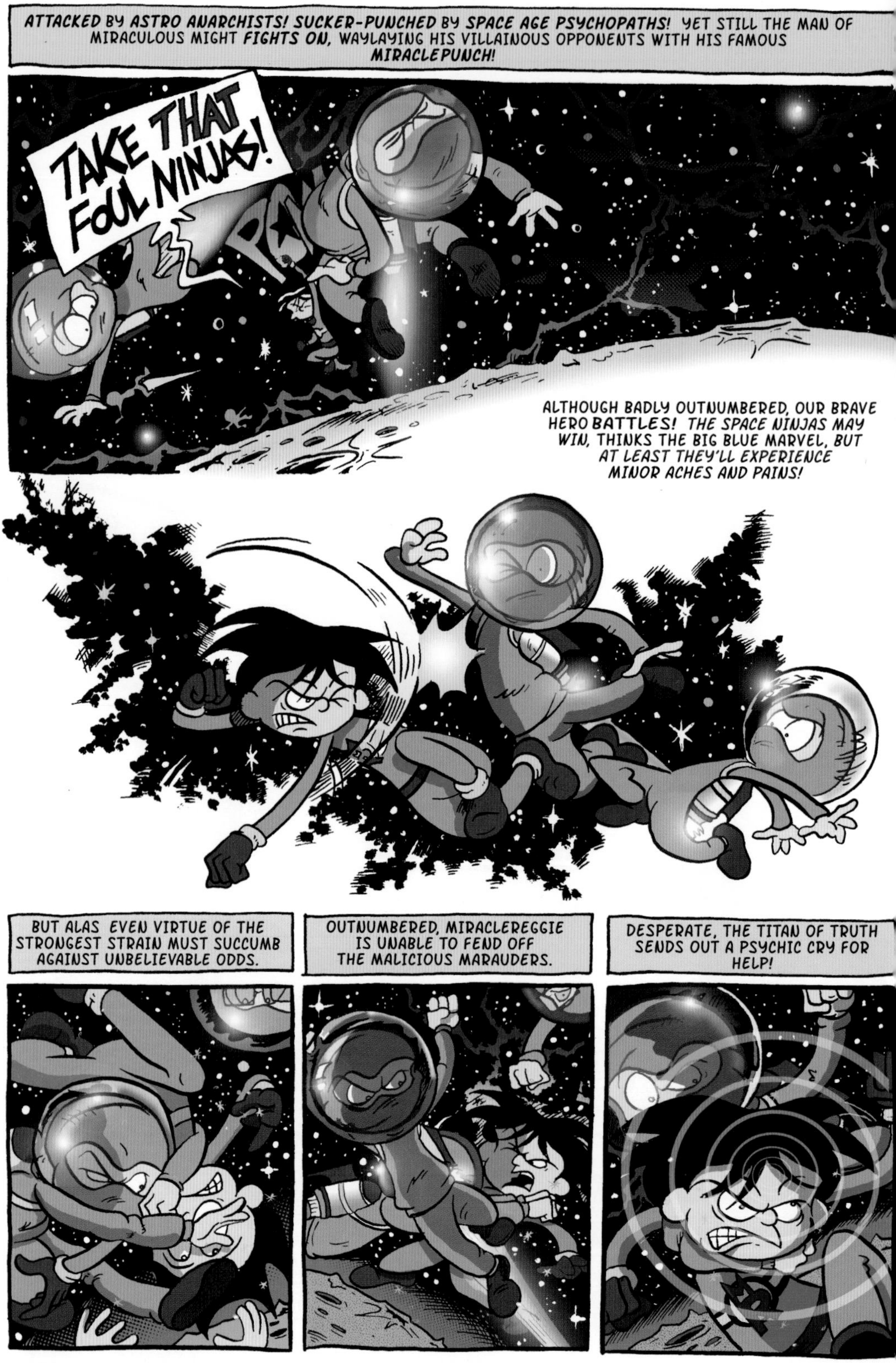
ATTACKED BY ASTRO ANARCHISTS! SUCKER-PUNCHED BY SPACE AGE PSYCHOPATHS! YET STILL THE MAN OF MIRACULOUS MIGHT FIGHTS ON, WAYLAYING HIS VILLAINOUS OPPONENTS WITH HIS FAMOUS MIRACLEPUNCH!
TAKE THAT FOUL NINJAS!
ALTHOUGH BADLY OUTNUMBERED, OUR BRAVE HERO BATTLES! THE SPACE NINJAS MAY WIN, THINKS THE BIG BLUE MARVEL, BUT AT LEAST THEY'LL EXPERIENCE MINOR ACHES AND PAINS!
BUT ALAS EVEN VIRTUE OF THE STRONGEST STRAIN MUST SUCCUMB AGAINST UNBELIEVABLE ODDS.
OUTNUMBERED, MIRACLEREGGIE IS UNABLE TO FEND OFF THE MALICIOUS MARAUDERS.
DESPERATE, THE TITAN OF TRUTH SENDS OUT A PSYCHIC CRY FOR HELP!

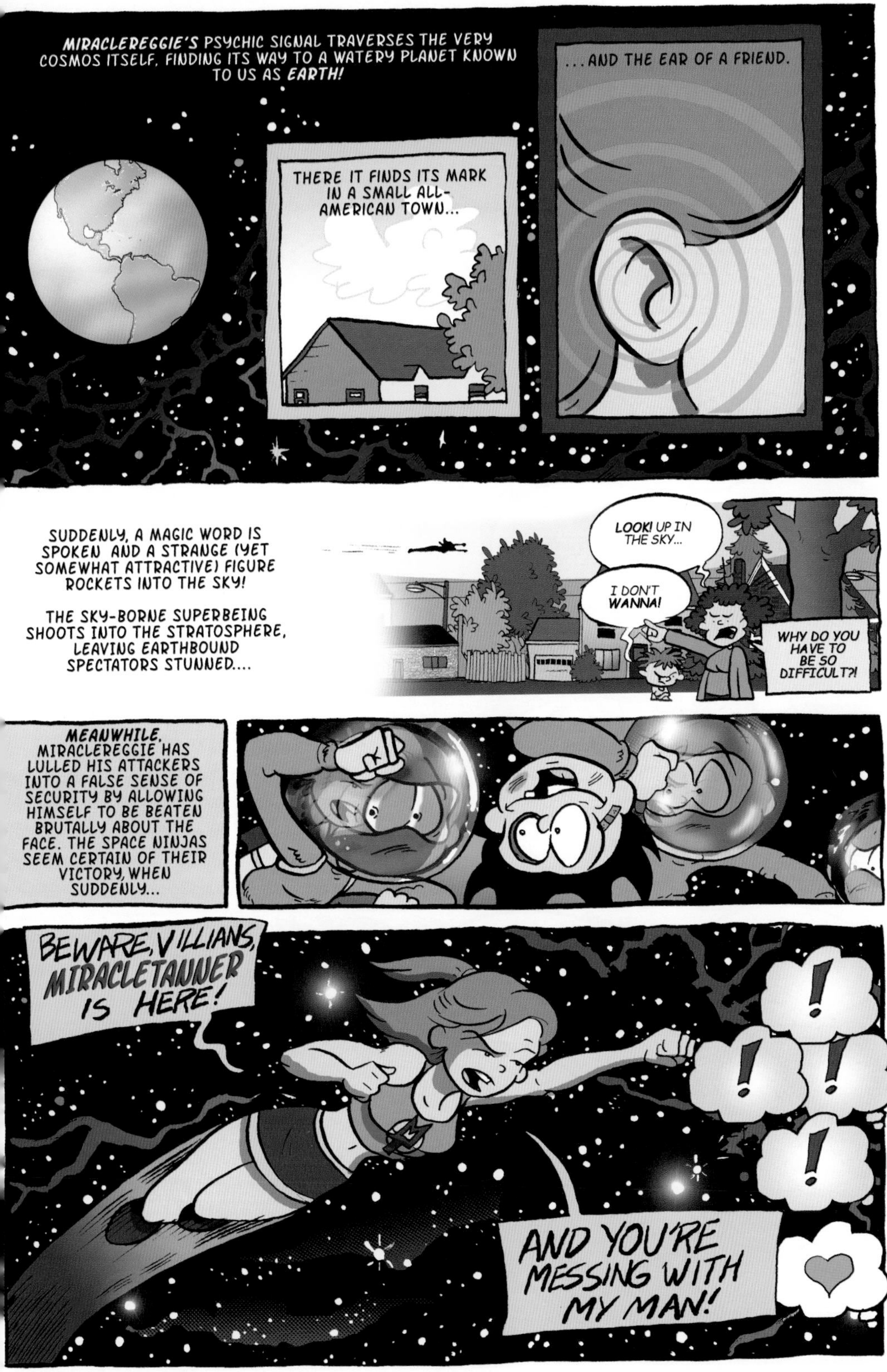
MIRACLEREGGIE'S PSYCHIC SIGNAL TRAVERSES THE VERY COSMOS ITSELF, FINDING ITS WAY TO A WATERY PLANET KNOWN TO US AS EARTH!
THERE IT FINDS ITS MARK IN A SMALL ALL-AMERICAN TOWN...
...AND THE EAR OF A FRIEND.
SUDDENLY, A MAGIC WORD IS SPOKEN AND A STRANGE (YET SOMEWHAT ATTRACTIVE) FIGURE ROCKETS INTO THE SKY!
THE SKY-BORNE SUPERBEING SHOOTS INTO THE STRATOSPHERE, LEAVING EARTHBOUND SPECTATORS STUNNED....
LOOK! UP IN THE SKY...
I DON'T WANNA!
WHY DO YOU HAVE TO BE SO DIFFICULT?!
MEANWHILE, MIRACLEREGGIE HAS LULLED HIS ATTACKERS INTO A FALSE SENSE OF SECURITY BY ALLOWING HIMSELF TO BE BEATEN BRUTALLY ABOUT THE FACE. THE SPACE NINJAS SEEM CERTAIN OF THEIR VICTORY, WHEN SUDDENLY...
BEWARE, VILLIANS, MIRACLETANNER IS HERE!
!
!
!
!
AND YOU'RE MESSING WITH MY MAN!

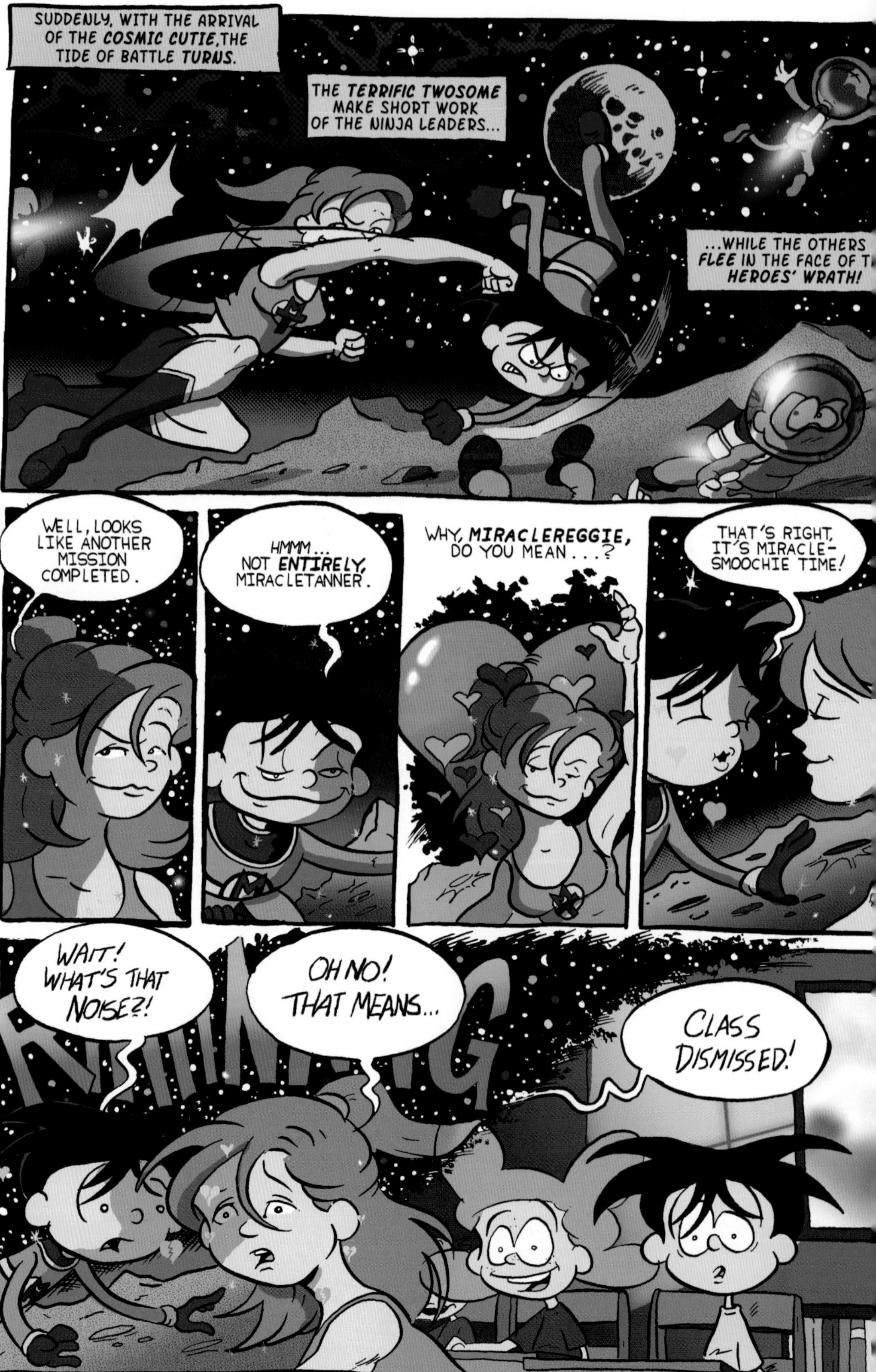
SUDDENLY, WITH THE ARRIVAL OF THE COSMIC CUTIE, THE TIDE OF BATTLE TURNS.
THE TERRIFIC TWOSOME MAKE SHORT WORK OF THE NINJA LEADERS...
...WHILE THE OTHERS FLEE IN THE FACE OF THE HEROES' WRATH!
WELL, LOOKS LIKE ANOTHER MISSION COMPLETED.
HMMM... NOT ENTIRELY, MIRACLETANNER.
WHY, MIRACLEREGGIE, DO YOU MEAN...?
THAT'S RIGHT, IT'S MIRACLE-SMOOCHIE TIME!
WAIT! WHAT'S THAT NOISE?!
OH NO! THAT MEANS...
CLASS DISMISSED!

AND THAT WAS IT. GRADE FOUR.

JOE McCART[...] ELEMENTA[...] "Weeding out t[...] wrong element[...] since 1952"

THERE IS NOTHING IN THE WORLD LIKE THE LAST DAY OF SCHOOL.

I WISH I COULD DESCRIBE IT BETTER, BUT IT'S HARD, Y'KNOW?

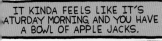

IT KINDA FEELS LIKE IT'S SATURDAY MORNING AND YOU HAVE A BOWL OF APPLE JACKS.

AND YOU'RE WATCHING CARTOONS AND IT'S ALL GOOD ONES....

AND THE CEREAL HAS MADE THE MILK ALL PINK AND SWEET....

AND MONDAY IS A HOLIDAY, AND IT'S GONNA SNOW ON TUESDAY, AND IT FEELS LIKE TIME IS STANDING STILL.

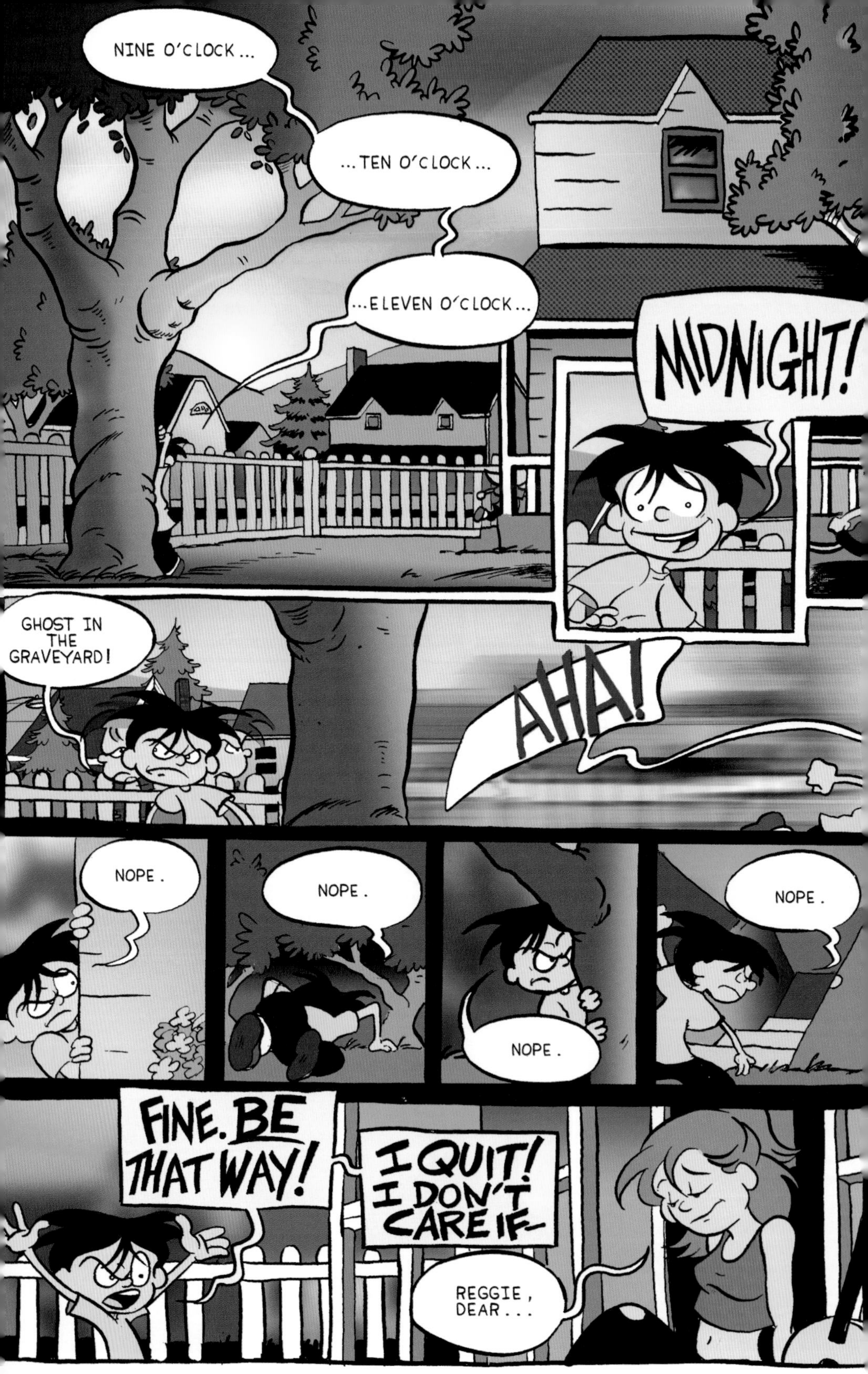
NINE O'CLOCK...
...TEN O'CLOCK...
...ELEVEN O'CLOCK...
MIDNIGHT!
GHOST IN THE GRAVEYARD!
AHA!
NOPE.
NOPE.
NOPE.
NOPE.
NOPE.
FINE. BE THAT WAY!
I QUIT! I DON'T CARE IF—
REGGIE, DEAR...

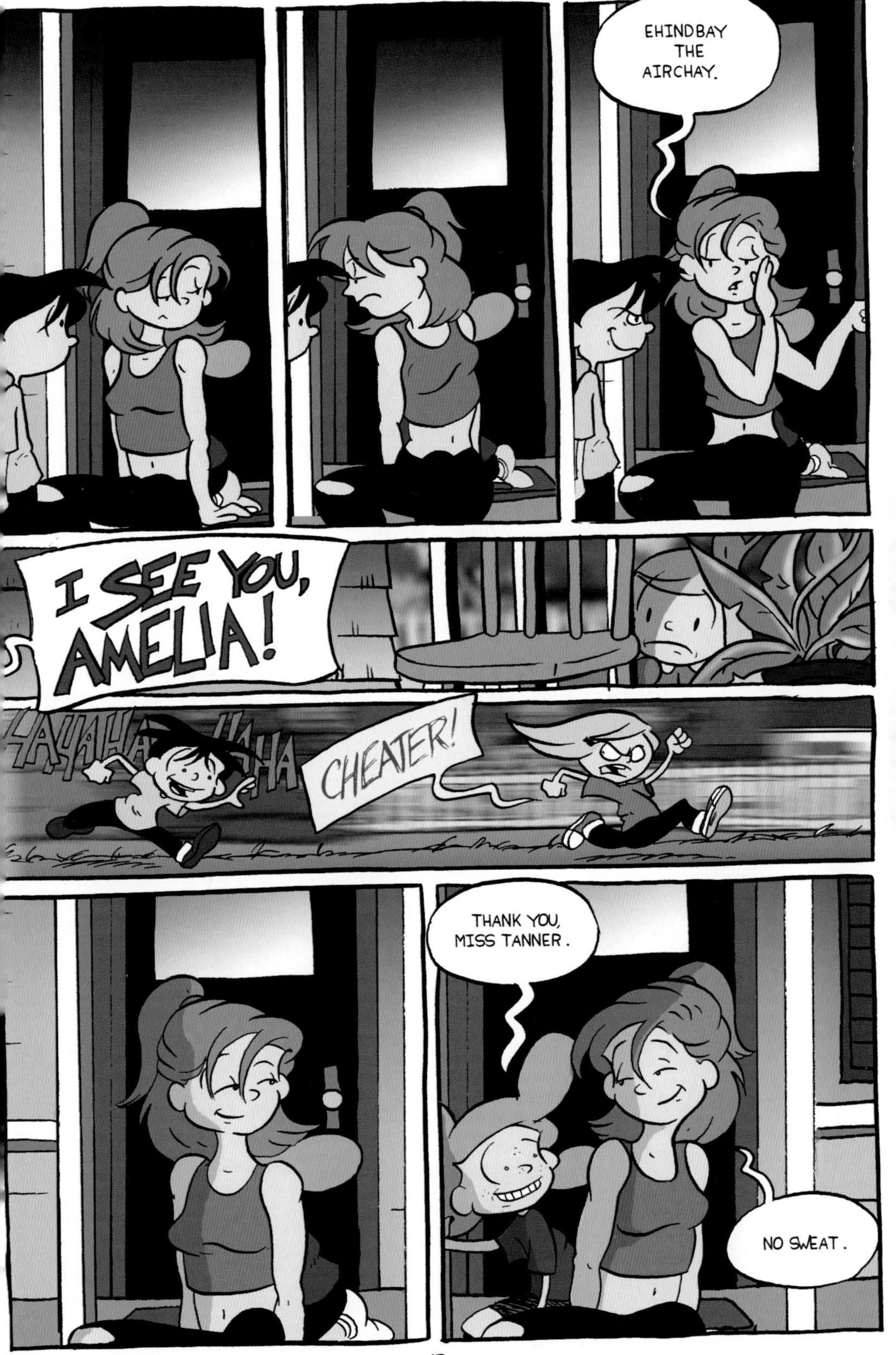
EHINDBAY THE AIRCHAY.
I SEE YOU, AMELIA!
HAHAHA HAHA
CHEATER!
THANK YOU, MISS TANNER.
NO SWEAT.

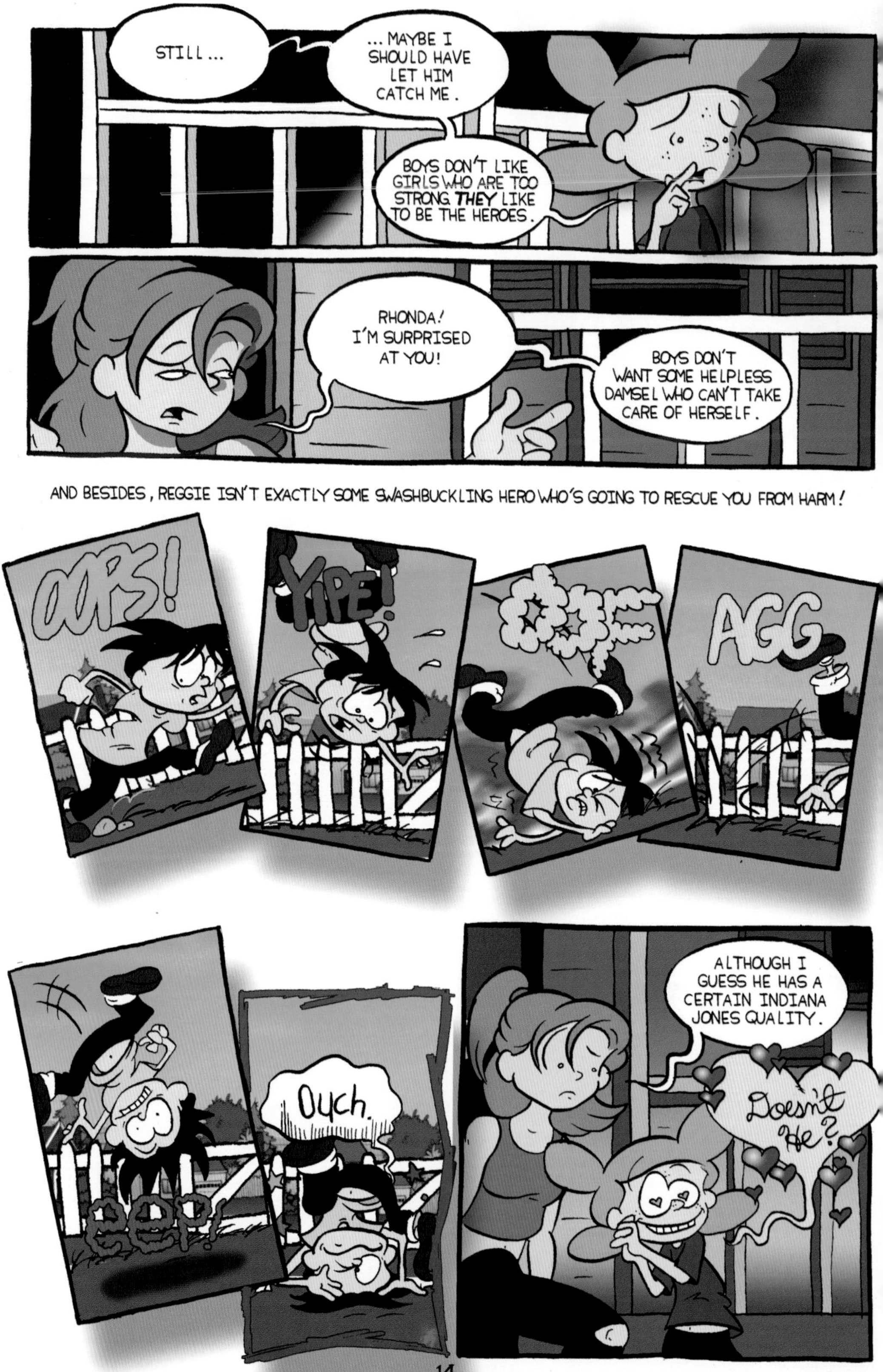
STILL ...
... MAYBE I SHOULD HAVE LET HIM CATCH ME.
BOYS DON'T LIKE GIRLS WHO ARE TOO STRONG. THEY LIKE TO BE THE HEROES.
RHONDA! I'M SURPRISED AT YOU!
BOYS DON'T WANT SOME HELPLESS DAMSEL WHO CAN'T TAKE CARE OF HERSELF.
AND BESIDES, REGGIE ISN'T EXACTLY SOME SWASHBUCKLING HERO WHO'S GOING TO RESCUE YOU FROM HARM!
OOPS!
YIPE!
AGG
Ouch.
ALTHOUGH I GUESS HE HAS A CERTAIN INDIANA JONES QUALITY.
Doesn't He?

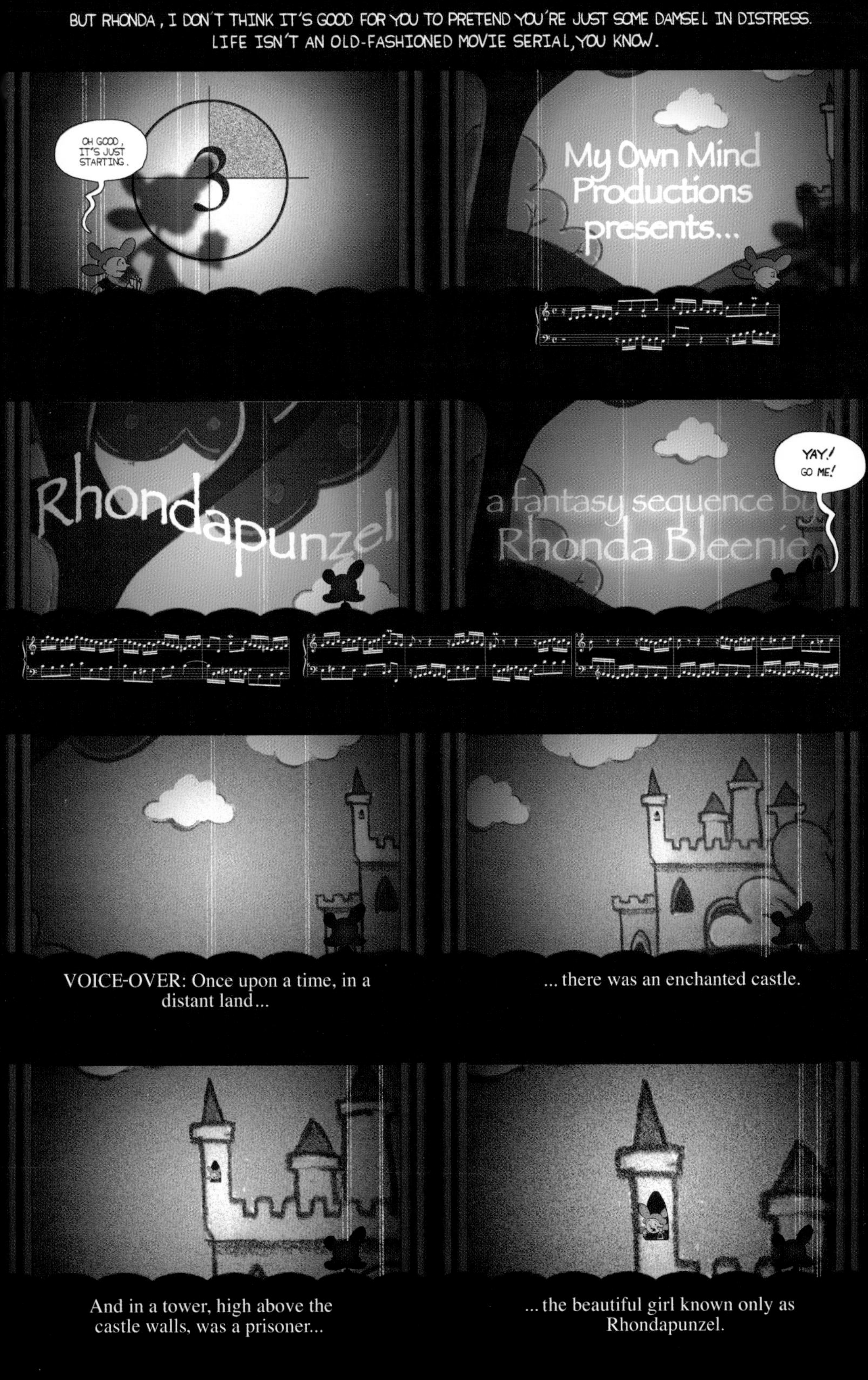
BUT RHONDA, I DON'T THINK IT'S GOOD FOR YOU TO PRETEND YOU'RE JUST SOME DAMSEL IN DISTRESS. LIFE ISN'T AN OLD-FASHIONED MOVIE SERIAL, YOU KNOW.
OH GOOD, IT'S JUST STARTING.
3
My Own Mind Productions presents...
Rhondapunzel
a fantasy sequence by Rhonda Bleenie
YAY! GO ME!
VOICE-OVER: Once upon a time, in a distant land...
... there was an enchanted castle.
And in a tower, high above the castle walls, was a prisoner...
... the beautiful girl known only as Rhondapunzel.

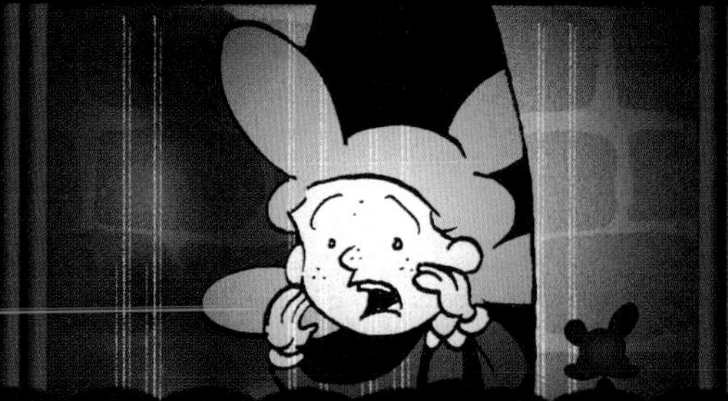

RHONDAPUNZEL: Help! Help! I, Rhondapunzel, am trapped in this tower, and in need of rescuing. (Eligible princes only need apply.)

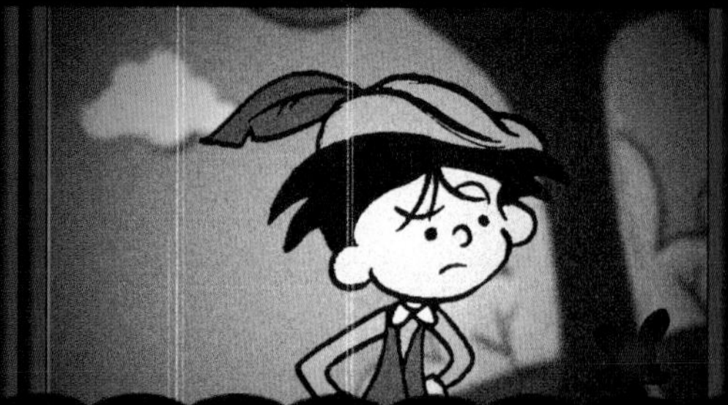

REGINALD: Hark! What doth cometh on yon morn breeze? Zounds! 'Tis the cry of a hot chick in distress!

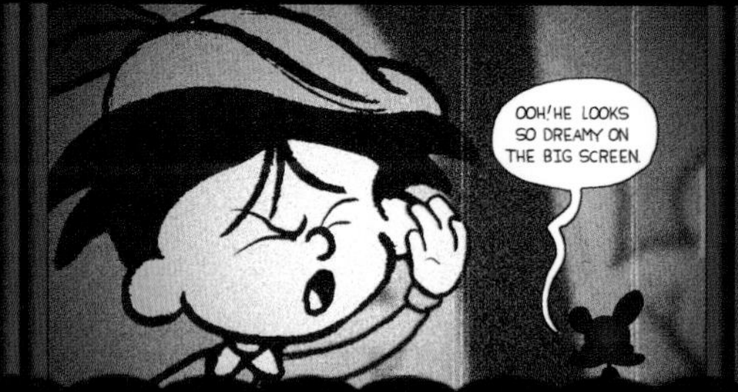
OOH! HE LOOKS SO DREAMY ON THE BIG SCREEN.

REGINALD: Fear not, fair hottie! For Reginald of the Woods is here! Lower your hair and I shall climb up to rescue you anon!

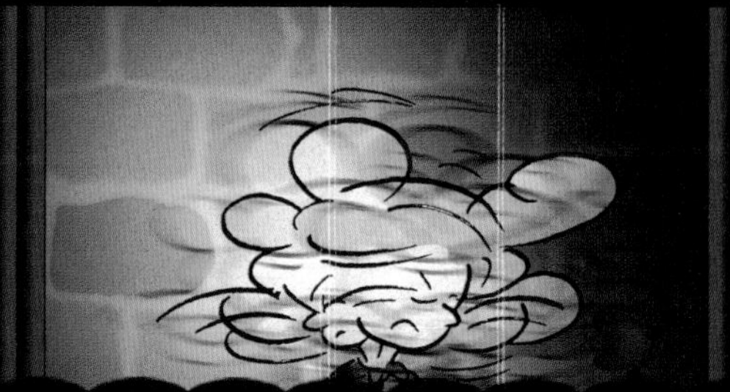

SFX: (Whip Whip Whip)

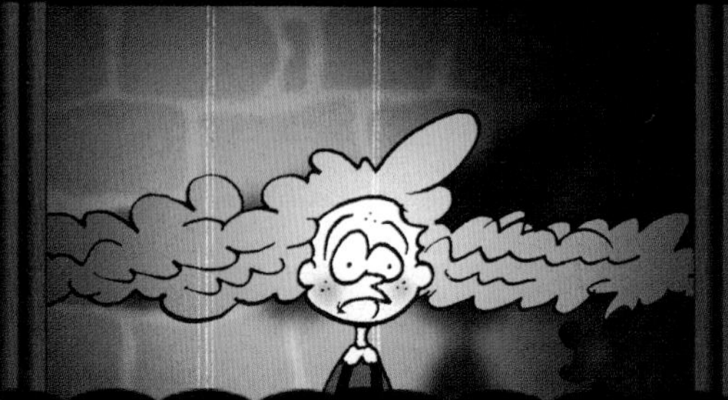

SFX: (Sproing!)
RHONDAPUNZEL: How embarrassing!

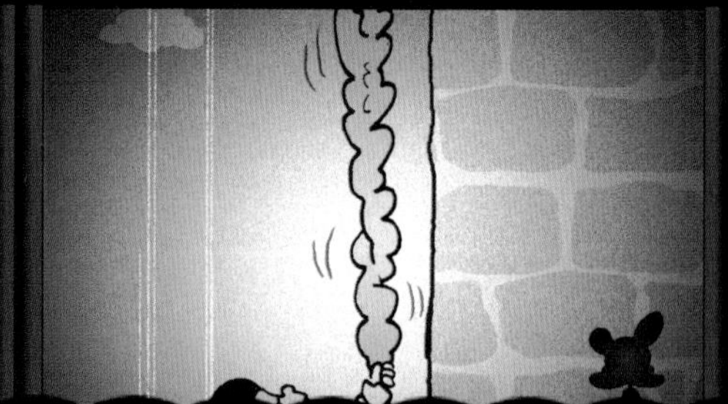

SFX: (Tug Tug)

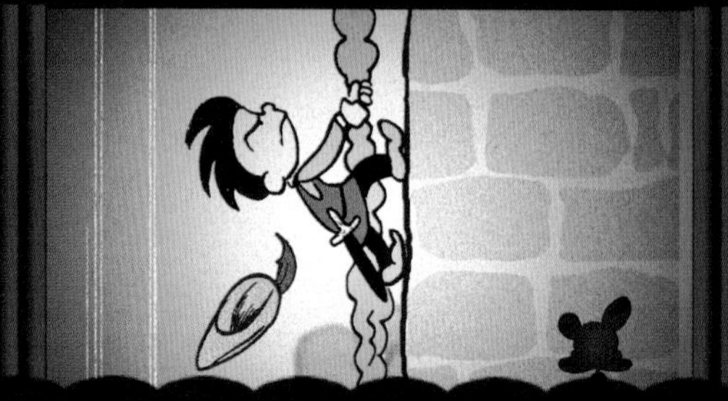

REGINALD: Huff! Huff!

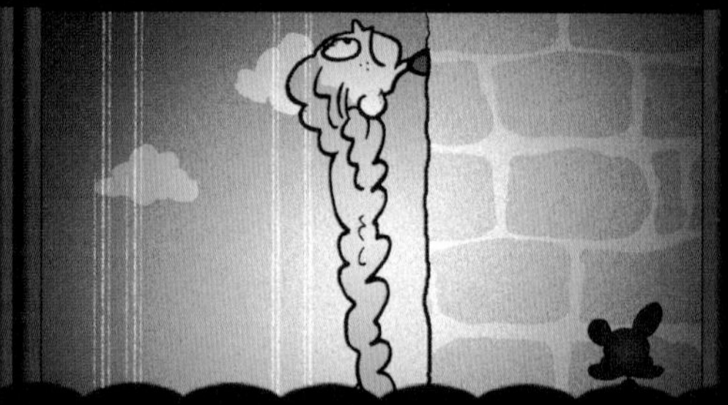

RHONDAPUNZEL: Ouch! Ouch!

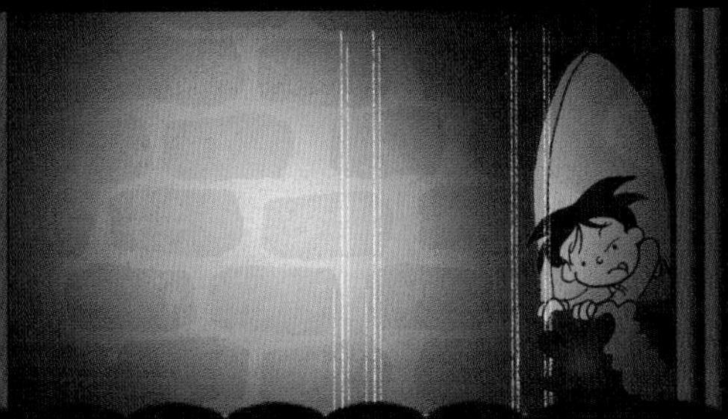

REGINALD: Take heart, fair maiden! For I, Reginald of the Woods, have come to save you.

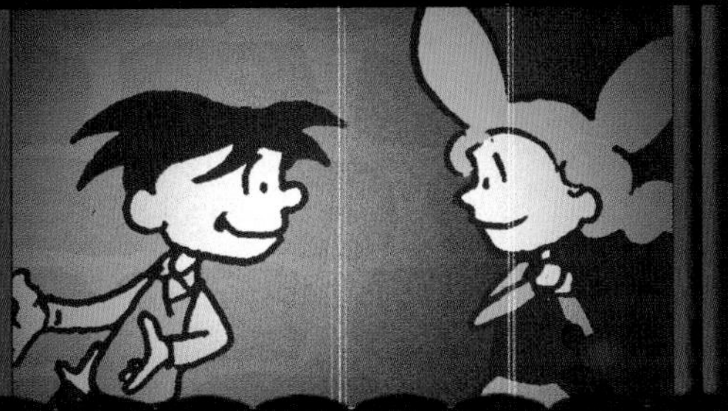

RHONDAPUNZEL: I knew that if I waited long enough, a handsome prince would come to rescue me.

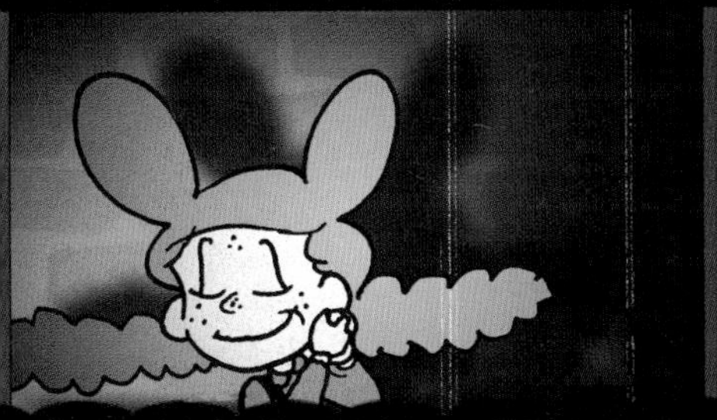

RHONDAPUNZEL: You ARE a prince, aren't you?

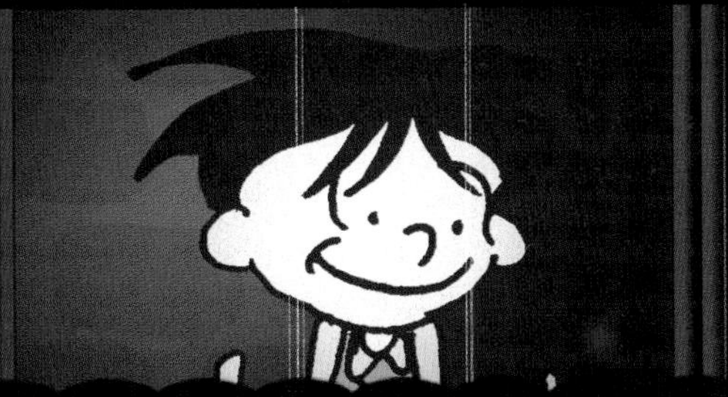

REGINALD: Well, not exactly, but my dad has most of his albums.

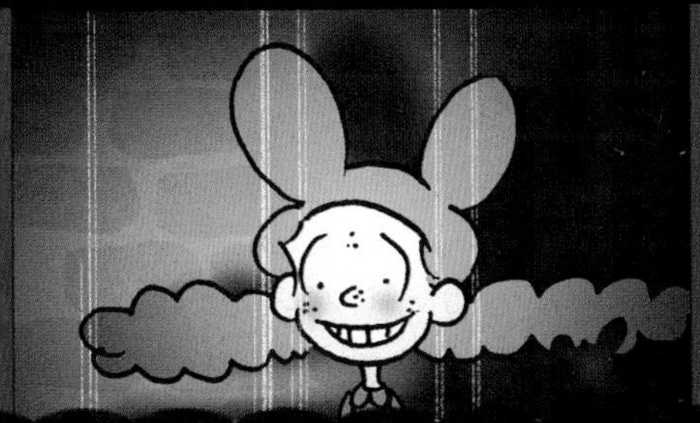

RHONDAPUNZEL: Close enough!

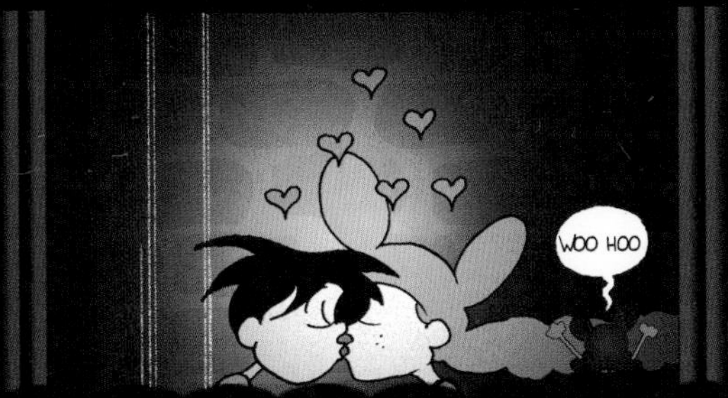
WOO HOO

SFX: Smoooooooooooooch!!

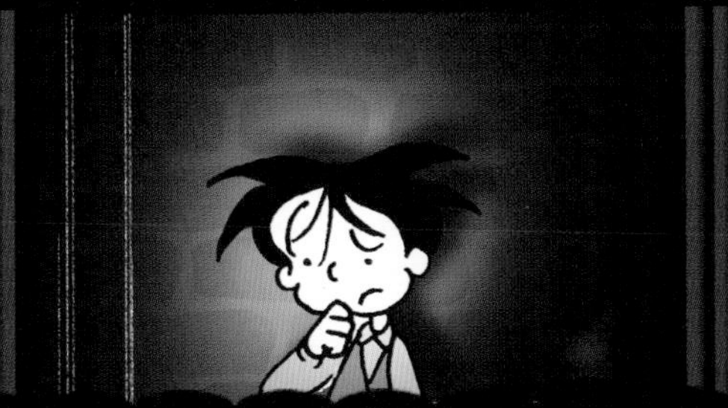

REGINALD: Hmmm...I just thought of something.
RHONDAPUNZEL: Yes, my love?

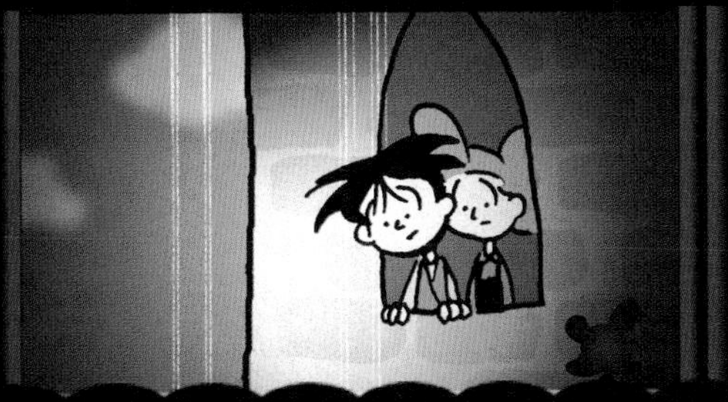

REGINALD: Now that I've rescued you, who is gonna rescue me?

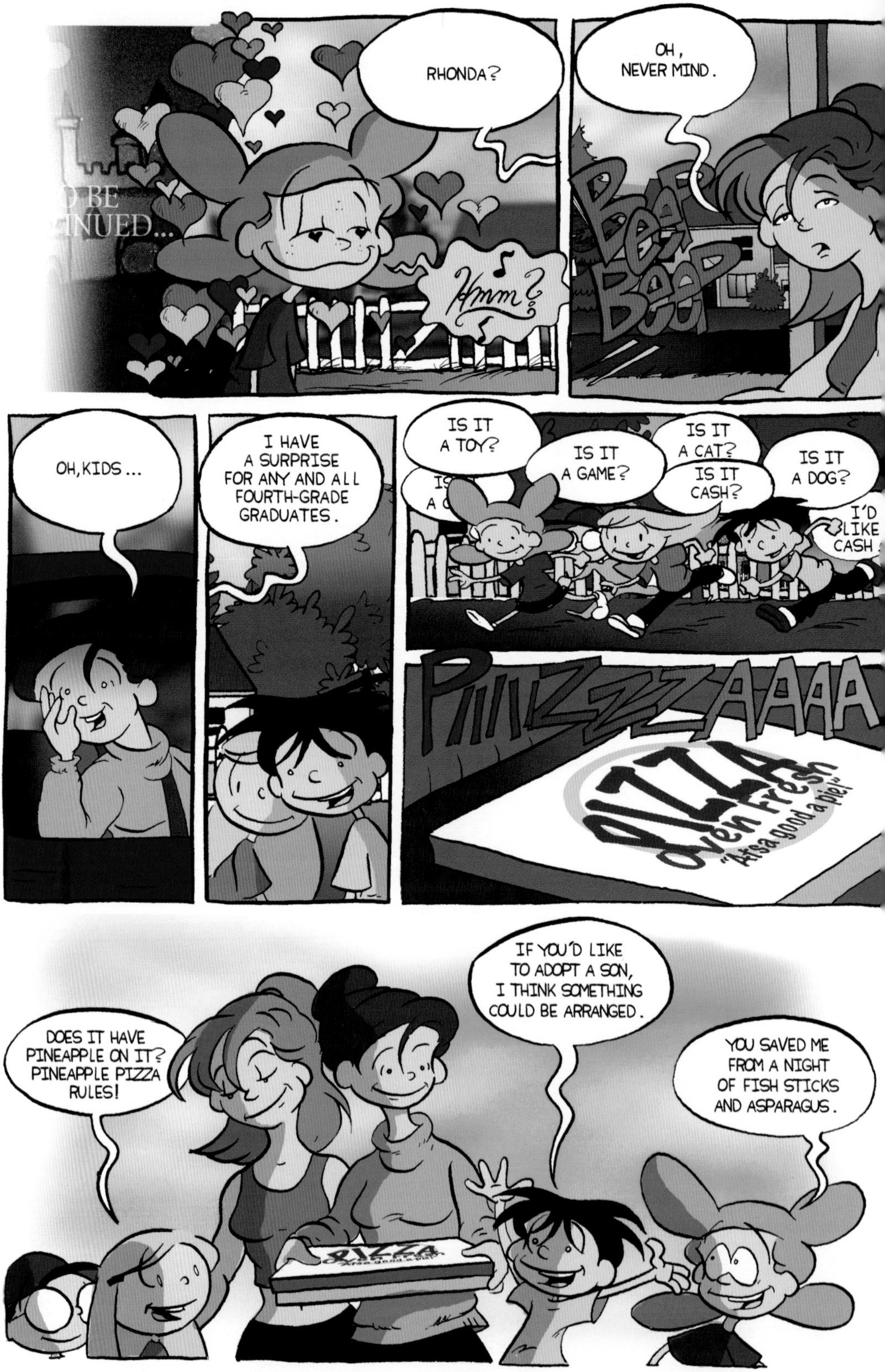
RHONDA?
Hmm?
OH, NEVER MIND.
BEEP BEEP
OH, KIDS ...
I HAVE A SURPRISE FOR ANY AND ALL FOURTH-GRADE GRADUATES.
IS IT A TOY?
IS IT A GAME?
IS IT A CAT?
IS IT CASH?
IS IT A DOG?
I'D LIKE CASH
PIIIIZZZZAAAA
PIZZA
Oven Fresh
"Atsa good a pie!"
DOES IT HAVE PINEAPPLE ON IT? PINEAPPLE PIZZA RULES!
IF YOU'D LIKE TO ADOPT A SON, I THINK SOMETHING COULD BE ARRANGED.
YOU SAVED ME FROM A NIGHT OF FISH STICKS AND ASPARAGUS.

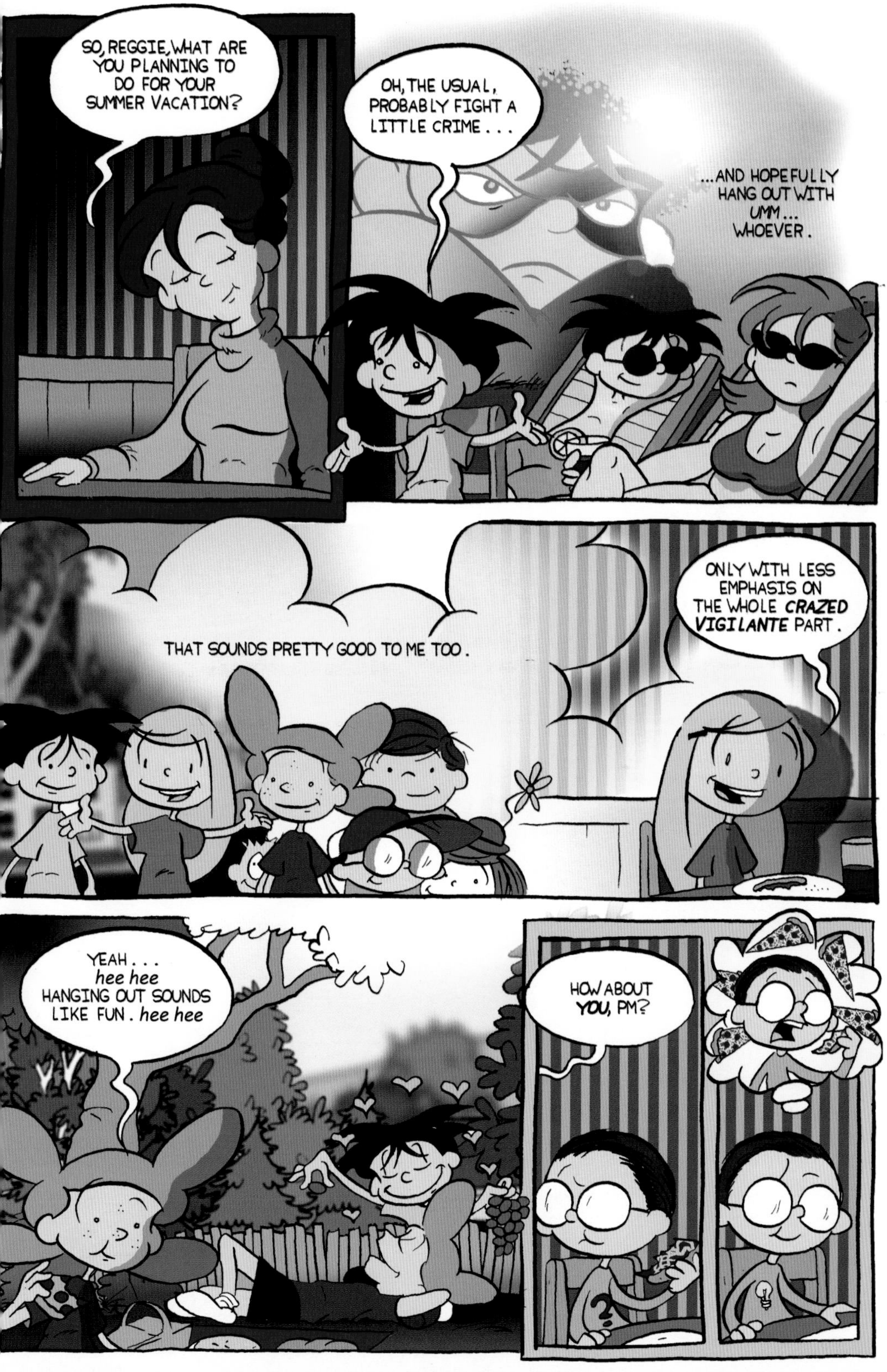
SO, REGGIE, WHAT ARE YOU PLANNING TO DO FOR YOUR SUMMER VACATION?
OH, THE USUAL, PROBABLY FIGHT A LITTLE CRIME . . .
...AND HOPEFULLY HANG OUT WITH UMM... WHOEVER.
THAT SOUNDS PRETTY GOOD TO ME TOO.
ONLY WITH LESS EMPHASIS ON THE WHOLE CRAZED VIGILANTE PART.
YEAH . . . hee hee HANGING OUT SOUNDS LIKE FUN. hee hee
HOW ABOUT YOU, PM?

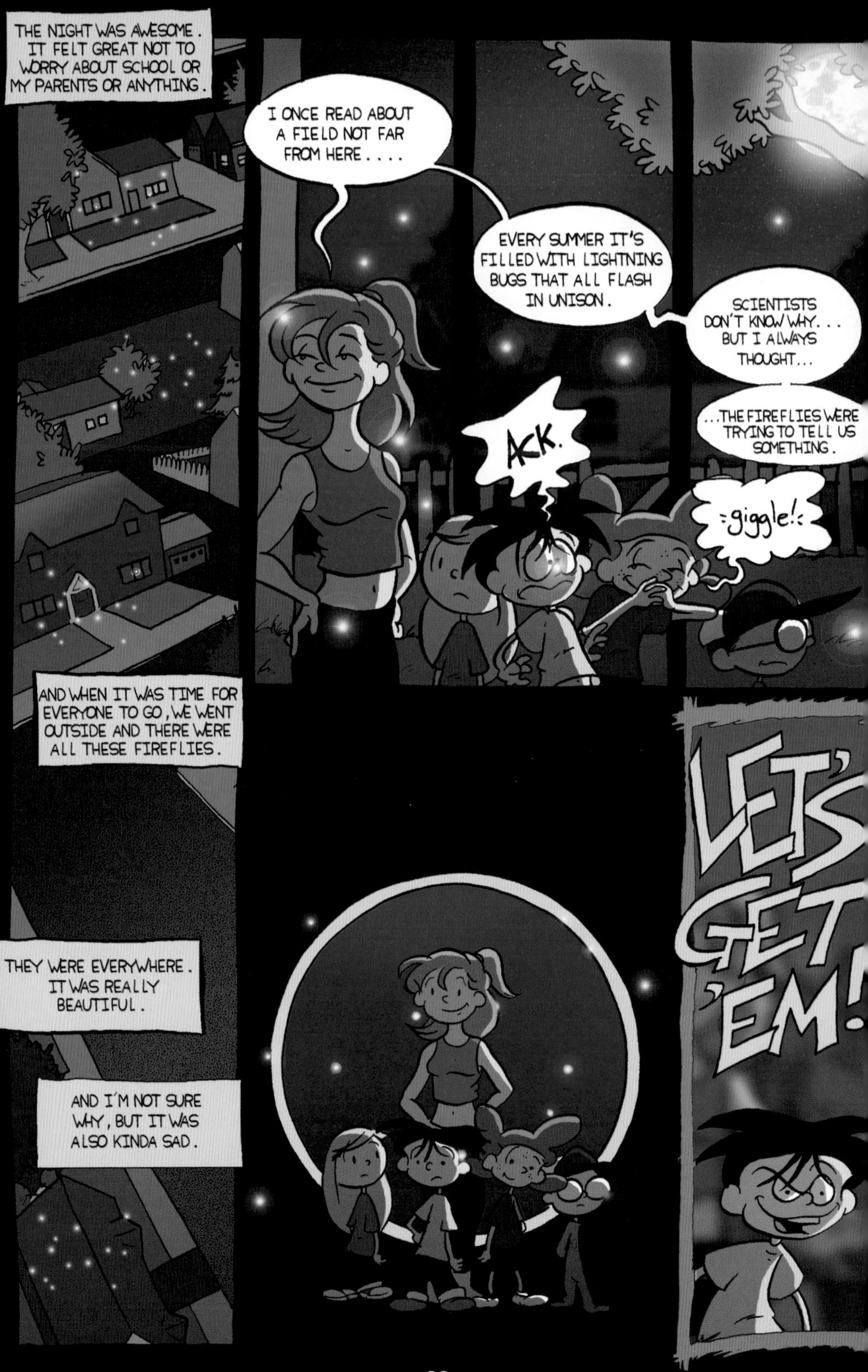
THE NIGHT WAS AWESOME. IT FELT GREAT NOT TO WORRY ABOUT SCHOOL OR MY PARENTS OR ANYTHING.
AND WHEN IT WAS TIME FOR EVERYONE TO GO, WE WENT OUTSIDE AND THERE WERE ALL THESE FIREFLIES.
THEY WERE EVERYWHERE. IT WAS REALLY BEAUTIFUL.
AND I'M NOT SURE WHY, BUT IT WAS ALSO KINDA SAD.
I ONCE READ ABOUT A FIELD NOT FAR FROM HERE....
EVERY SUMMER IT'S FILLED WITH LIGHTNING BUGS THAT ALL FLASH IN UNISON.
SCIENTISTS DON'T KNOW WHY... BUT I ALWAYS THOUGHT...
...THE FIREFLIES WERE TRYING TO TELL US SOMETHING.
ACK.
giggle!
LET'S GET 'EM!

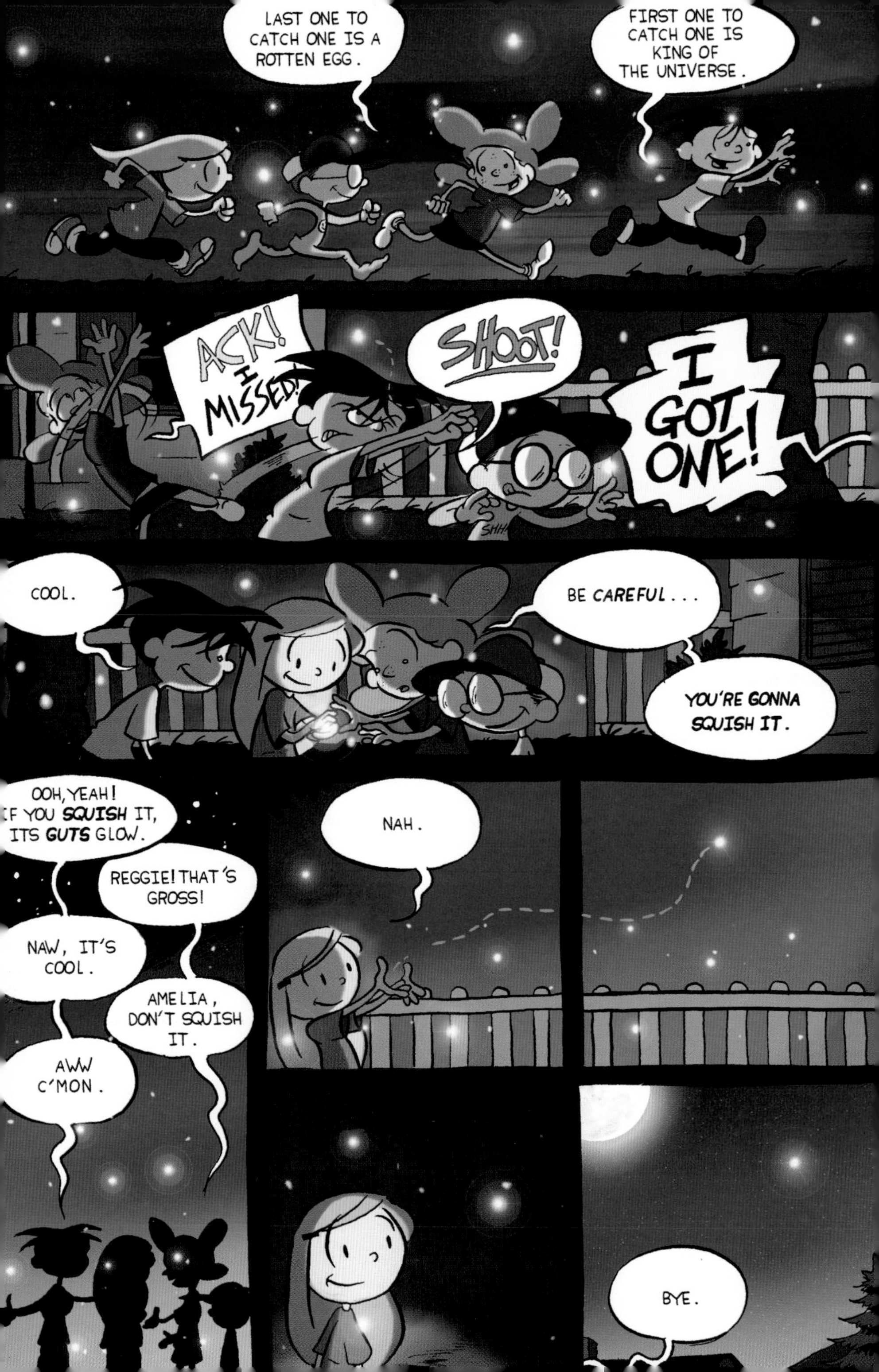

LAST ONE TO CATCH ONE IS A ROTTEN EGG.
FIRST ONE TO CATCH ONE IS KING OF THE UNIVERSE.
ACK! I MISSED!
SHOOT!
I GOT ONE!
SHH
COOL.
BE CAREFUL...
YOU'RE GONNA SQUISH IT.
OOH, YEAH! IF YOU SQUISH IT, ITS GUTS GLOW.
REGGIE! THAT'S GROSS!
NAW, IT'S COOL.
AMELIA, DON'T SQUISH IT.
AWW C'MON.
NAH.
BYE.

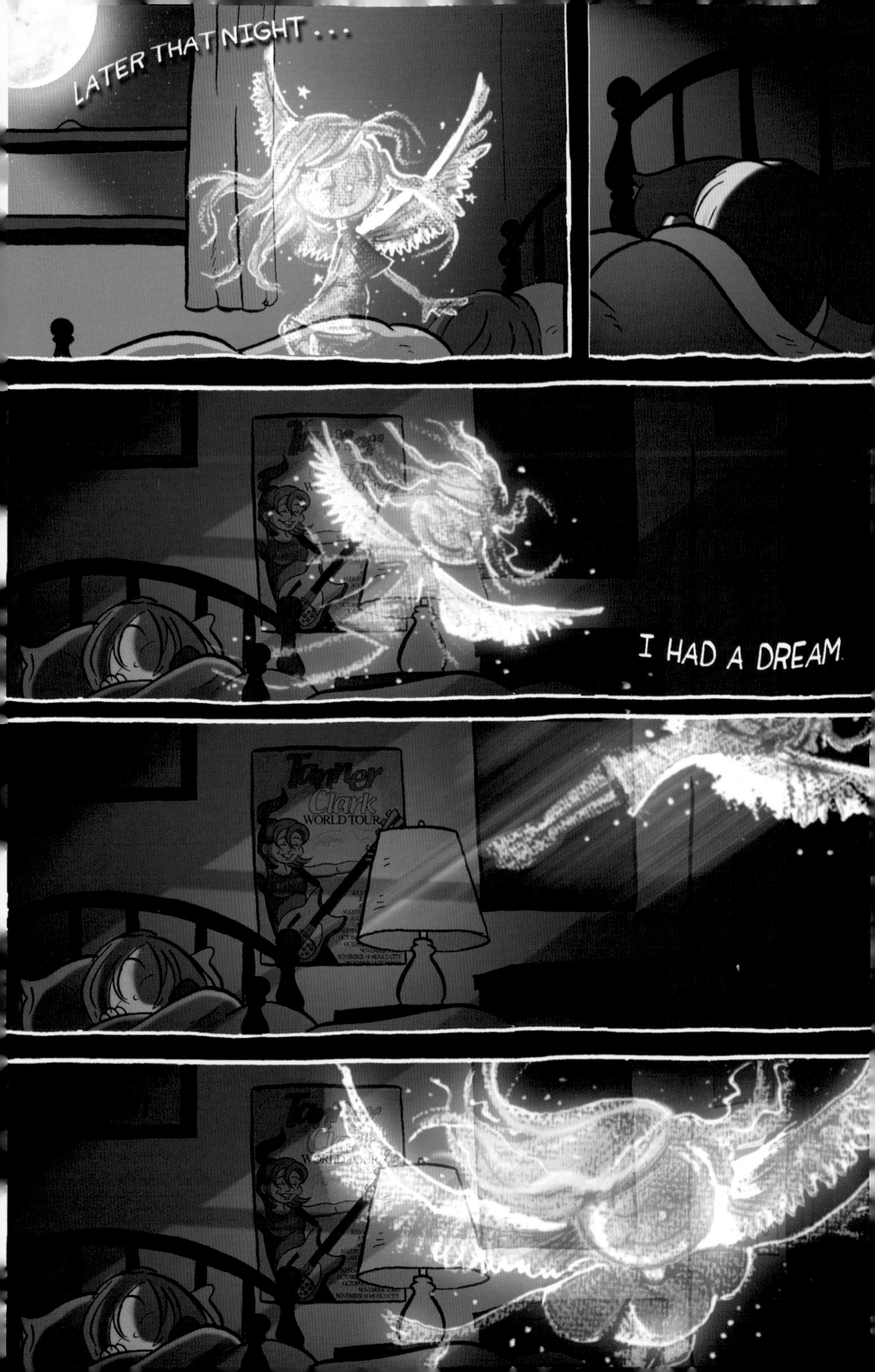
LATER THAT NIGHT . . .
I HAD A DREAM.

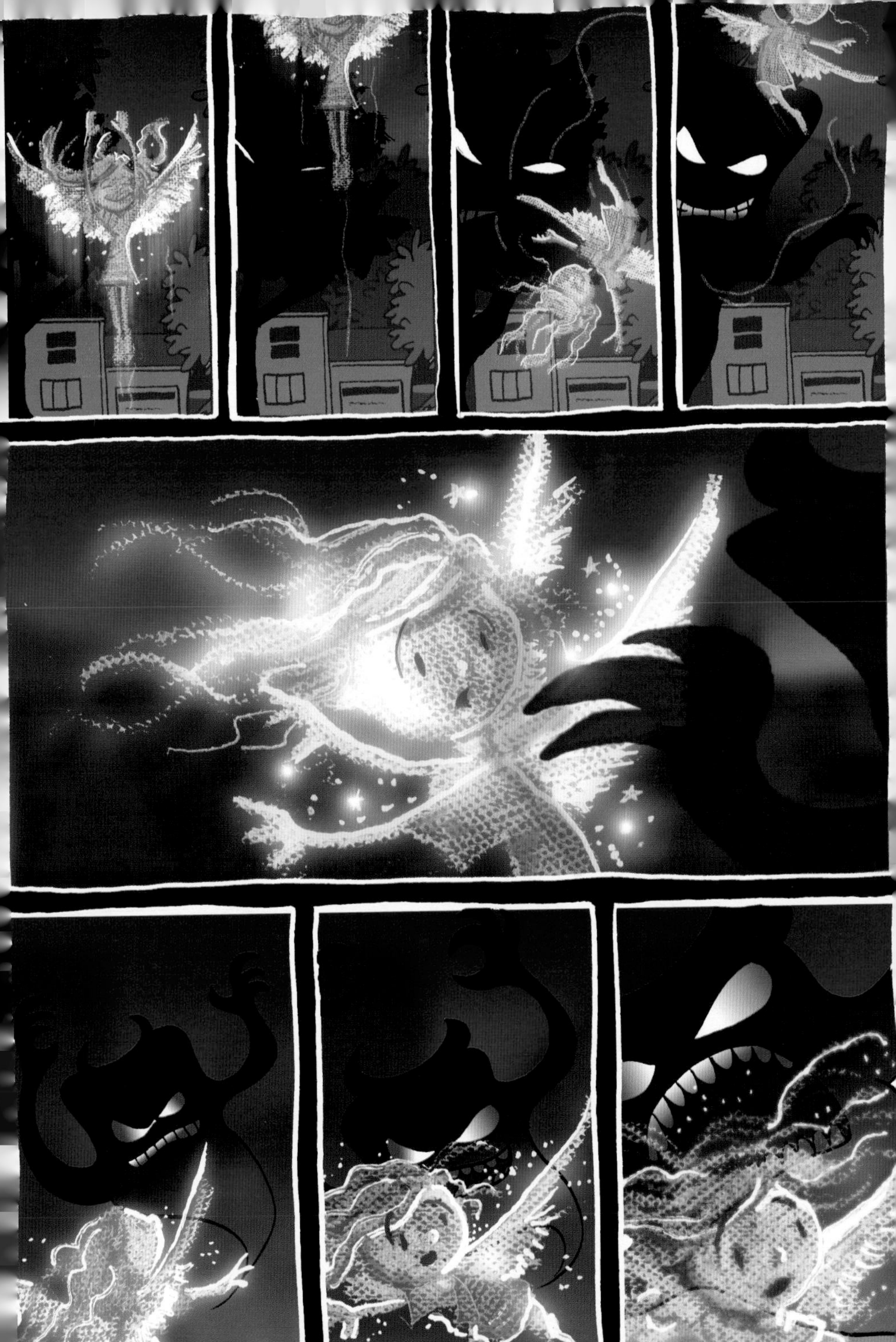

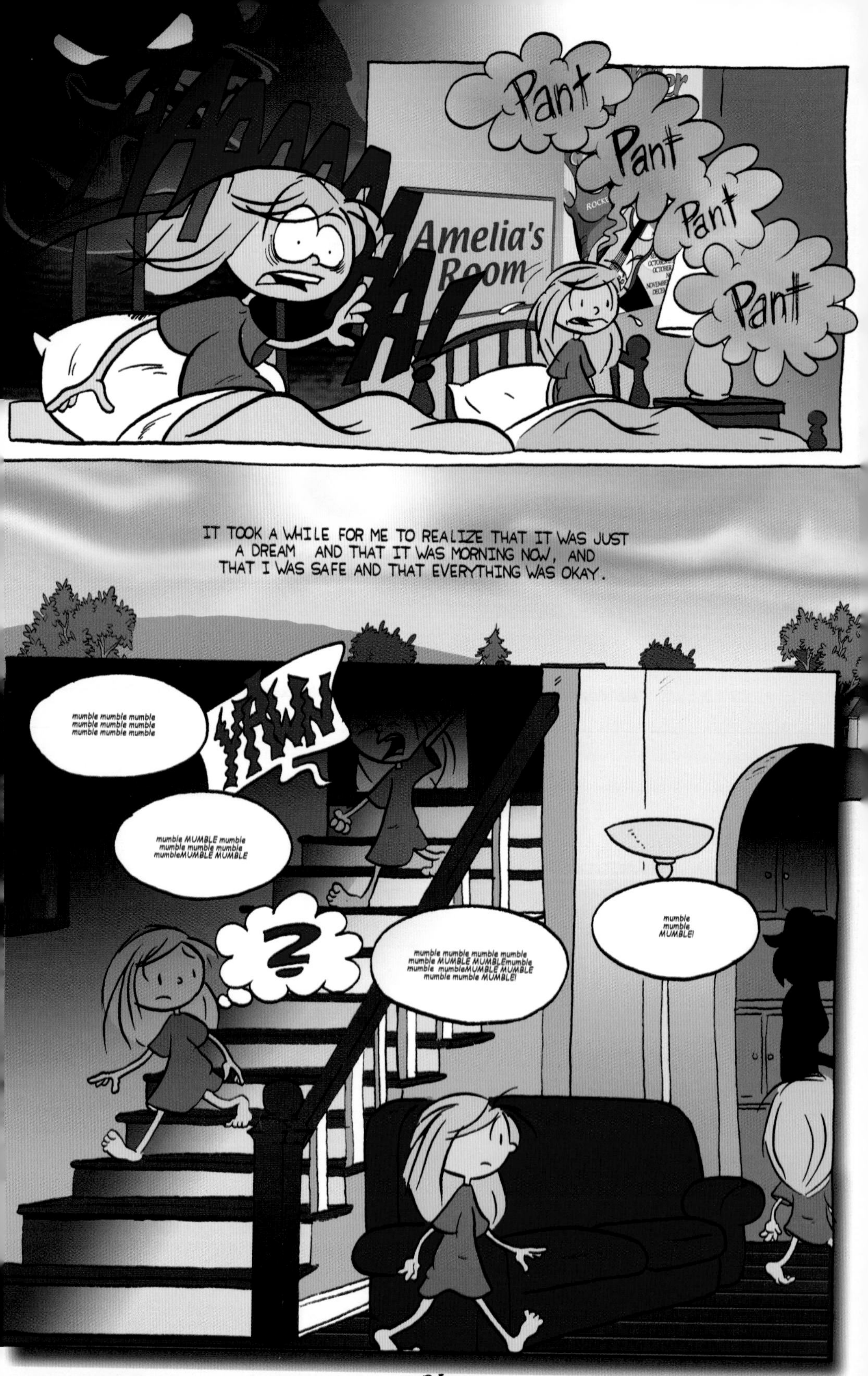
Amelia's Room
Pant
Pant
Pant
Pant
IT TOOK A WHILE FOR ME TO REALIZE THAT IT WAS JUST A DREAM AND THAT IT WAS MORNING NOW, AND THAT I WAS SAFE AND THAT EVERYTHING WAS OKAY.
mumble mumble mumble mumble mumble mumble mumble mumble mumble
YAWN
mumble MUMBLE mumble mumble mumble mumble mumbleMUMBLE MUMBLE
Z
mumble mumble mumble mumble mumble MUMBLE MUMBLEmumble mumble mumbleMUMBLE MUMBLE mumble mumble MUMBLE!
mumble mumble MUMBLE!

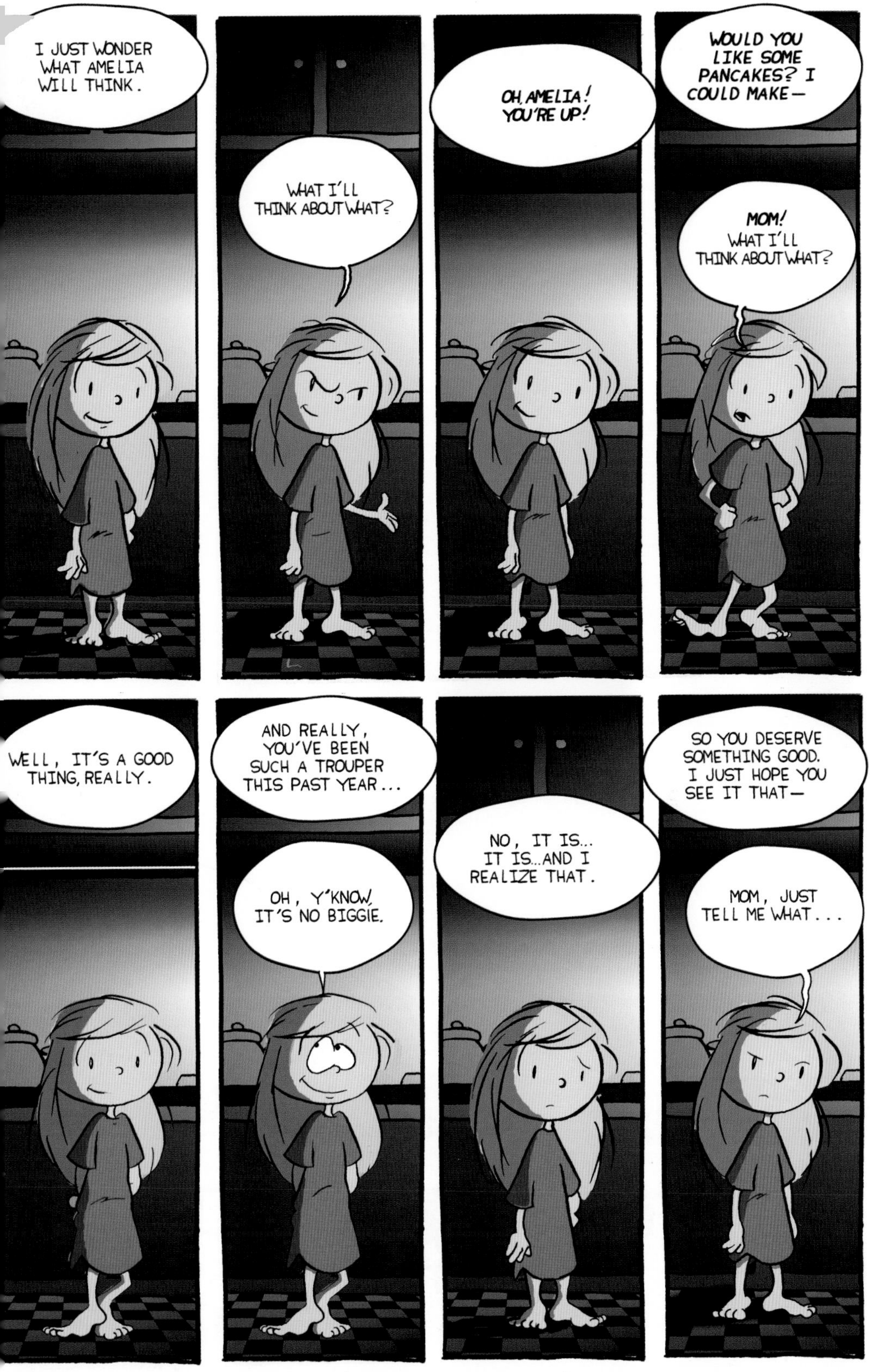
I JUST WONDER WHAT AMELIA WILL THINK.
WHAT I'LL THINK ABOUT WHAT?
OH, AMELIA! YOU'RE UP!
WOULD YOU LIKE SOME PANCAKES? I COULD MAKE—
MOM! WHAT I'LL THINK ABOUT WHAT?
WELL, IT'S A GOOD THING, REALLY.
AND REALLY, YOU'VE BEEN SUCH A TROUPER THIS PAST YEAR...
OH, Y'KNOW, IT'S NO BIGGIE.
NO, IT IS... IT IS...AND I REALIZE THAT.
SO YOU DESERVE SOMETHING GOOD. I JUST HOPE YOU SEE IT THAT—
MOM, JUST TELL ME WHAT...

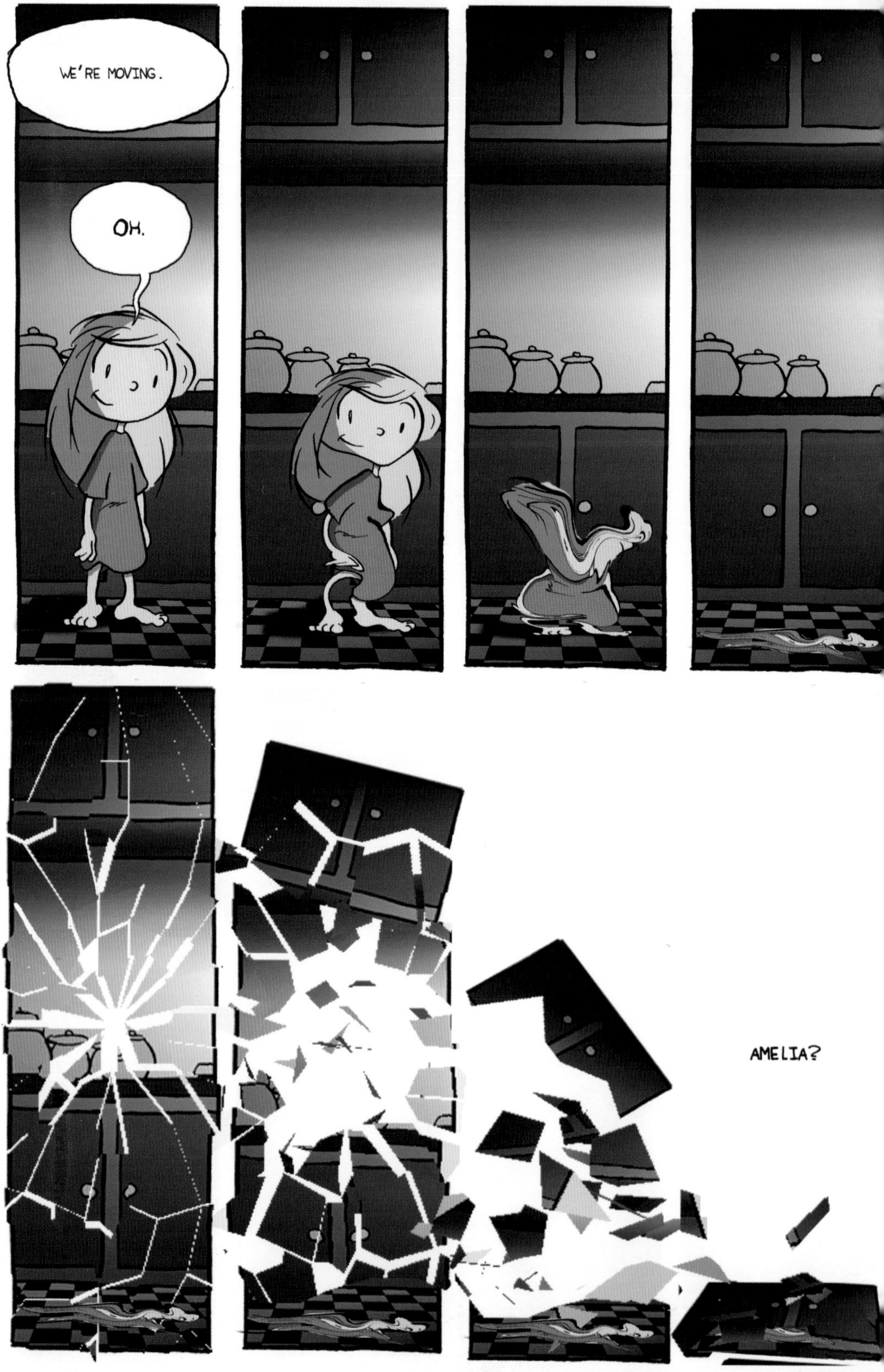
WE'RE MOVING.
OH.
AMELIA?

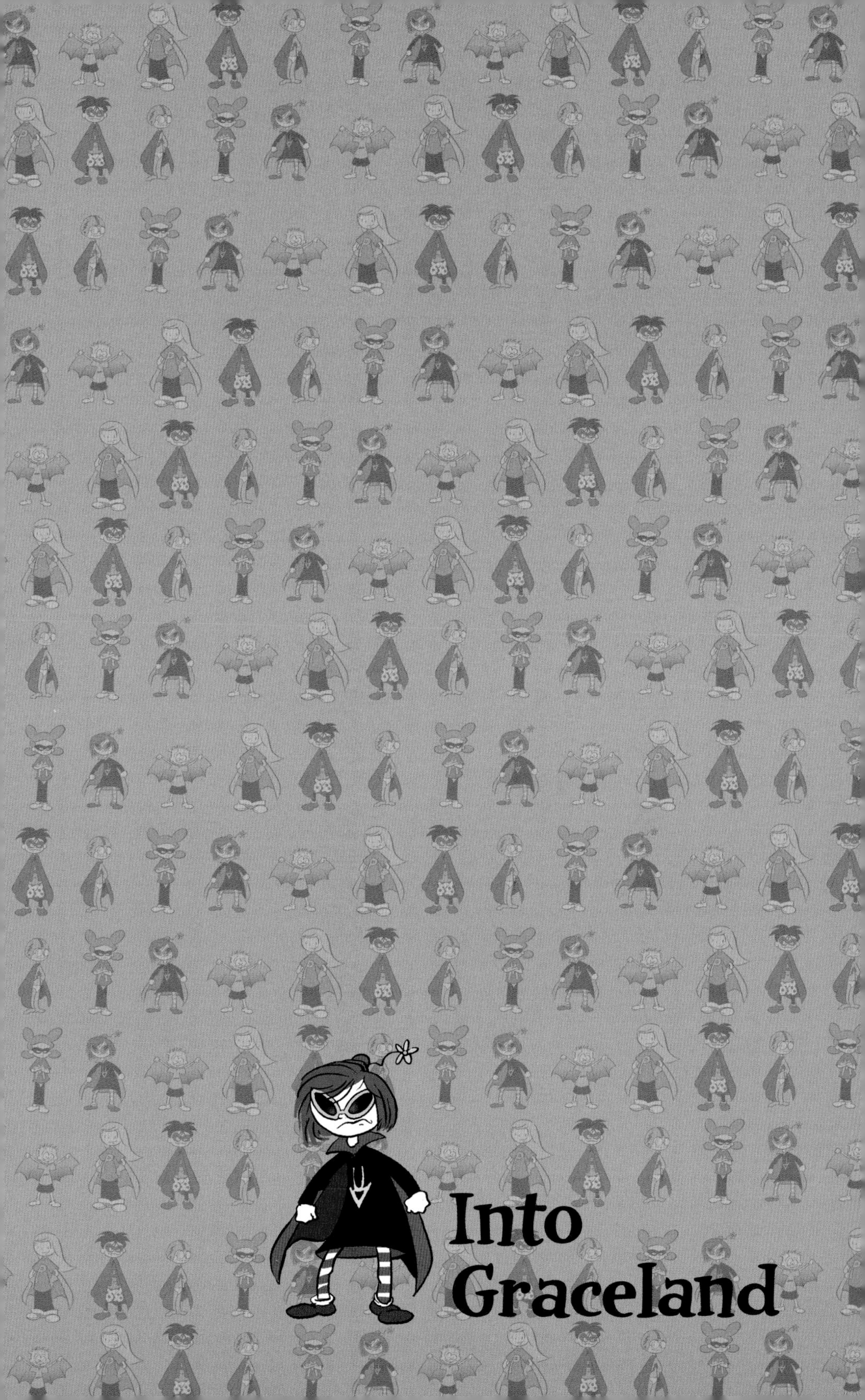

Into Graceland

MOVING?

AT FIRST I JUST FIGURED
I **HEARD** HER WRONG.

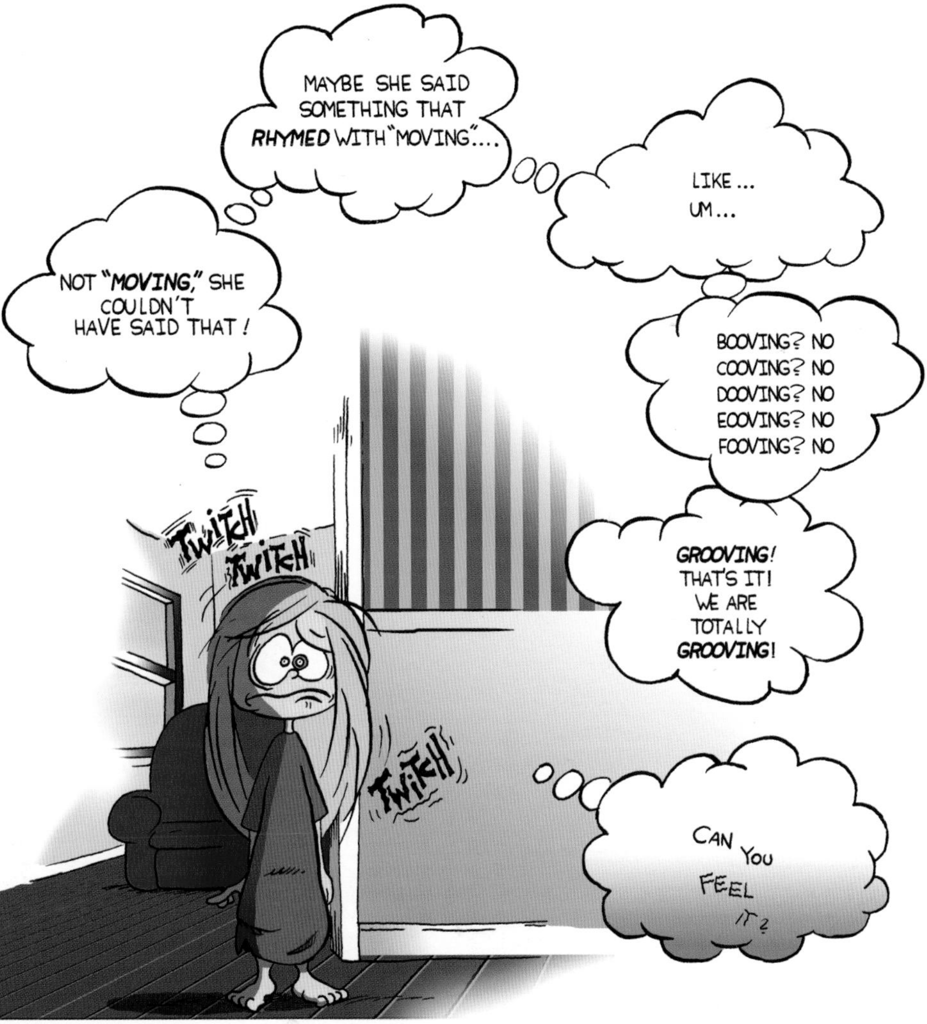
NOT "**MOVING**," SHE COULDN'T HAVE SAID THAT!
MAYBE SHE SAID SOMETHING THAT **RHYMED** WITH "MOVING"....
LIKE... UM...
BOOVING? NO
COOVING? NO
DOOVING? NO
EOOVING? NO
FOOVING? NO
GROOVING! THAT'S IT! WE ARE TOTALLY **GROOVING**!
TWITCH
TWITCH
TWITCH
CAN YOU FEEL IT?

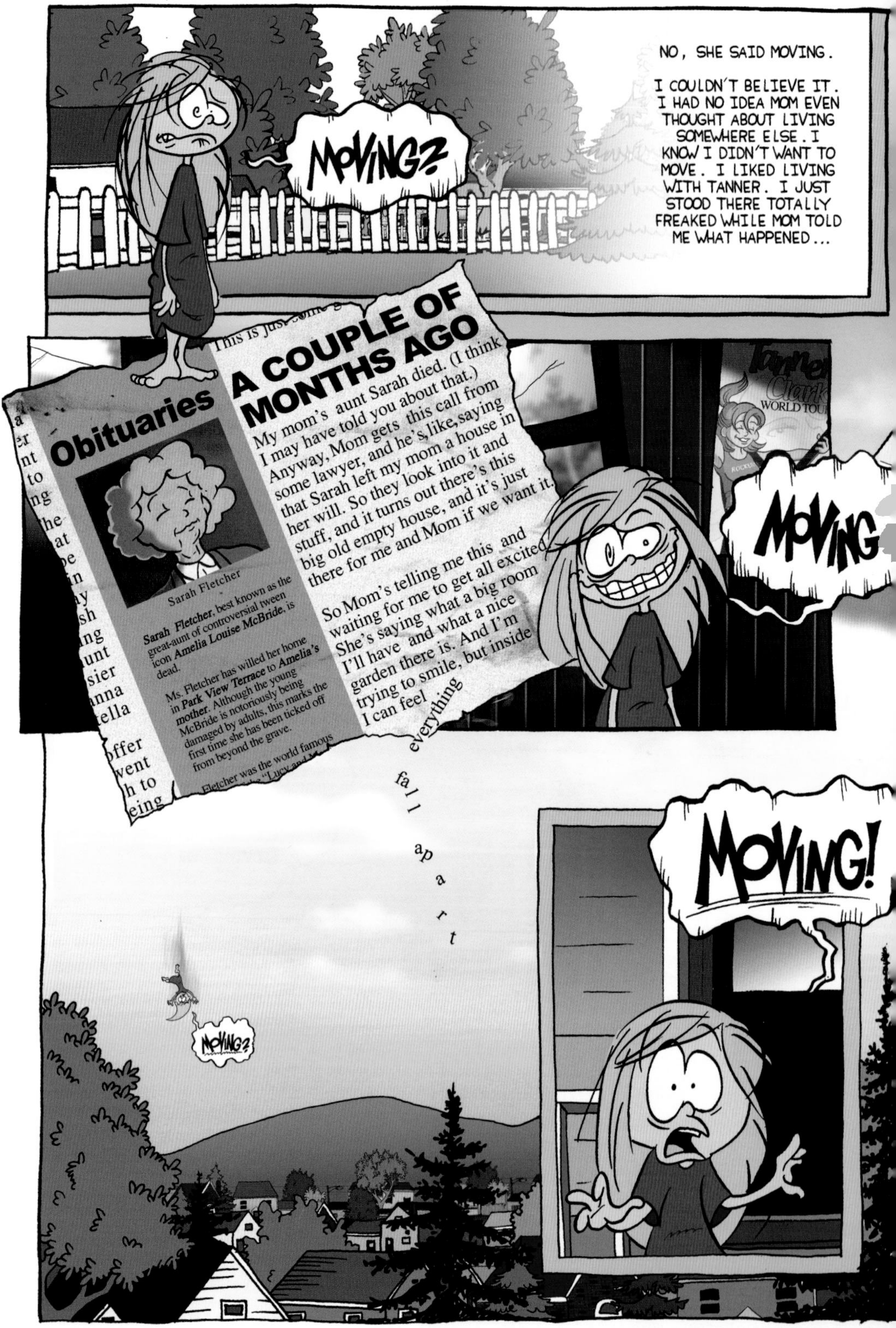
NO, SHE SAID MOVING.
I COULDN'T BELIEVE IT. I HAD NO IDEA MOM EVEN THOUGHT ABOUT LIVING SOMEWHERE ELSE. I KNOW I DIDN'T WANT TO MOVE. I LIKED LIVING WITH TANNER. I JUST STOOD THERE TOTALLY FREAKED WHILE MOM TOLD ME WHAT HAPPENED...
MOVING?
A COUPLE OF MONTHS AGO
My mom's aunt Sarah died. (I think I may have told you about that.) Anyway, Mom gets this call from some lawyer, and he's, like, saying that Sarah left my mom a house in her will. So they look into it and stuff, and it turns out there's this big old empty house, and it's just there for me and Mom if we want it.
So Mom's telling me this and waiting for me to get all excited. She's saying what a big room I'll have and what a nice garden there is. And I'm trying to smile, but inside I can feel everything fall apart
Obituaries
Sarah Fletcher
Sarah Fletcher, best known as the great-aunt of controversial tween icon Amelia Louise McBride, is dead.
Ms. Fletcher has willed her home in Park View Terrace to Amelia's mother. Although the young McBride is notoriously being damaged by adults, this marks the first time she has been ticked off from beyond the grave.
Fletcher was the world famous
Tanner Clark WORLD TOUR
MOVING
MOVING!
MOVING?

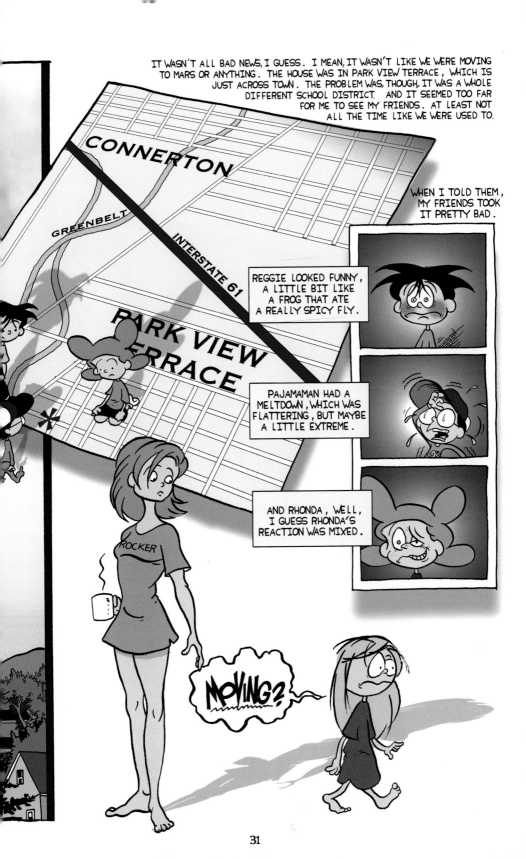

IT WASN'T ALL BAD NEWS, I GUESS. I MEAN, IT WASN'T LIKE WE WERE MOVING TO MARS OR ANYTHING. THE HOUSE WAS IN PARK VIEW TERRACE, WHICH IS JUST ACROSS TOWN. THE PROBLEM WAS, THOUGH, IT WAS A WHOLE DIFFERENT SCHOOL DISTRICT. AND IT SEEMED TOO FAR FOR ME TO SEE MY FRIENDS. AT LEAST NOT ALL THE TIME LIKE WE WERE USED TO.

WHEN I TOLD THEM, MY FRIENDS TOOK IT PRETTY BAD.

REGGIE LOOKED FUNNY, A LITTLE BIT LIKE A FROG THAT ATE A REALLY SPICY FLY.

PAJAMAMAN HAD A MELTDOWN, WHICH WAS FLATTERING, BUT MAYBE A LITTLE EXTREME.

AND RHONDA, WELL, I GUESS RHONDA'S REACTION WAS MIXED.

CONNERTON

GREENBELT

INTERSTATE 61

PARK VIEW TERRACE

ROCKER

MOVING?

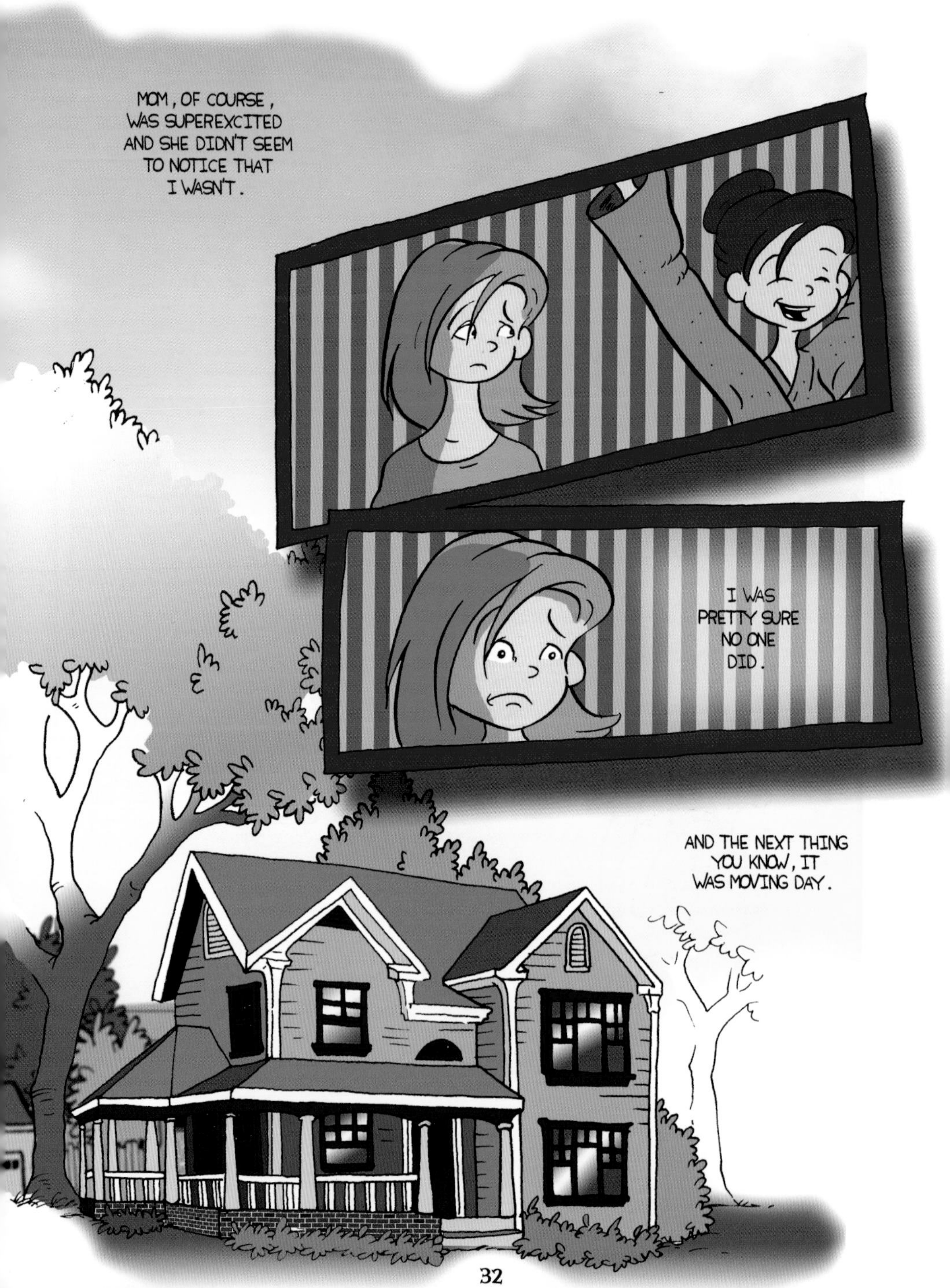
MOM, OF COURSE, WAS SUPEREXCITED AND SHE DIDN'T SEEM TO NOTICE THAT I WASN'T.
I WAS PRETTY SURE NO ONE DID.
AND THE NEXT THING YOU KNOW, IT WAS MOVING DAY.

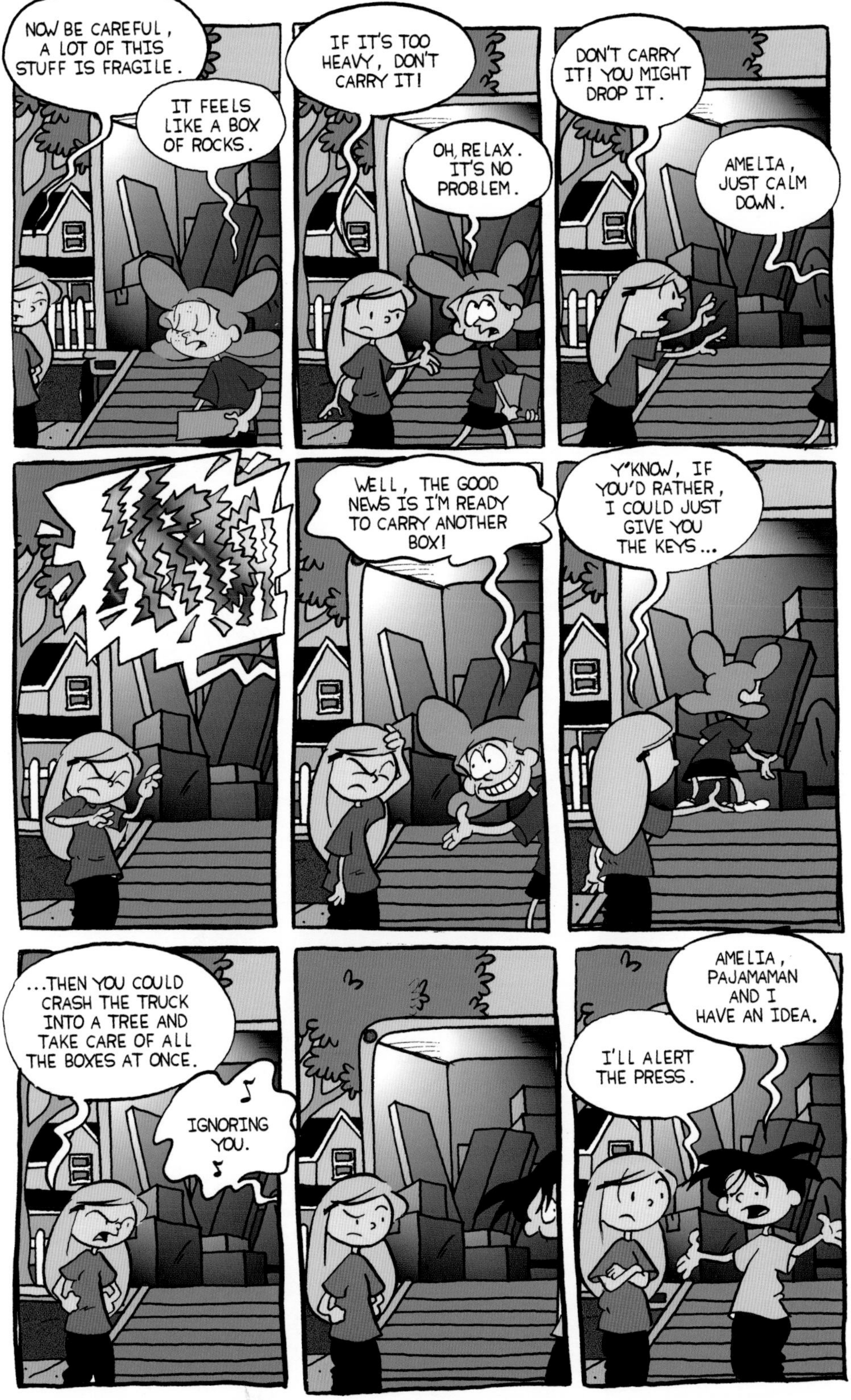
NOW BE CAREFUL, A LOT OF THIS STUFF IS FRAGILE.
IT FEELS LIKE A BOX OF ROCKS.
IF IT'S TOO HEAVY, DON'T CARRY IT!
OH, RELAX. IT'S NO PROBLEM.
DON'T CARRY IT! YOU MIGHT DROP IT.
AMELIA, JUST CALM DOWN.
WELL, THE GOOD NEWS IS I'M READY TO CARRY ANOTHER BOX!
Y'KNOW, IF YOU'D RATHER, I COULD JUST GIVE YOU THE KEYS...
...THEN YOU COULD CRASH THE TRUCK INTO A TREE AND TAKE CARE OF ALL THE BOXES AT ONCE.
IGNORING YOU.
AMELIA, PAJAMAMAN AND I HAVE AN IDEA.
I'LL ALERT THE PRESS.

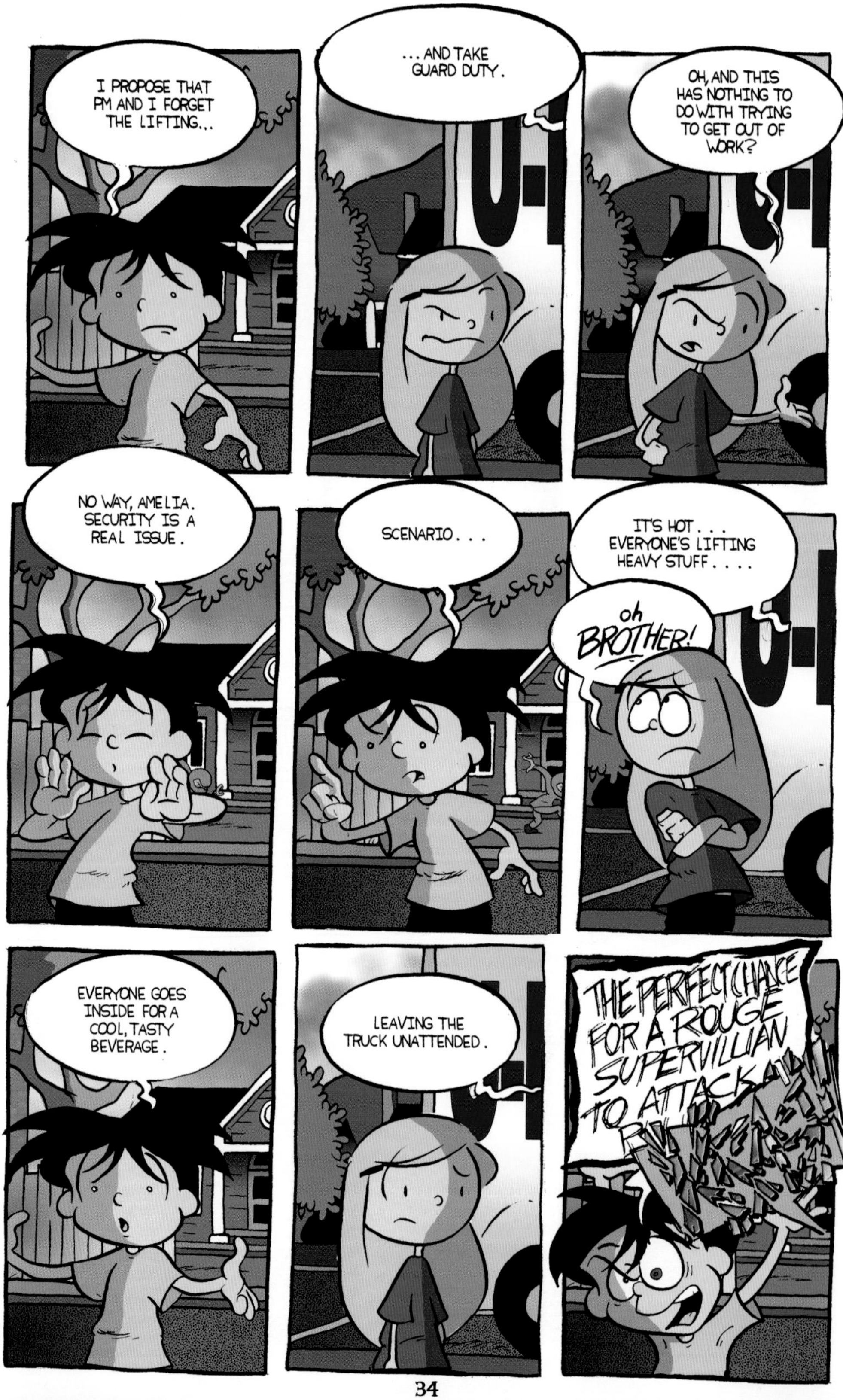
I PROPOSE THAT PM AND I FORGET THE LIFTING...
...AND TAKE GUARD DUTY.
OH, AND THIS HAS NOTHING TO DO WITH TRYING TO GET OUT OF WORK?
NO WAY, AMELIA. SECURITY IS A REAL ISSUE.
SCENARIO...
IT'S HOT... EVERYONE'S LIFTING HEAVY STUFF....
oh BROTHER!
EVERYONE GOES INSIDE FOR A COOL, TASTY BEVERAGE.
LEAVING THE TRUCK UNATTENDED.
THE PERFECT CHANCE FOR A ROUGE SUPERVILLIAN TO ATTACK

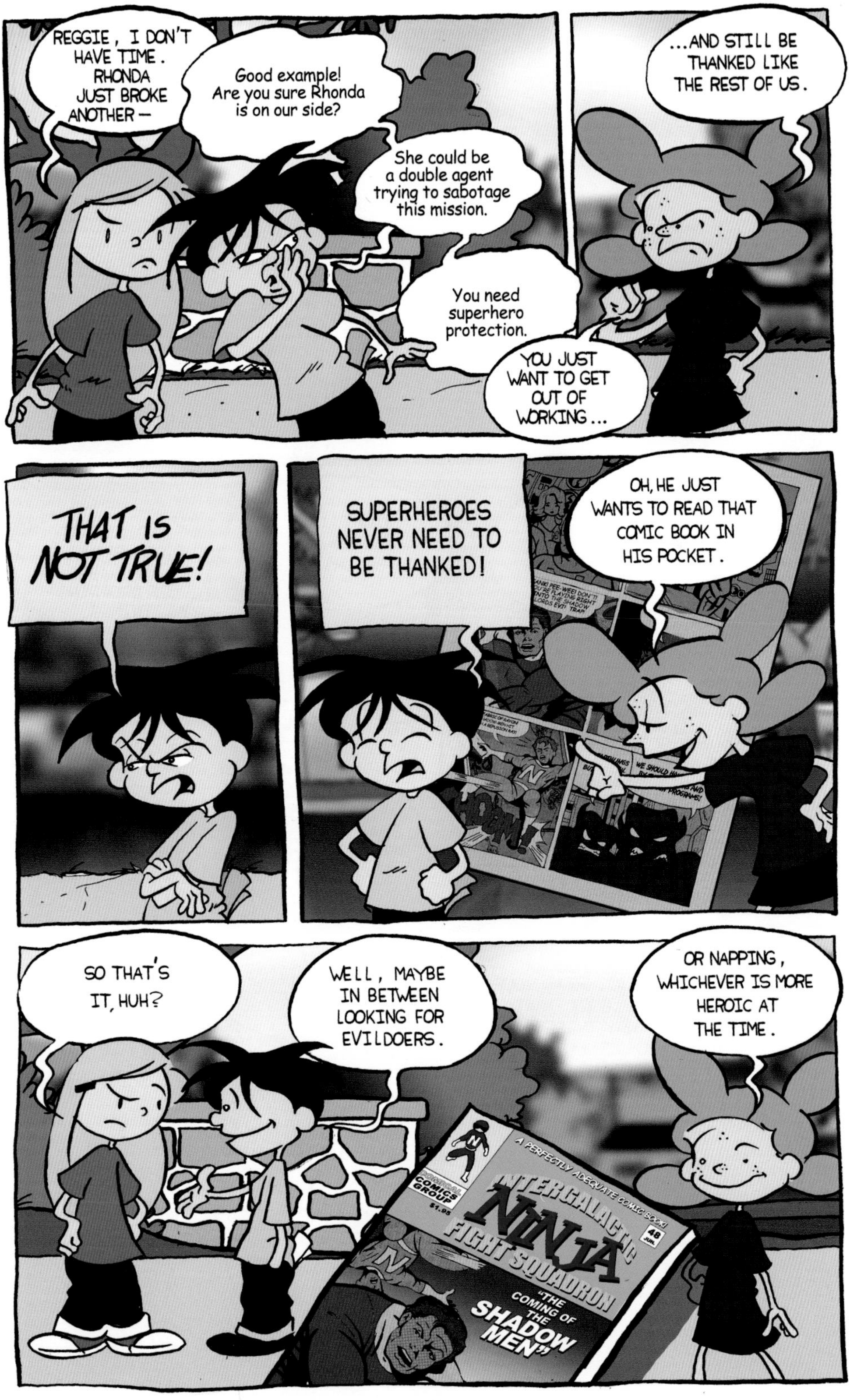
REGGIE, I DON'T HAVE TIME. RHONDA JUST BROKE ANOTHER—
Good example! Are you sure Rhonda is on our side?
She could be a double agent trying to sabotage this mission.
You need superhero protection.
YOU JUST WANT TO GET OUT OF WORKING...
...AND STILL BE THANKED LIKE THE REST OF US.
THAT IS NOT TRUE!
SUPERHEROES NEVER NEED TO BE THANKED!
OH, HE JUST WANTS TO READ THAT COMIC BOOK IN HIS POCKET.
SO THAT'S IT, HUH?
WELL, MAYBE IN BETWEEN LOOKING FOR EVILDOERS.
OR NAPPING, WHICHEVER IS MORE HEROIC AT THE TIME.
A PERFECTLY ADEQUATE COMIC BOOK!
COMICAL COMICS GROUP
$1.95
48 JUN.
INTERGALACTIC NINJA FIGHT SQUADRON
"THE COMING OF THE SHADOW MEN"

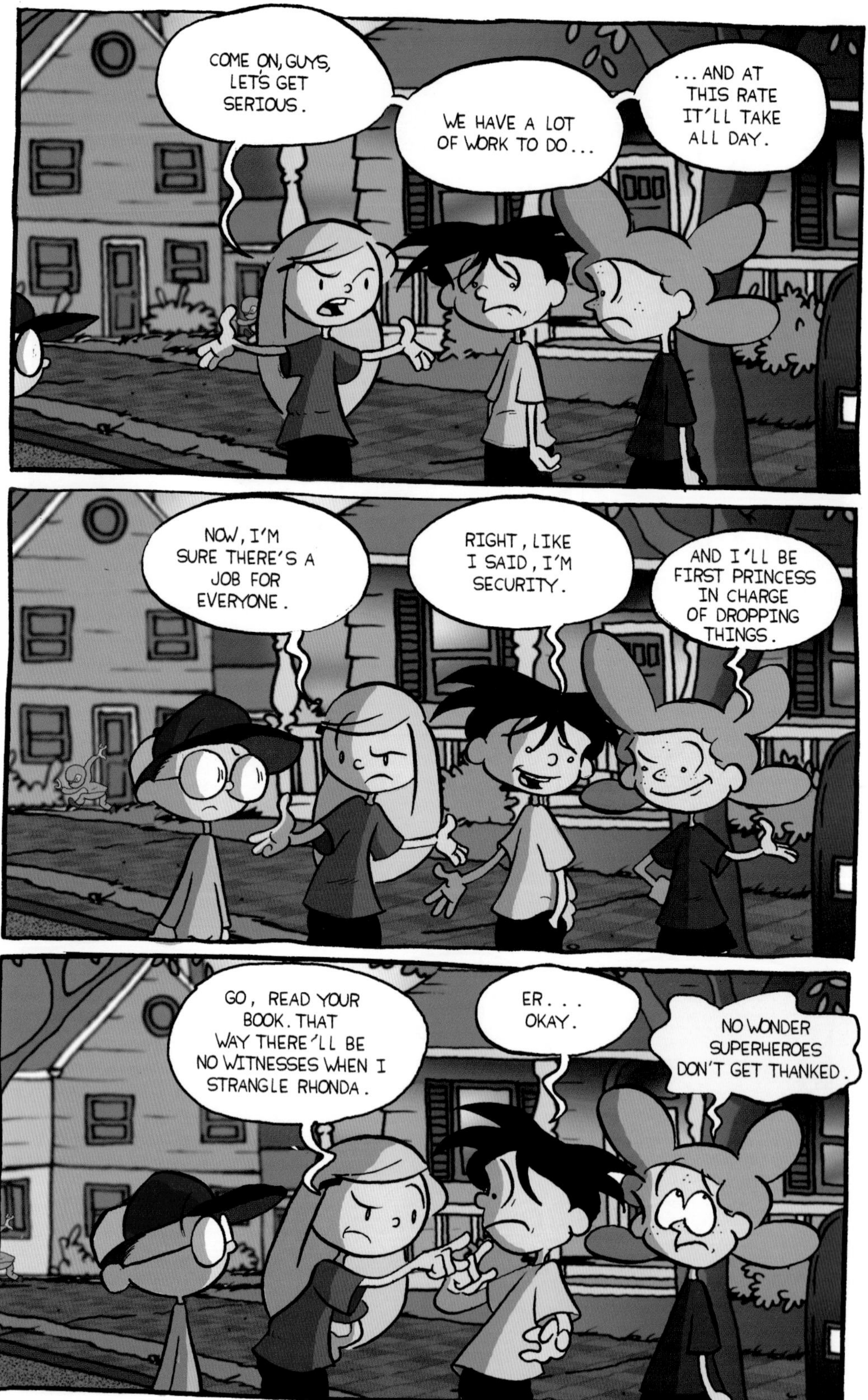
COME ON, GUYS, LET'S GET SERIOUS.
WE HAVE A LOT OF WORK TO DO...
...AND AT THIS RATE IT'LL TAKE ALL DAY.
NOW, I'M SURE THERE'S A JOB FOR EVERYONE.
RIGHT, LIKE I SAID, I'M SECURITY.
AND I'LL BE FIRST PRINCESS IN CHARGE OF DROPPING THINGS.
GO, READ YOUR BOOK. THAT WAY THERE'LL BE NO WITNESSES WHEN I STRANGLE RHONDA.
ER... OKAY.
NO WONDER SUPERHEROES DON'T GET THANKED.

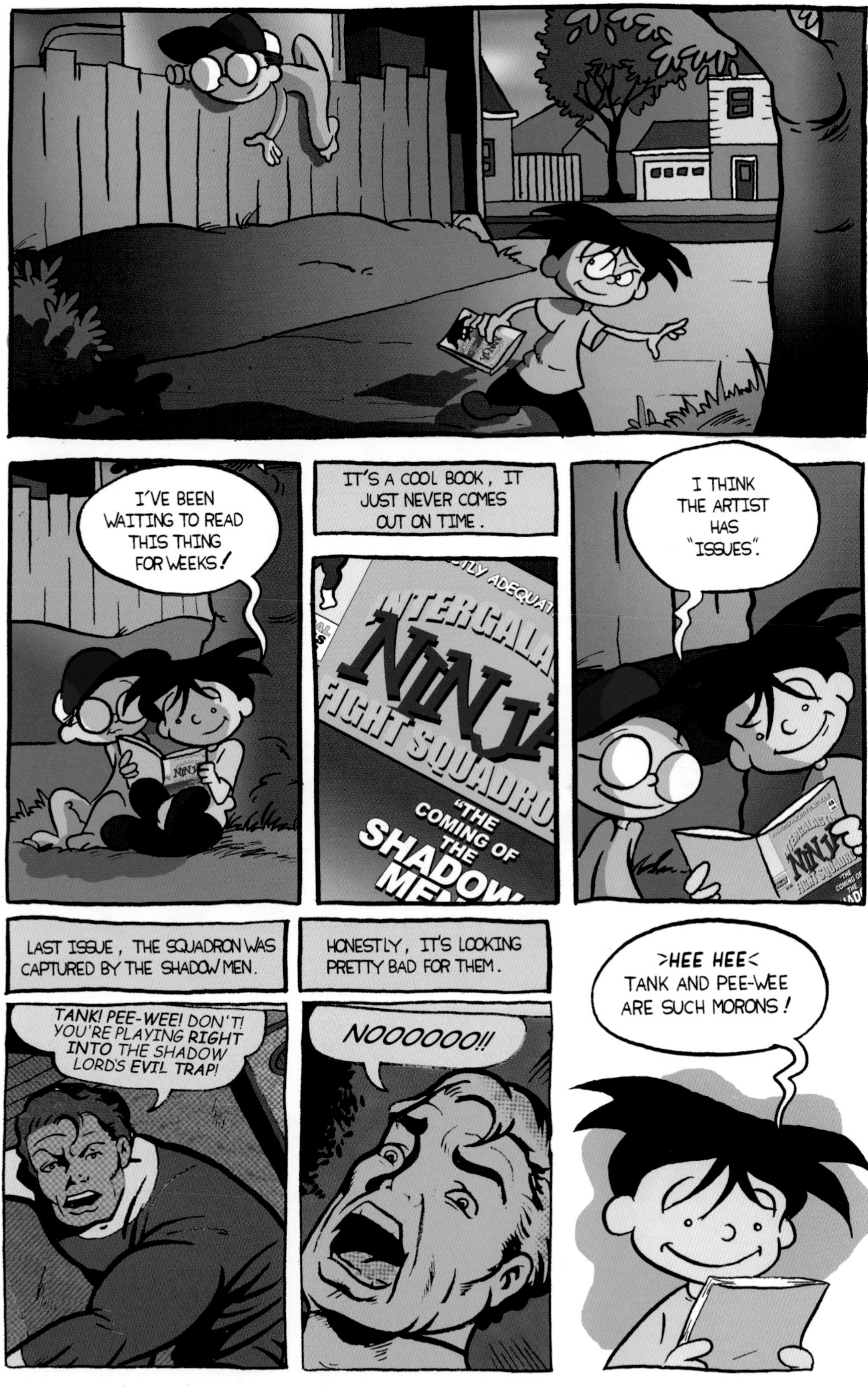
I'VE BEEN WAITING TO READ THIS THING FOR WEEKS!
IT'S A COOL BOOK, IT JUST NEVER COMES OUT ON TIME.
INTERGALA
NINJA
FIGHT SQUADRO
"THE COMING OF THE SHADOW ME
I THINK THE ARTIST HAS "ISSUES".
LAST ISSUE, THE SQUADRON WAS CAPTURED BY THE SHADOW MEN.
HONESTLY, IT'S LOOKING PRETTY BAD FOR THEM.
TANK! PEE-WEE! DON'T! YOU'RE PLAYING RIGHT INTO THE SHADOW LORD'S EVIL TRAP!
NOOOOOO!!
>HEE HEE< TANK AND PEE-WEE ARE SUCH MORONS!

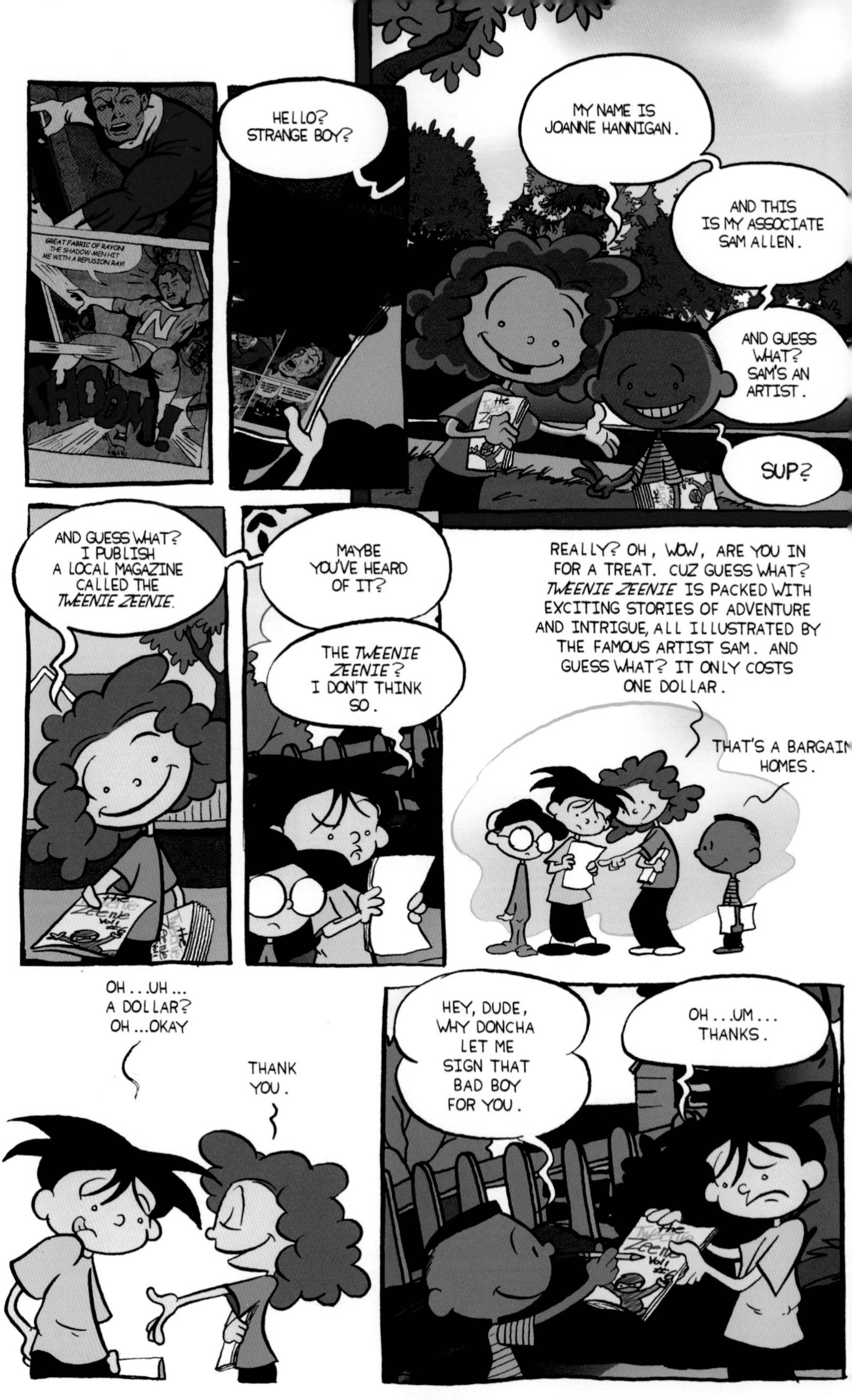
GREAT FABRIC OF RAYON! THE SHADOW-MEN HIT ME WITH A REPUSION RAY!
HELLO? STRANGE BOY?
MY NAME IS JOANNE HANNIGAN.
AND THIS IS MY ASSOCIATE SAM ALLEN.
AND GUESS WHAT? SAM'S AN ARTIST.
SUP?
AND GUESS WHAT? I PUBLISH A LOCAL MAGAZINE CALLED THE *TWEENIE ZEENIE*.
MAYBE YOU'VE HEARD OF IT?
THE *TWEENIE ZEENIE*? I DON'T THINK SO.
REALLY? OH, WOW, ARE YOU IN FOR A TREAT. CUZ GUESS WHAT? *TWEENIE ZEENIE* IS PACKED WITH EXCITING STORIES OF ADVENTURE AND INTRIGUE, ALL ILLUSTRATED BY THE FAMOUS ARTIST SAM. AND GUESS WHAT? IT ONLY COSTS ONE DOLLAR.
THAT'S A BARGAIN HOMES.
OH...UH... A DOLLAR? OH...OKAY
THANK YOU.
HEY, DUDE, WHY DONCHA LET ME SIGN THAT BAD BOY FOR YOU.
OH...UM... THANKS.

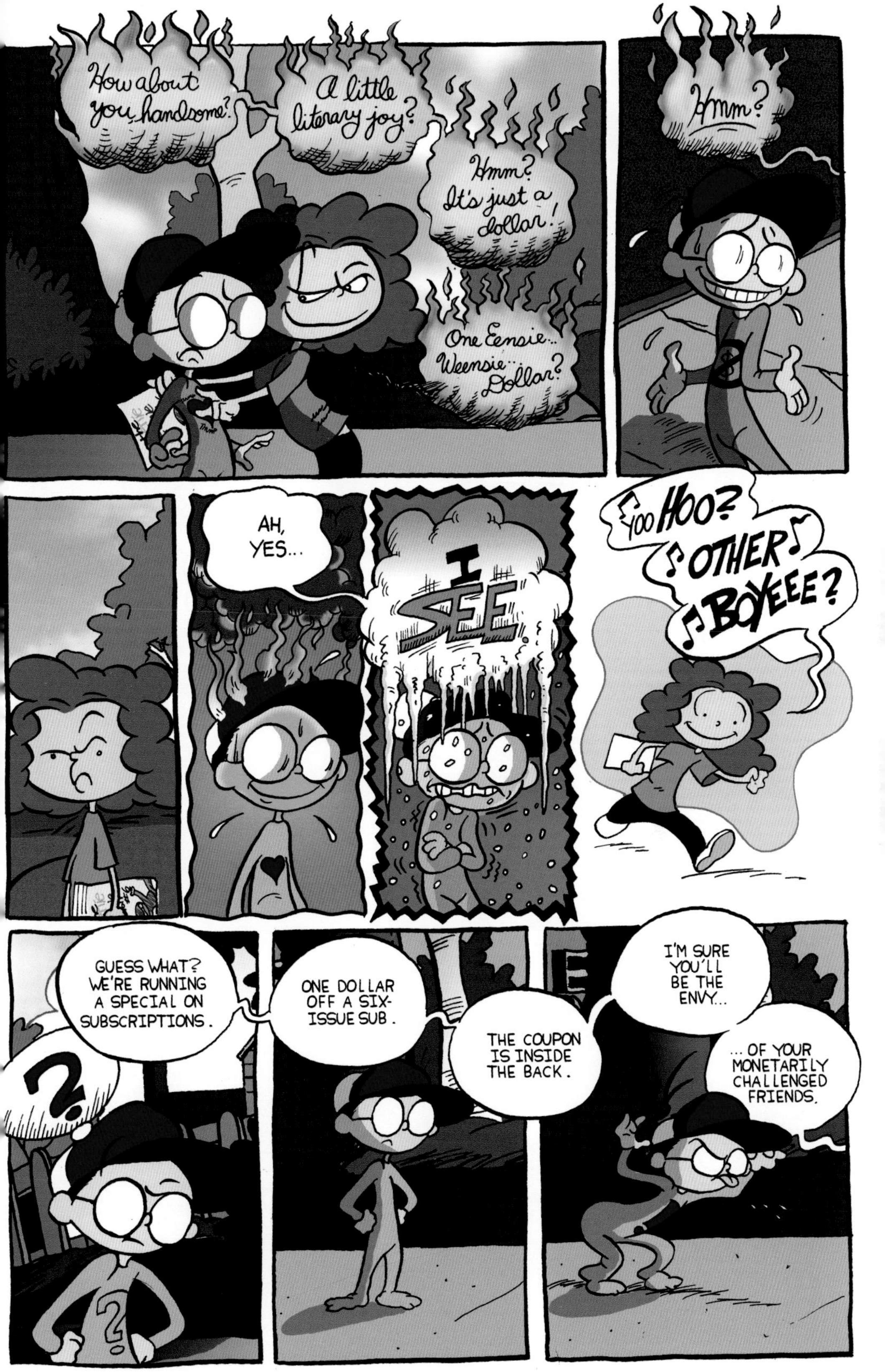
How about you, handsome?
A little literary joy?
Hmm? It's just a dollar!
One Eensie... Weensie... Dollar?
Hmm?
AH, YES...
I SEE.
YOO HOO? OTHER BOYEEE?
GUESS WHAT? WE'RE RUNNING A SPECIAL ON SUBSCRIPTIONS.
ONE DOLLAR OFF A SIX-ISSUE SUB.
THE COUPON IS INSIDE THE BACK.
I'M SURE YOU'LL BE THE ENVY...
... OF YOUR MONETARILY CHALLENGED FRIENDS.

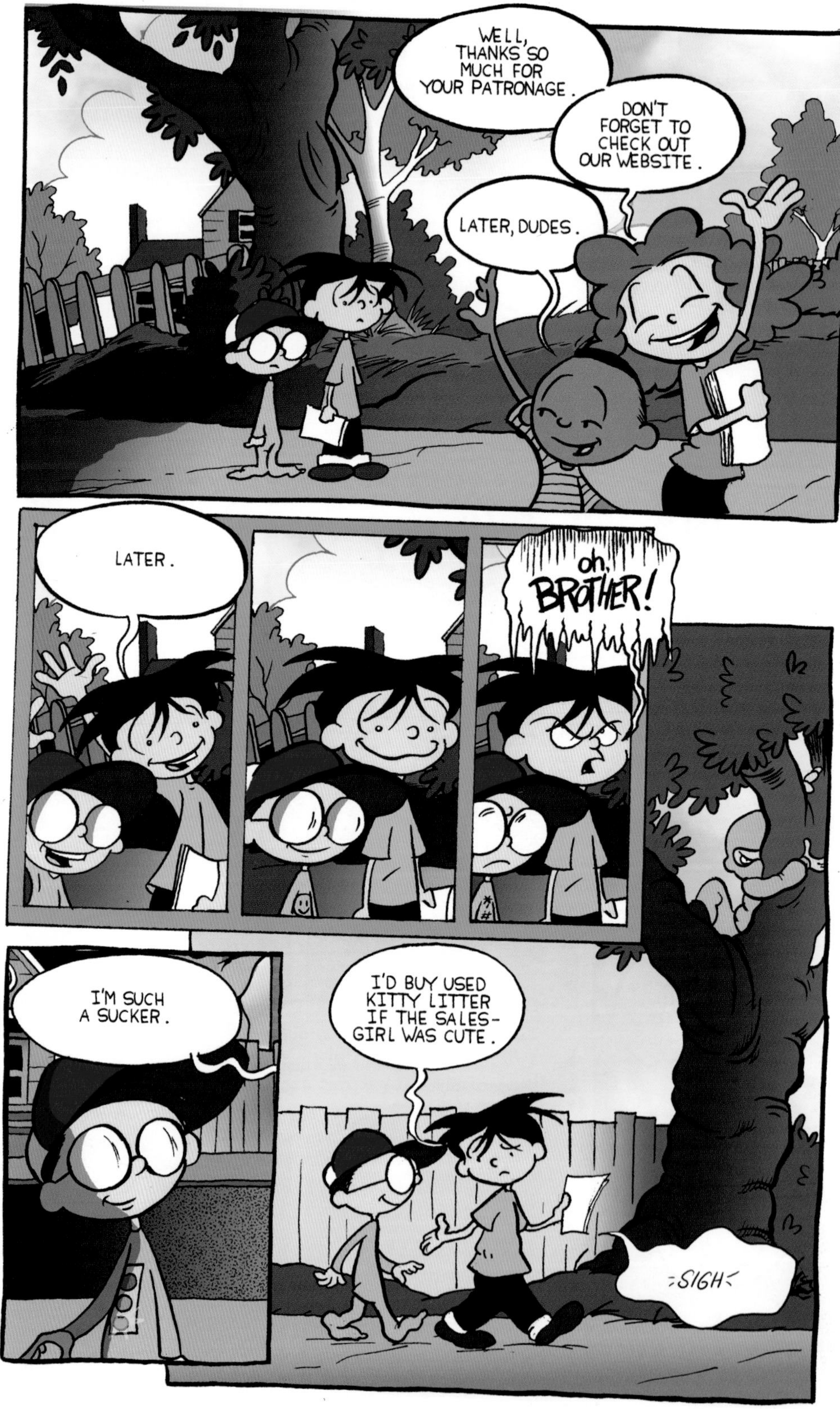
WELL, THANKS SO MUCH FOR YOUR PATRONAGE.
DON'T FORGET TO CHECK OUT OUR WEBSITE.
LATER, DUDES.
LATER.
oh, BROTHER!
I'M SUCH A SUCKER.
I'D BUY USED KITTY LITTER IF THE SALES-GIRL WAS CUTE.
SIGH

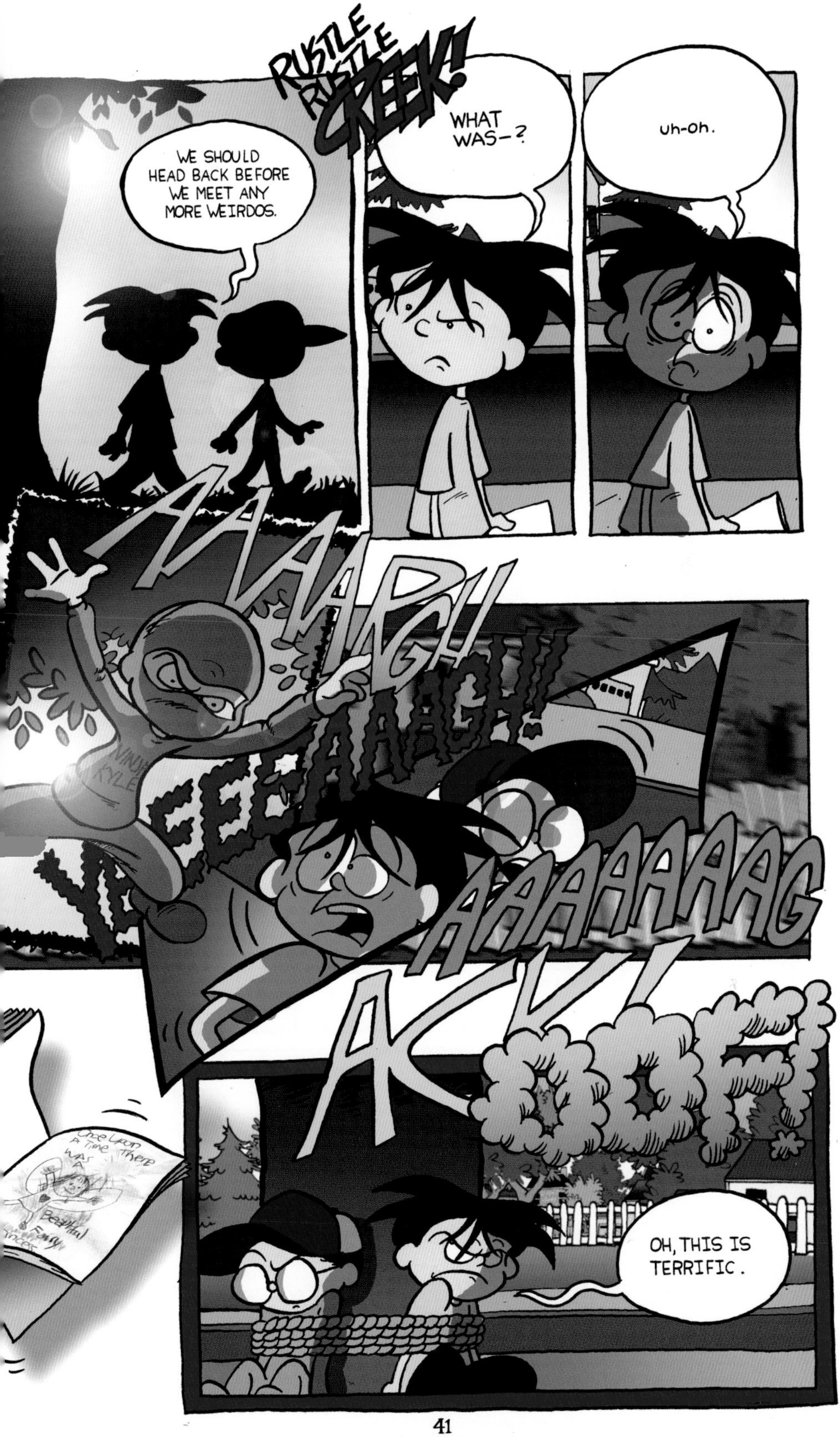
RUSTLE
RUSTLE
CREEK!
WE SHOULD HEAD BACK BEFORE WE MEET ANY MORE WEIRDOS.
WHAT WAS—?
uh-oh.
AAAARGH!!
YEEEAAAGH!!
AAAAAAAAG
ACK!
OOF!
Once Upon A Time There WAS A Beautiful Fairy
OH, THIS IS TERRIFIC.

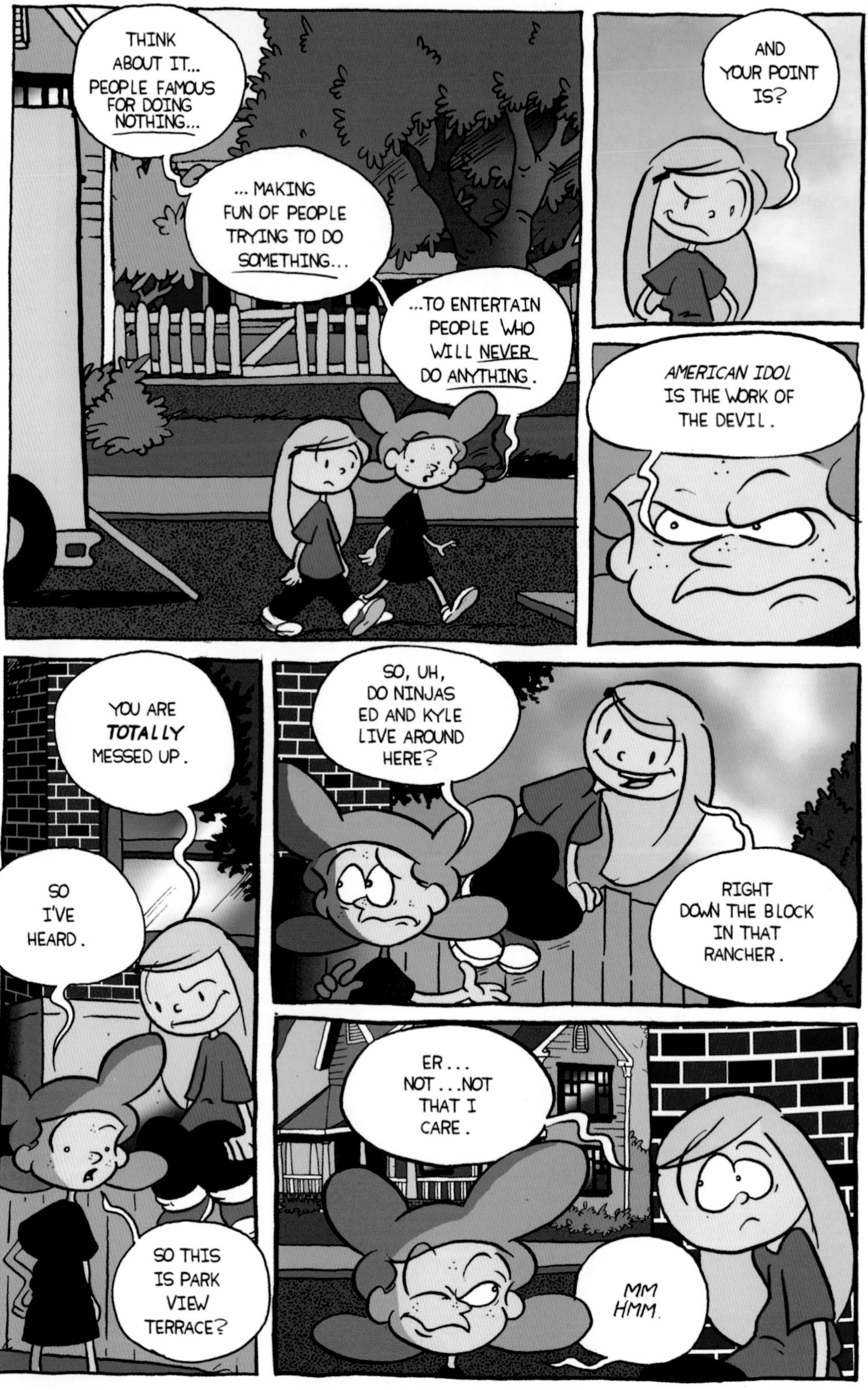
THINK ABOUT IT... PEOPLE FAMOUS FOR DOING NOTHING...
... MAKING FUN OF PEOPLE TRYING TO DO SOMETHING...
...TO ENTERTAIN PEOPLE WHO WILL NEVER DO ANYTHING.
AND YOUR POINT IS?
AMERICAN IDOL IS THE WORK OF THE DEVIL.
YOU ARE **TOTALLY** MESSED UP.
SO I'VE HEARD.
SO THIS IS PARK VIEW TERRACE?
SO, UH, DO NINJAS ED AND KYLE LIVE AROUND HERE?
RIGHT DOWN THE BLOCK IN THAT RANCHER.
ER... NOT...NOT THAT I CARE.
MM HMM.

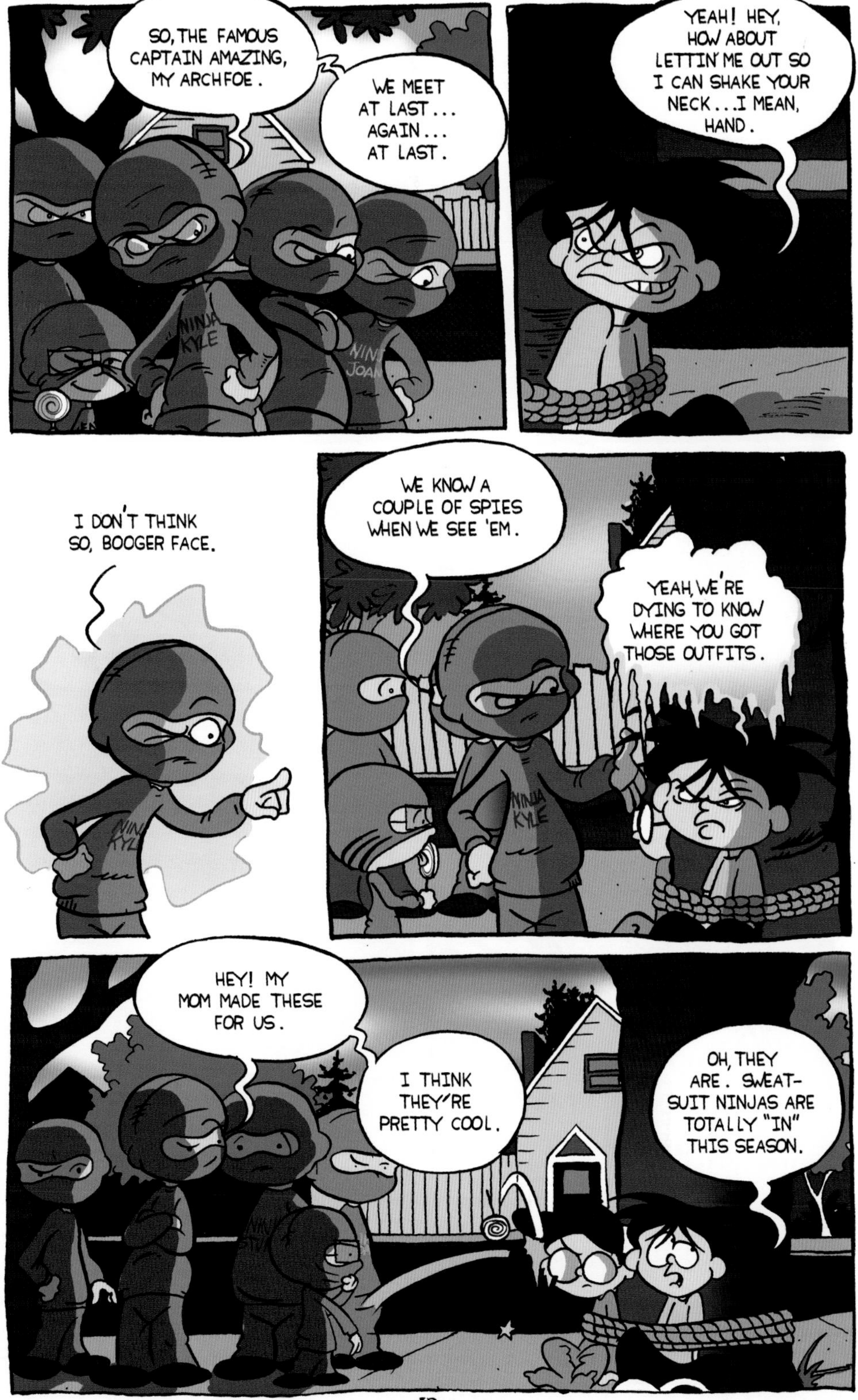
SO, THE FAMOUS CAPTAIN AMAZING, MY ARCHFOE.
WE MEET AT LAST... AGAIN... AT LAST.
YEAH! HEY, HOW ABOUT LETTIN' ME OUT SO I CAN SHAKE YOUR NECK...I MEAN, HAND.
I DON'T THINK SO, BOOGER FACE.
WE KNOW A COUPLE OF SPIES WHEN WE SEE 'EM.
YEAH, WE'RE DYING TO KNOW WHERE YOU GOT THOSE OUTFITS.
HEY! MY MOM MADE THESE FOR US.
I THINK THEY'RE PRETTY COOL.
OH, THEY ARE. SWEAT-SUIT NINJAS ARE TOTALLY "IN" THIS SEASON.

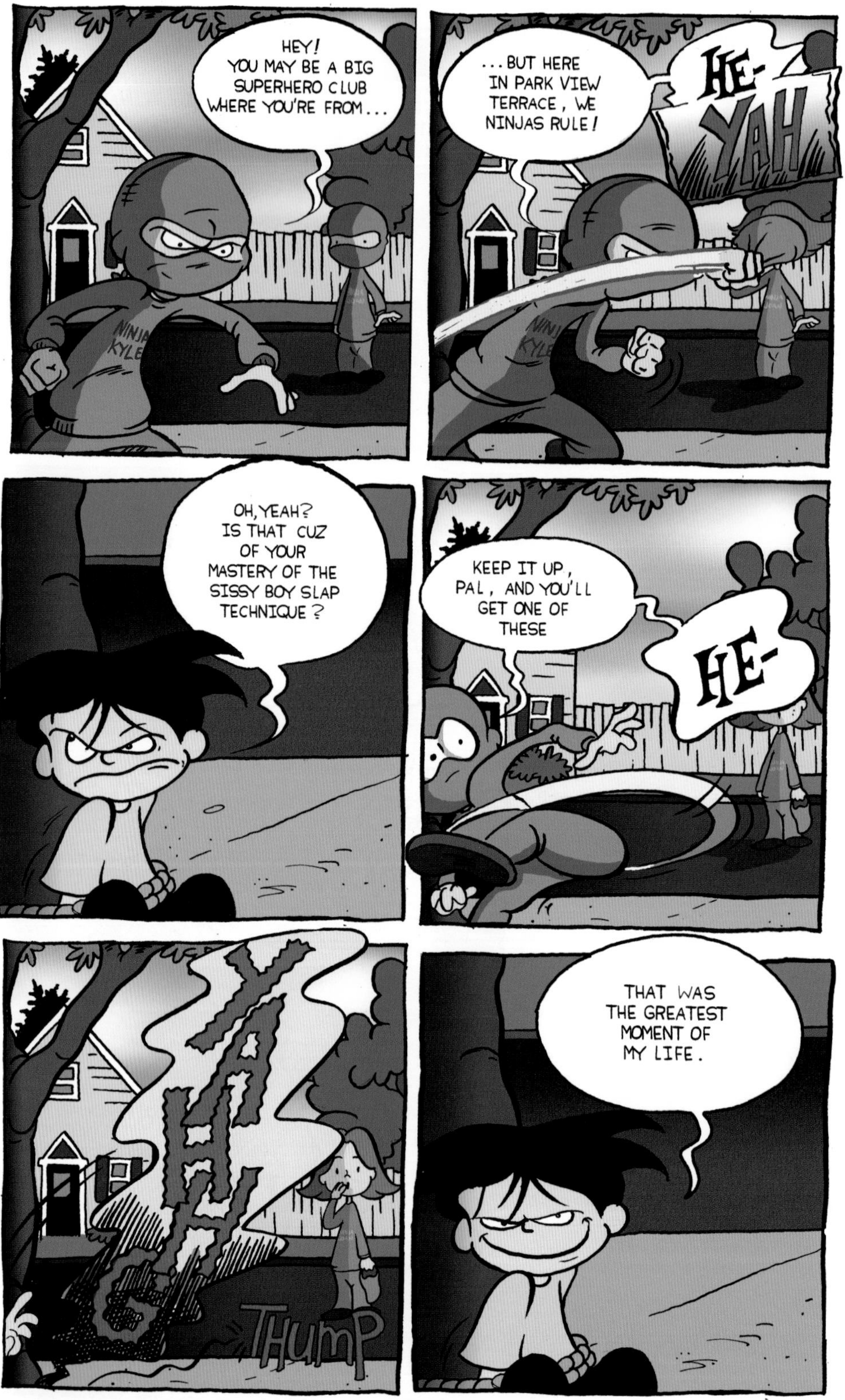
HEY! YOU MAY BE A BIG SUPERHERO CLUB WHERE YOU'RE FROM...
NINJA KYLE
...BUT HERE IN PARK VIEW TERRACE, WE NINJAS RULE!
HE-YAH
OH, YEAH? IS THAT CUZ OF YOUR MASTERY OF THE SISSY BOY SLAP TECHNIQUE?
KEEP IT UP, PAL, AND YOU'LL GET ONE OF THESE
HE-
YAH
THUMP
THAT WAS THE GREATEST MOMENT OF MY LIFE.

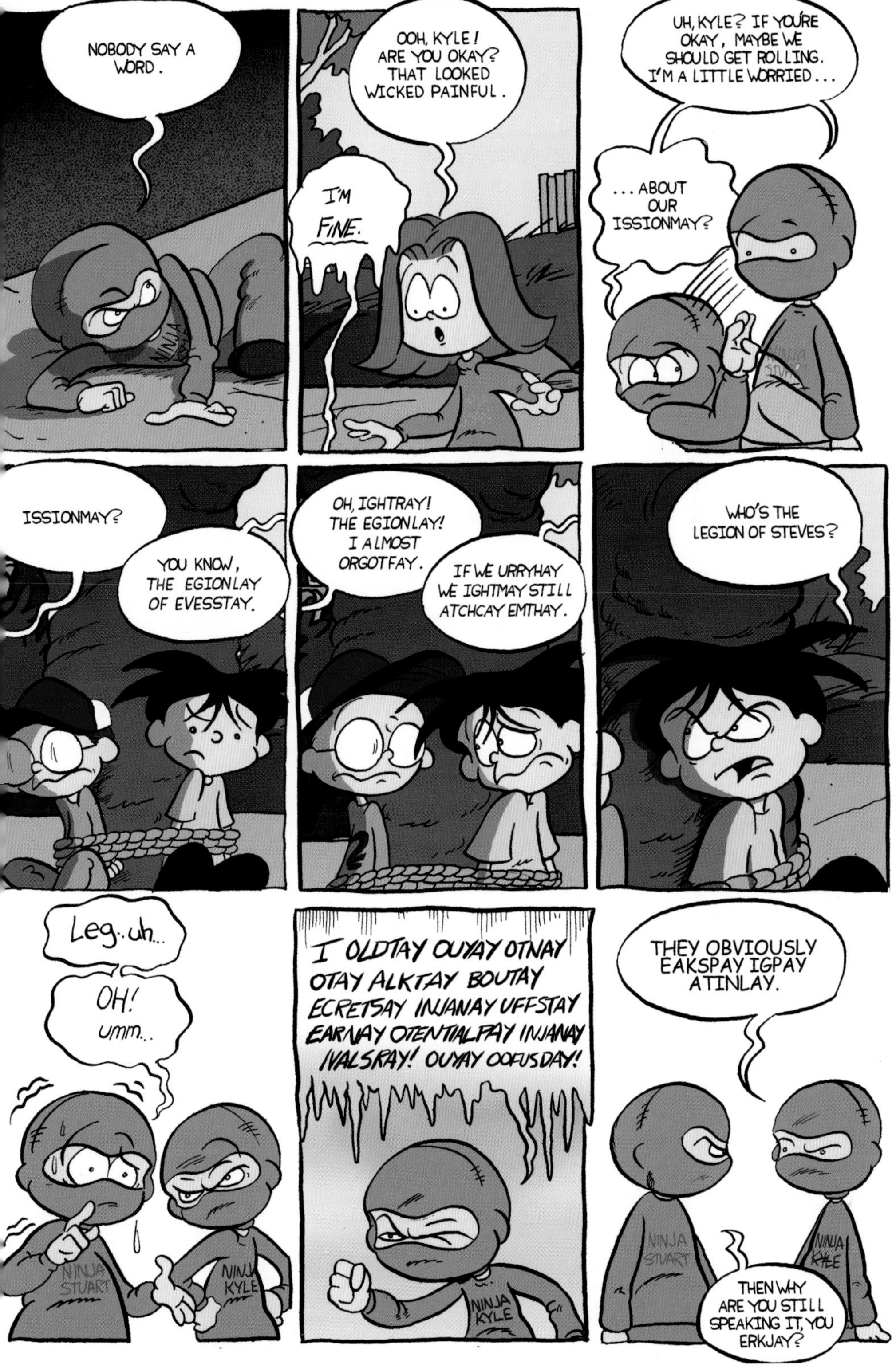
NOBODY SAY A WORD.
OOH, KYLE! ARE YOU OKAY? THAT LOOKED WICKED PAINFUL.
I'M FINE.
UH, KYLE? IF YOU'RE OKAY, MAYBE WE SHOULD GET ROLLING. I'M A LITTLE WORRIED...
...ABOUT OUR ISSIONMAY?
NINJA STUART
ISSIONMAY?
YOU KNOW, THE EGIONLAY OF EVESSTAY.
OH, IGHTRAY! THE EGIONLAY! I ALMOST ORGOTFAY.
IF WE URRYHAY WE IGHTMAY STILL ATCHCAY EMTHAY.
WHO'S THE LEGION OF STEVES?
Leg..uh...
OH! umm...
NINJA STUART
NINJA KYLE
I OLDTAY OUYAY OTNAY OTAY ALKTAY BOUTAY ECRETSAY INJANAY UFFSTAY EARNAY OTENTIALPAY INJANAY IVALSRAY! OUYAY OOFUSDAY!
NINJA KYLE
THEY OBVIOUSLY EAKSPAY IGPAY ATINLAY.
NINJA STUART
NINJA KYLE
THEN WHY ARE YOU STILL SPEAKING IT, YOU ERKJAY?

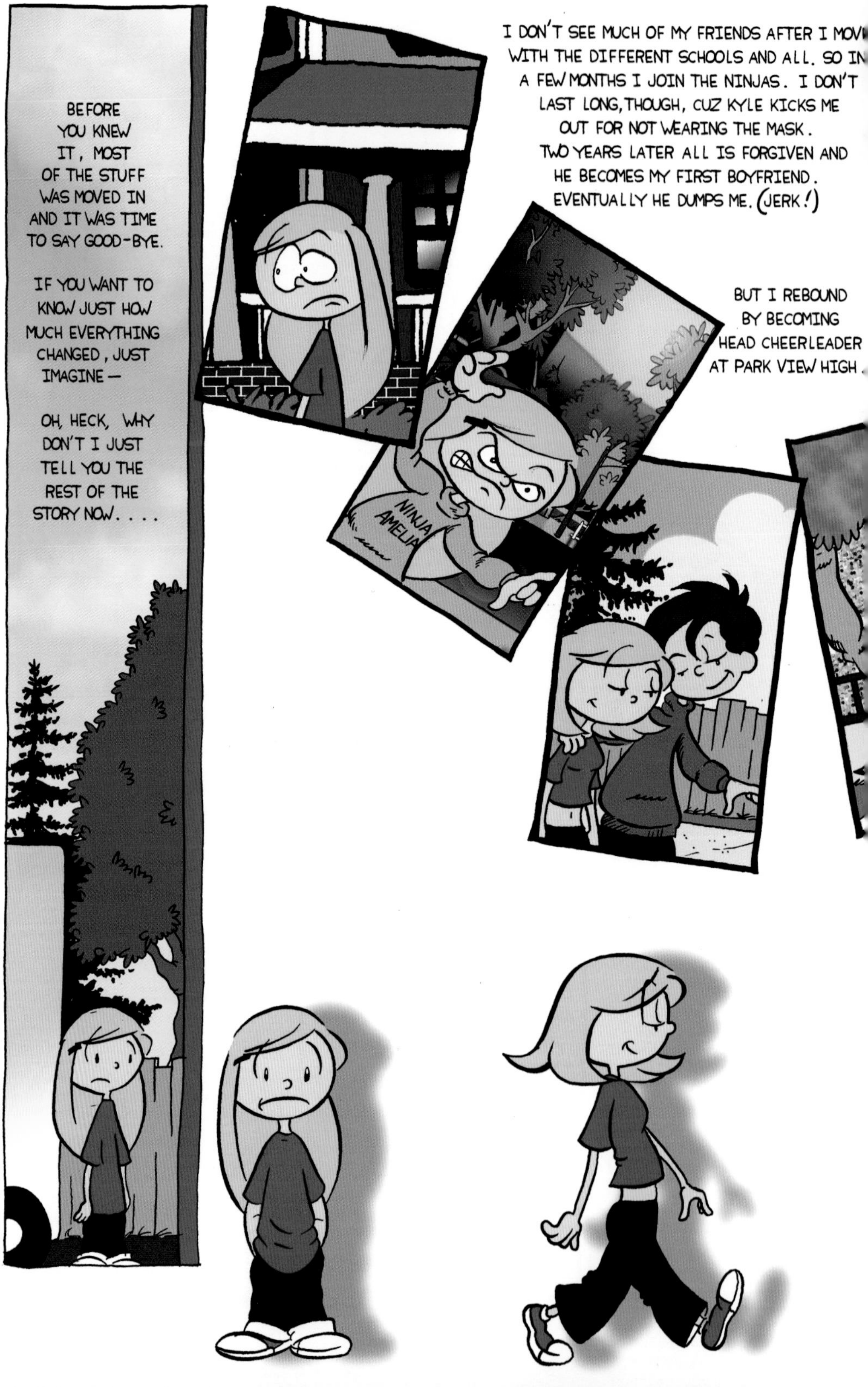
BEFORE YOU KNEW IT, MOST OF THE STUFF WAS MOVED IN AND IT WAS TIME TO SAY GOOD-BYE.
IF YOU WANT TO KNOW JUST HOW MUCH EVERYTHING CHANGED, JUST IMAGINE—
OH, HECK, WHY DON'T I JUST TELL YOU THE REST OF THE STORY NOW. . . .
I DON'T SEE MUCH OF MY FRIENDS AFTER I MOV WITH THE DIFFERENT SCHOOLS AND ALL. SO IN A FEW MONTHS I JOIN THE NINJAS. I DON'T LAST LONG, THOUGH, CUZ KYLE KICKS ME OUT FOR NOT WEARING THE MASK. TWO YEARS LATER ALL IS FORGIVEN AND HE BECOMES MY FIRST BOYFRIEND. EVENTUALLY HE DUMPS ME. (JERK!)
NINJA AMELIA
BUT I REBOUND BY BECOMING HEAD CHEERLEADER AT PARK VIEW HIGH.

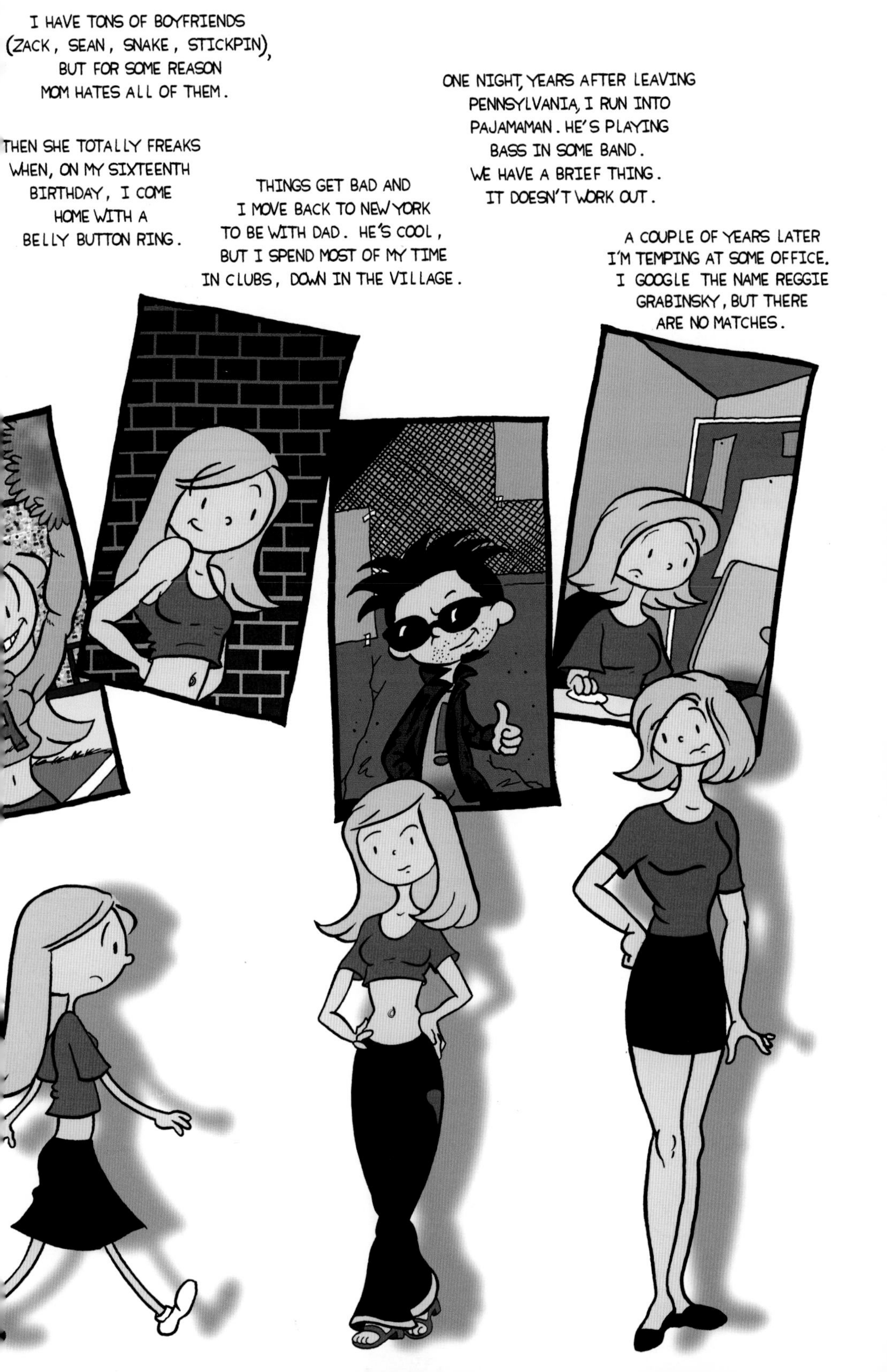
I HAVE TONS OF BOYFRIENDS (ZACK, SEAN, SNAKE, STICKPIN), BUT FOR SOME REASON MOM HATES ALL OF THEM.
THEN SHE TOTALLY FREAKS WHEN, ON MY SIXTEENTH BIRTHDAY, I COME HOME WITH A BELLY BUTTON RING.
THINGS GET BAD AND I MOVE BACK TO NEW YORK TO BE WITH DAD. HE'S COOL, BUT I SPEND MOST OF MY TIME IN CLUBS, DOWN IN THE VILLAGE.
ONE NIGHT, YEARS AFTER LEAVING PENNSYLVANIA, I RUN INTO PAJAMAMAN. HE'S PLAYING BASS IN SOME BAND.
WE HAVE A BRIEF THING.
IT DOESN'T WORK OUT.
A COUPLE OF YEARS LATER I'M TEMPING AT SOME OFFICE. I GOOGLE THE NAME REGGIE GRABINSKY, BUT THERE ARE NO MATCHES.

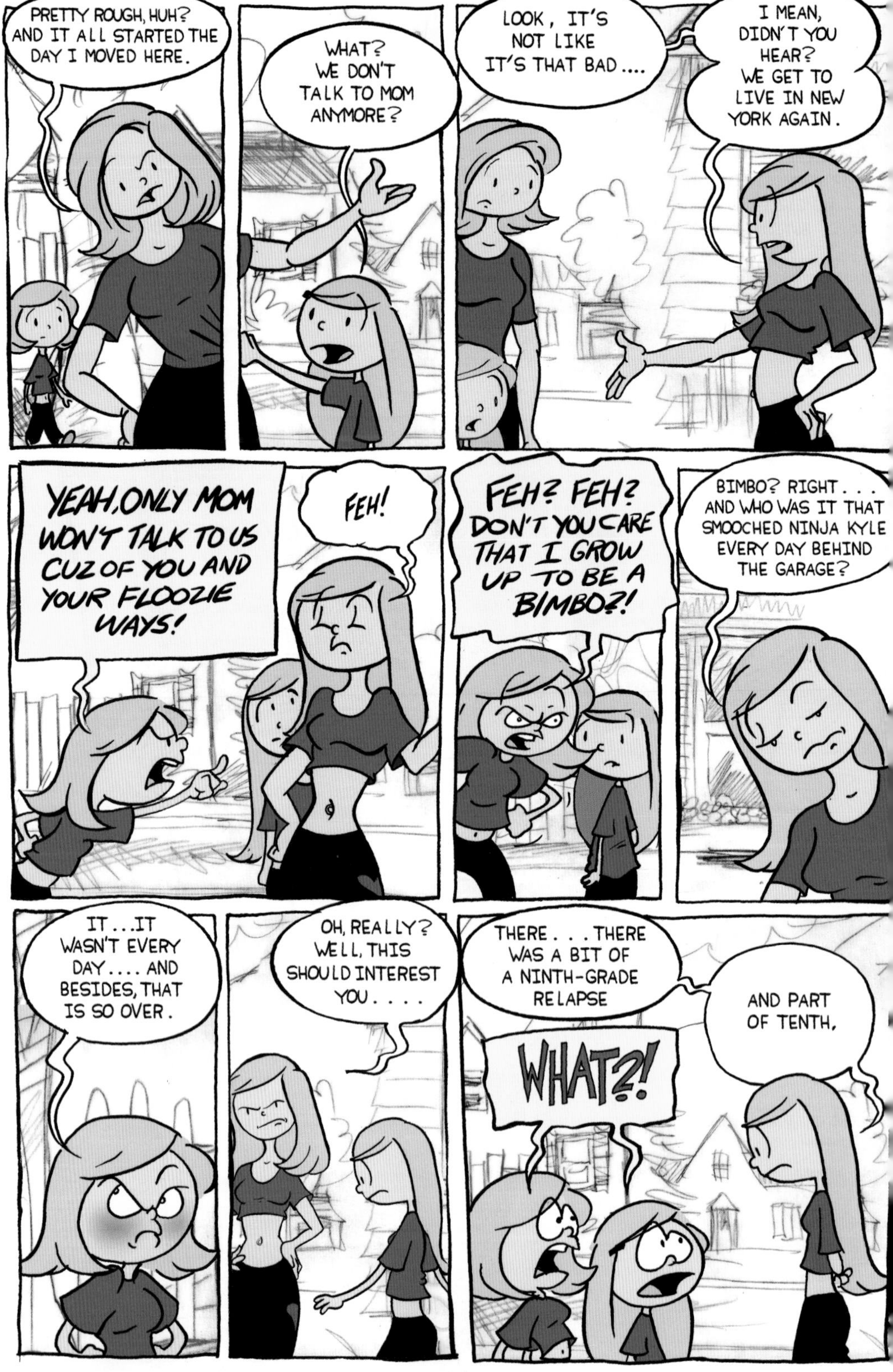
PRETTY ROUGH, HUH? AND IT ALL STARTED THE DAY I MOVED HERE.
WHAT? WE DON'T TALK TO MOM ANYMORE?
LOOK, IT'S NOT LIKE IT'S THAT BAD....
I MEAN, DIDN'T YOU HEAR? WE GET TO LIVE IN NEW YORK AGAIN.
YEAH, ONLY MOM WON'T TALK TO US CUZ OF YOU AND YOUR FLOOZIE WAYS!
FEH!
FEH? FEH? DON'T YOU CARE THAT I GROW UP TO BE A BIMBO?!
BIMBO? RIGHT... AND WHO WAS IT THAT SMOOCHED NINJA KYLE EVERY DAY BEHIND THE GARAGE?
IT...IT WASN'T EVERY DAY.... AND BESIDES, THAT IS SO OVER.
OH, REALLY? WELL, THIS SHOULD INTEREST YOU....
THERE...THERE WAS A BIT OF A NINTH-GRADE RELAPSE
AND PART OF TENTH.
WHAT?!

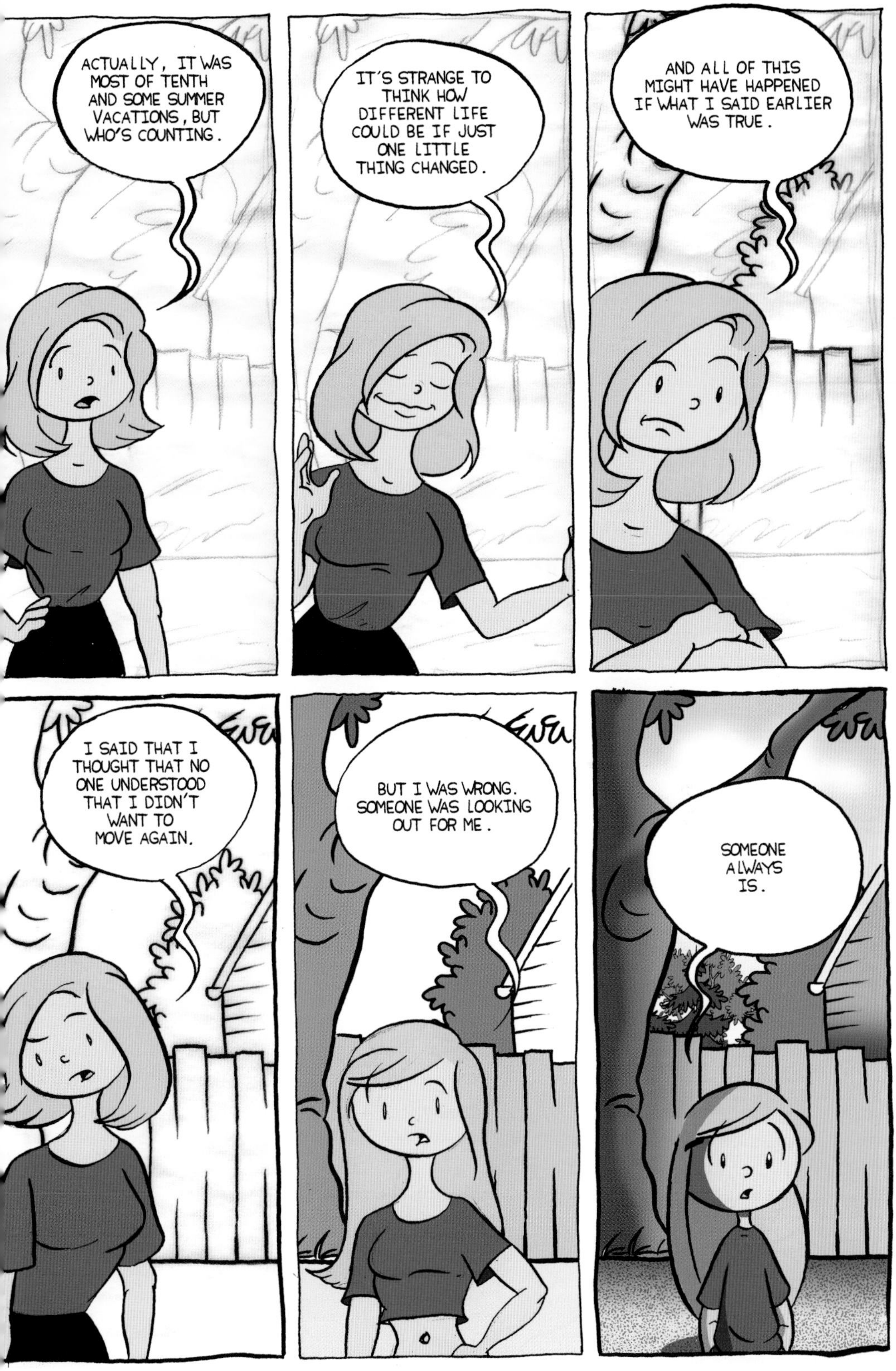
ACTUALLY, IT WAS MOST OF TENTH AND SOME SUMMER VACATIONS, BUT WHO'S COUNTING.
IT'S STRANGE TO THINK HOW DIFFERENT LIFE COULD BE IF JUST ONE LITTLE THING CHANGED.
AND ALL OF THIS MIGHT HAVE HAPPENED IF WHAT I SAID EARLIER WAS TRUE.
I SAID THAT I THOUGHT THAT NO ONE UNDERSTOOD THAT I DIDN'T WANT TO MOVE AGAIN.
BUT I WAS WRONG. SOMEONE WAS LOOKING OUT FOR ME.
SOMEONE ALWAYS IS.

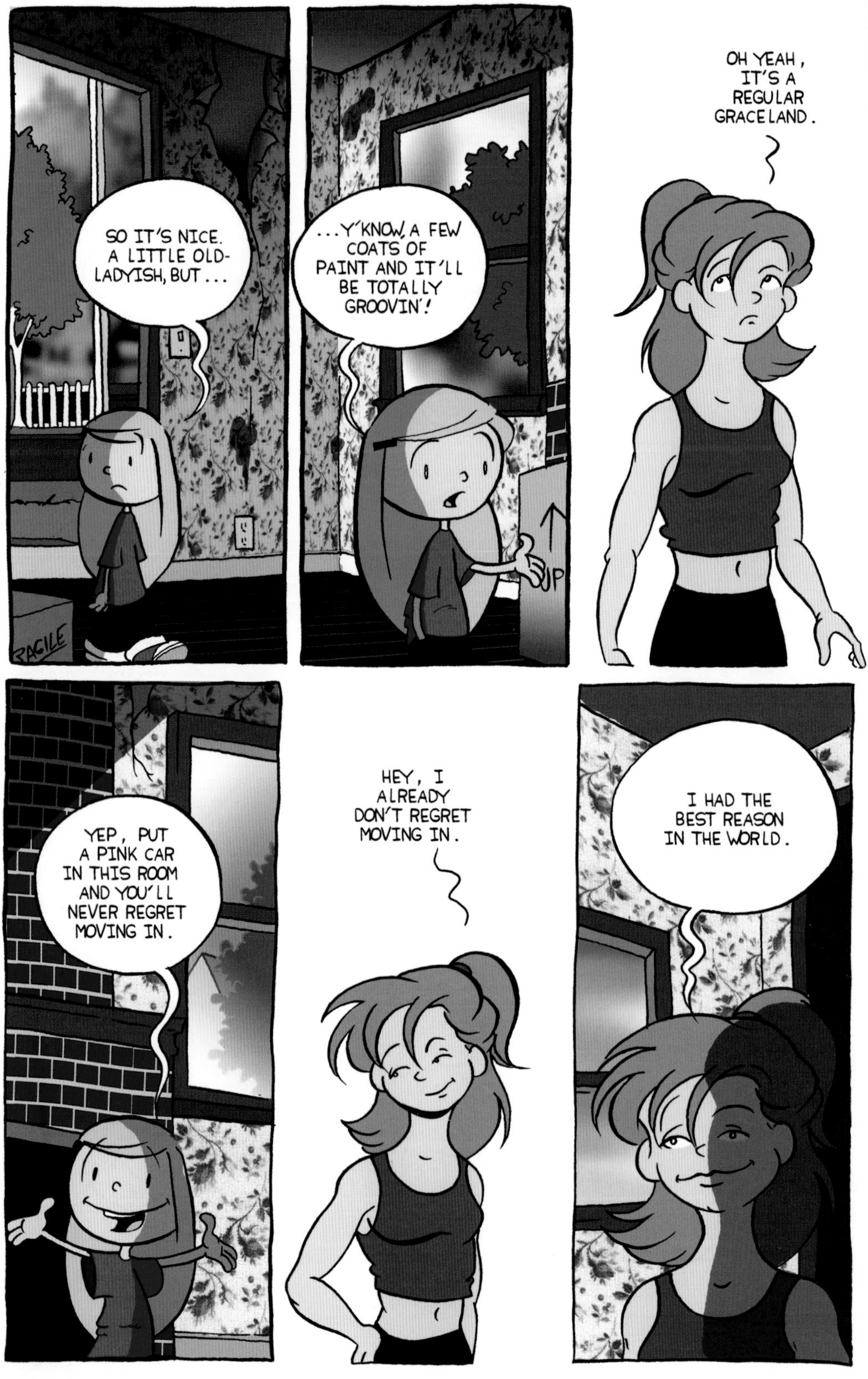
SO IT'S NICE. A LITTLE OLD-LADYISH, BUT . . .
. . . Y'KNOW, A FEW COATS OF PAINT AND IT'LL BE TOTALLY GROOVIN'!
UP
OH YEAH, IT'S A REGULAR GRACELAND.
YEP, PUT A PINK CAR IN THIS ROOM AND YOU'LL NEVER REGRET MOVING IN.
HEY, I ALREADY DON'T REGRET MOVING IN.
I HAD THE BEST REASON IN THE WORLD.

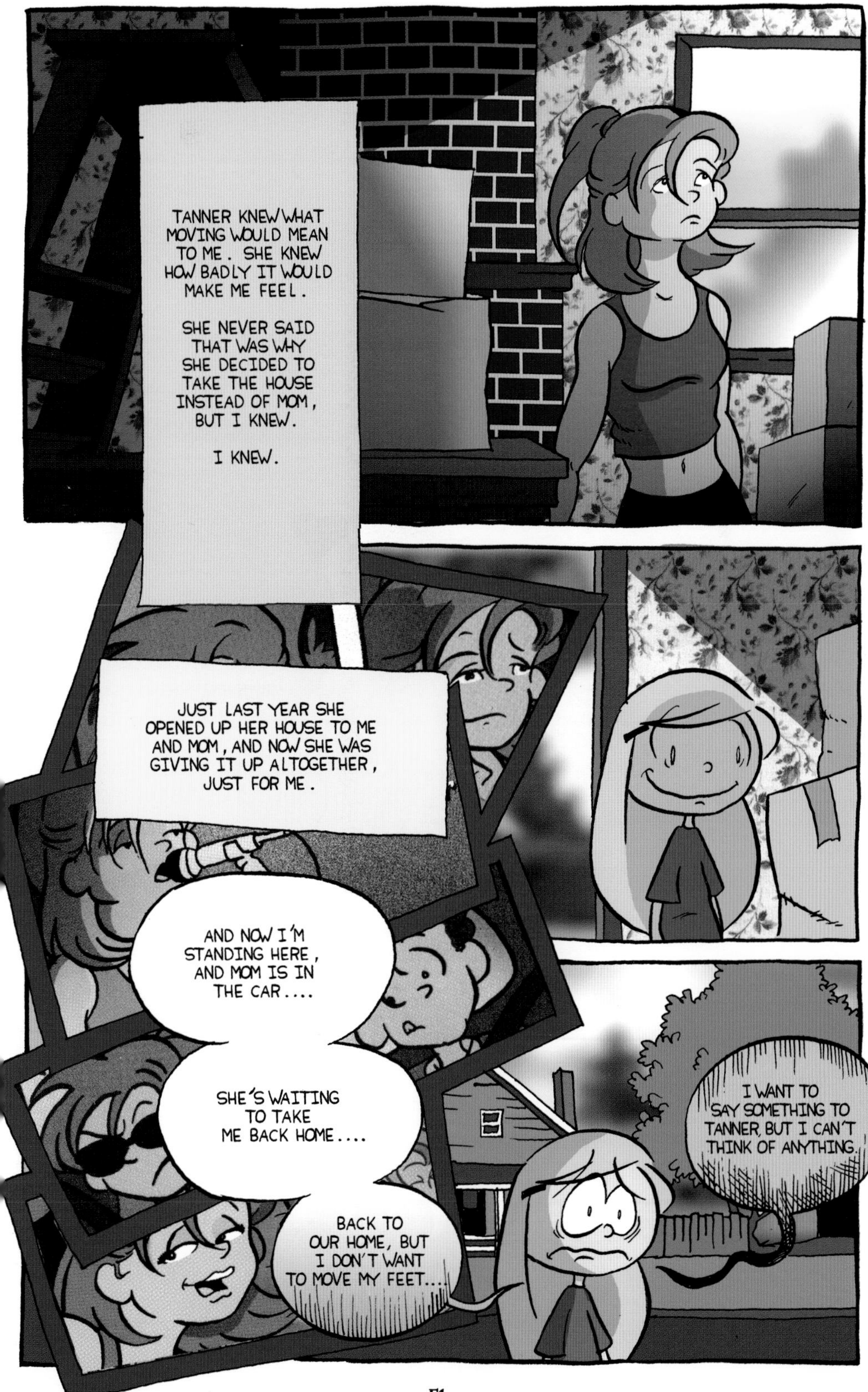
TANNER KNEW WHAT MOVING WOULD MEAN TO ME. SHE KNEW HOW BADLY IT WOULD MAKE ME FEEL.
SHE NEVER SAID THAT WAS WHY SHE DECIDED TO TAKE THE HOUSE INSTEAD OF MOM, BUT I KNEW.
I KNEW.
JUST LAST YEAR SHE OPENED UP HER HOUSE TO ME AND MOM, AND NOW SHE WAS GIVING IT UP ALTOGETHER, JUST FOR ME.
AND NOW I'M STANDING HERE, AND MOM IS IN THE CAR....
SHE'S WAITING TO TAKE ME BACK HOME....
BACK TO OUR HOME, BUT I DON'T WANT TO MOVE MY FEET...
I WANT TO SAY SOMETHING TO TANNER, BUT I CAN'T THINK OF ANYTHING.

SO I RUN BACK IN AND
I JUMP UP ON HER AND
I'M HUGGING HER AROUND
HER NECK AND I START
CRYING AND SHE STARTS
LAUGHING AND I
STILL CAN'T THINK
OF ANYTHING TO SAY.

BUT IT DOESN'T MATTER,
CUZ SUPERHEROES
NEVER NEED TO BE
THANKED ANYWAY.

Old Friends
Who Just Met

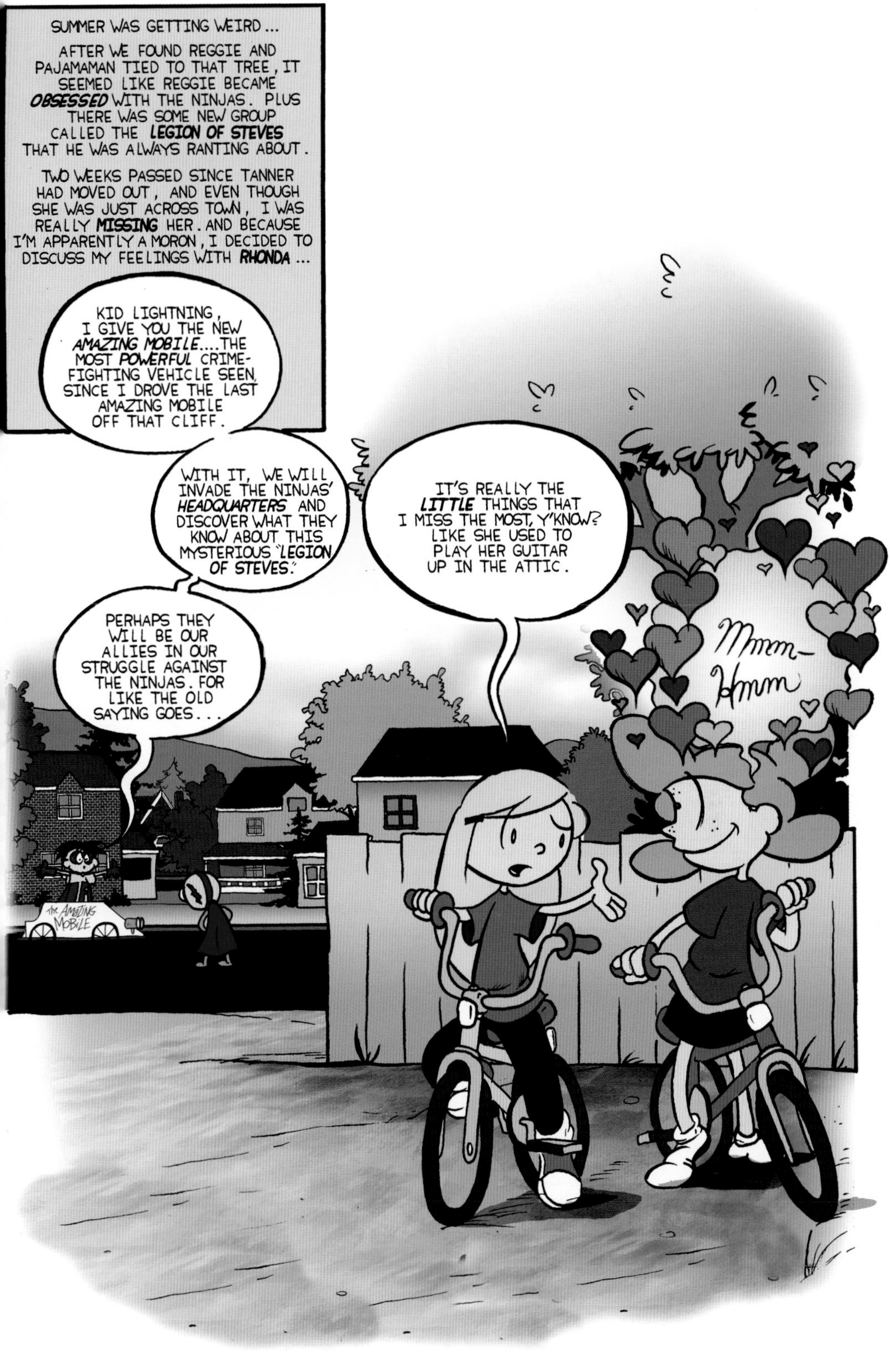
SUMMER WAS GETTING WEIRD...
AFTER WE FOUND REGGIE AND PAJAMAMAN TIED TO THAT TREE, IT SEEMED LIKE REGGIE BECAME **OBSESSED** WITH THE NINJAS. PLUS THERE WAS SOME NEW GROUP CALLED THE **LEGION OF STEVES** THAT HE WAS ALWAYS RANTING ABOUT.
TWO WEEKS PASSED SINCE TANNER HAD MOVED OUT, AND EVEN THOUGH SHE WAS JUST ACROSS TOWN, I WAS REALLY **MISSING** HER. AND BECAUSE I'M APPARENTLY A MORON, I DECIDED TO DISCUSS MY FEELINGS WITH **RHONDA**...
KID LIGHTNING, I GIVE YOU THE NEW ***AMAZING MOBILE***....THE MOST ***POWERFUL*** CRIME-FIGHTING VEHICLE SEEN, SINCE I DROVE THE LAST AMAZING MOBILE OFF THAT CLIFF.
WITH IT, WE WILL INVADE THE NINJAS' ***HEADQUARTERS*** AND DISCOVER WHAT THEY KNOW ABOUT THIS MYSTERIOUS "***LEGION OF STEVES***."
PERHAPS THEY WILL BE OUR ALLIES IN OUR STRUGGLE AGAINST THE NINJAS. FOR LIKE THE OLD SAYING GOES...
THE AMAZING MOBILE
IT'S REALLY THE ***LITTLE*** THINGS THAT I MISS THE MOST, Y'KNOW? LIKE SHE USED TO PLAY HER GUITAR UP IN THE ATTIC.
Mmm-Hmm

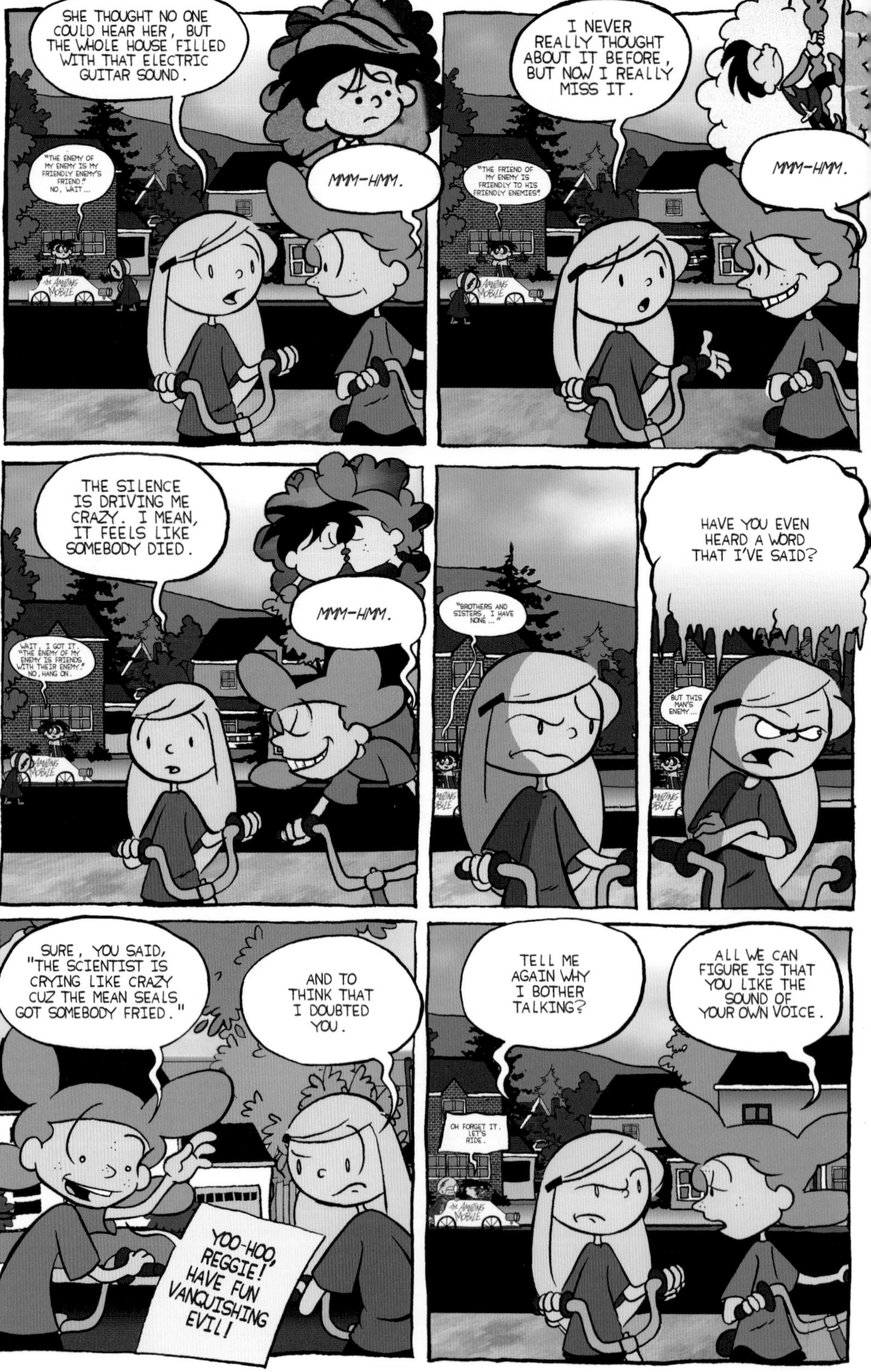
SHE THOUGHT NO ONE COULD HEAR HER, BUT THE WHOLE HOUSE FILLED WITH THAT ELECTRIC GUITAR SOUND.
"THE ENEMY OF MY ENEMY IS MY FRIENDLY ENEMY'S FRIEND." NO, WAIT...
MMM-HMM.
THE AMAZING MOBILE
I NEVER REALLY THOUGHT ABOUT IT BEFORE, BUT NOW I REALLY MISS IT.
"THE FRIEND OF MY ENEMY IS FRIENDLY TO HIS FRIENDLY ENEMIES."
MMM-HMM.
THE SILENCE IS DRIVING ME CRAZY. I MEAN, IT FEELS LIKE SOMEBODY DIED.
WAIT, I GOT IT. "THE ENEMY OF MY ENEMY IS FRIENDS WITH THEIR ENEMY." NO, HANG ON.
MMM-HMM.
"BROTHERS AND SISTERS, I HAVE NONE..."
HAVE YOU EVEN HEARD A WORD THAT I'VE SAID?
BUT THIS MAN'S ENEMY...
SURE, YOU SAID, "THE SCIENTIST IS CRYING LIKE CRAZY CUZ THE MEAN SEALS GOT SOMEBODY FRIED."
AND TO THINK THAT I DOUBTED YOU.
YOO-HOO, REGGIE! HAVE FUN VANQUISHING EVIL!
TELL ME AGAIN WHY I BOTHER TALKING?
ALL WE CAN FIGURE IS THAT YOU LIKE THE SOUND OF YOUR OWN VOICE.
OH FORGET IT. LET'S RIDE.

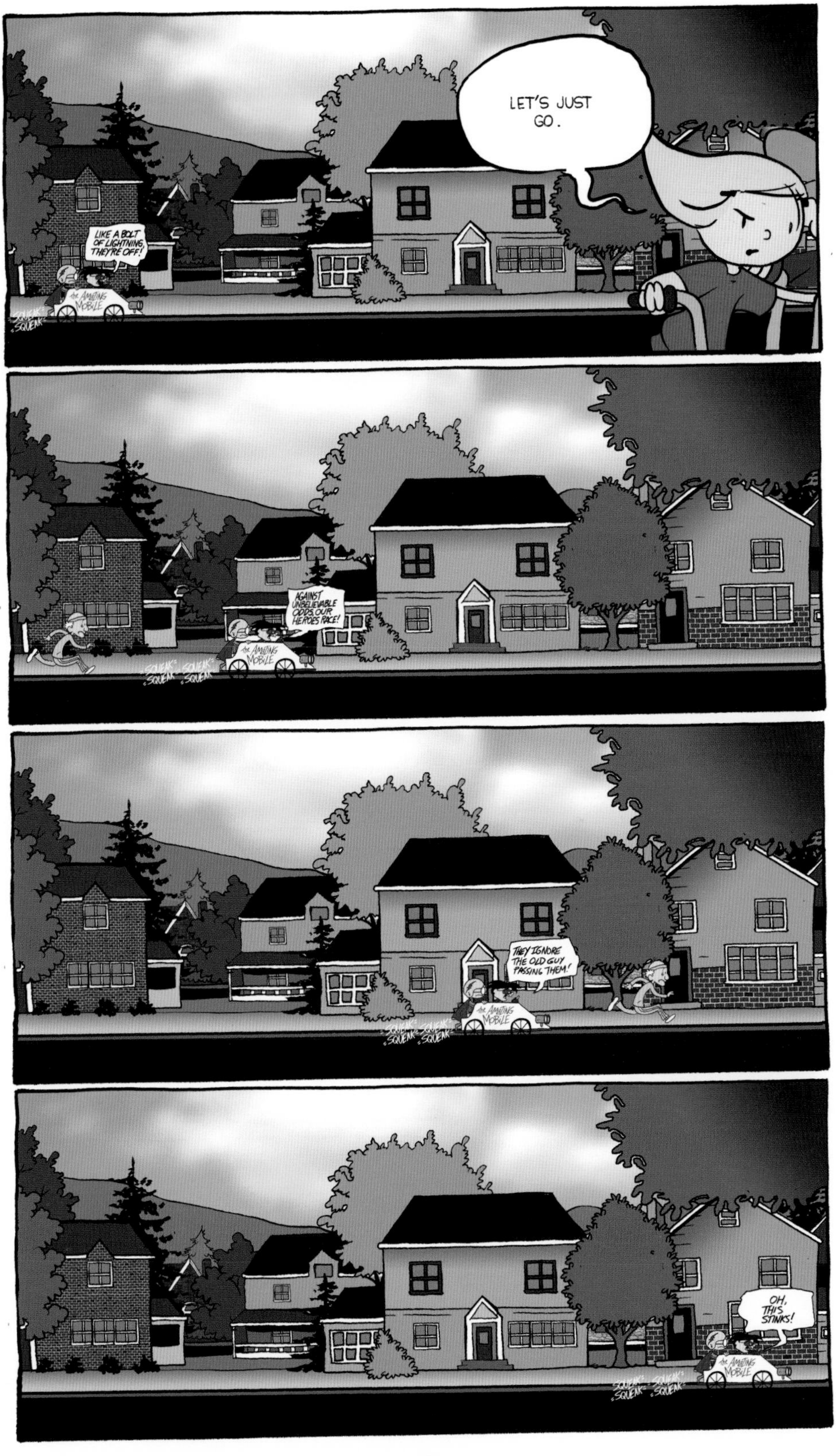
LIKE A BOLT OF LIGHTNING, THEY'RE OFF!
SQUEAK SQUEAK
LET'S JUST GO.
AGAINST UNBELIEVABLE ODDS, OUR HEROES RACE!
SQUEAK SQUEAK SQUEAK SQUEAK
THEY IGNORE THE OLD GUY PASSING THEM!
SQUEAK SQUEAK SQUEAK SQUEAK
OH, THIS STINKS!
SQUEAK SQUEAK SQUEAK SQUEAK

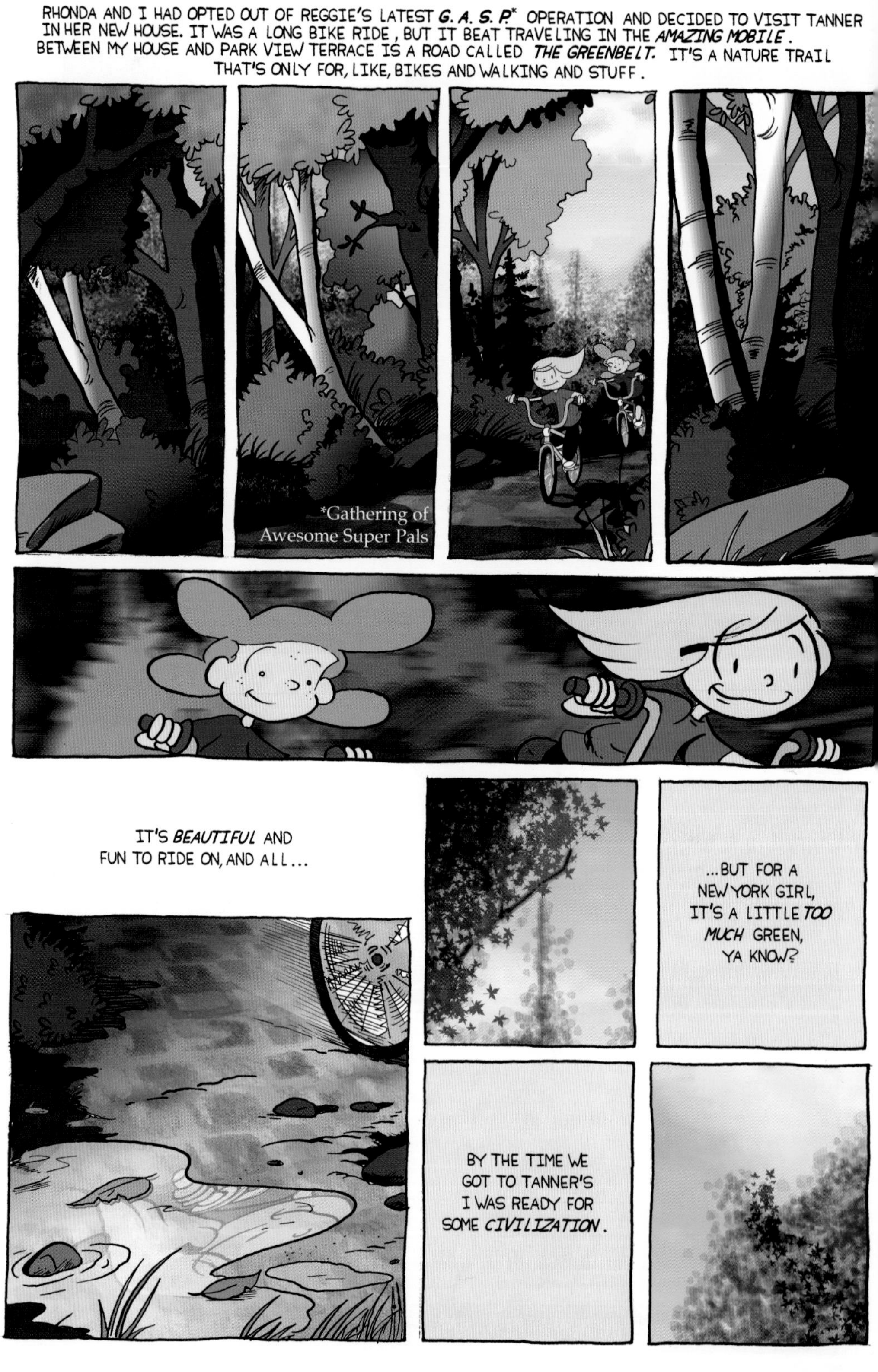
RHONDA AND I HAD OPTED OUT OF REGGIE'S LATEST G. A. S. P.* OPERATION AND DECIDED TO VISIT TANNER IN HER NEW HOUSE. IT WAS A LONG BIKE RIDE, BUT IT BEAT TRAVELING IN THE AMAZING MOBILE. BETWEEN MY HOUSE AND PARK VIEW TERRACE IS A ROAD CALLED THE GREENBELT. IT'S A NATURE TRAIL THAT'S ONLY FOR, LIKE, BIKES AND WALKING AND STUFF.
*Gathering of Awesome Super Pals
IT'S BEAUTIFUL AND FUN TO RIDE ON, AND ALL...
...BUT FOR A NEW YORK GIRL, IT'S A LITTLE TOO MUCH GREEN, YA KNOW?
BY THE TIME WE GOT TO TANNER'S I WAS READY FOR SOME CIVILIZATION.

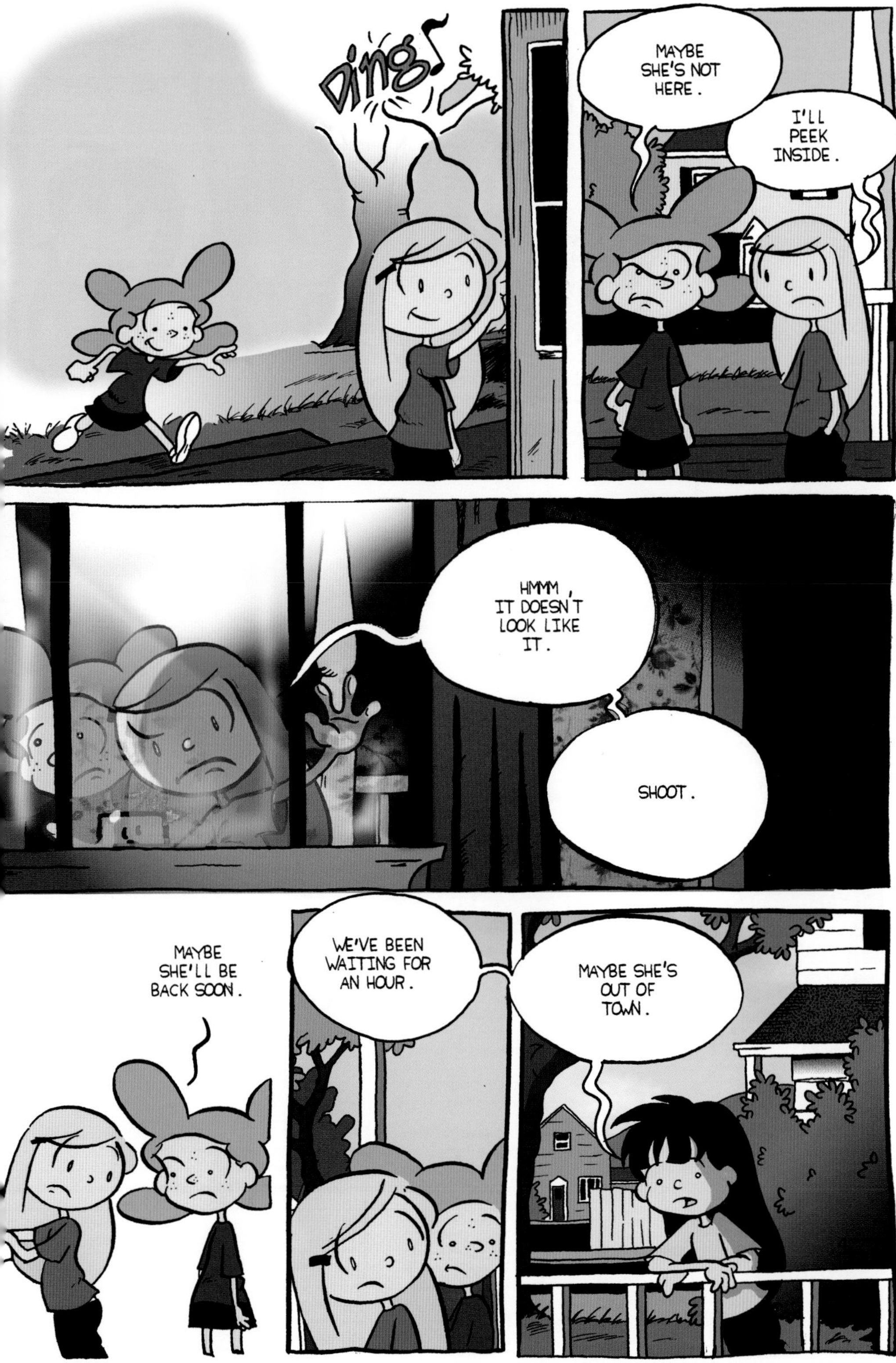

DING
MAYBE SHE'S NOT HERE.
I'LL PEEK INSIDE.
HMMM, IT DOESN'T LOOK LIKE IT.
SHOOT.
MAYBE SHE'LL BE BACK SOON.
WE'VE BEEN WAITING FOR AN HOUR.
MAYBE SHE'S OUT OF TOWN.

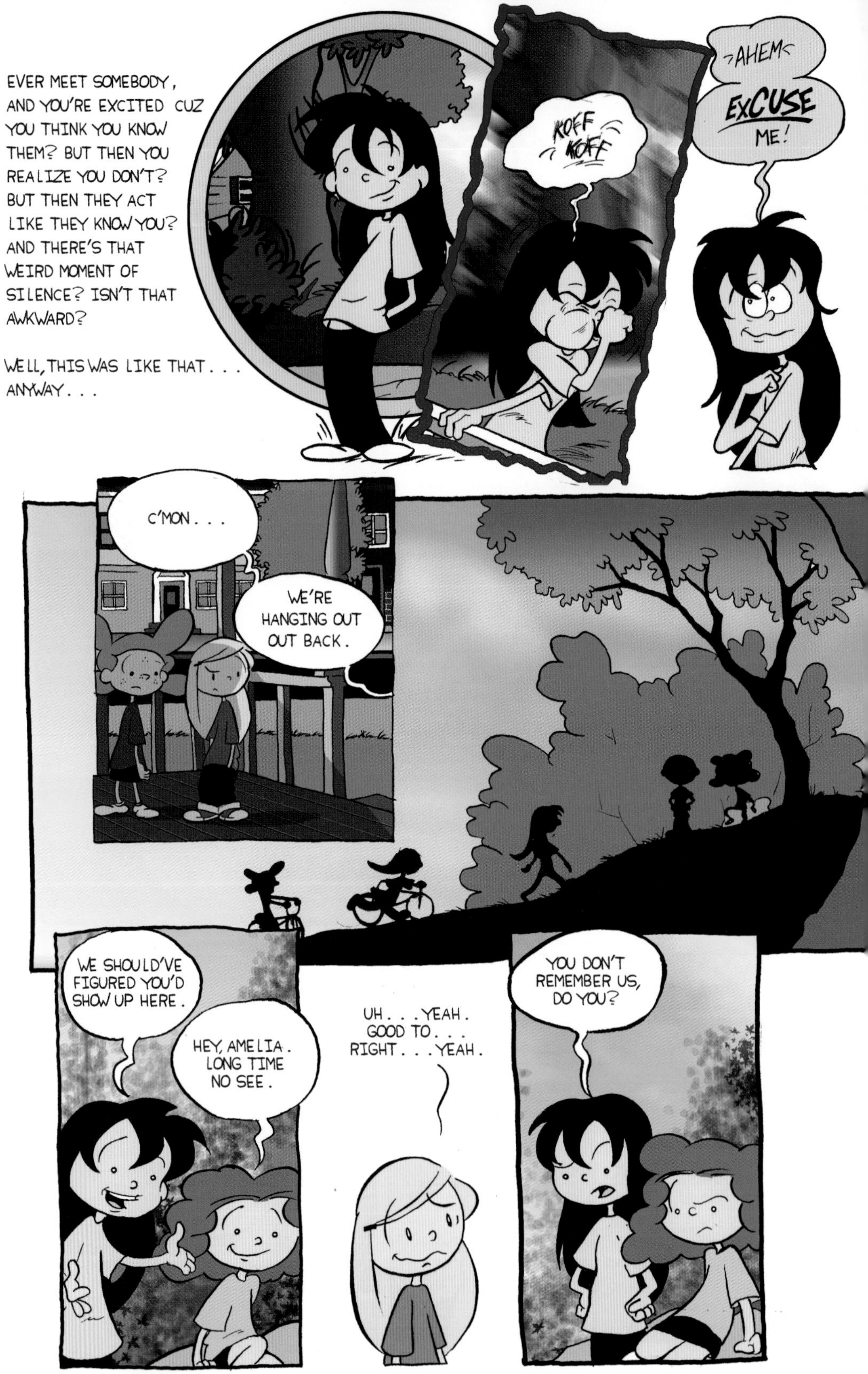
EVER MEET SOMEBODY, AND YOU'RE EXCITED CUZ YOU THINK YOU KNOW THEM? BUT THEN YOU REALIZE YOU DON'T? BUT THEN THEY ACT LIKE THEY KNOW YOU? AND THERE'S THAT WEIRD MOMENT OF SILENCE? ISN'T THAT AWKWARD?
WELL, THIS WAS LIKE THAT . . . ANYWAY . . .
KOFF KOFF
AHEM
EXCUSE ME!
C'MON . . .
WE'RE HANGING OUT OUT BACK.
WE SHOULD'VE FIGURED YOU'D SHOW UP HERE.
HEY, AMELIA. LONG TIME NO SEE.
UH . . . YEAH. GOOD TO . . . RIGHT . . . YEAH.
YOU DON'T REMEMBER US, DO YOU?

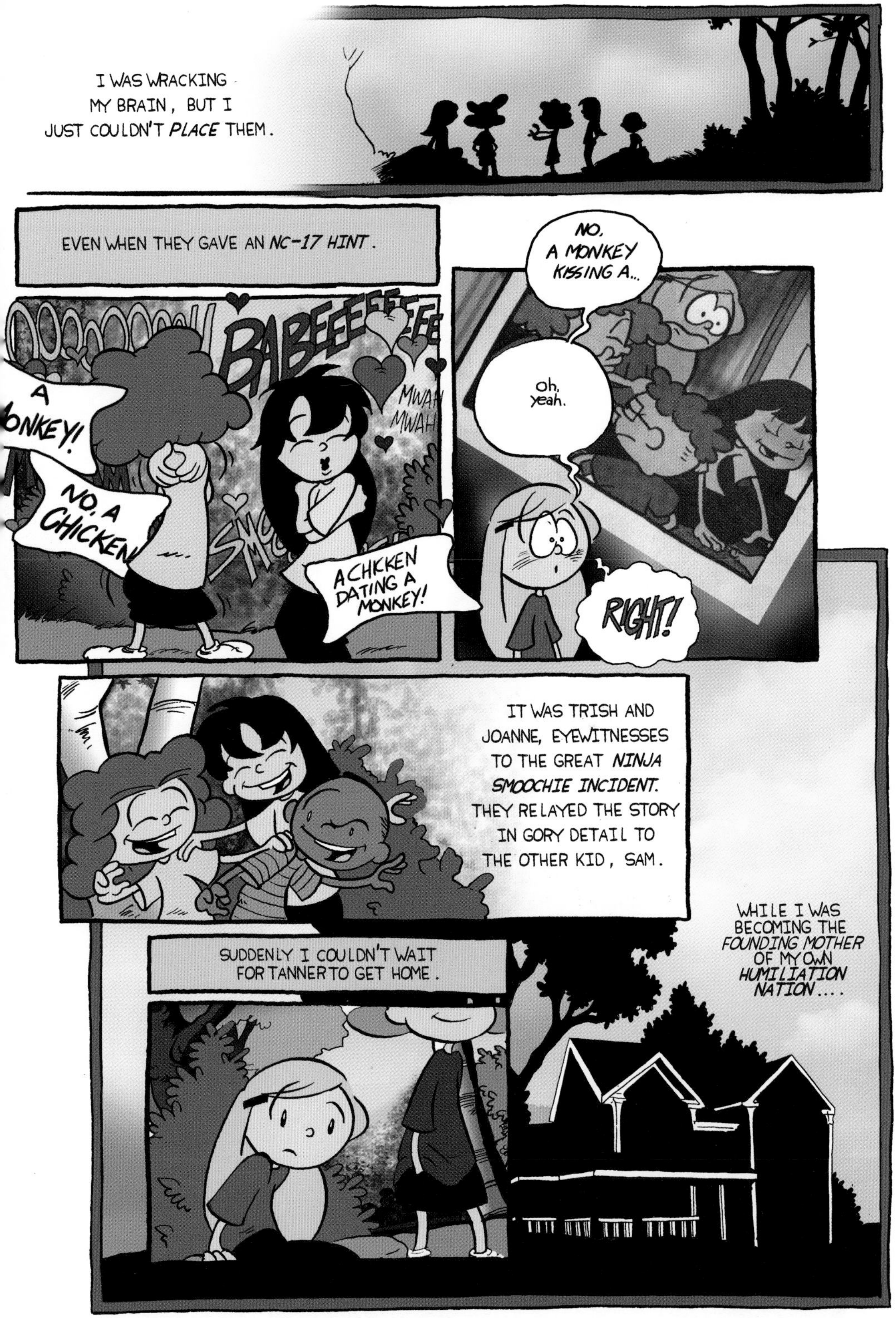
I WAS WRACKING MY BRAIN, BUT I JUST COULDN'T PLACE THEM.
EVEN WHEN THEY GAVE AN NC-17 HINT.
OOOOOOOOOO!!
BABEEEEEEEEEE
A MONKEY!
NO, A CHICKEN
MWAH MWAH
A CHICKEN DATING A MONKEY!
NO, A MONKEY KISSING A...
oh, yeah.
RIGHT!
IT WAS TRISH AND JOANNE, EYEWITNESSES TO THE GREAT NINJA SMOOCHIE INCIDENT. THEY RELAYED THE STORY IN GORY DETAIL TO THE OTHER KID, SAM.
WHILE I WAS BECOMING THE FOUNDING MOTHER OF MY OWN HUMILIATION NATION....
SUDDENLY I COULDN'T WAIT FOR TANNER TO GET HOME.

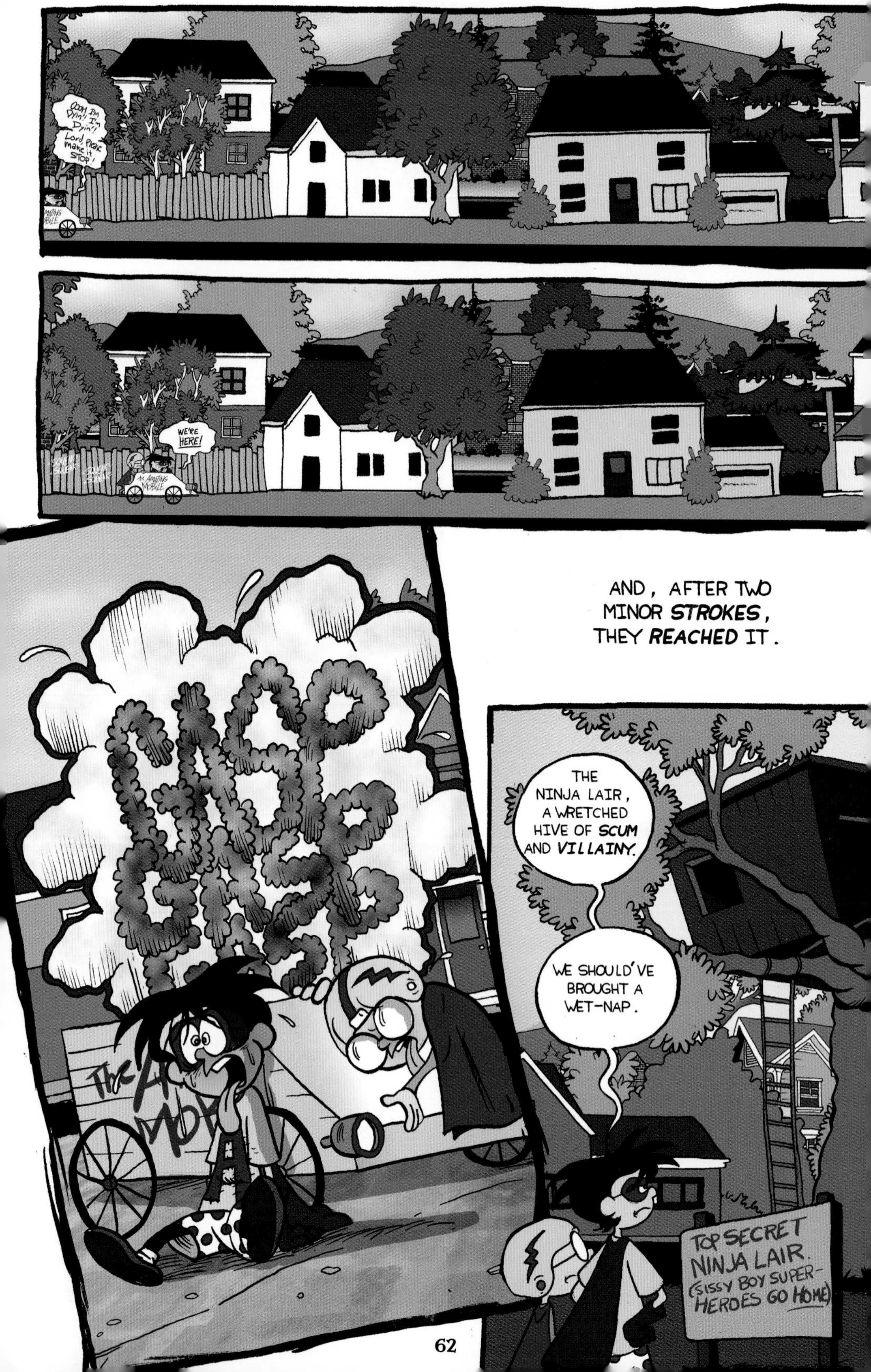

OOOH I'm Dyin'! I'm Dyin'!
Lord, Please make it STOP!
SQUEAK SQUEAK
SQUEAK SQUEAK
WE'RE HERE!
the AMAZING MOBILE
AND, AFTER TWO MINOR STROKES, THEY REACHED IT.
GASP GASP
THE NINJA LAIR, A WRETCHED HIVE OF SCUM AND VILLAINY.
WE SHOULD'VE BROUGHT A WET-NAP.
TOP SECRET NINJA LAIR (SISSY BOY SUPER-HEROES GO HOME)

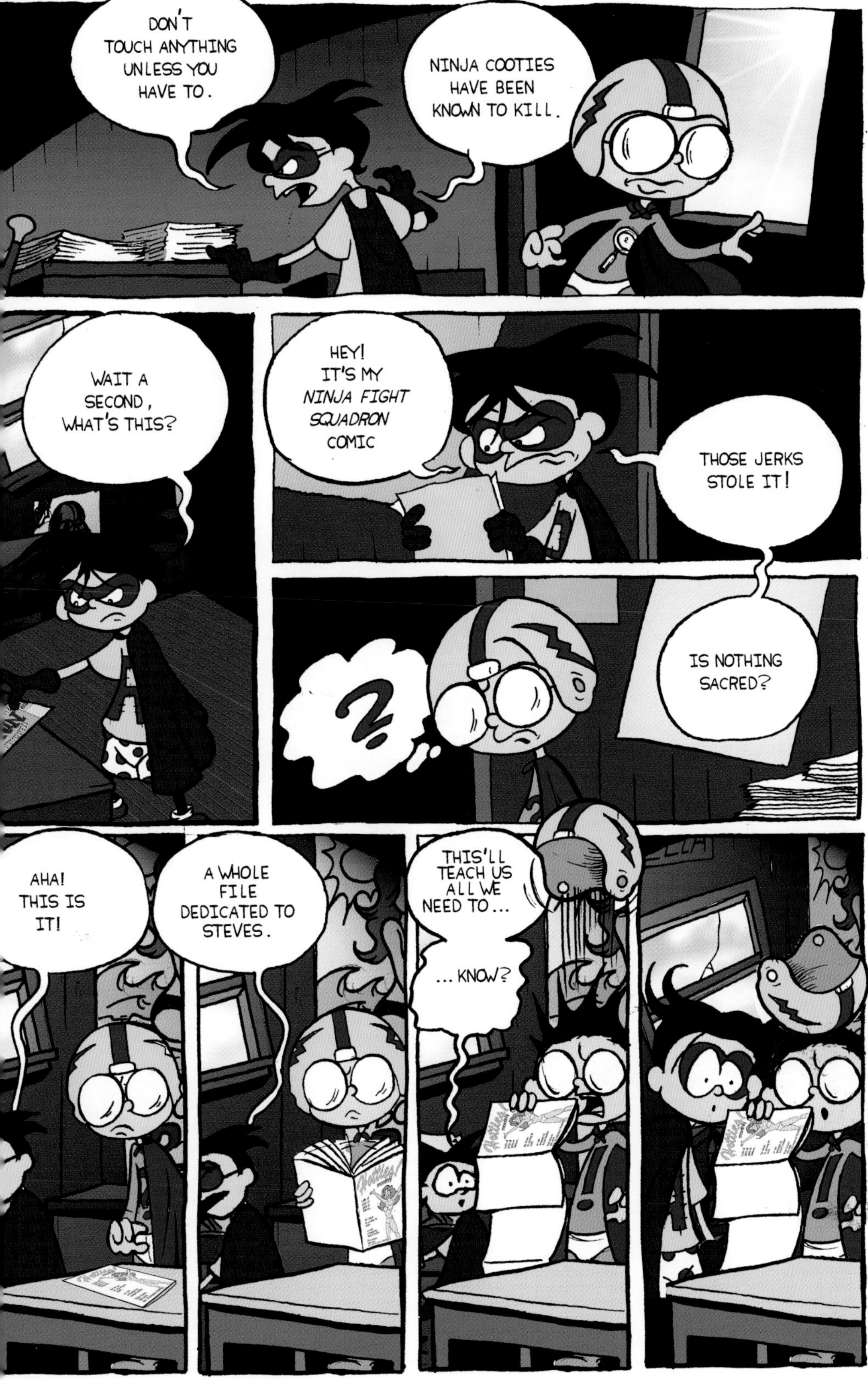
DON'T TOUCH ANYTHING UNLESS YOU HAVE TO.
NINJA COOTIES HAVE BEEN KNOWN TO KILL.
WAIT A SECOND, WHAT'S THIS?
HEY! IT'S MY *NINJA FIGHT SQUADRON* COMIC
THOSE JERKS STOLE IT!
IS NOTHING SACRED?
?
AHA! THIS IS IT!
A WHOLE FILE DEDICATED TO STEVES.
THIS'LL TEACH US ALL WE NEED TO...
...KNOW?

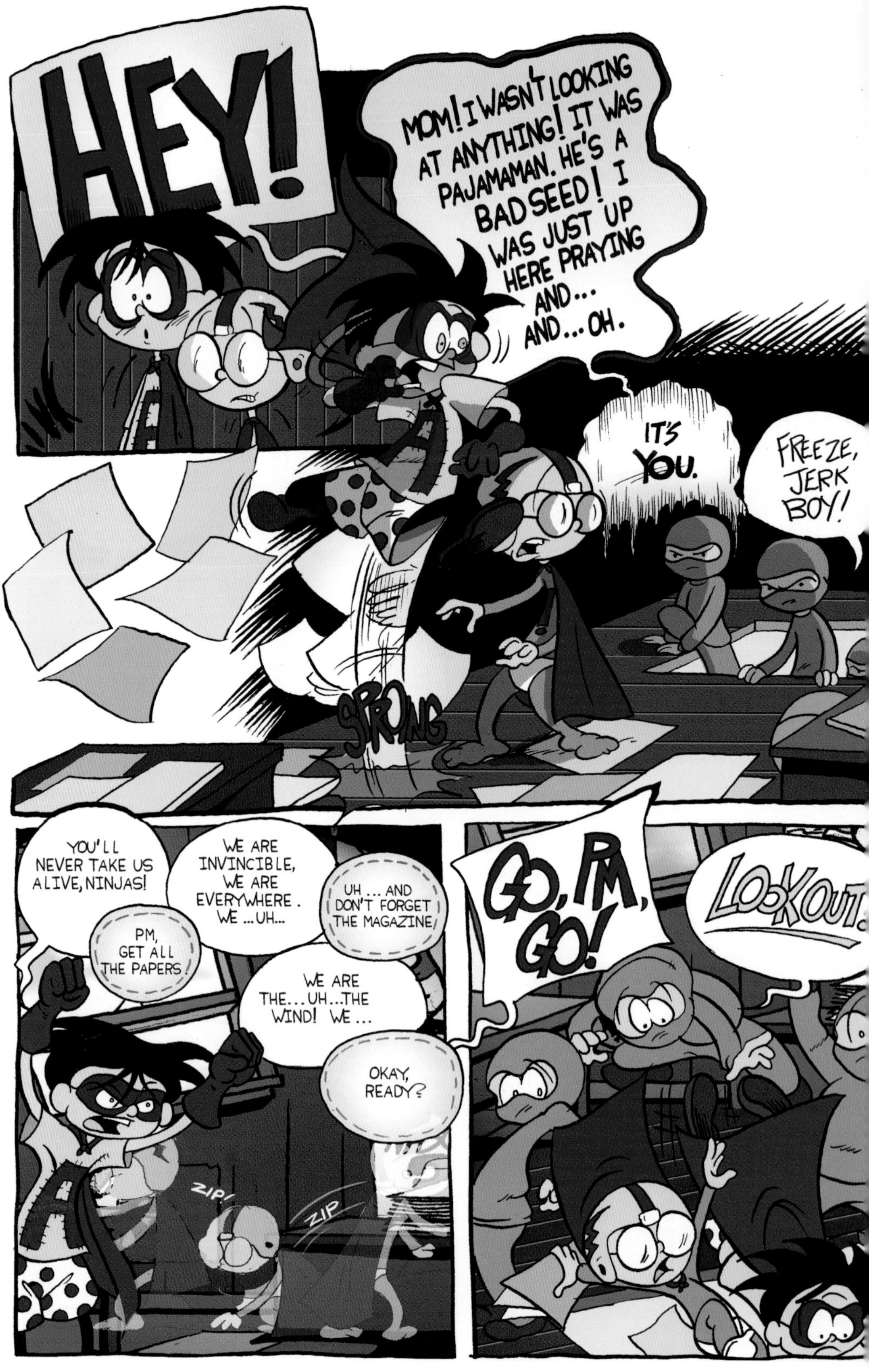
HEY!
MOM! I WASN'T LOOKING AT ANYTHING! IT WAS PAJAMAMAN. HE'S A BAD SEED! I WAS JUST UP HERE PRAYING AND... AND... OH.
IT'S YOU.
FREEZE, JERK BOY!
SPROING
YOU'LL NEVER TAKE US ALIVE, NINJAS!
WE ARE INVINCIBLE, WE ARE EVERYWHERE. WE ...UH...
PM, GET ALL THE PAPERS.
UH ... AND DON'T FORGET THE MAGAZINE
WE ARE THE... UH... THE WIND! WE ...
OKAY, READY?
ZIP!
ZIP
GO, PM, GO!
LOOKOUT!

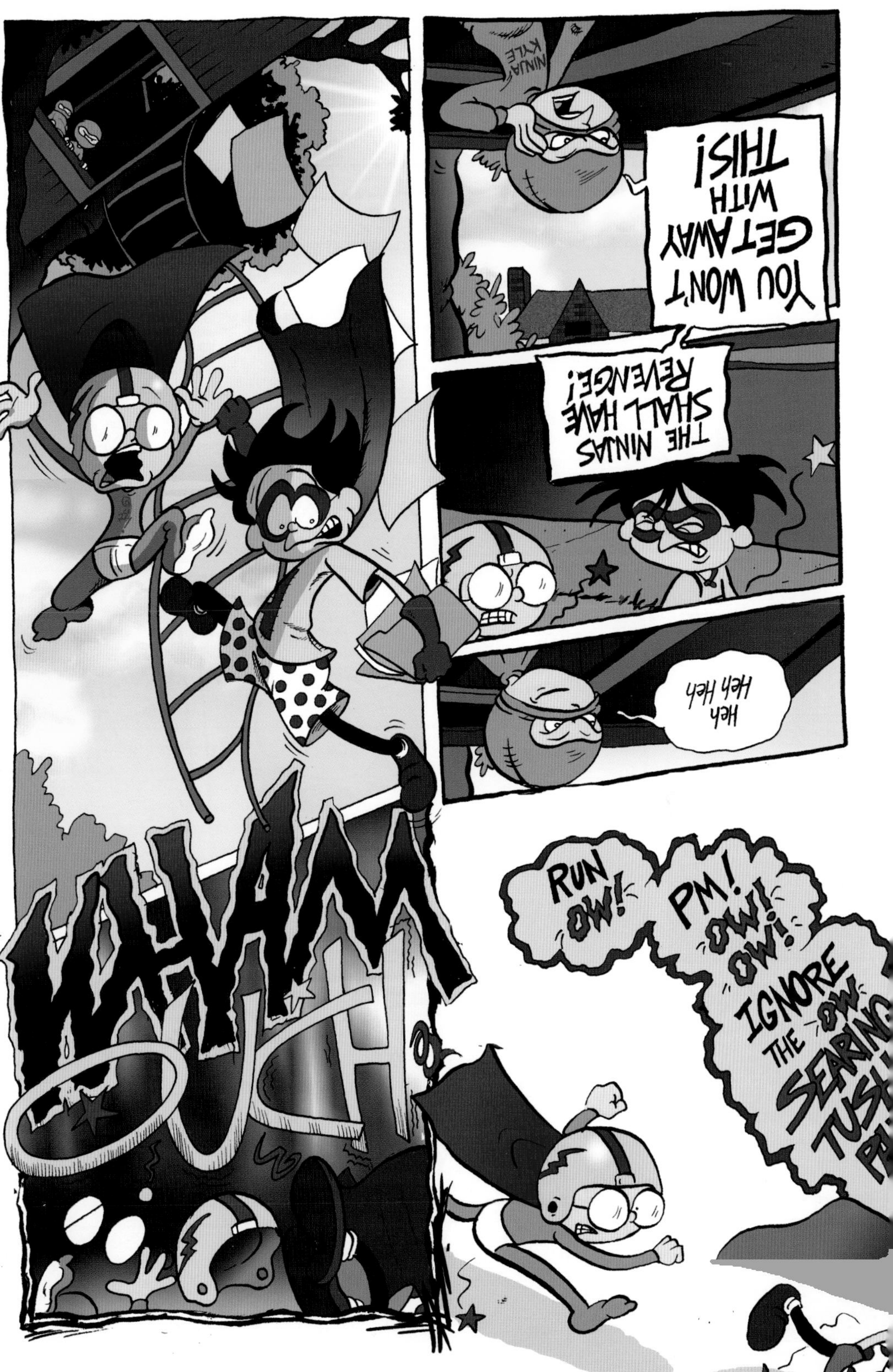
NINJA KYLE
YOU WON'T GET AWAY WITH THIS!
THE NINJAS SHALL HAVE REVENGE!
Heh Heh Heh
WHAM
OUCH
RUN OW!
PM! OW! OW!
IGNORE THE OW SEARIN TUSH P

AND SPEAKING OF ***PAINS IN THE BUTT***. . .I FIGURED THE BEST WAY TO STOP BEING EMBARRASSED WAS TO START DOING THE EMBARRASSING. SO I TURNED THE SPOTLIGHT ON MY GOOD FRIEND RHONDA

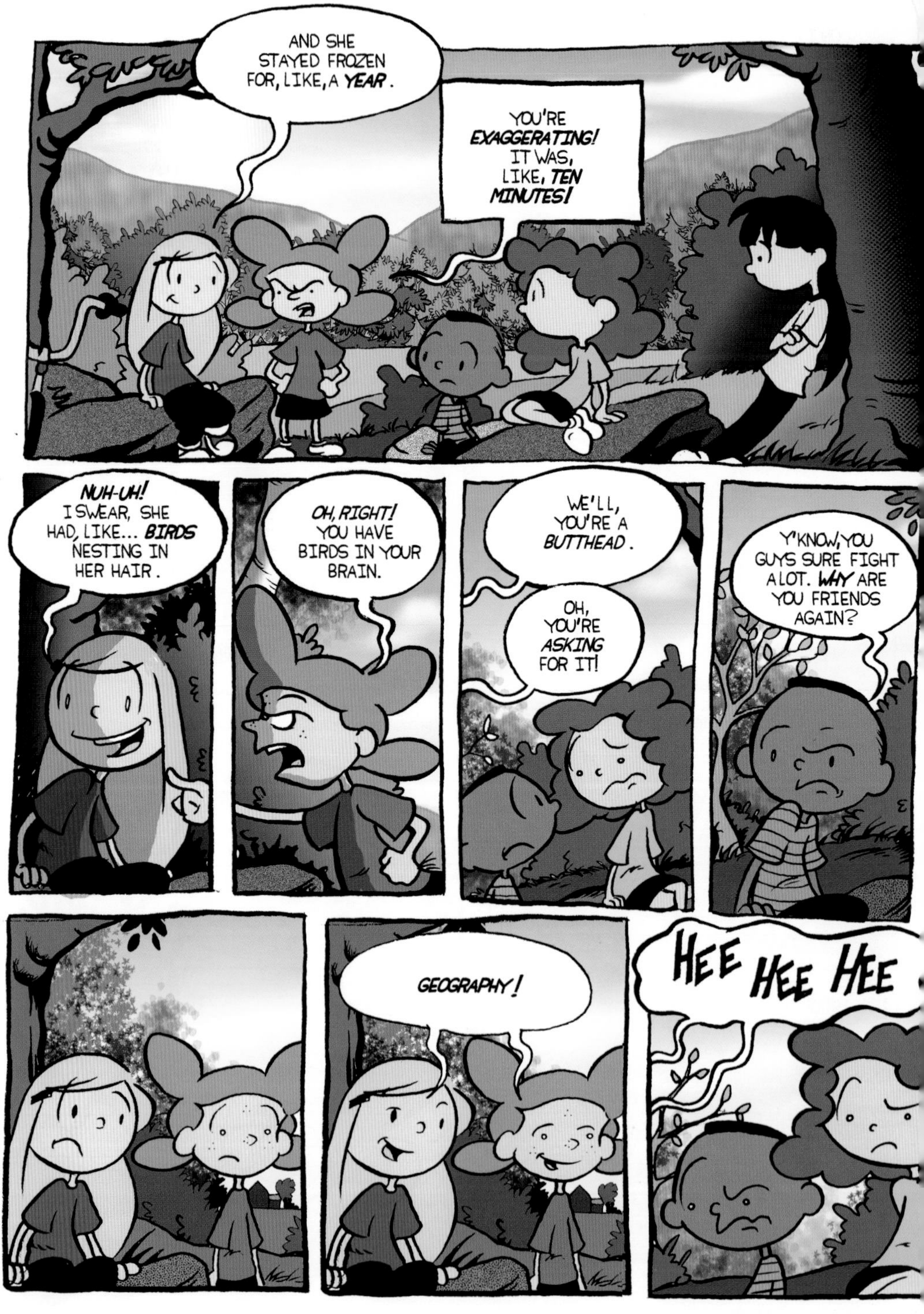

AND SHE STAYED FROZEN FOR, LIKE, A ***YEAR***.
YOU'RE ***EXAGGERATING!*** IT WAS, LIKE, ***TEN MINUTES!***
NUH-UH! I SWEAR, SHE HAD, LIKE... ***BIRDS*** NESTING IN HER HAIR.
OH, RIGHT! YOU HAVE BIRDS IN YOUR BRAIN.
WE'LL, YOU'RE A ***BUTTHEAD***.
OH, YOU'RE ***ASKING*** FOR IT!
Y'KNOW, YOU GUYS SURE FIGHT ALOT. ***WHY*** ARE YOU FRIENDS AGAIN?
GEOGRAPHY!
HEE HEE HEE

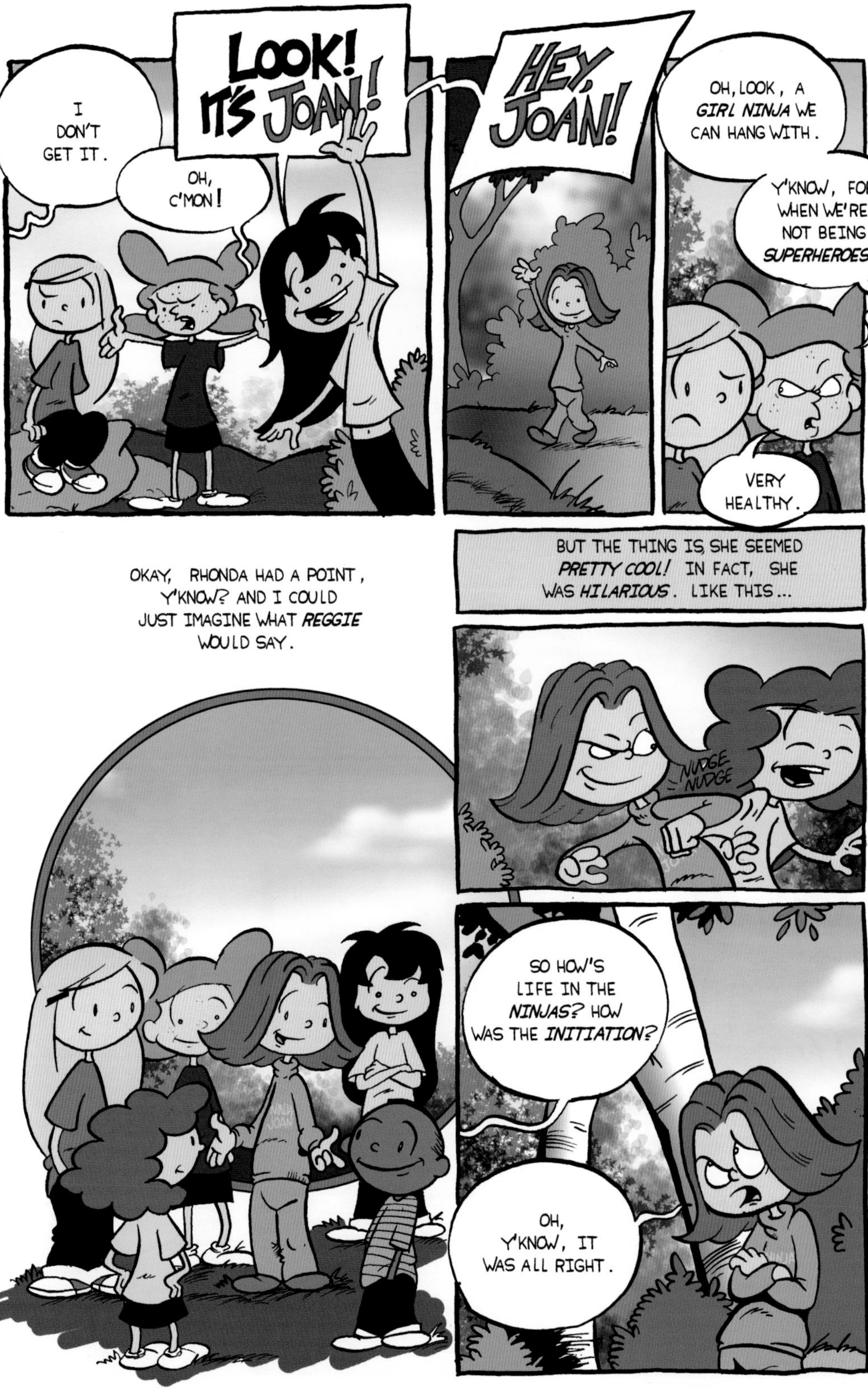
I DON'T GET IT.
LOOK! IT'S JOAN!
OH, C'MON!
HEY, JOAN!
OH, LOOK, A *GIRL NINJA* WE CAN HANG WITH.
Y'KNOW, FOR WHEN WE'RE NOT BEING *SUPERHEROES*.
VERY HEALTHY.
OKAY, RHONDA HAD A POINT, Y'KNOW? AND I COULD JUST IMAGINE WHAT *REGGIE* WOULD SAY.
BUT THE THING IS, SHE SEEMED *PRETTY COOL!* IN FACT, SHE WAS *HILARIOUS*. LIKE THIS...
NUDGE NUDGE
SO HOW'S LIFE IN THE *NINJAS?* HOW WAS THE *INITIATION?*
OH, Y'KNOW, IT WAS ALL RIGHT.

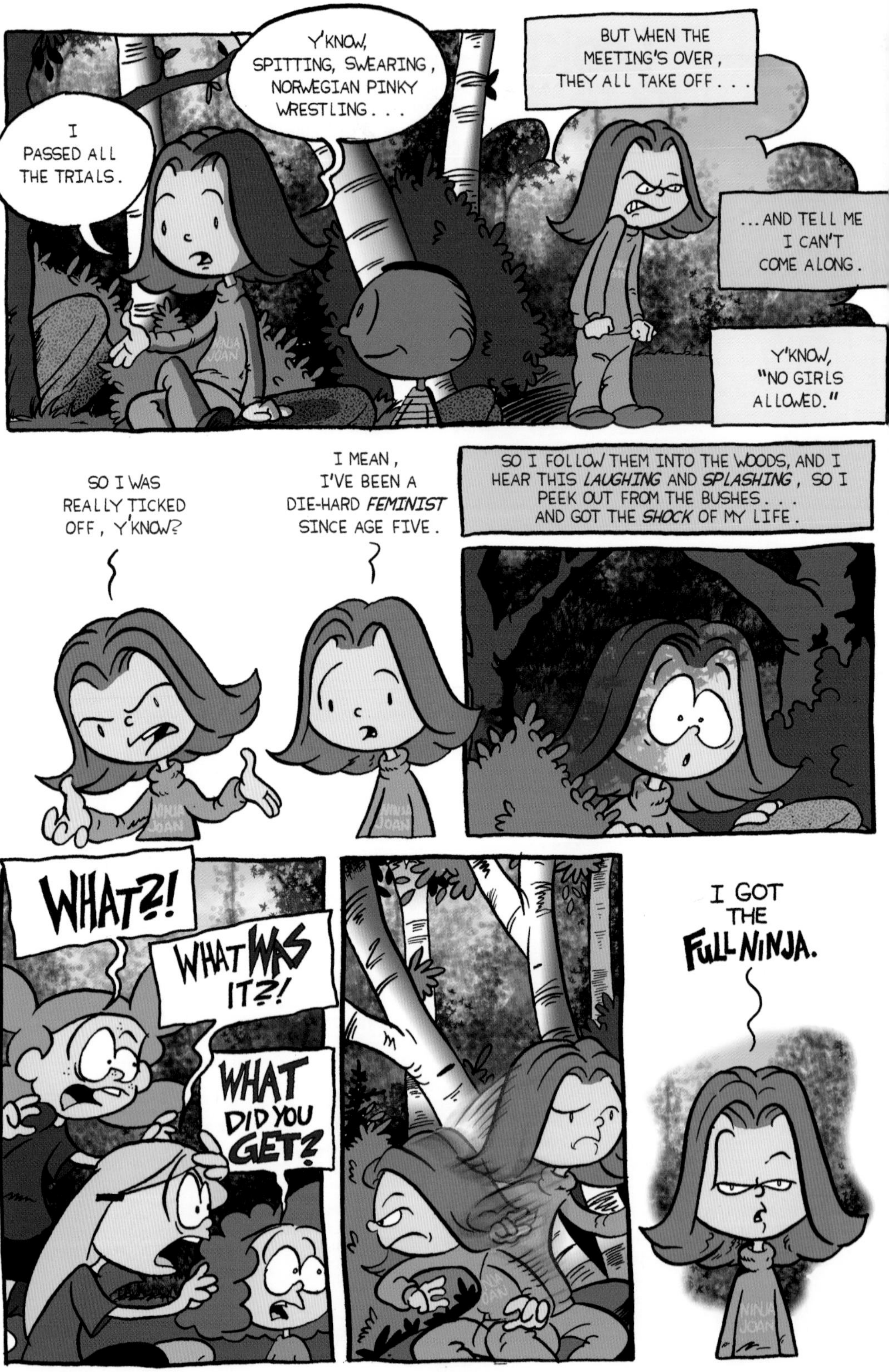
I PASSED ALL THE TRIALS.
Y'KNOW, SPITTING, SWEARING, NORWEGIAN PINKY WRESTLING . . .
BUT WHEN THE MEETING'S OVER, THEY ALL TAKE OFF . . .
. . . AND TELL ME I CAN'T COME ALONG.
Y'KNOW, "NO GIRLS ALLOWED."
SO I WAS REALLY TICKED OFF, Y'KNOW?
I MEAN, I'VE BEEN A DIE-HARD FEMINIST SINCE AGE FIVE.
SO I FOLLOW THEM INTO THE WOODS, AND I HEAR THIS LAUGHING AND SPLASHING, SO I PEEK OUT FROM THE BUSHES . . . AND GOT THE SHOCK OF MY LIFE.
WHAT?!
WHAT WAS IT?!
WHAT DID YOU GET?
I GOT THE FULL NINJA.

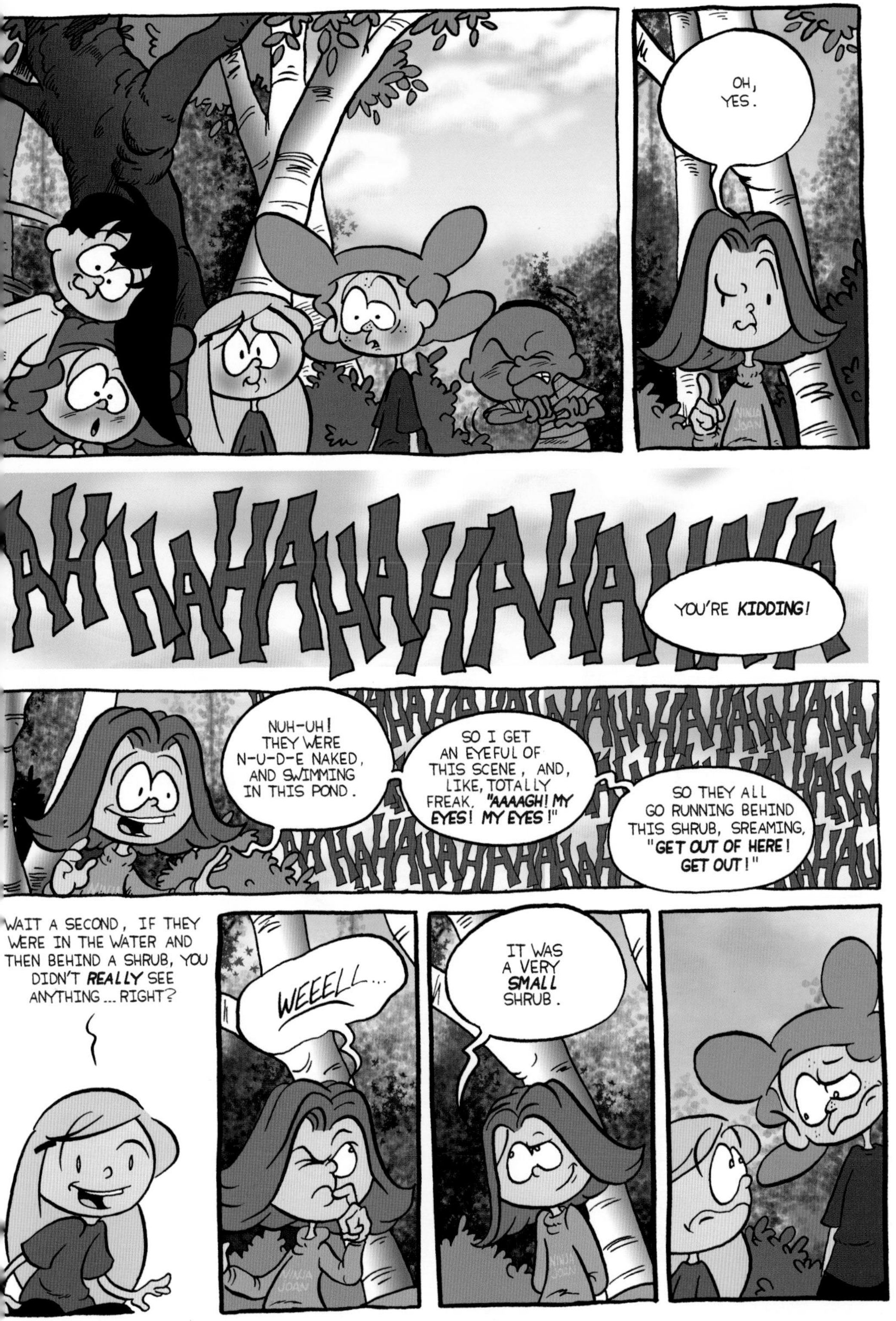
OH, YES.
AHHAHAHAHAHAHAHAHA
YOU'RE **KIDDING**!
NUH-UH! THEY WERE N-U-D-E NAKED, AND SWIMMING IN THIS POND.
SO I GET AN EYEFUL OF THIS SCENE, AND, LIKE, TOTALLY FREAK. **"AAAAGH! MY EYES! MY EYES!"**
SO THEY ALL GO RUNNING BEHIND THIS SHRUB, SREAMING, "**GET OUT OF HERE! GET OUT!**"
WAIT A SECOND, IF THEY WERE IN THE WATER AND THEN BEHIND A SHRUB, YOU DIDN'T ***REALLY*** SEE ANYTHING ... RIGHT?
WEEELL...
IT WAS A VERY ***SMALL*** SHRUB.

WHY DON'T I GIVE YOU A MINUTE TO ERASE THAT HORRIBLE IMAGE. OKAY, READY? LET'S CONTINUE.

WE ENDED UP HANGING OUT FOR A LONG TIME, AND IT WAS KINDA COOL. JOAN WAS EASILY THE MOST NORMAL NINJA I'D MET YET, AND EVERYONE ELSE SEEMED NICE TOO. SO WHEN NINJA JOAN HAD TO GO HOME, WE DIDN'T MIND BEING HIJACKED OVER TO JOANNE'S HOUSE.

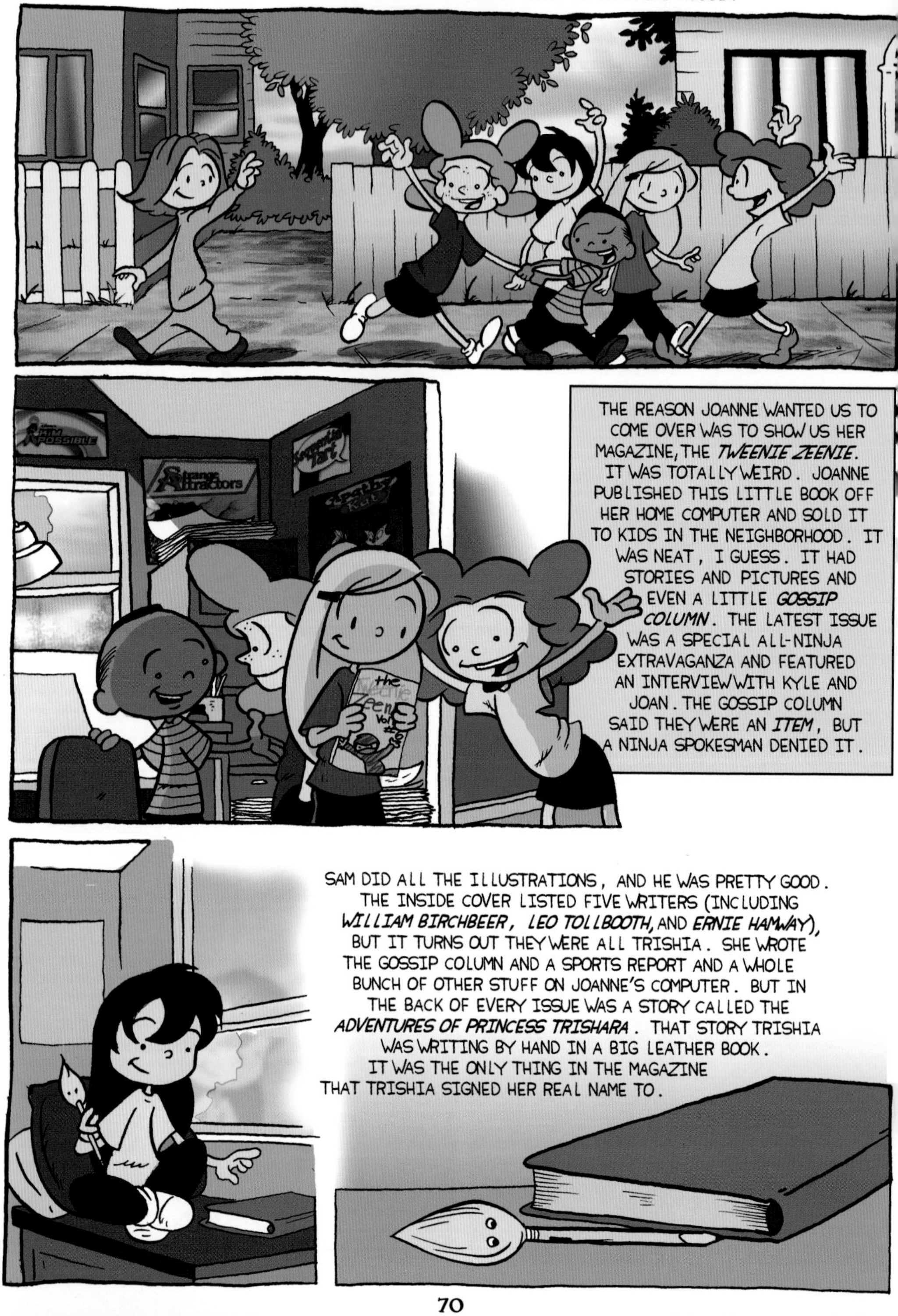

THE REASON JOANNE WANTED US TO COME OVER WAS TO SHOW US HER MAGAZINE, THE *TWEENIE ZEENIE*. IT WAS TOTALLY WEIRD. JOANNE PUBLISHED THIS LITTLE BOOK OFF HER HOME COMPUTER AND SOLD IT TO KIDS IN THE NEIGHBORHOOD. IT WAS NEAT, I GUESS. IT HAD STORIES AND PICTURES AND EVEN A LITTLE *GOSSIP COLUMN*. THE LATEST ISSUE WAS A SPECIAL ALL-NINJA EXTRAVAGANZA AND FEATURED AN INTERVIEW WITH KYLE AND JOAN. THE GOSSIP COLUMN SAID THEY WERE AN *ITEM*, BUT A NINJA SPOKESMAN DENIED IT.
KIM POSSIBLE
Strange Attractors
SAM DID ALL THE ILLUSTRATIONS, AND HE WAS PRETTY GOOD. THE INSIDE COVER LISTED FIVE WRITERS (INCLUDING *WILLIAM BIRCHBEER*, *LEO TOLLBOOTH*, AND *ERNIE HAMWAY*), BUT IT TURNS OUT THEY WERE ALL TRISHIA. SHE WROTE THE GOSSIP COLUMN AND A SPORTS REPORT AND A WHOLE BUNCH OF OTHER STUFF ON JOANNE'S COMPUTER. BUT IN THE BACK OF EVERY ISSUE WAS A STORY CALLED THE *ADVENTURES OF PRINCESS TRISHARA*. THAT STORY TRISHIA WAS WRITING BY HAND IN A BIG LEATHER BOOK. IT WAS THE ONLY THING IN THE MAGAZINE THAT TRISHIA SIGNED HER REAL NAME TO.

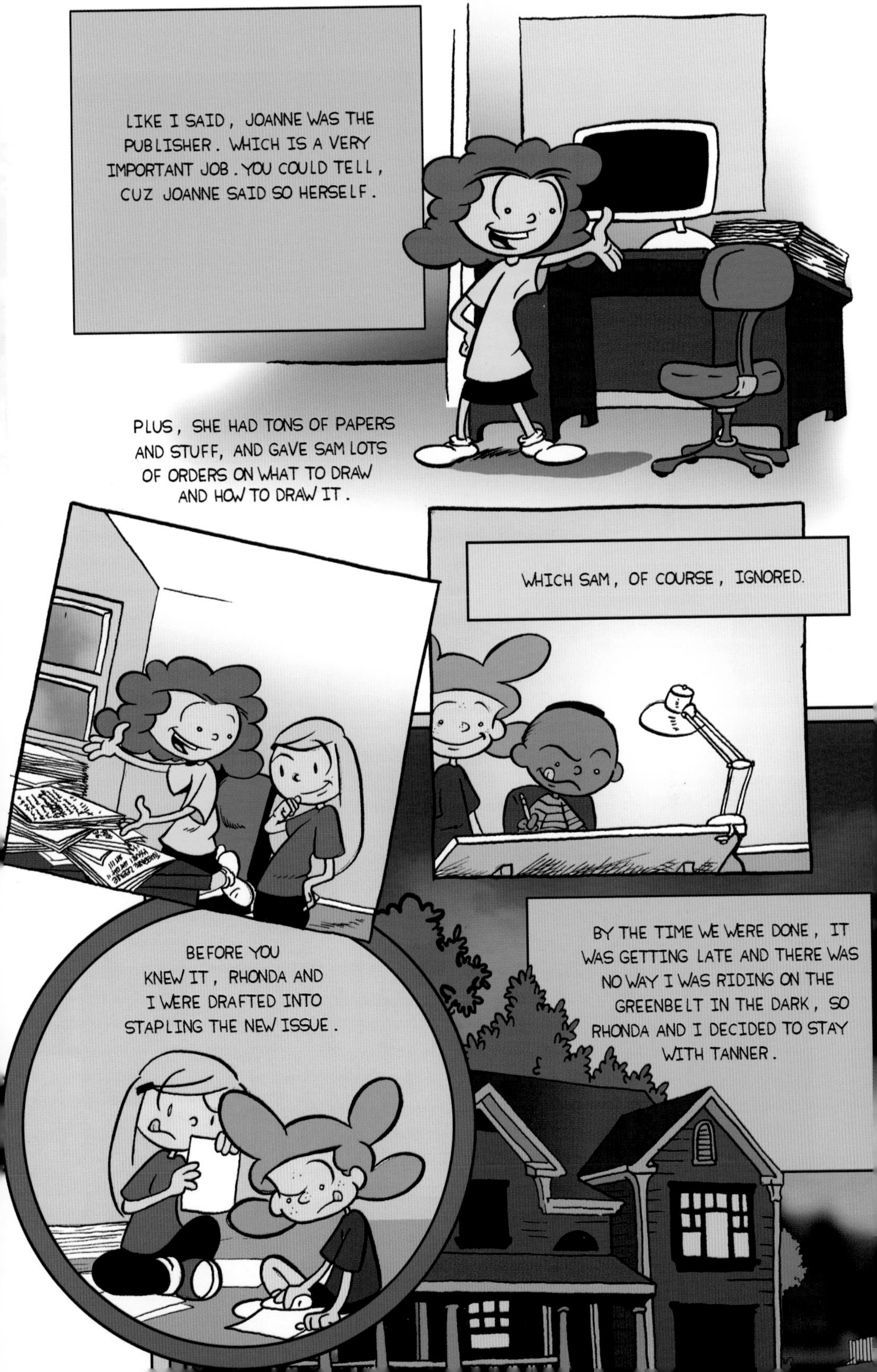
LIKE I SAID, JOANNE WAS THE PUBLISHER. WHICH IS A VERY IMPORTANT JOB. YOU COULD TELL, CUZ JOANNE SAID SO HERSELF.
PLUS, SHE HAD TONS OF PAPERS AND STUFF, AND GAVE SAM LOTS OF ORDERS ON WHAT TO DRAW AND HOW TO DRAW IT.
WHICH SAM, OF COURSE, IGNORED.
BEFORE YOU KNEW IT, RHONDA AND I WERE DRAFTED INTO STAPLING THE NEW ISSUE.
BY THE TIME WE WERE DONE, IT WAS GETTING LATE AND THERE WAS NO WAY I WAS RIDING ON THE GREENBELT IN THE DARK, SO RHONDA AND I DECIDED TO STAY WITH TANNER.

BUT WHILE RHONDA SAWED LOGS, I READ EVERY CHAPTER OF ***TRISHARA***. I GOTTA ADMIT, I WAS KINDA READING IT CUZ I THOUGHT IT MIGHT BE ***MOCKABLE***. BUT IT WAS COOL. REALLY, REALLY COOL, IN FACT. THERE WERE WIZARDS AND FAIRIES AND DRAGONS AND Y'KNOW... ***OH MY!***

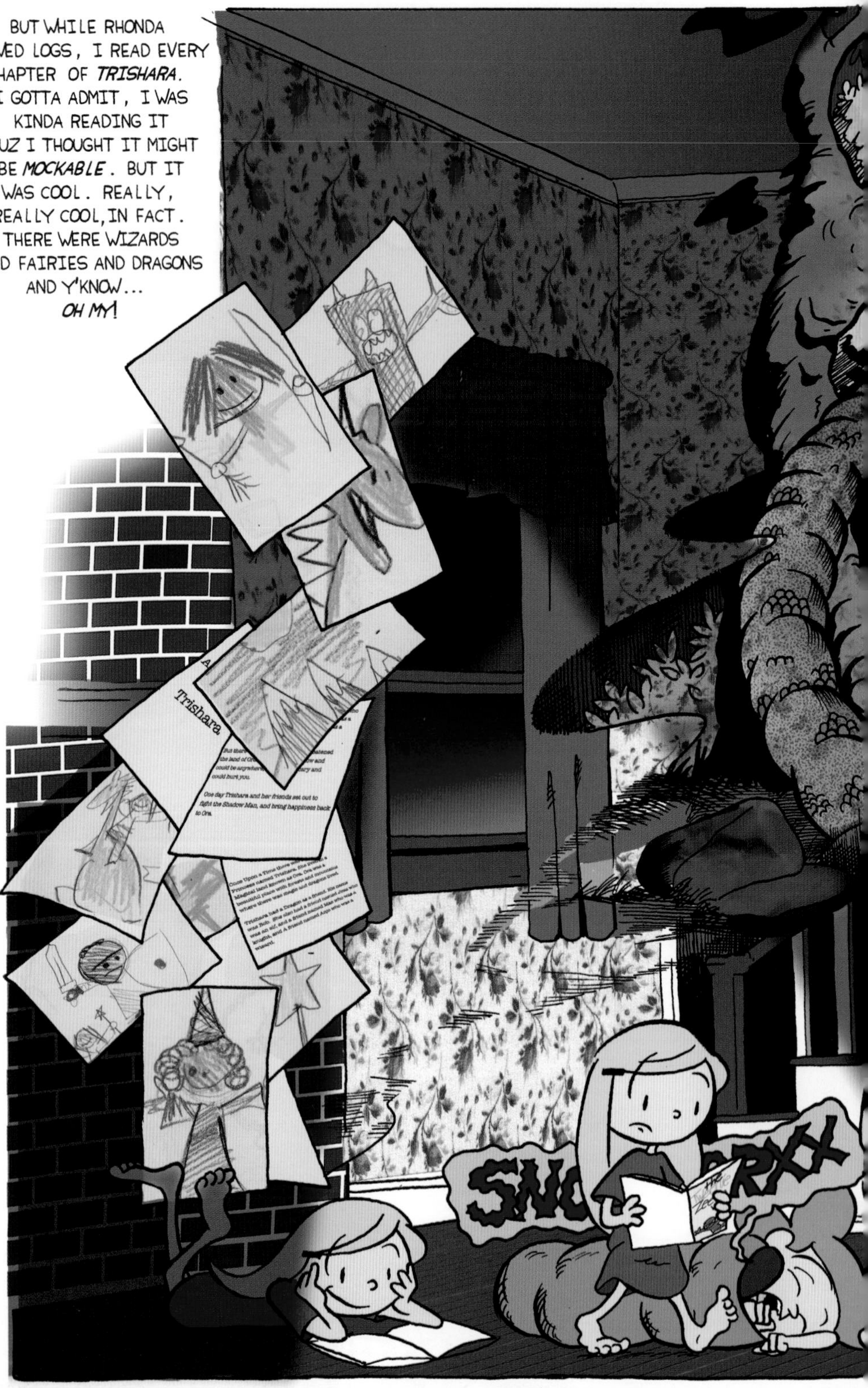
Trishara
One day Trishara and her friends set out to fight the Shadow Man, and bring happiness back to Ora.

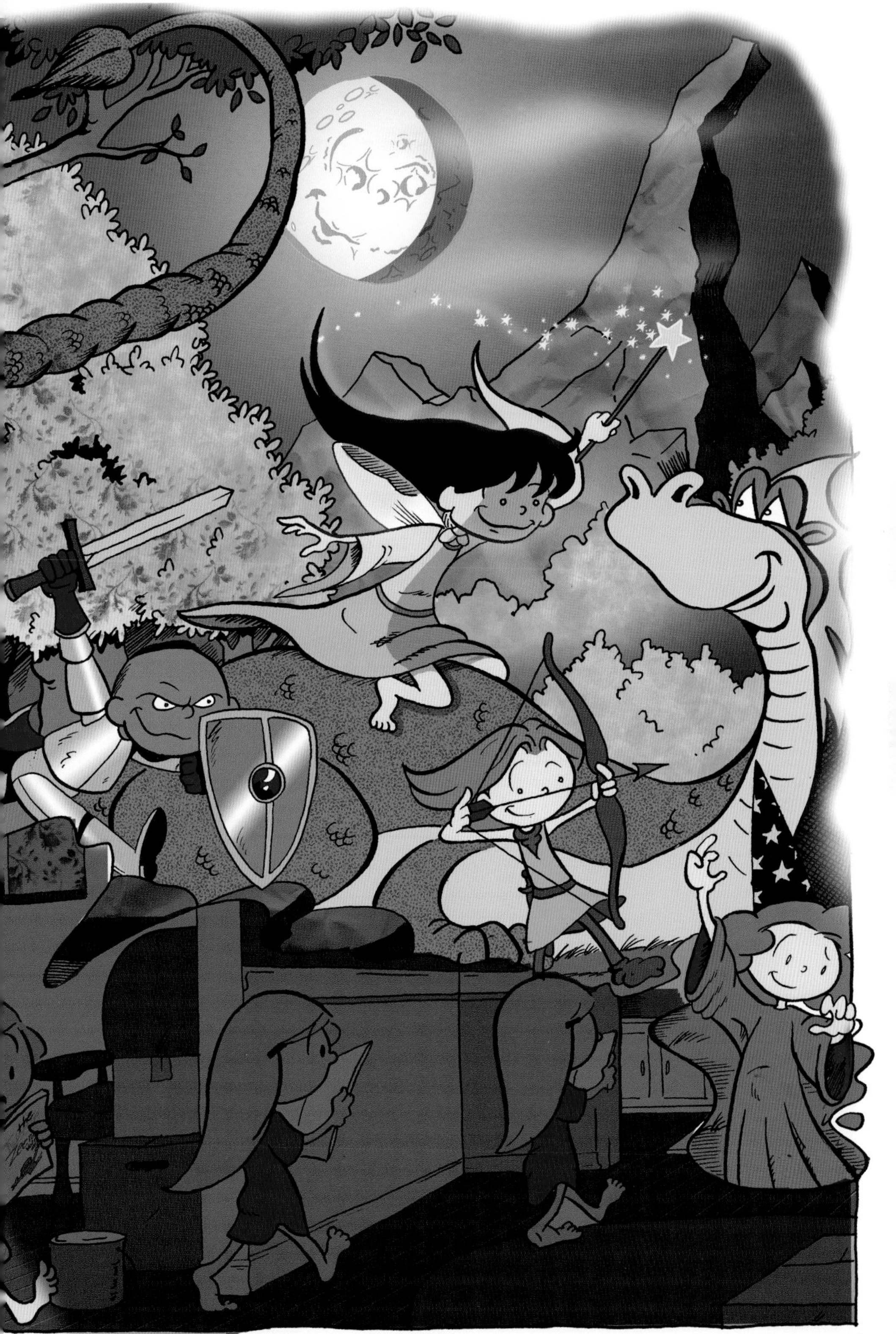

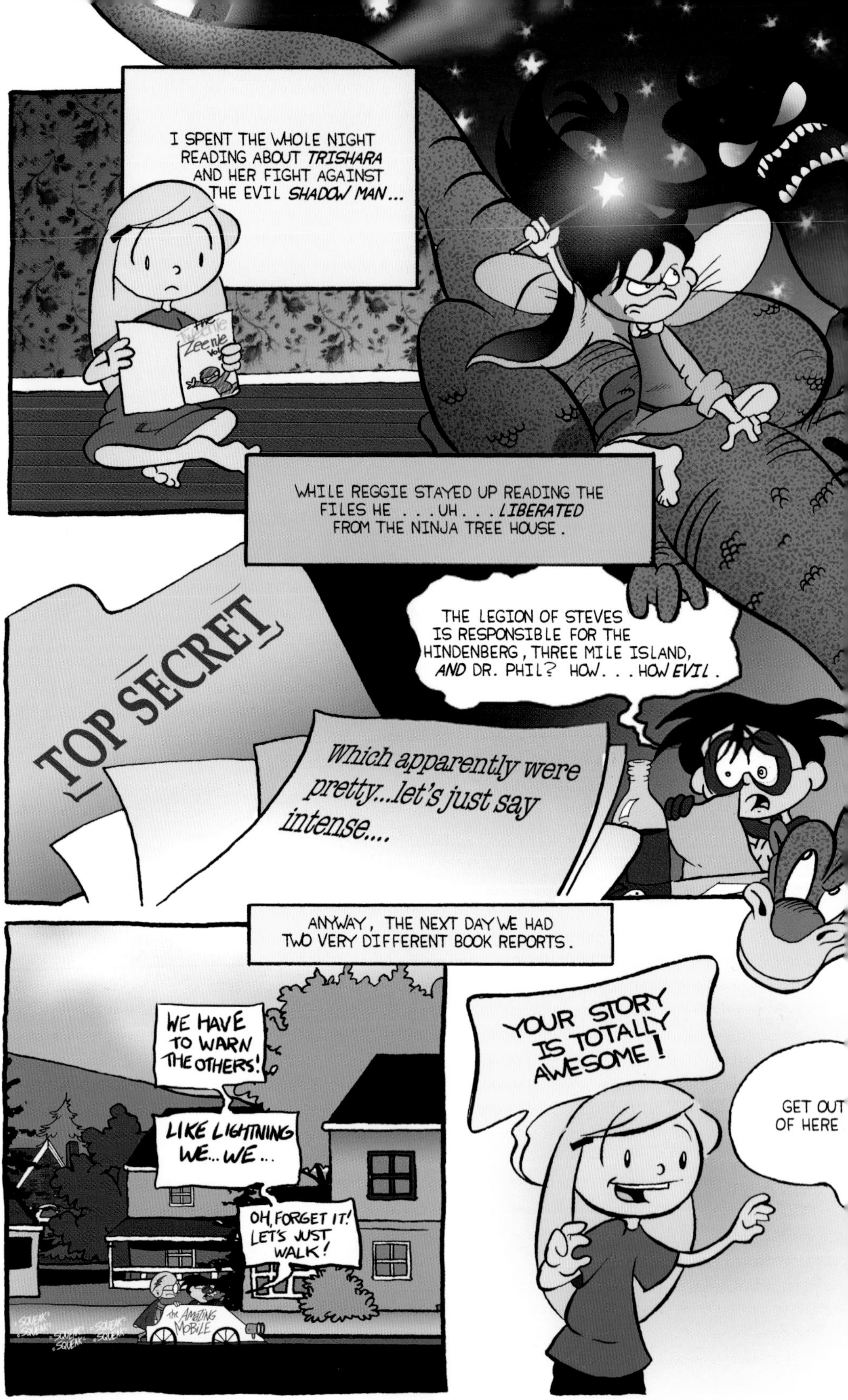
I SPENT THE WHOLE NIGHT READING ABOUT *TRISHARA* AND HER FIGHT AGAINST THE EVIL *SHADOW MAN*...
WHILE REGGIE STAYED UP READING THE FILES HE . . . UH . . . *LIBERATED* FROM THE NINJA TREE HOUSE.
TOP SECRET
THE LEGION OF STEVES IS RESPONSIBLE FOR THE HINDENBERG, THREE MILE ISLAND, *AND* DR. PHIL? HOW. . . HOW *EVIL*.
Which apparently were pretty...let's just say intense....
ANYWAY, THE NEXT DAY WE HAD TWO VERY DIFFERENT BOOK REPORTS.
WE HAVE TO WARN THE OTHERS!
LIKE LIGHTNING WE... WE...
OH, FORGET IT! LET'S JUST WALK!
The Amazing Mobile
SQUEAK SQUEAK
YOUR STORY IS TOTALLY AWESOME!
GET OUT OF HERE

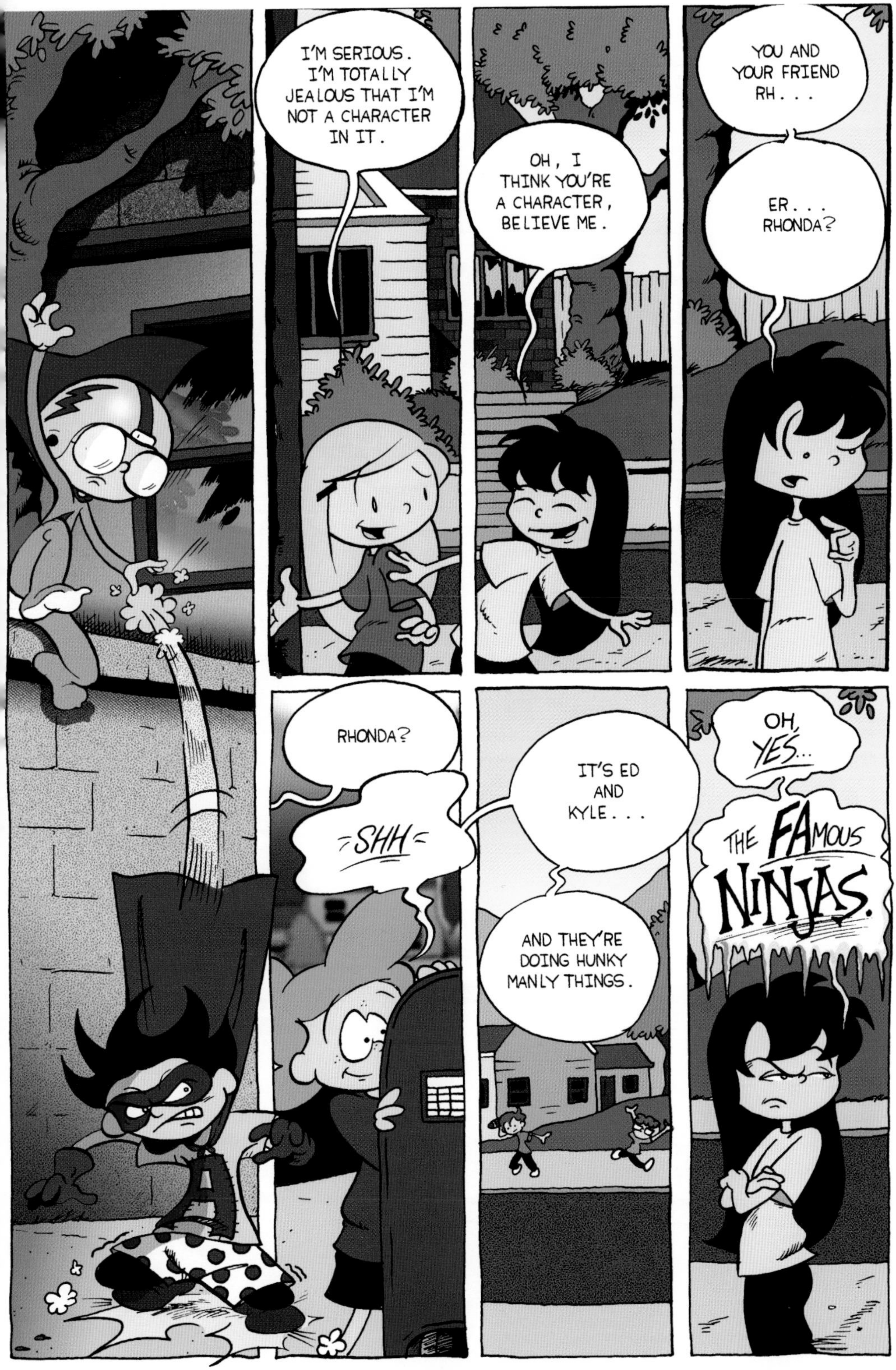
I'M SERIOUS. I'M TOTALLY JEALOUS THAT I'M NOT A CHARACTER IN IT.
OH, I THINK YOU'RE A CHARACTER, BELIEVE ME.
YOU AND YOUR FRIEND RH . . .
ER . . . RHONDA?
RHONDA?
SHH
IT'S ED AND KYLE . . .
AND THEY'RE DOING HUNKY MANLY THINGS.
OH, YES...
THE FAMOUS NINJAS.

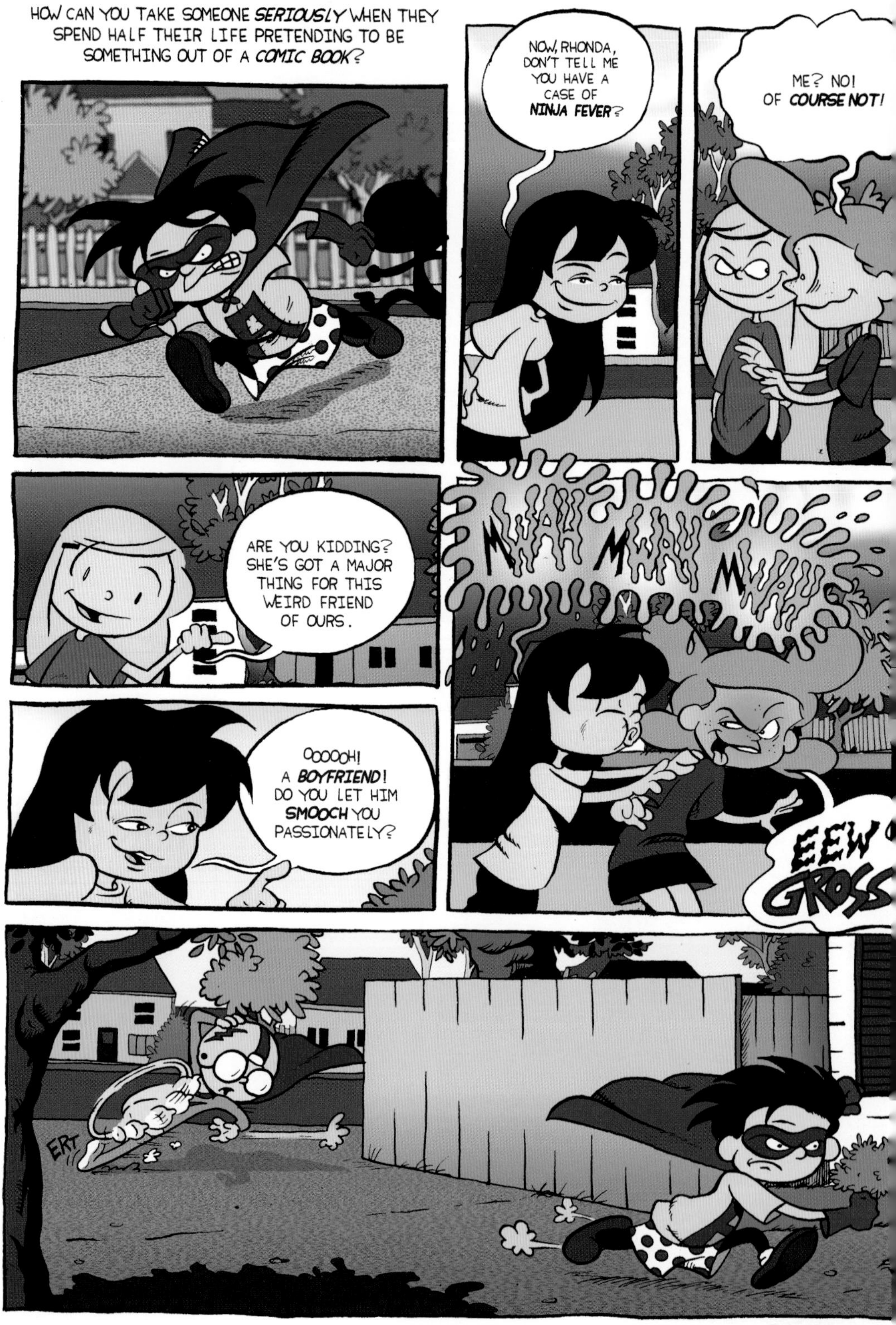
HOW CAN YOU TAKE SOMEONE SERIOUSLY WHEN THEY SPEND HALF THEIR LIFE PRETENDING TO BE SOMETHING OUT OF A COMIC BOOK?
NOW, RHONDA, DON'T TELL ME YOU HAVE A CASE OF NINJA FEVER?
ME? NO! OF COURSE NOT!
ARE YOU KIDDING? SHE'S GOT A MAJOR THING FOR THIS WEIRD FRIEND OF OURS.
OOOOOH! A BOYFRIEND! DO YOU LET HIM SMOOCH YOU PASSIONATELY?
MWAH MWAH MWAH
EEW GROSS
ERT

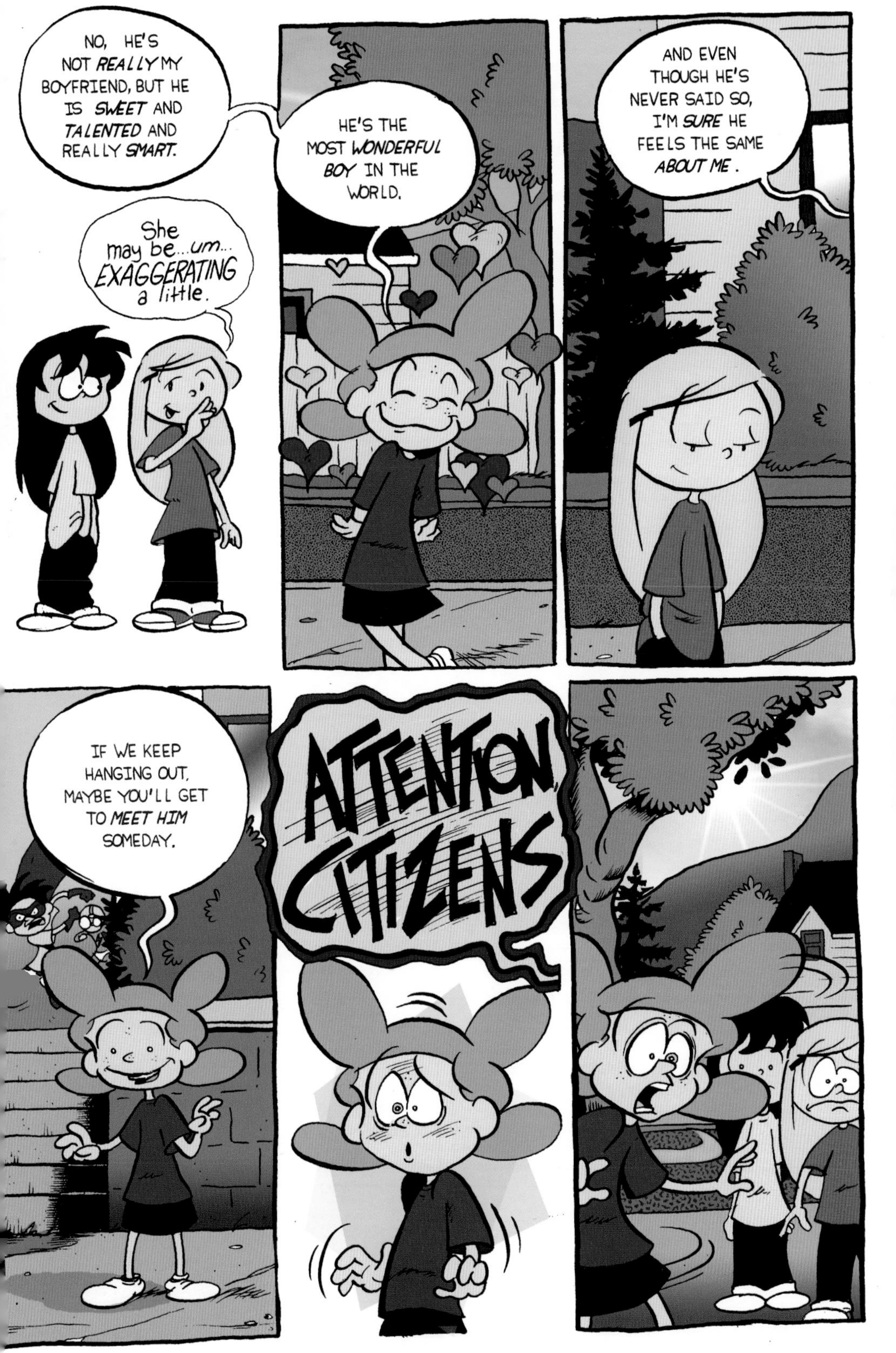
NO, HE'S NOT REALLY MY BOYFRIEND, BUT HE IS SWEET AND TALENTED AND REALLY SMART.
She may be...um... EXAGGERATING a little.
HE'S THE MOST WONDERFUL BOY IN THE WORLD.
AND EVEN THOUGH HE'S NEVER SAID SO, I'M SURE HE FEELS THE SAME ABOUT ME.
IF WE KEEP HANGING OUT, MAYBE YOU'LL GET TO MEET HIM SOMEDAY.
ATTENTION CITIZENS

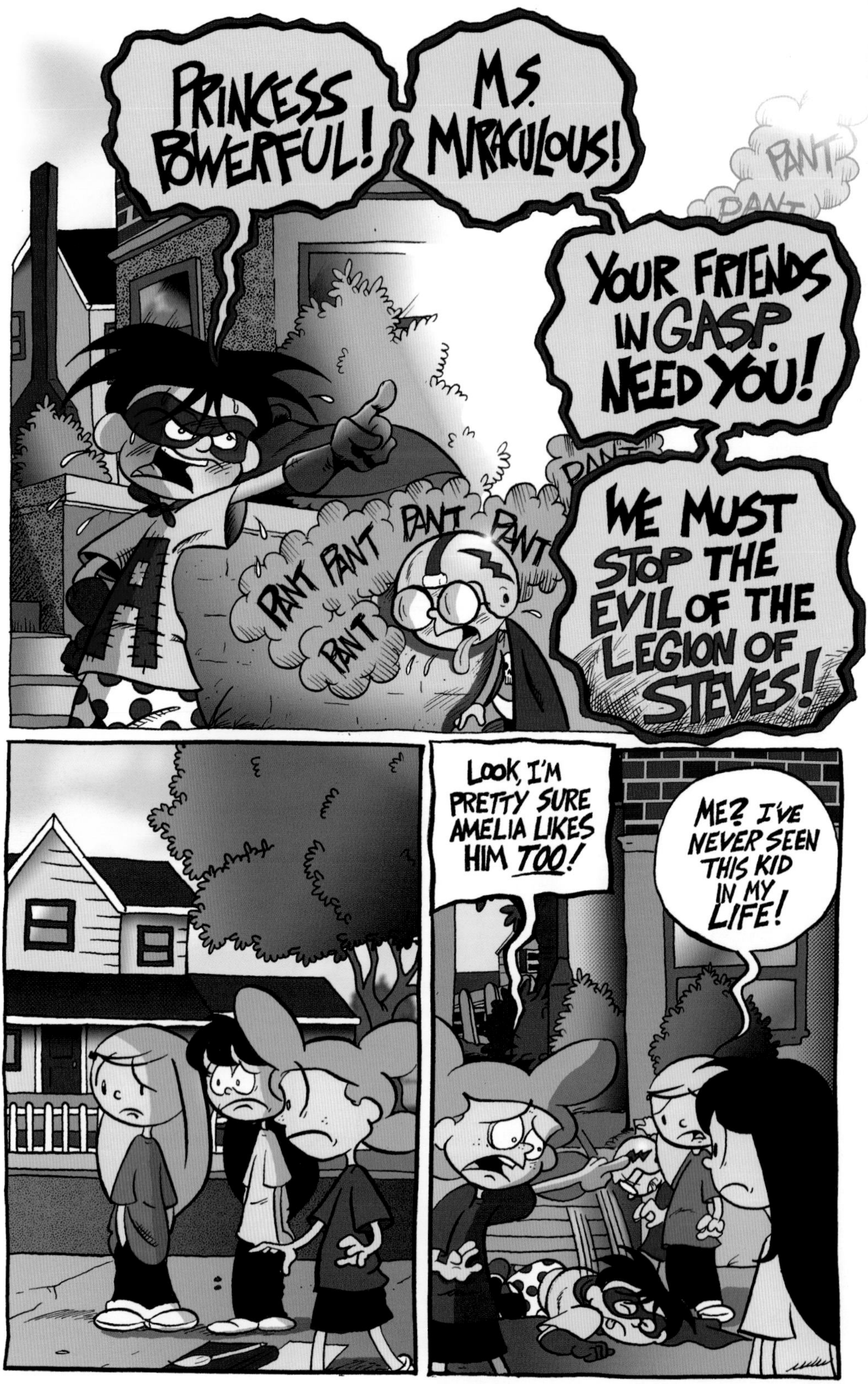
PRINCESS POWERFUL!
M.S. MIRACULOUS!
PANT
YOUR FRIENDS IN G.A.S.P. NEED YOU!
WE MUST STOP THE EVIL OF THE LEGION OF STEVES!
PANT PANT PANT PANT PANT
LOOK, I'M PRETTY SURE AMELIA LIKES HIM TOO!
ME? I'VE NEVER SEEN THIS KID IN MY LIFE!

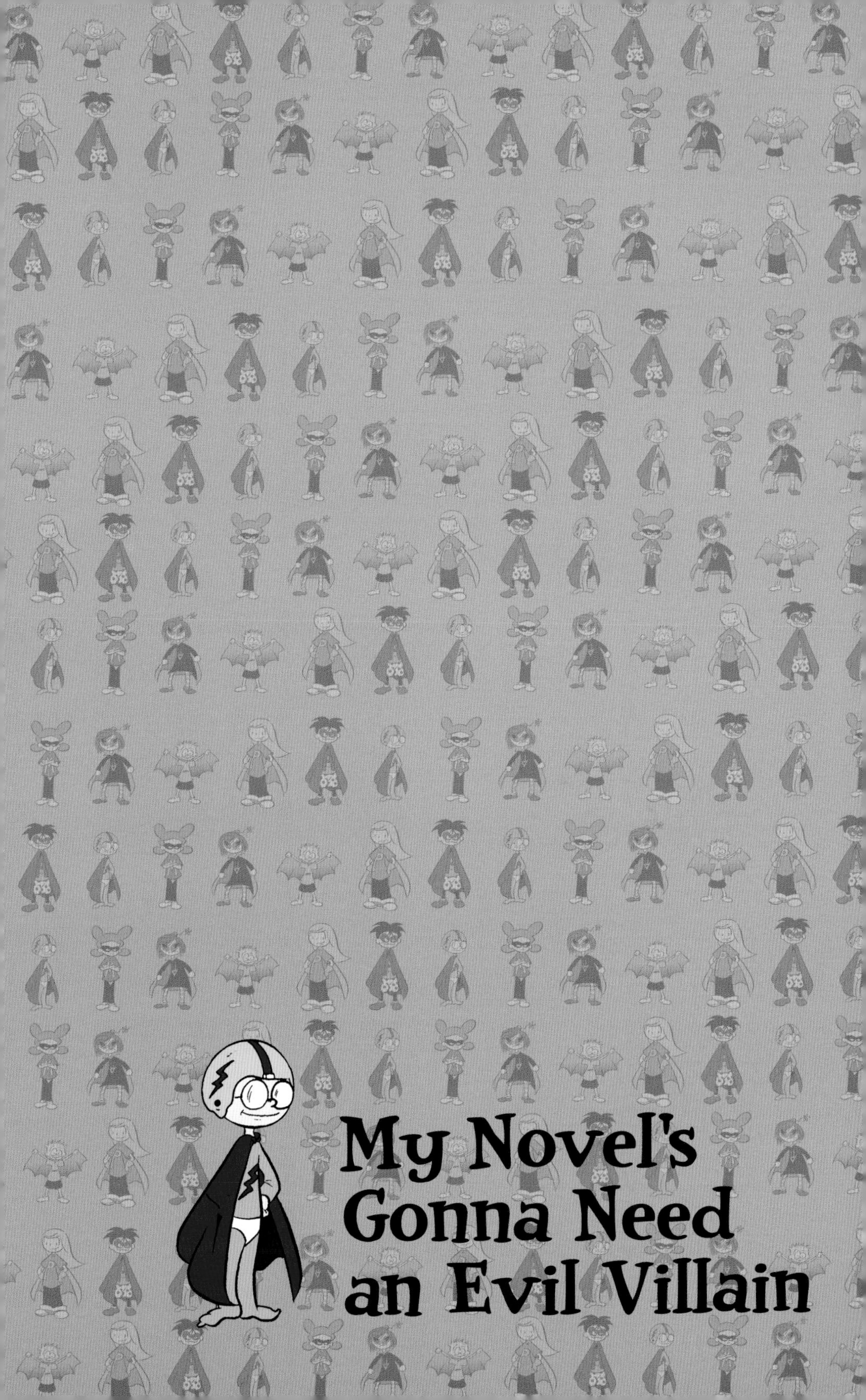

My Novel's Gonna Need an Evil Villain

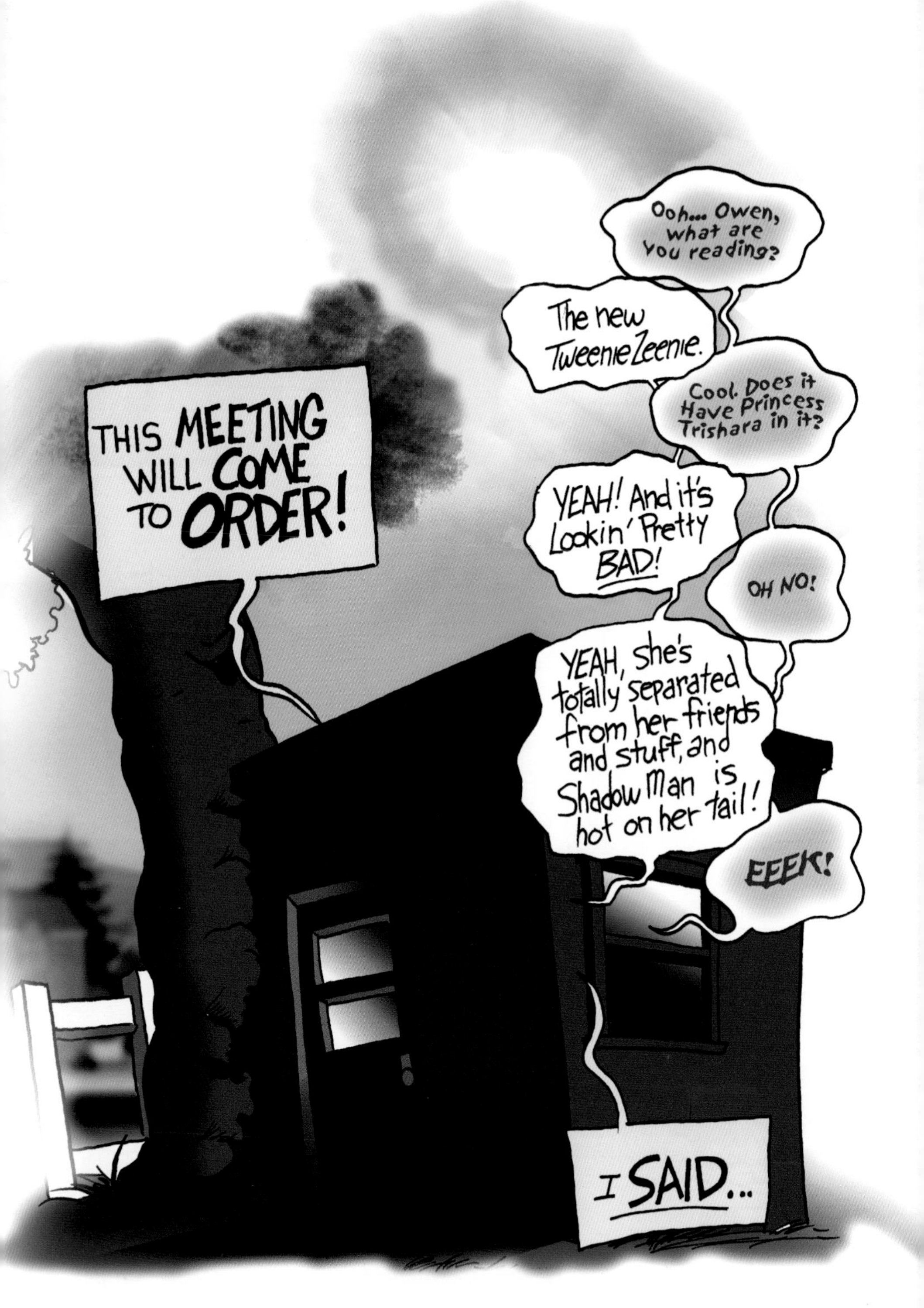
THIS MEETING WILL COME TO ORDER!
Ooh... Owen, what are you reading?
The new Tweenie Zeenie.
Cool. Does it have Princess Trishara in it?
YEAH! And it's Lookin' Pretty BAD!
OH NO!
YEAH, she's totally separated from her friends and stuff, and Shadow Man is hot on her tail!
EEEK!
I SAID...

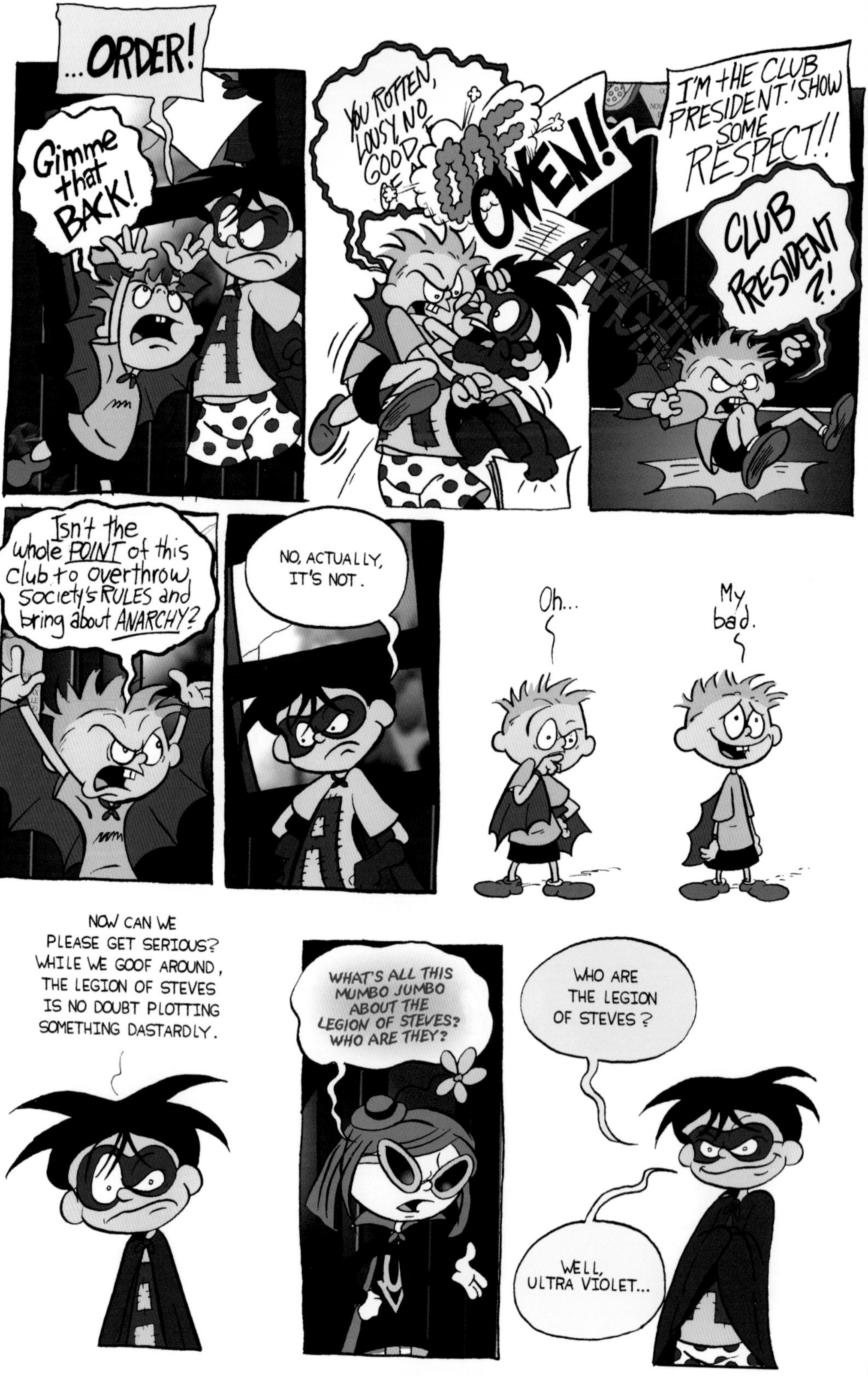

...ORDER!
Gimme that BACK!
YOU ROTTEN, LOUSY, NO GOOD...
OOF
OWEN!
AAAGH!
I'M THE CLUB PRESIDENT! SHOW SOME RESPECT!!
CLUB PRESIDENT ?!
Isn't the whole POINT of this club to overthrow society's RULES and bring about ANARCHY?
NO, ACTUALLY, IT'S NOT.
Oh...
My bad.
NOW CAN WE PLEASE GET SERIOUS? WHILE WE GOOF AROUND, THE LEGION OF STEVES IS NO DOUBT PLOTTING SOMETHING DASTARDLY.
WHAT'S ALL THIS MUMBO JUMBO ABOUT THE LEGION OF STEVES? WHO ARE THEY?
WHO ARE THE LEGION OF STEVES?
WELL, ULTRA VIOLET...

I'M GLAD YOU ASKED . . .

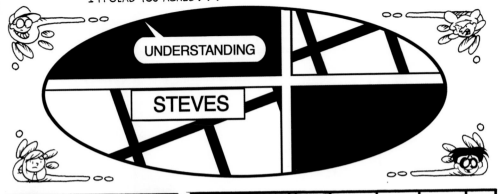

UNDERSTANDING
STEVES
HI. I'M **CAPTAIN AMAZING**.
FOR SOME TIME NOW, I'VE BEEN WORKING TO STAMP OUT EVIL.
BUT UNTIL RECENTLY, I BELIEVED THAT EVIL WAS A **RANDOMLY OCCURRING PHENOMENON**.
AND **NOT** THE RESULT OF A SINGLE ORGANIZATION OR GROUP.
EVIL
HOWEVER, NEW INFORMATION HAS REVEALED THAT, IN FACT, ALL OF THE **EVIL**, ALL OF THE **SUFFERING**, ALL OF THE **GENERAL POOPINESS** THAT OCCURS ANYWHERE IN THE WORLD...
...IS CAUSED BY GUYS NAMED **STEVE**.
UH-OH.
STEVE
ALLOW ME TO ELABORATE.

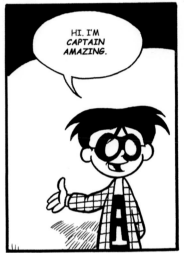

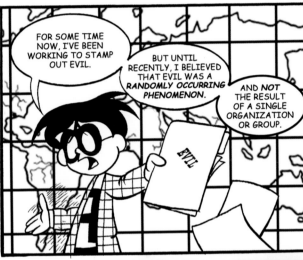

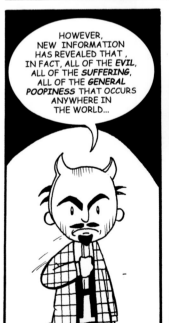

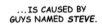

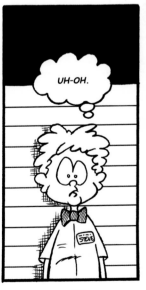

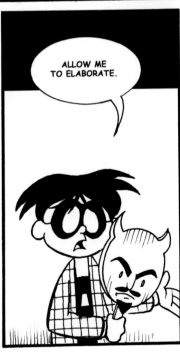

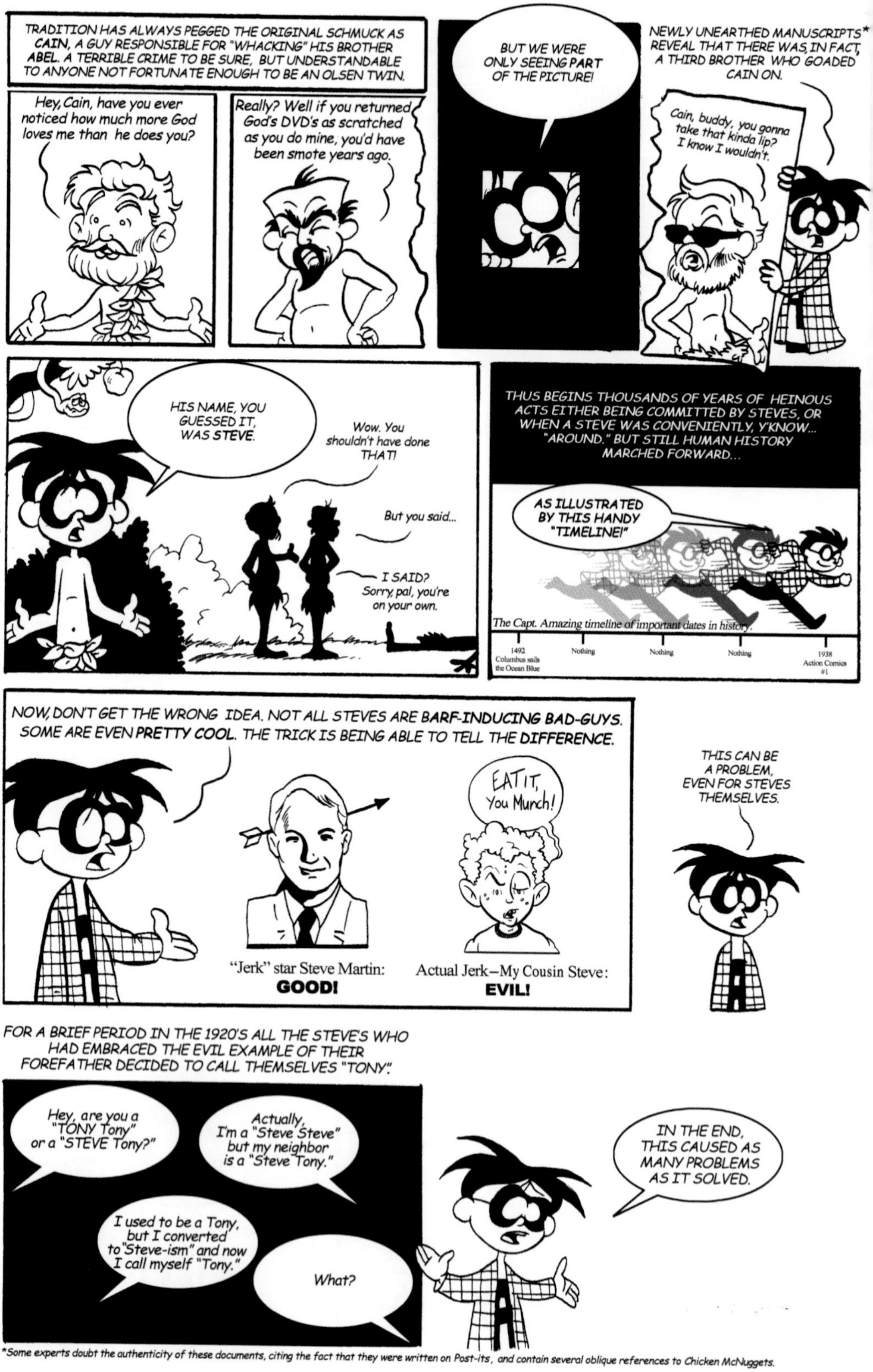
TRADITION HAS ALWAYS PEGGED THE ORIGINAL SCHMUCK AS CAIN, A GUY RESPONSIBLE FOR "WHACKING" HIS BROTHER ABEL. A TERRIBLE CRIME TO BE SURE, BUT UNDERSTANDABLE TO ANYONE NOT FORTUNATE ENOUGH TO BE AN OLSEN TWIN.
Hey, Cain, have you ever noticed how much more God loves me than he does you?
Really? Well if you returned God's DVD's as scratched as you do mine, you'd have been smote years ago.
BUT WE WERE ONLY SEEING PART OF THE PICTURE!
NEWLY UNEARTHED MANUSCRIPTS* REVEAL THAT THERE WAS, IN FACT, A THIRD BROTHER WHO GOADED CAIN ON.
Cain, buddy, you gonna take that kinda lip? I know I wouldn't.
HIS NAME, YOU GUESSED IT, WAS STEVE.
Wow. You shouldn't have done THAT!
But you said...
I SAID? Sorry, pal, you're on your own.
THUS BEGINS THOUSANDS OF YEARS OF HEINOUS ACTS EITHER BEING COMMITTED BY STEVES, OR WHEN A STEVE WAS CONVENIENTLY, Y'KNOW... "AROUND." BUT STILL HUMAN HISTORY MARCHED FORWARD...
AS ILLUSTRATED BY THIS HANDY "TIMELINE!"
The Capt. Amazing timeline of important dates in history.
1492 Columbus sails the Ocean Blue
Nothing
Nothing
Nothing
1938 Action Comics #1
NOW, DON'T GET THE WRONG IDEA. NOT ALL STEVES ARE BARF-INDUCING BAD-GUYS. SOME ARE EVEN PRETTY COOL. THE TRICK IS BEING ABLE TO TELL THE DIFFERENCE.
EAT IT, You Munch!
"Jerk" star Steve Martin: GOOD!
Actual Jerk–My Cousin Steve: EVIL!
THIS CAN BE A PROBLEM, EVEN FOR STEVES THEMSELVES.
FOR A BRIEF PERIOD IN THE 1920'S ALL THE STEVE'S WHO HAD EMBRACED THE EVIL EXAMPLE OF THEIR FOREFATHER DECIDED TO CALL THEMSELVES "TONY".
Hey, are you a "TONY Tony" or a "STEVE Tony?"
Actually, I'm a "Steve Steve" but my neighbor is a "Steve Tony."
I used to be a Tony, but I converted to "Steve-ism" and now I call myself "Tony."
What?
IN THE END, THIS CAUSED AS MANY PROBLEMS AS IT SOLVED.

*Some experts doubt the authenticity of these documents, citing the fact that they were written on Post-its, and contain several oblique references to Chicken McNuggets.

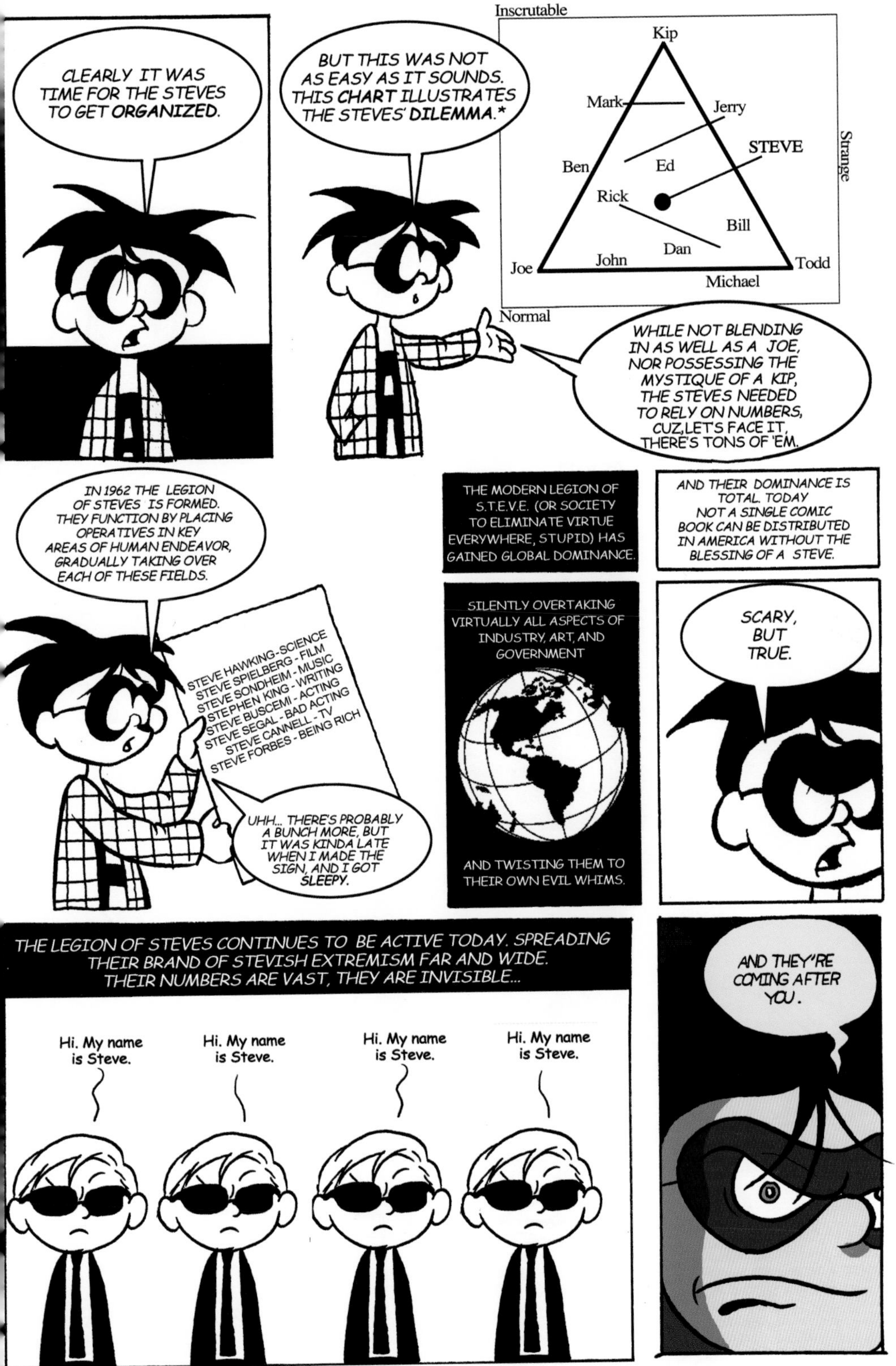
CLEARLY IT WAS TIME FOR THE STEVES TO GET ORGANIZED.
BUT THIS WAS NOT AS EASY AS IT SOUNDS. THIS CHART ILLUSTRATES THE STEVES' DILEMMA.*
Inscrutable
Strange
Normal
Kip
Mark
Jerry
STEVE
Ben
Ed
Rick
Bill
Dan
John
Joe
Todd
Michael
WHILE NOT BLENDING IN AS WELL AS A JOE, NOR POSSESSING THE MYSTIQUE OF A KIP, THE STEVES NEEDED TO RELY ON NUMBERS, CUZ, LET'S FACE IT, THERE'S TONS OF 'EM.
IN 1962 THE LEGION OF STEVES IS FORMED. THEY FUNCTION BY PLACING OPERATIVES IN KEY AREAS OF HUMAN ENDEAVOR, GRADUALLY TAKING OVER EACH OF THESE FIELDS.
STEVE HAWKING - SCIENCE
STEVE SPIELBERG - FILM
STEVE SONDHEIM - MUSIC
STEPHEN KING - WRITING
STEVE BUSCEMI - ACTING
STEVE SEGAL - BAD ACTING
STEVE CANNELL - TV
STEVE FORBES - BEING RICH
UHH... THERE'S PROBABLY A BUNCH MORE, BUT IT WAS KINDA LATE WHEN I MADE THE SIGN, AND I GOT SLEEPY.
THE MODERN LEGION OF S.T.E.V.E. (OR SOCIETY TO ELIMINATE VIRTUE EVERYWHERE, STUPID) HAS GAINED GLOBAL DOMINANCE.
AND THEIR DOMINANCE IS TOTAL. TODAY NOT A SINGLE COMIC BOOK CAN BE DISTRIBUTED IN AMERICA WITHOUT THE BLESSING OF A STEVE.
SILENTLY OVERTAKING VIRTUALLY ALL ASPECTS OF INDUSTRY, ART, AND GOVERNMENT
AND TWISTING THEM TO THEIR OWN EVIL WHIMS.
SCARY, BUT TRUE.
THE LEGION OF STEVES CONTINUES TO BE ACTIVE TODAY. SPREADING THEIR BRAND OF STEVISH EXTREMISM FAR AND WIDE. THEIR NUMBERS ARE VAST, THEY ARE INVISIBLE...
Hi. My name is Steve.
Hi. My name is Steve.
Hi. My name is Steve.
Hi. My name is Steve.
AND THEY'RE COMING AFTER YOU.

*Actually, this chart makes no sense, but it always looks more official when you have a chart.

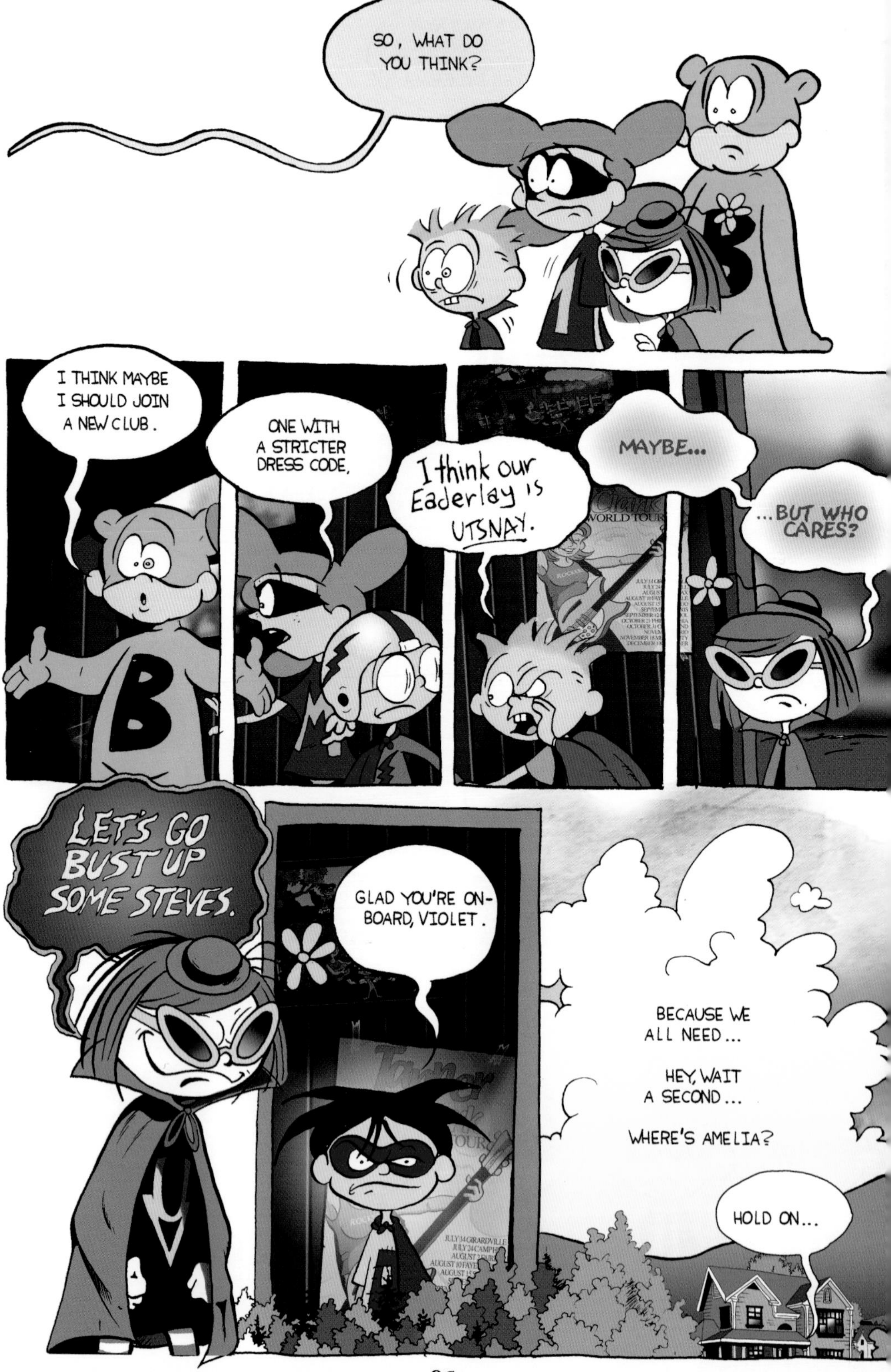
SO, WHAT DO YOU THINK?
I THINK MAYBE I SHOULD JOIN A NEW CLUB.
ONE WITH A STRICTER DRESS CODE.
I think our Eaderlay is UTSNAY.
MAYBE...
...BUT WHO CARES?
LET'S GO BUST UP SOME STEVES.
GLAD YOU'RE ON-BOARD, VIOLET.
BECAUSE WE ALL NEED...
HEY, WAIT A SECOND...
WHERE'S AMELIA?
HOLD ON...

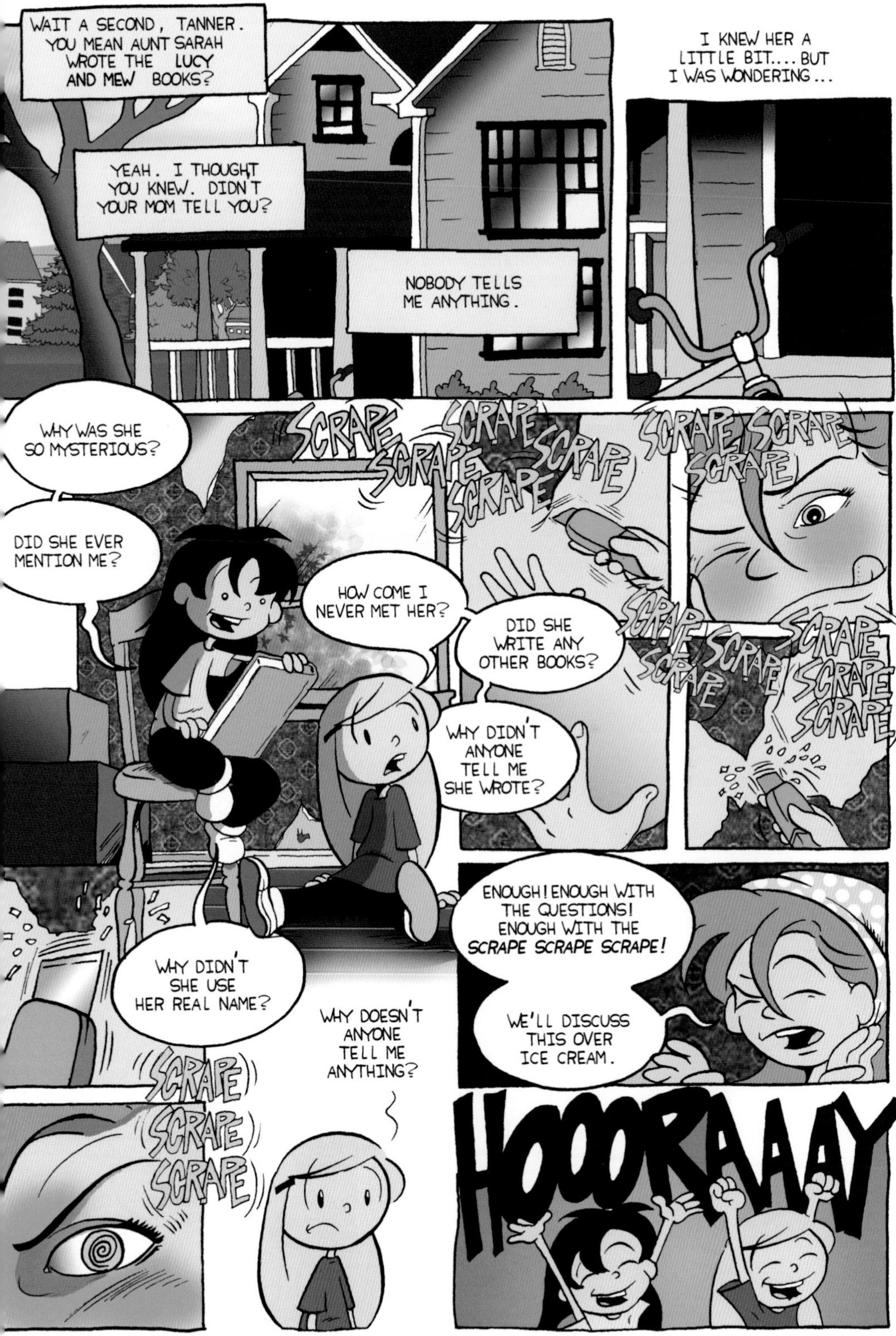

WAIT A SECOND, TANNER. YOU MEAN AUNT SARAH WROTE THE LUCY AND MEW BOOKS?
YEAH. I THOUGHT YOU KNEW. DIDN'T YOUR MOM TELL YOU?
NOBODY TELLS ME ANYTHING.
I KNEW HER A LITTLE BIT.... BUT I WAS WONDERING...
WHY WAS SHE SO MYSTERIOUS?
DID SHE EVER MENTION ME?
HOW COME I NEVER MET HER?
DID SHE WRITE ANY OTHER BOOKS?
WHY DIDN'T ANYONE TELL ME SHE WROTE?
SCRAPE SCRAPE SCRAPE SCRAPE SCRAPE SCRAPE
SCRAPE SCRAPE SCRAPE
SCRAPE SCRAPE SCRAPE SCRAPE SCRAPE SCRAPE
WHY DIDN'T SHE USE HER REAL NAME?
WHY DOESN'T ANYONE TELL ME ANYTHING?
ENOUGH! ENOUGH WITH THE QUESTIONS! ENOUGH WITH THE SCRAPE SCRAPE SCRAPE!
WE'LL DISCUSS THIS OVER ICE CREAM.
SCRAPE SCRAPE SCRAPE
HOOORAAAY

See, the thing about Sarah is, she was, well, very Sarah-ish, you know? She totally was her own person. She wanted to be a writer, so she wrote. And those Lucy and Mew books were superpopular. When I was a kid, they made Softee Chicken look pretty much like…well, like Softee Chicken. But Sarah didn't want to be famous. That's why she used the pen name. Some people knew her for years and never knew what she did.

Now, here's the interesting part. When she was just twenty and living in New York City, Sarah met her one true love, another aspiring writer named Hugh S. Travers. They were inseparable. Everything was perfect except that the better Sarah's career went, the worse Hugh's did. Still, that didn't stop their love. They lived a very New York life—same street, different buildings. Together when they wanted, apart when they needed.

And they vowed never to get married.

So everything's going along normally. Sarah's selling zillions of books. Hugh's collecting rejection slips. Then one day Hugh's mother gets sick. Really sick. Hugh needs to go back to Pennsylvania, to the town where he grew up, to take care of her. So, on the night before he leaves, he does the unthinkable and asks Sarah to marry him. Of course, she says no. Hugh is heartbroken, but he has responsibilities and leaves New York, never to return.

Five years pass. Sarah has no contact with Hugh, but she never forgets him. She writes another book called *Lucy and Mew: Against Unbelievable Odds*. It's totally a mash note to Hugh, but written so that only he would understand. Sarah has no idea if he'll ever see it. He does. He gets it. They reconnect, and it's still magic.

She moves to Pennsylvania. To Hugh's hometown. To this TOWN. She buys this house, and they live happily ever after. Unmarried, on the same street and in two different houses.

When Hugh died, Sarah didn't spend much time here, but she kept the house.

I moved here in large part to be near Sarah. My sister moved here to stay with me, and she brought Amelia along with her.

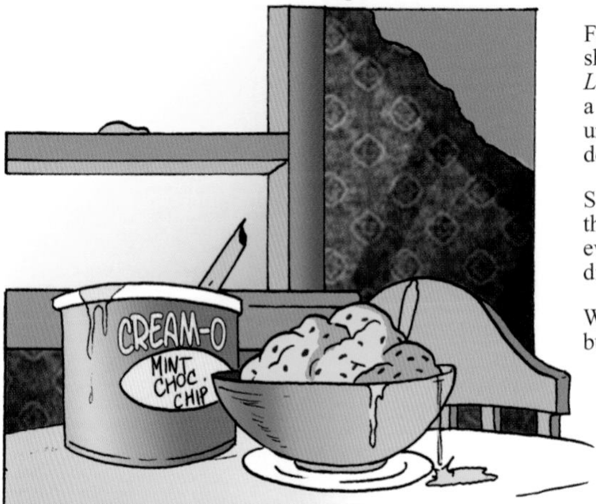
CREAM-O
MINT CHOC CHIP

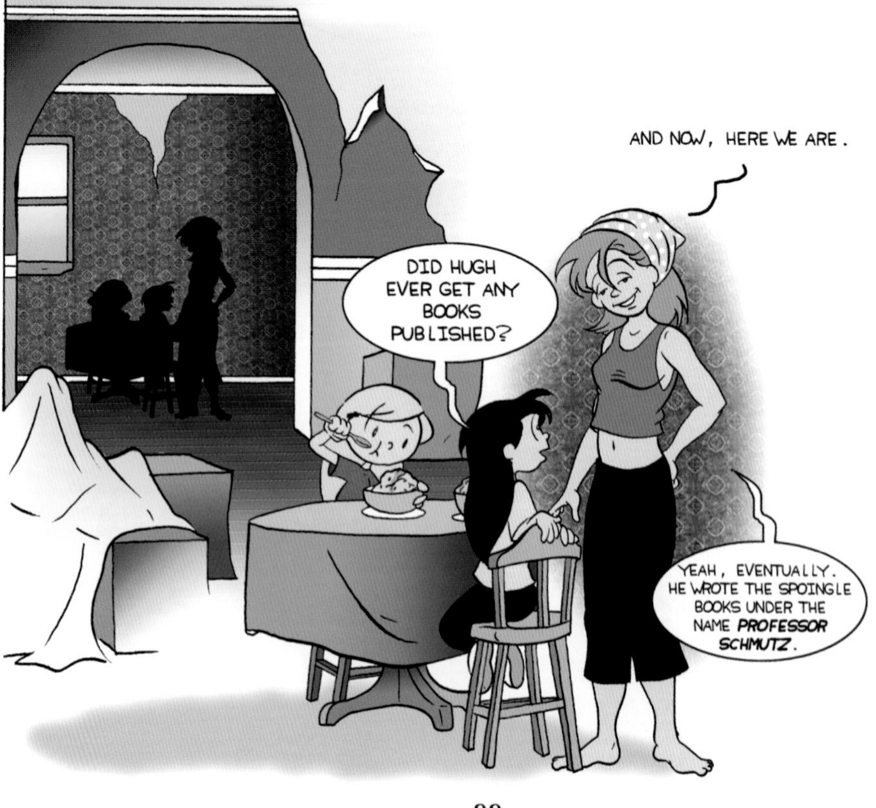
AND NOW, HERE WE ARE.
DID HUGH EVER GET ANY BOOKS PUBLISHED?
YEAH, EVENTUALLY. HE WROTE THE SPOINGLE BOOKS UNDER THE NAME **PROFESSOR SCHMUTZ**.

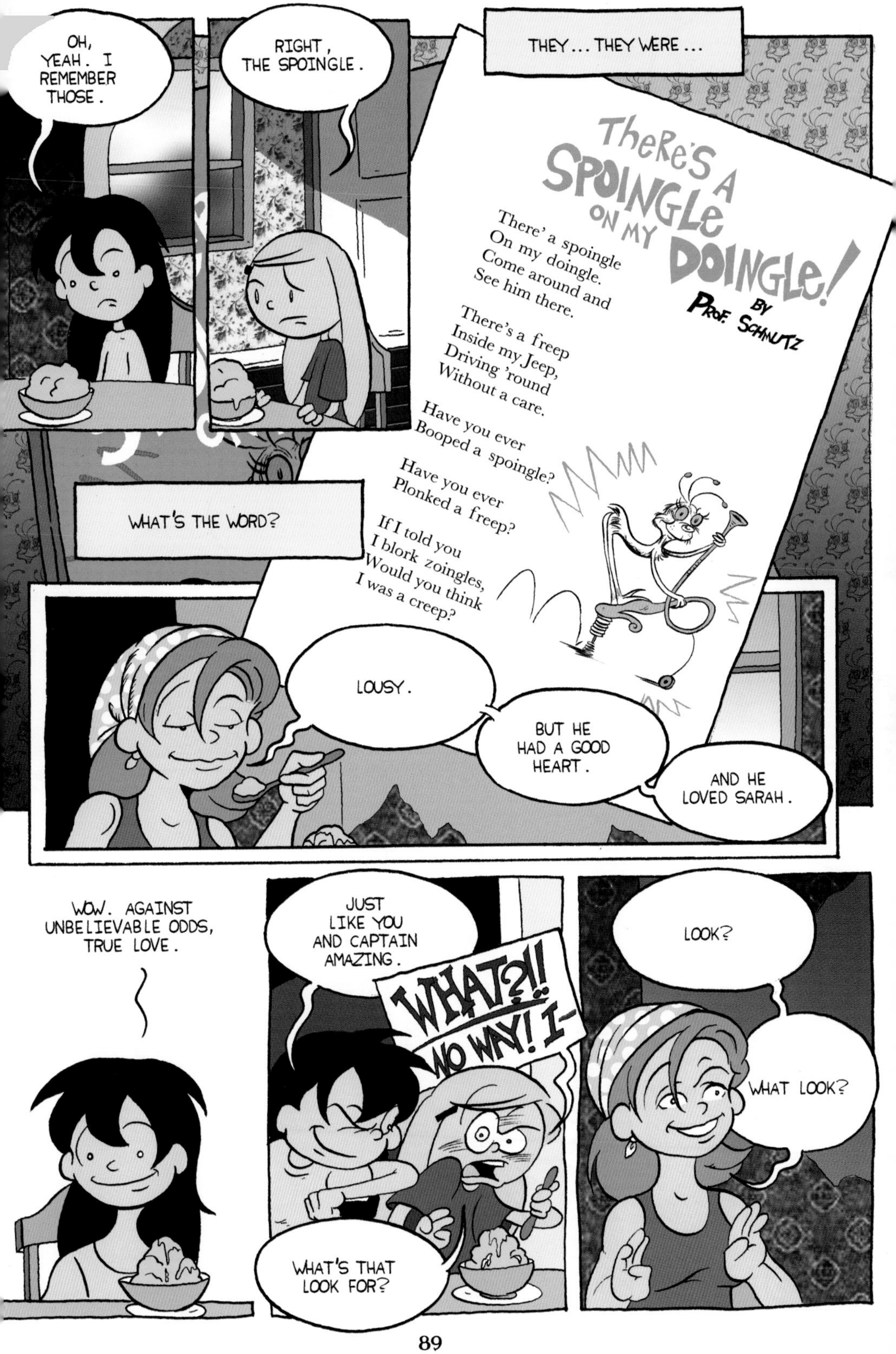
OH, YEAH. I REMEMBER THOSE.
RIGHT, THE SPOINGLE.
THEY... THEY WERE...
There's a Spoingle on my Doingle!
By Prof. Schmutz
There' a spoingle
On my doingle.
Come around and
See him there.
There's a freep
Inside my Jeep,
Driving 'round
Without a care.
Have you ever
Booped a spoingle?
Have you ever
Plonked a freep?
If I told you
I blork zoingles,
Would you think
I was a creep?
WHAT'S THE WORD?
LOUSY.
BUT HE HAD A GOOD HEART.
AND HE LOVED SARAH.
WOW. AGAINST UNBELIEVABLE ODDS, TRUE LOVE.
JUST LIKE YOU AND CAPTAIN AMAZING.
WHAT?!! NO WAY! I-
WHAT'S THAT LOOK FOR?
LOOK?
WHAT LOOK?

I'M JUST THINKING OF ALL WE DO FOR LOVE.

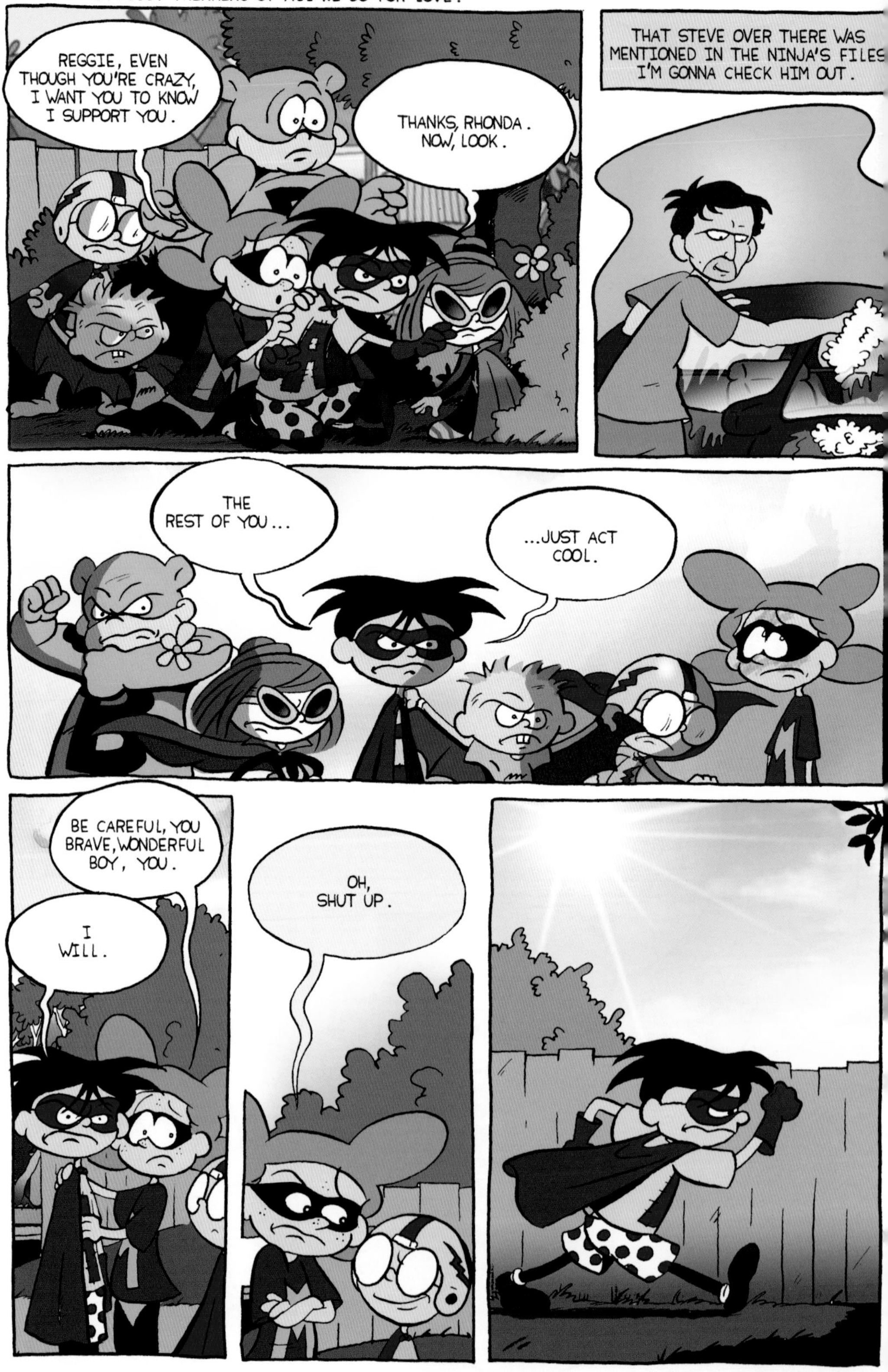
REGGIE, EVEN THOUGH YOU'RE CRAZY, I WANT YOU TO KNOW I SUPPORT YOU.
THANKS, RHONDA. NOW, LOOK.
THAT STEVE OVER THERE WAS MENTIONED IN THE NINJA'S FILES. I'M GONNA CHECK HIM OUT.
THE REST OF YOU...
...JUST ACT COOL.
BE CAREFUL, YOU BRAVE, WONDERFUL BOY, YOU.
I WILL.
OH, SHUT UP.

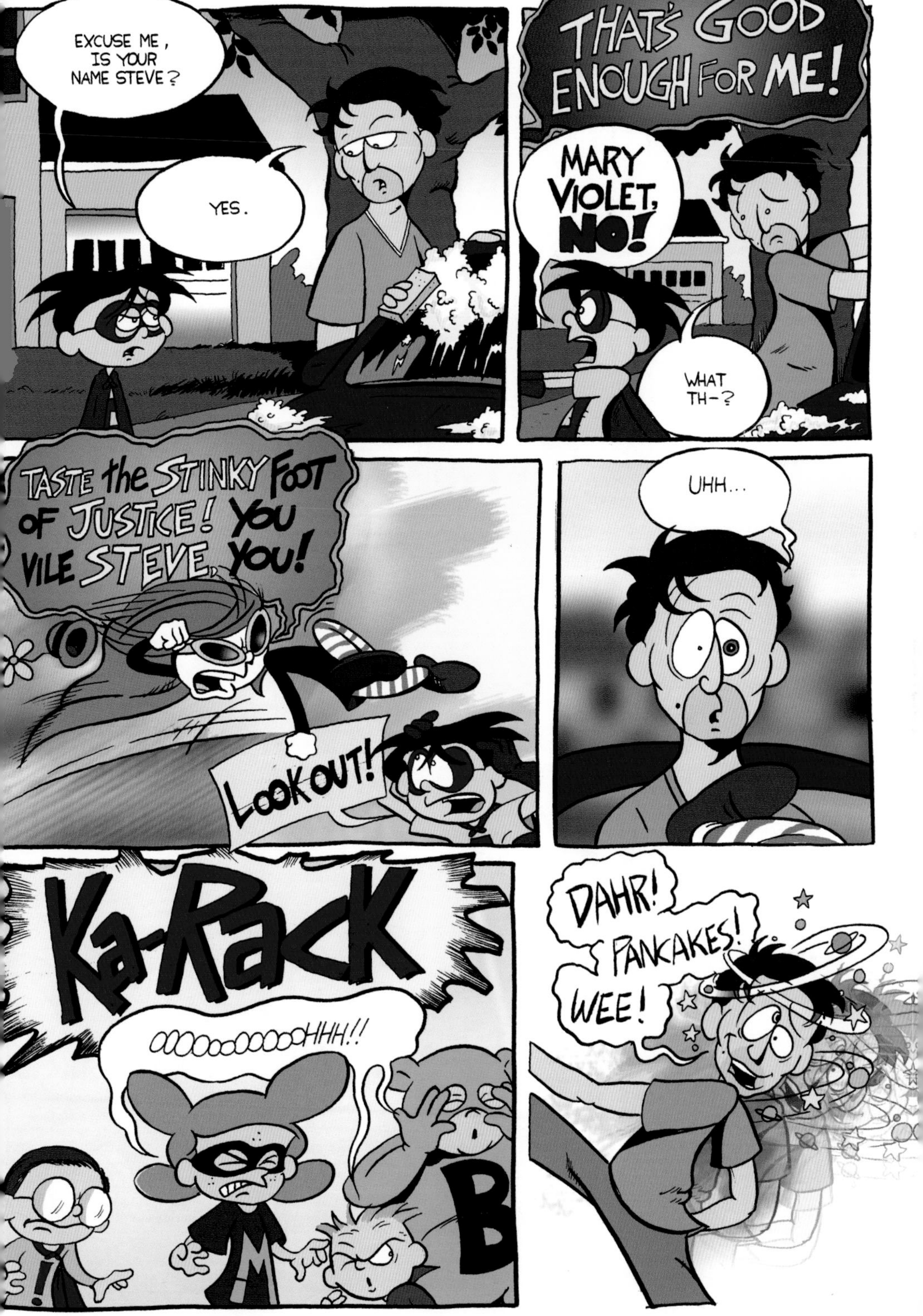
EXCUSE ME, IS YOUR NAME STEVE?
YES.
THAT'S GOOD ENOUGH FOR ME!
MARY VIOLET, NO!
WHAT TH-?
TASTE the STINKY FOOT OF JUSTICE! YOU VILE STEVE, YOU!
LOOK OUT!
UHH...
KA-RACK
OOOOOOOOOOOHHH!!
DAHR! PANKAKES! WEE!

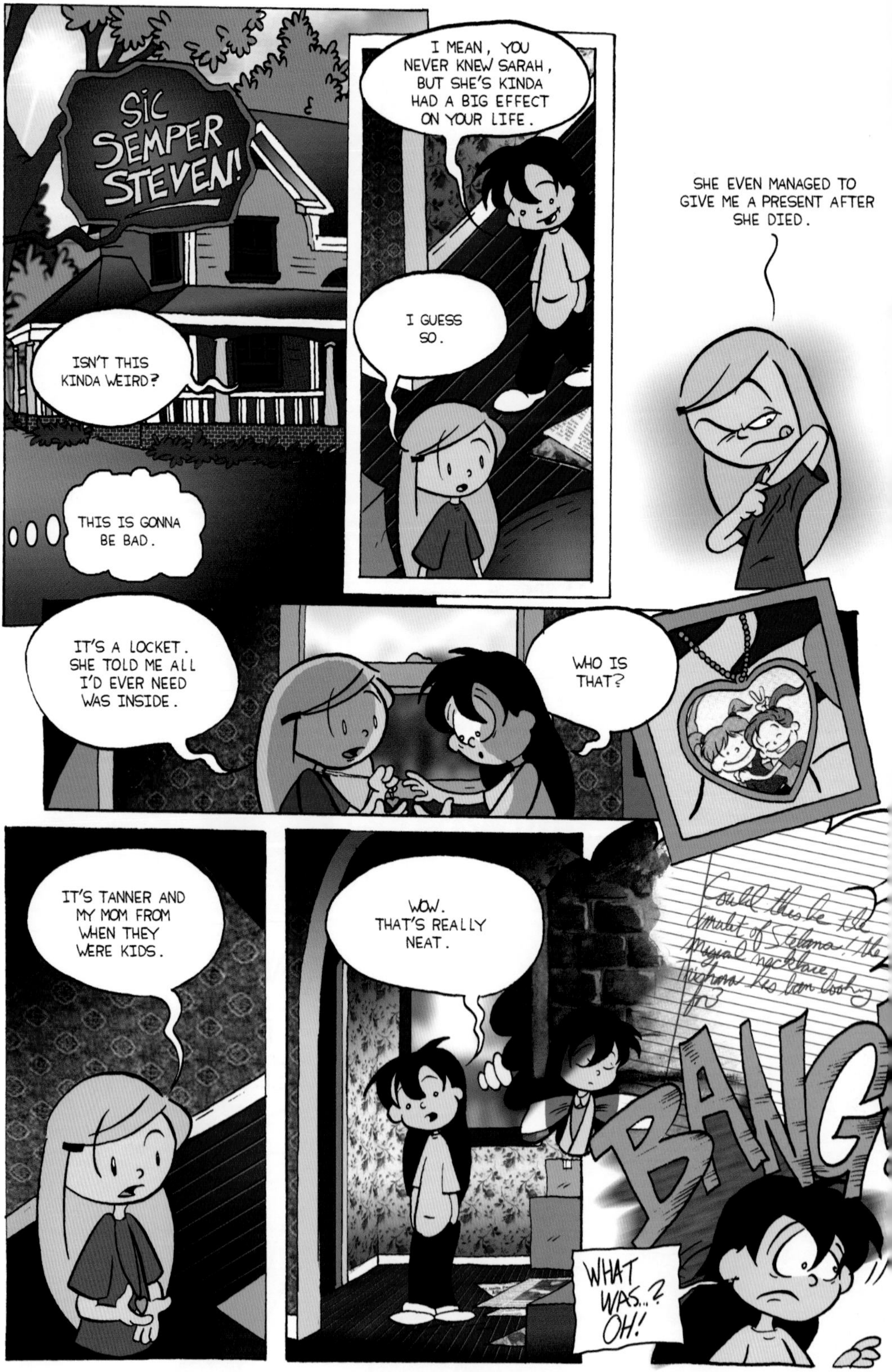
Sic SEMPER STEVEN!
ISN'T THIS KINDA WEIRD?
THIS IS GONNA BE BAD.
I MEAN, YOU NEVER KNEW SARAH, BUT SHE'S KINDA HAD A BIG EFFECT ON YOUR LIFE.
I GUESS SO.
SHE EVEN MANAGED TO GIVE ME A PRESENT AFTER SHE DIED.
IT'S A LOCKET. SHE TOLD ME ALL I'D EVER NEED WAS INSIDE.
WHO IS THAT?
IT'S TANNER AND MY MOM FROM WHEN THEY WERE KIDS.
WOW. THAT'S REALLY NEAT.
BANG
WHAT WAS..? OH!

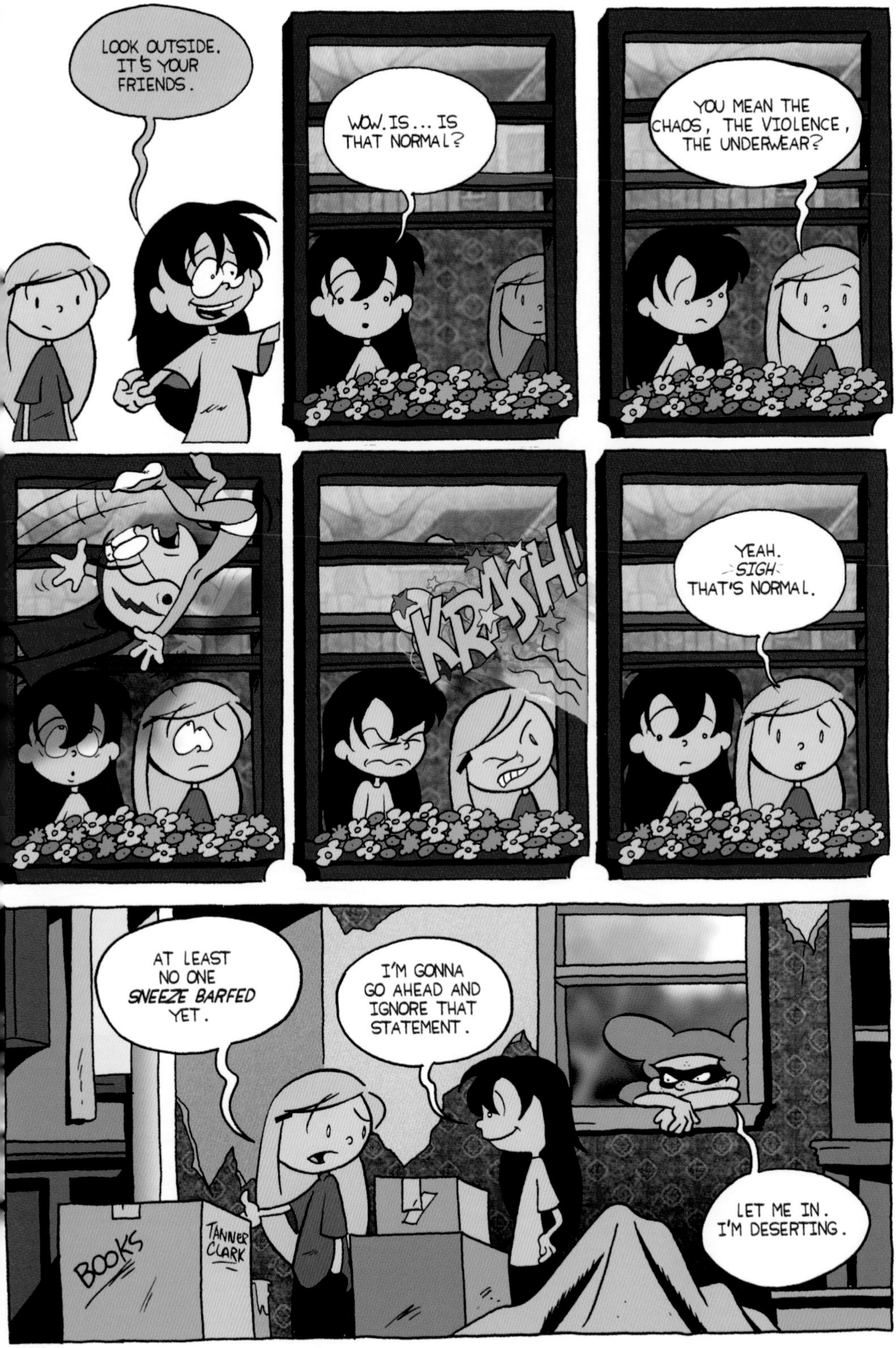
LOOK OUTSIDE. IT'S YOUR FRIENDS.
WOW. IS... IS THAT NORMAL?
YOU MEAN THE CHAOS, THE VIOLENCE, THE UNDERWEAR?
KRASH!
YEAH. SIGH THAT'S NORMAL.
AT LEAST NO ONE SNEEZE BARFED YET.
I'M GONNA GO AHEAD AND IGNORE THAT STATEMENT.
LET ME IN. I'M DESERTING.
BOOKS
TANNER CLARK

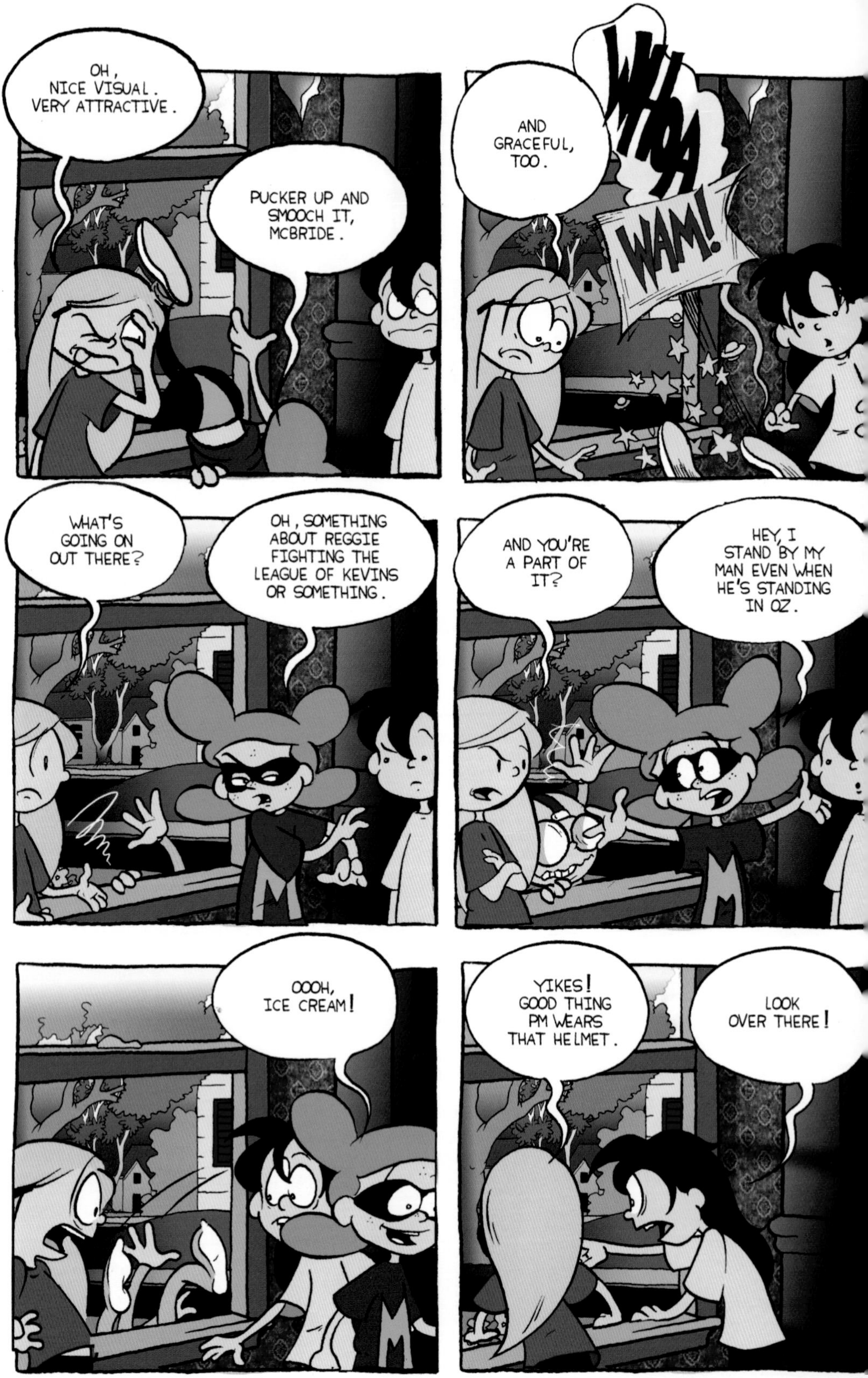

OH, NICE VISUAL. VERY ATTRACTIVE.
PUCKER UP AND SMOOCH IT, MCBRIDE.
AND GRACEFUL, TOO.
WHOA
WAM!
WHAT'S GOING ON OUT THERE?
OH, SOMETHING ABOUT REGGIE FIGHTING THE LEAGUE OF KEVINS OR SOMETHING.
AND YOU'RE A PART OF IT?
HEY, I STAND BY MY MAN EVEN WHEN HE'S STANDING IN OZ.
OOOH, ICE CREAM!
YIKES! GOOD THING PM WEARS THAT HELMET.
LOOK OVER THERE!

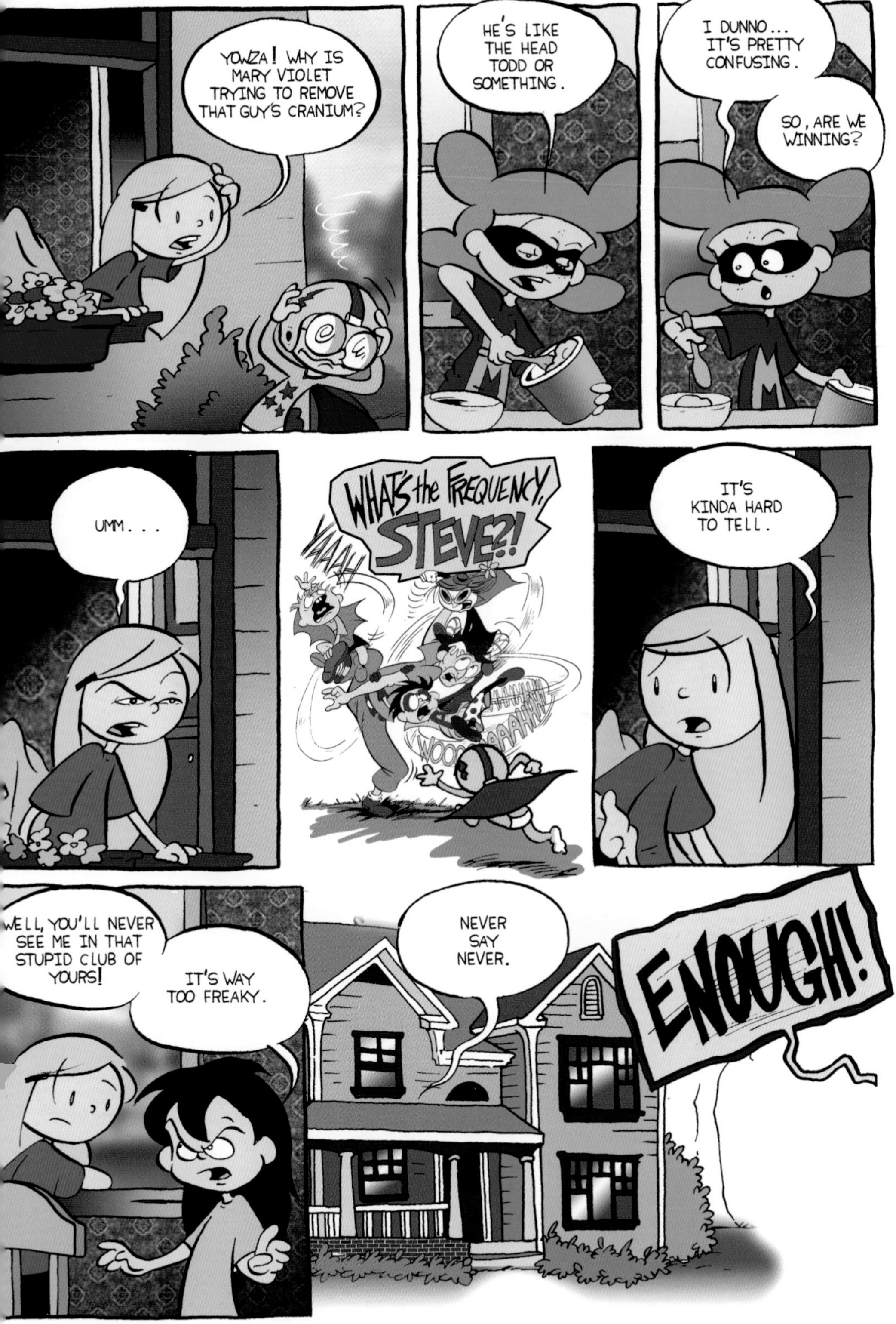

YOWZA! WHY IS MARY VIOLET TRYING TO REMOVE THAT GUY'S CRANIUM?
HE'S LIKE THE HEAD TODD OR SOMETHING.
I DUNNO... IT'S PRETTY CONFUSING.
SO, ARE WE WINNING?
UMM...
WHAT'S the FREQUENCY, STEVE?!
YAAAH
AAAHHH
WOOO
IT'S KINDA HARD TO TELL.
WELL, YOU'LL NEVER SEE ME IN THAT STUPID CLUB OF YOURS!
IT'S WAY TOO FREAKY.
NEVER SAY NEVER.
ENOUGH!

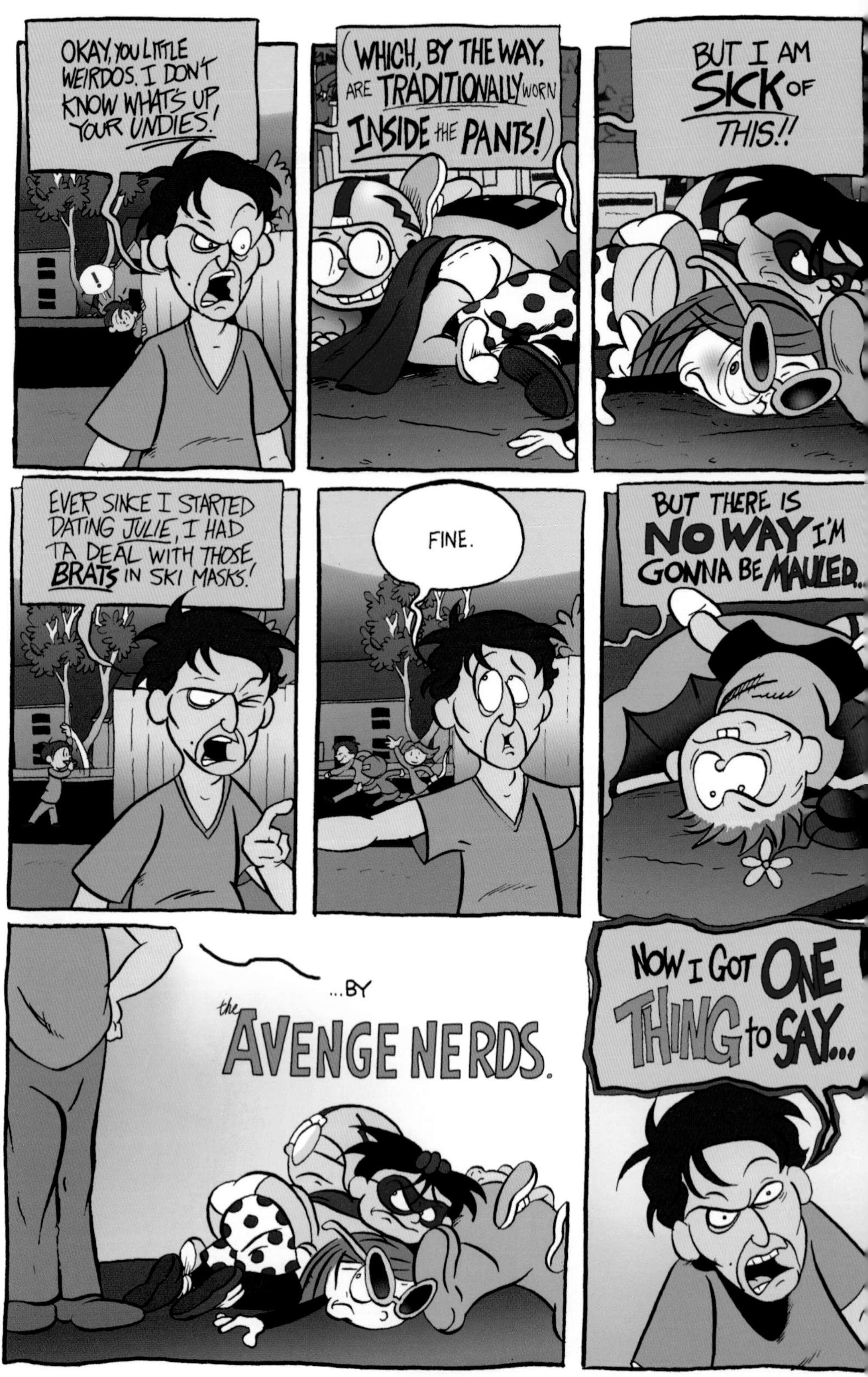
OKAY, YOU LITTLE WEIRDOS. I DON'T KNOW WHAT'S UP YOUR UNDIES!
!
(WHICH, BY THE WAY, ARE TRADITIONALLY WORN INSIDE THE PANTS!)
BUT I AM SICK OF THIS!!
EVER SINCE I STARTED DATING JULIE, I HAD TA DEAL WITH THOSE BRATS IN SKI MASKS!
FINE.
BUT THERE IS NO WAY I'M GONNA BE MAULED...
...BY
the AVENGE NERDS.
NOW I GOT ONE THING to SAY...

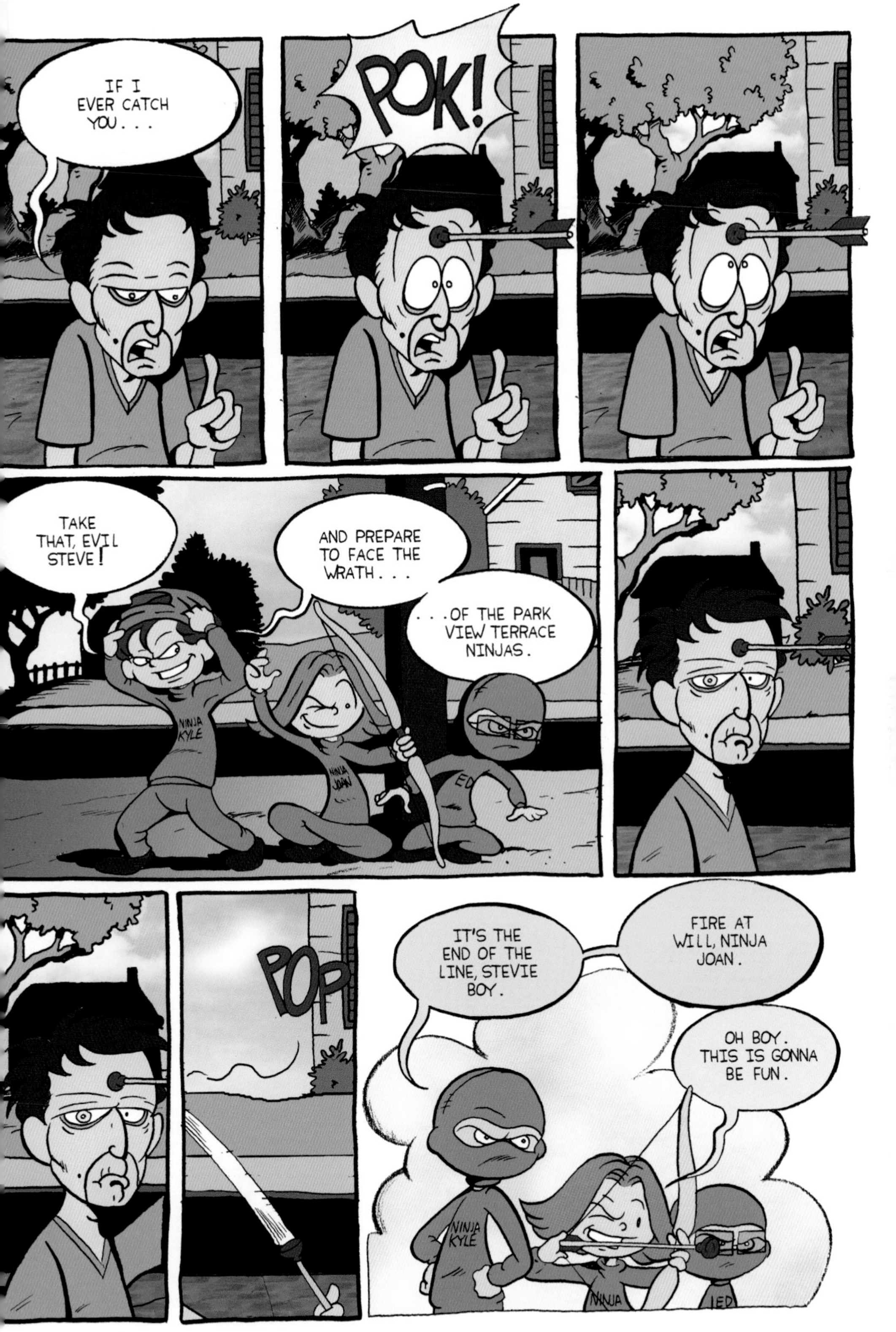
IF I EVER CATCH YOU . . .
POK!
TAKE THAT, EVIL STEVE!
AND PREPARE TO FACE THE WRATH . . .
. . .OF THE PARK VIEW TERRACE NINJAS.
NINJA KYLE
NINJA JOAN
ED
POP
IT'S THE END OF THE LINE, STEVIE BOY.
FIRE AT WILL, NINJA JOAN.
OH BOY. THIS IS GONNA BE FUN.
NINJA KYLE
NINJA
ED

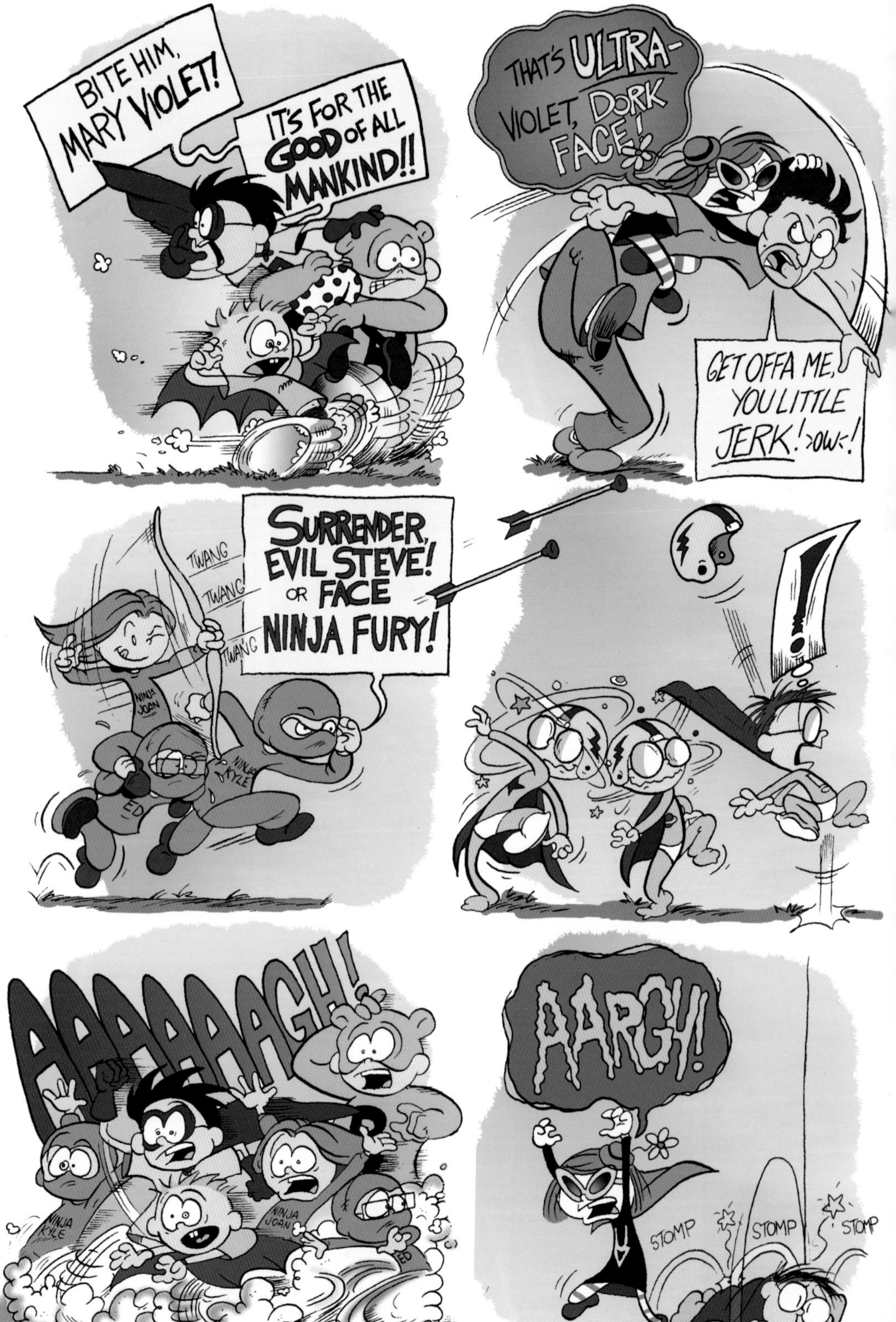
BITE HIM, MARY VIOLET!
IT'S FOR THE GOOD OF ALL MANKIND!!
THAT'S ULTRA-VIOLET, DORK FACE!
GET OFFA ME, YOU LITTLE JERK! >OW<!
SURRENDER, EVIL STEVE! OR FACE NINJA FURY!
TWANG
TWANG
TWANG
NINJA JOAN
NINJA KYLE
ED
!
AAAAAAGH!
NINJA KYLE
NINJA JOAN
ED
AARGH!
STOMP
STOMP
STOMP

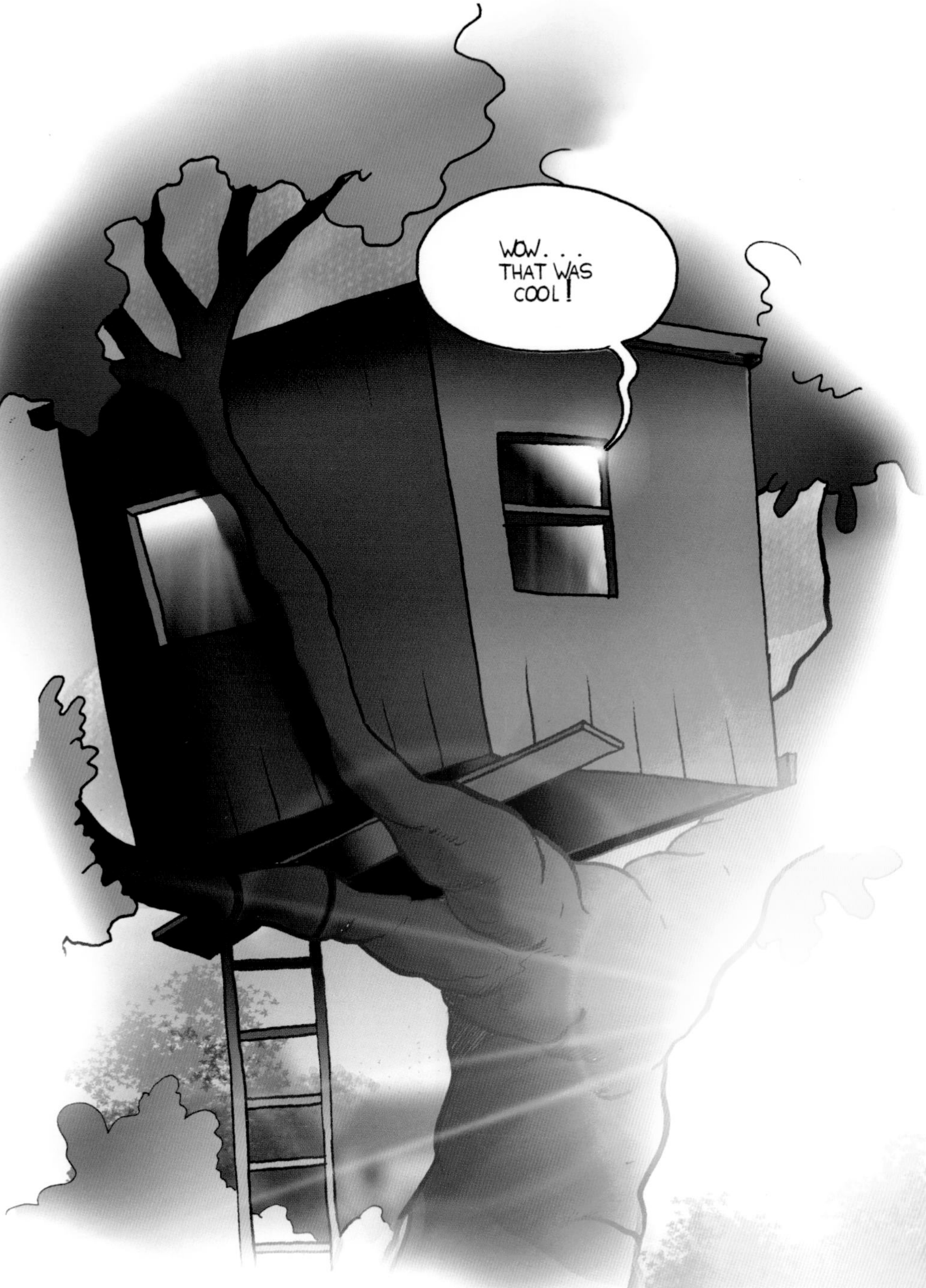
WOW. . . THAT WAS COOL!

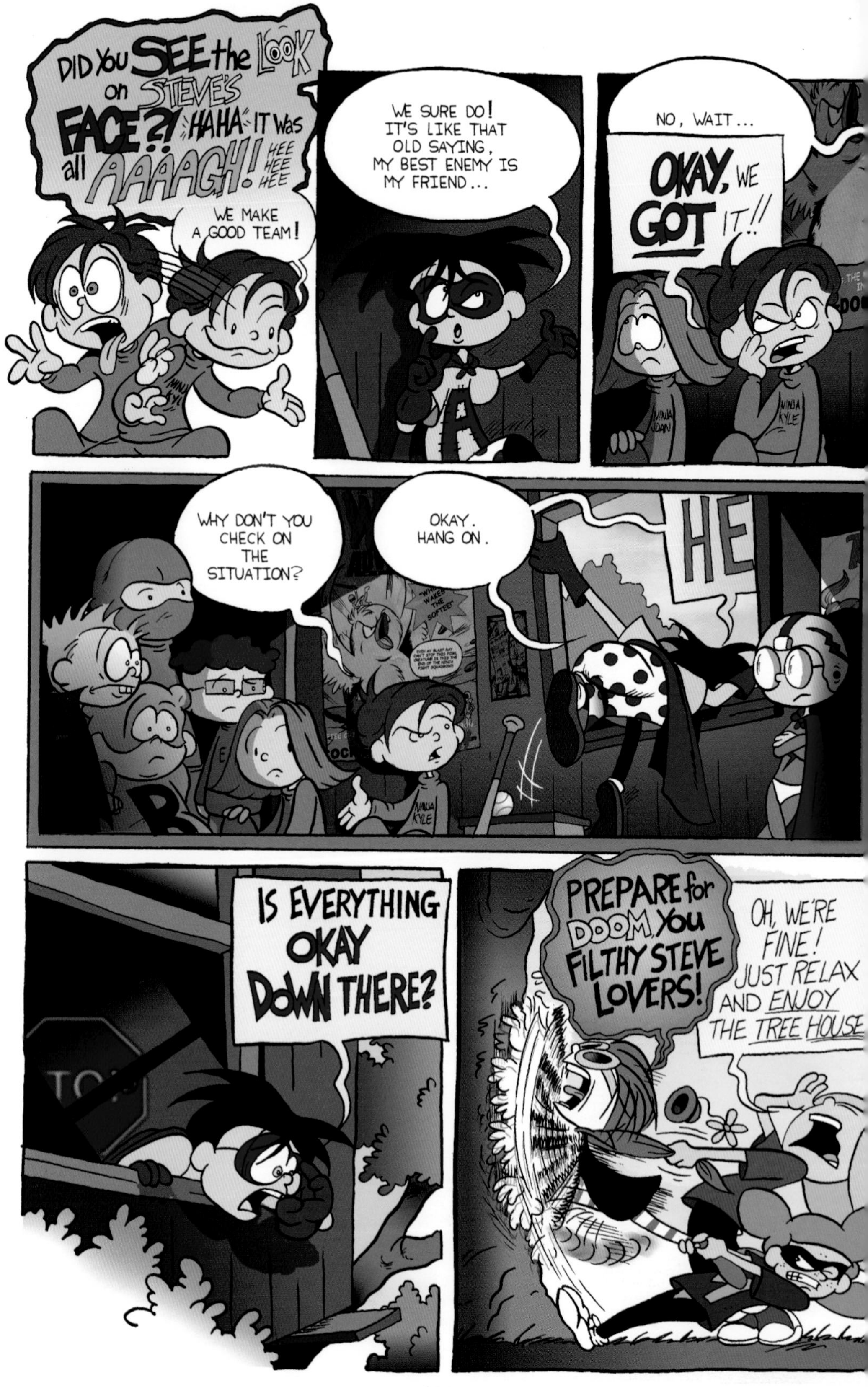

DID YOU SEE THE LOOK ON STEVE'S FACE?! HAHA IT WAS ALL AAAAGH! HEE HEE HEE
WE MAKE A GOOD TEAM!
WE SURE DO! IT'S LIKE THAT OLD SAYING, MY BEST ENEMY IS MY FRIEND...
NO, WAIT...
OKAY, WE GOT IT!!
WHY DON'T YOU CHECK ON THE SITUATION?
OKAY. HANG ON.
IS EVERYTHING OKAY DOWN THERE?
PREPARE FOR DOOM, YOU FILTHY STEVE LOVERS!
OH, WE'RE FINE! JUST RELAX AND ENJOY THE TREE HOUSE

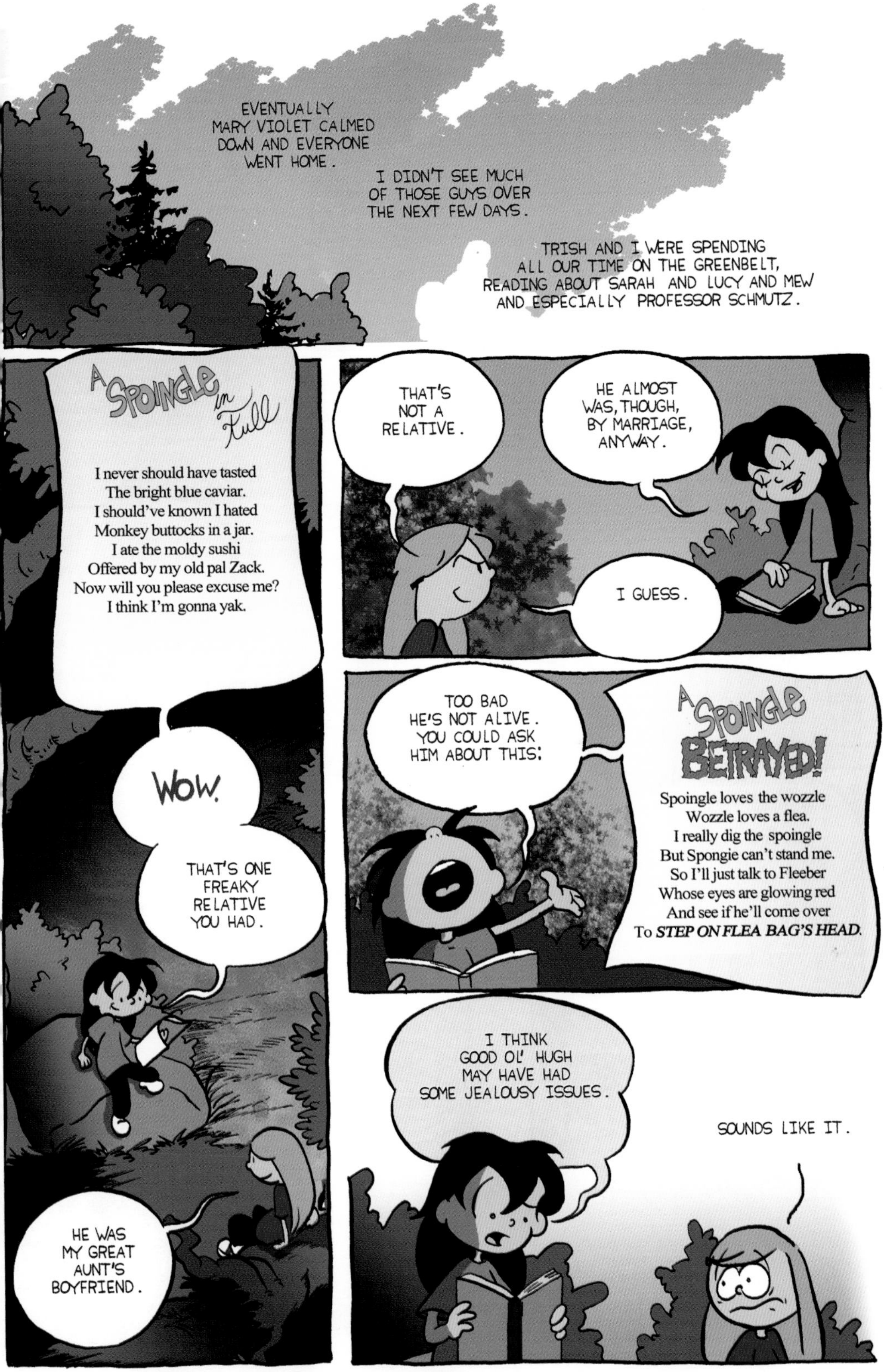

EVENTUALLY MARY VIOLET CALMED DOWN AND EVERYONE WENT HOME.
I DIDN'T SEE MUCH OF THOSE GUYS OVER THE NEXT FEW DAYS.
TRISH AND I WERE SPENDING ALL OUR TIME ON THE GREENBELT, READING ABOUT SARAH AND LUCY AND MEW AND ESPECIALLY PROFESSOR SCHMUTZ.
A Spoingle in Full
I never should have tasted
The bright blue caviar.
I should've known I hated
Monkey buttocks in a jar.
I ate the moldy sushi
Offered by my old pal Zack.
Now will you please excuse me?
I think I'm gonna yak.
WOW.
THAT'S ONE FREAKY RELATIVE YOU HAD.
HE WAS MY GREAT AUNT'S BOYFRIEND.
THAT'S NOT A RELATIVE.
HE ALMOST WAS, THOUGH, BY MARRIAGE, ANYWAY.
I GUESS.
TOO BAD HE'S NOT ALIVE. YOU COULD ASK HIM ABOUT THIS:
A Spoingle BETRAYED!
Spoingle loves the wozzle
Wozzle loves a flea.
I really dig the spoingle
But Spongie can't stand me.
So I'll just talk to Fleeber
Whose eyes are glowing red
And see if he'll come over
To STEP ON FLEA BAG'S HEAD.
I THINK GOOD OL' HUGH MAY HAVE HAD SOME JEALOUSY ISSUES.
SOUNDS LIKE IT.

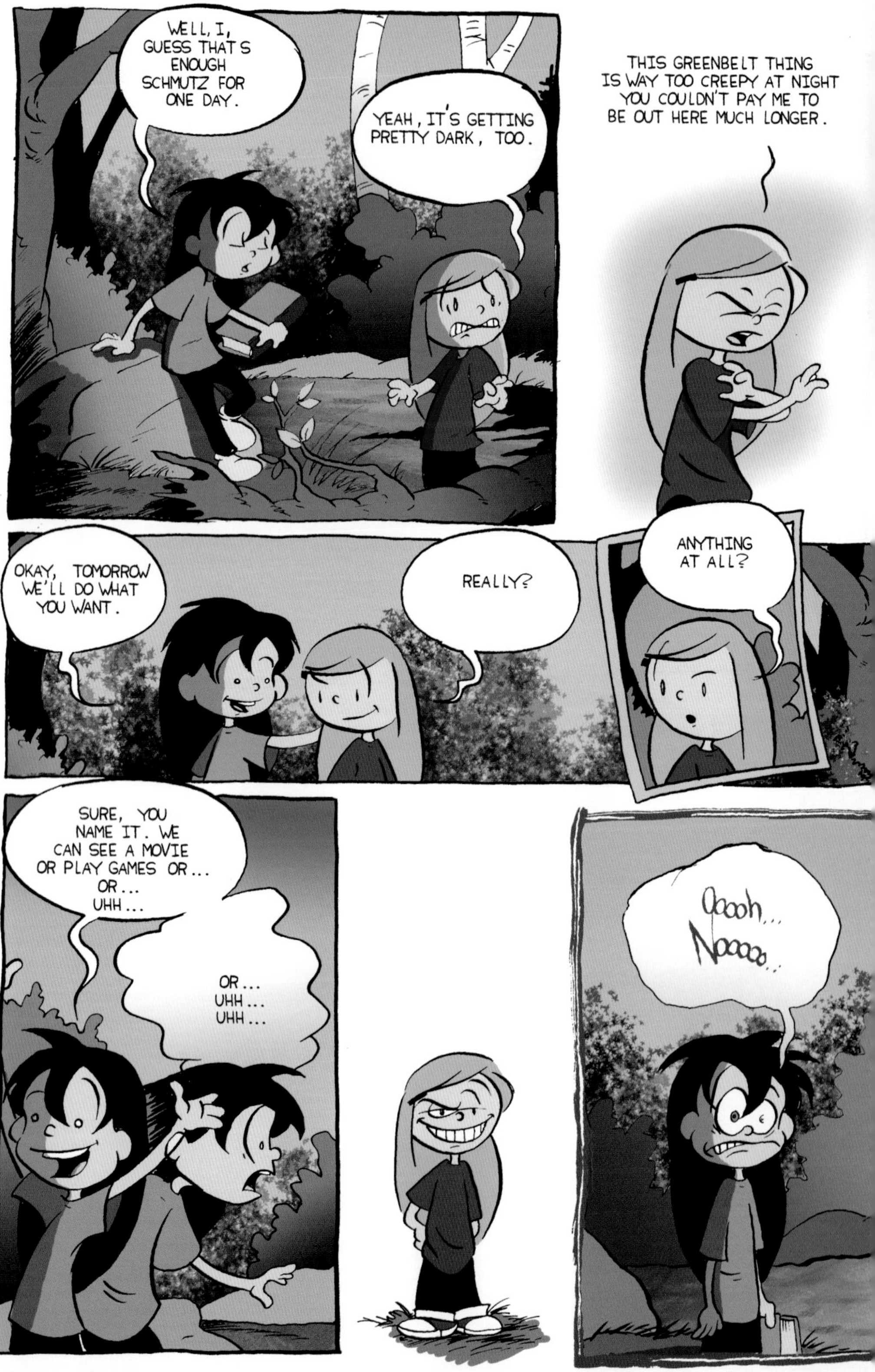
WELL, I, GUESS THAT'S ENOUGH SCHMUTZ FOR ONE DAY.
YEAH, IT'S GETTING PRETTY DARK, TOO.
THIS GREENBELT THING IS WAY TOO CREEPY AT NIGHT YOU COULDN'T PAY ME TO BE OUT HERE MUCH LONGER.
OKAY, TOMORROW WE'LL DO WHAT YOU WANT.
REALLY?
ANYTHING AT ALL?
SURE, YOU NAME IT. WE CAN SEE A MOVIE OR PLAY GAMES OR... OR... UHH...
OR... UHH... UHH...
Ooooh... Noooo...

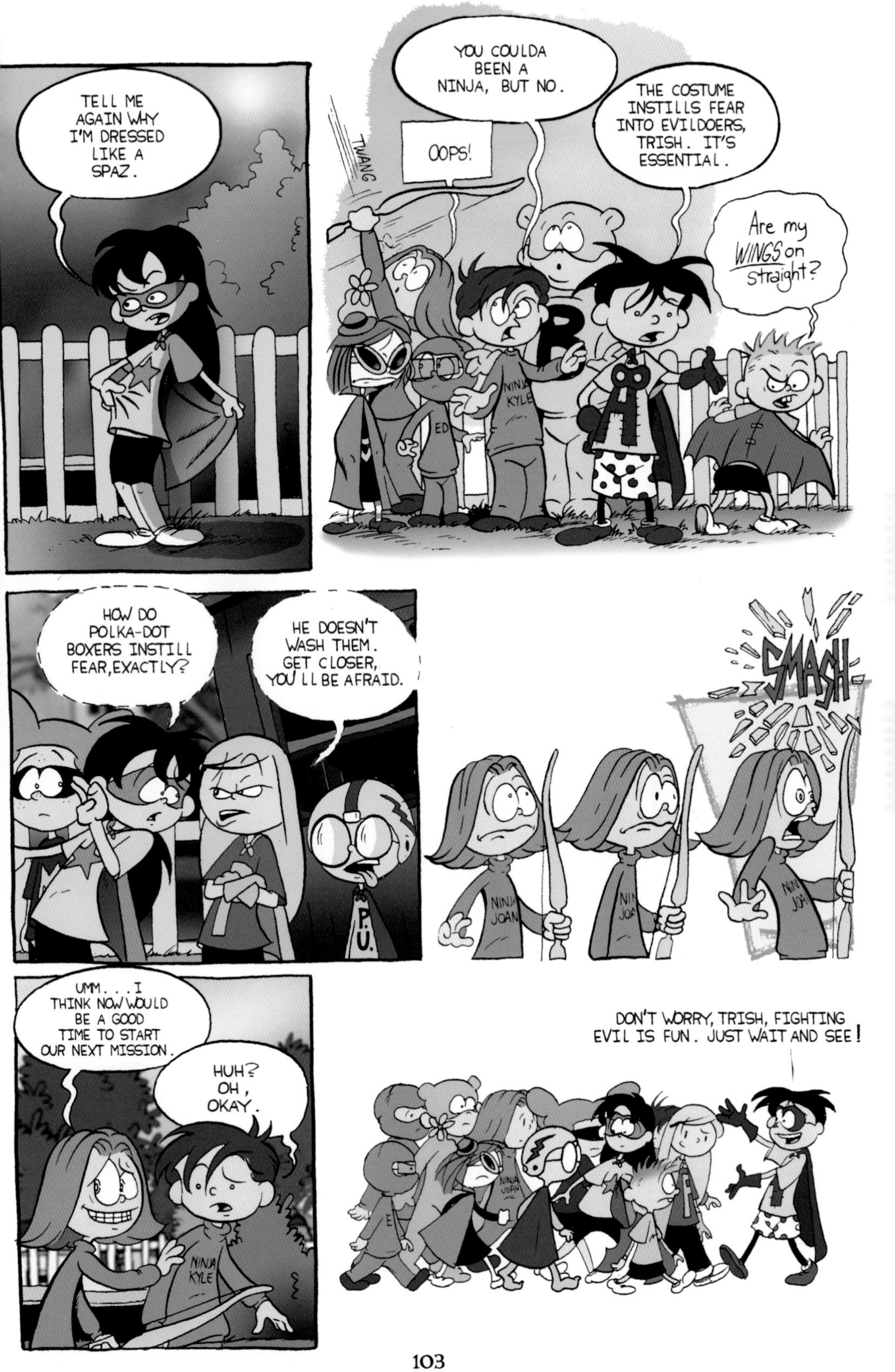
TELL ME AGAIN WHY I'M DRESSED LIKE A SPAZ.
YOU COULDA BEEN A NINJA, BUT NO.
TWANG
OOPS!
THE COSTUME INSTILLS FEAR INTO EVILDOERS, TRISH. IT'S ESSENTIAL.
Are my WINGS on straight?
NINJA KYLE
ED
HOW DO POLKA-DOT BOXERS INSTILL FEAR, EXACTLY?
HE DOESN'T WASH THEM. GET CLOSER, YOU'LL BE AFRAID.
P.U.
SMASH
UMM...I THINK NOW WOULD BE A GOOD TIME TO START OUR NEXT MISSION.
HUH? OH, OKAY.
NINJA KYLE
DON'T WORRY, TRISH, FIGHTING EVIL IS FUN. JUST WAIT AND SEE!

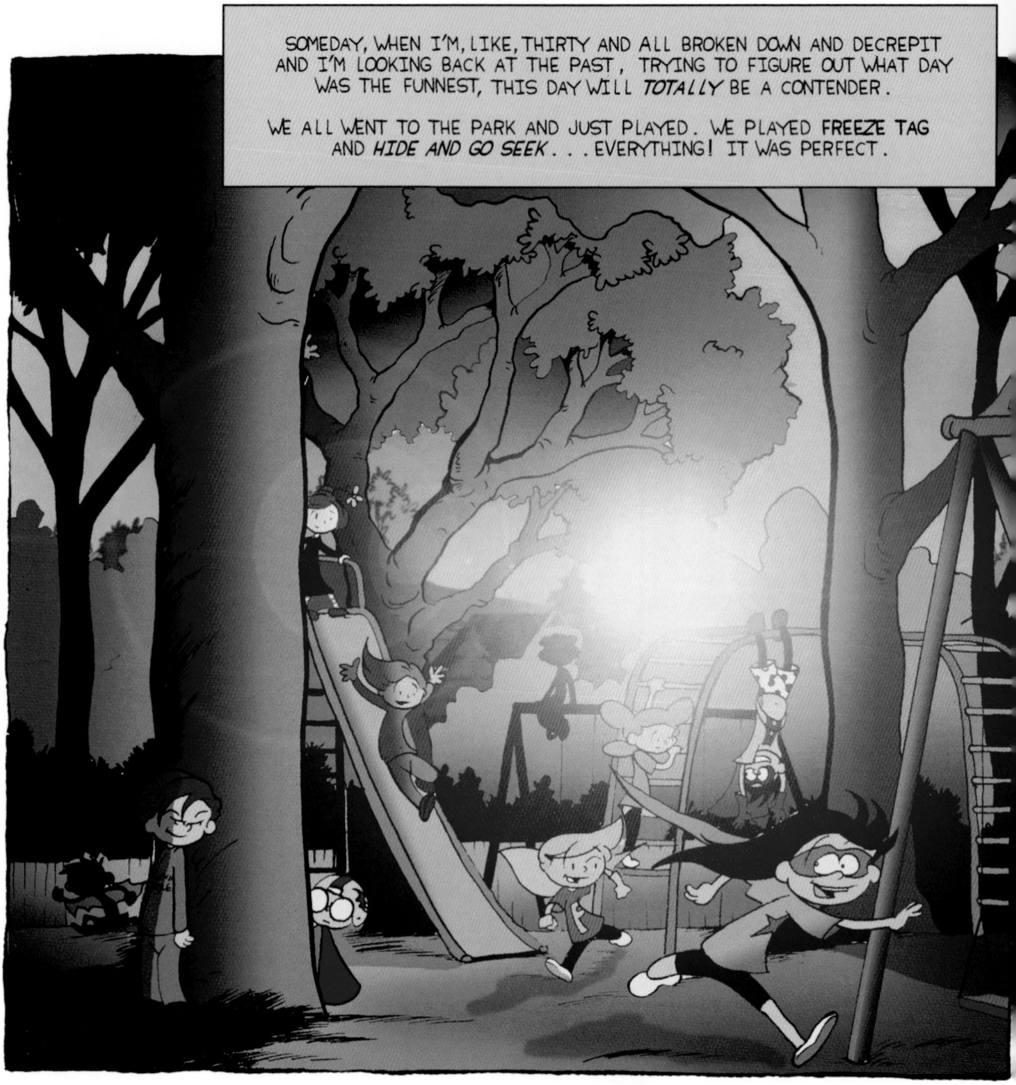
SOMEDAY, WHEN I'M, LIKE, THIRTY AND ALL BROKEN DOWN AND DECREPIT AND I'M LOOKING BACK AT THE PAST, TRYING TO FIGURE OUT WHAT DAY WAS THE FUNNEST, THIS DAY WILL *TOTALLY* BE A CONTENDER.
WE ALL WENT TO THE PARK AND JUST PLAYED. WE PLAYED **FREEZE TAG** AND ***HIDE AND GO SEEK***. . . EVERYTHING! IT WAS PERFECT.

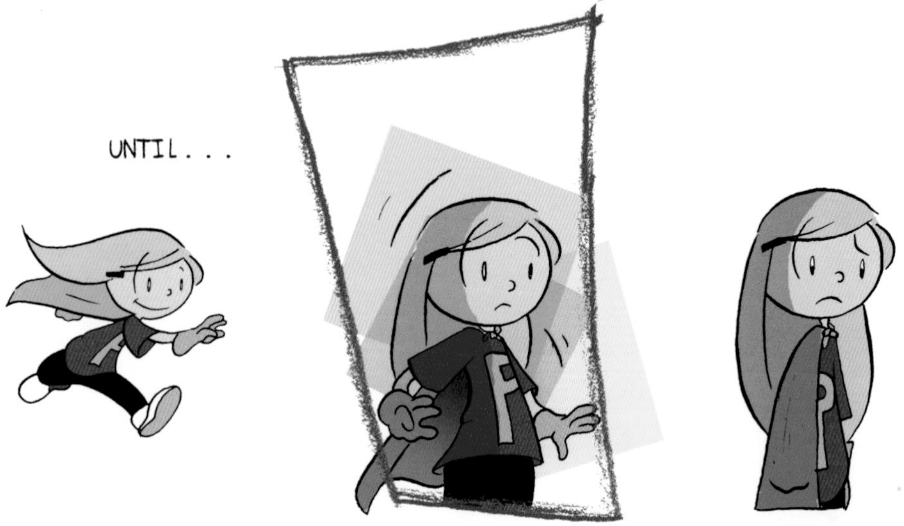
UNTIL. . .

WHAT'S GOING ON?

WHAT'S GOING ON? DID ANYONE EVER TELL YOU THAT YOU'RE A TROUBLEMAKER, LITTLE GIRL?

EVERYBODY TELLS ME THAT.

WHAT'S GOING ON?

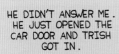
HE DIDN'T ANSWER ME. HE JUST OPENED THE CAR DOOR AND TRISH GOT IN.

SHE DIDN'T SAY ANYTHING, EITHER.

SHE JUST LOOKED...

HELPLESS, I GUESS.

AND KINDA SCARED.

AND THEN THEY WERE GONE.

AFTER THAT, NO ONE SAW TRISHIA FOR WEEKS.

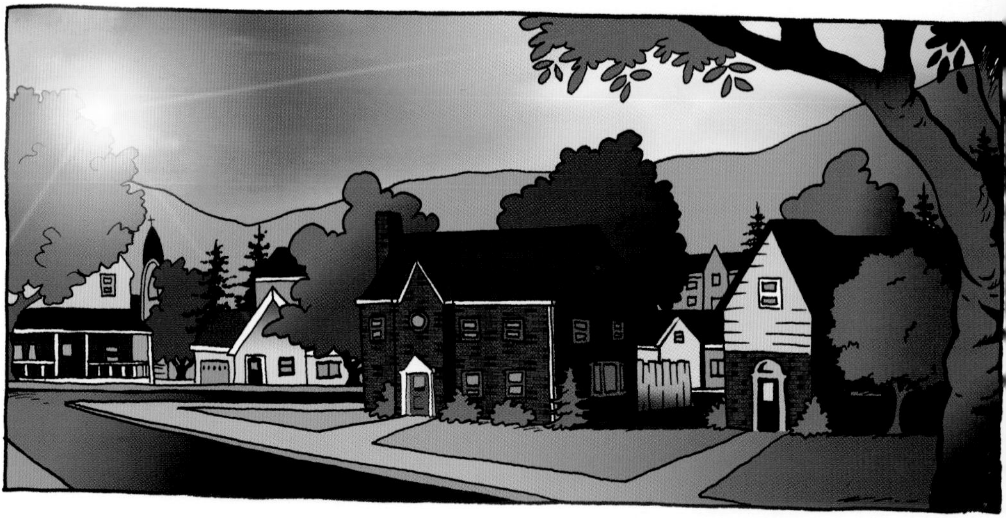

IT RAINED OFF AND ON, WHICH ALWAYS STINKS DURING SUMMER VACATION.

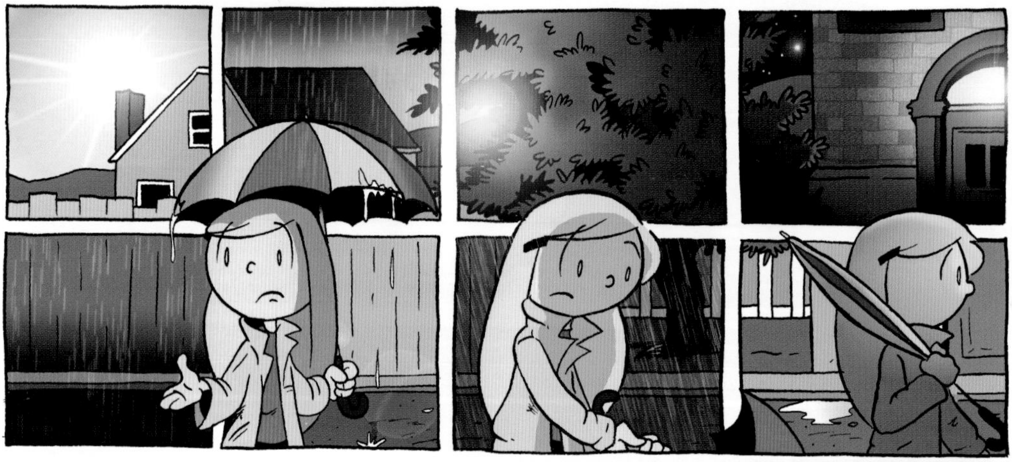

ONE DAY JOANNE
SHOWED UP WITH
THE NEW *TWEENIE ZEENIE*.
EVERYONE WANTED TO KNOW
WHAT HAPPENED TO
PRINCESS TRISHARA.

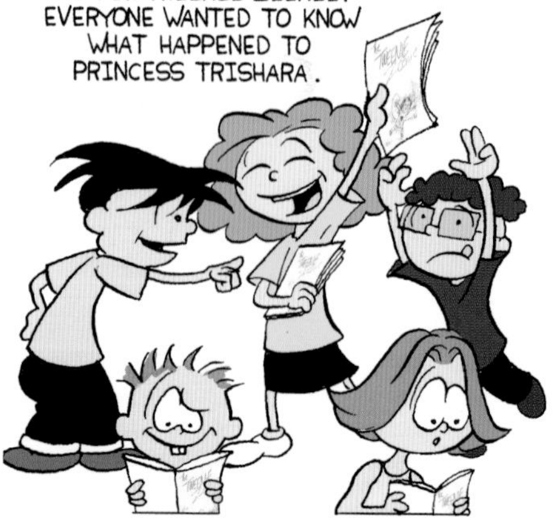

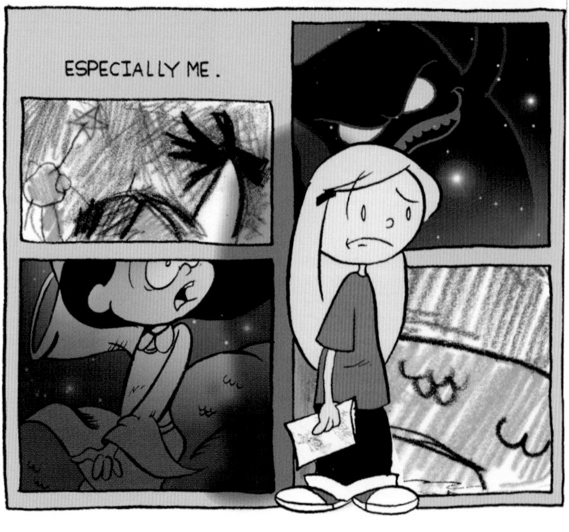
ESPECIALLY ME.

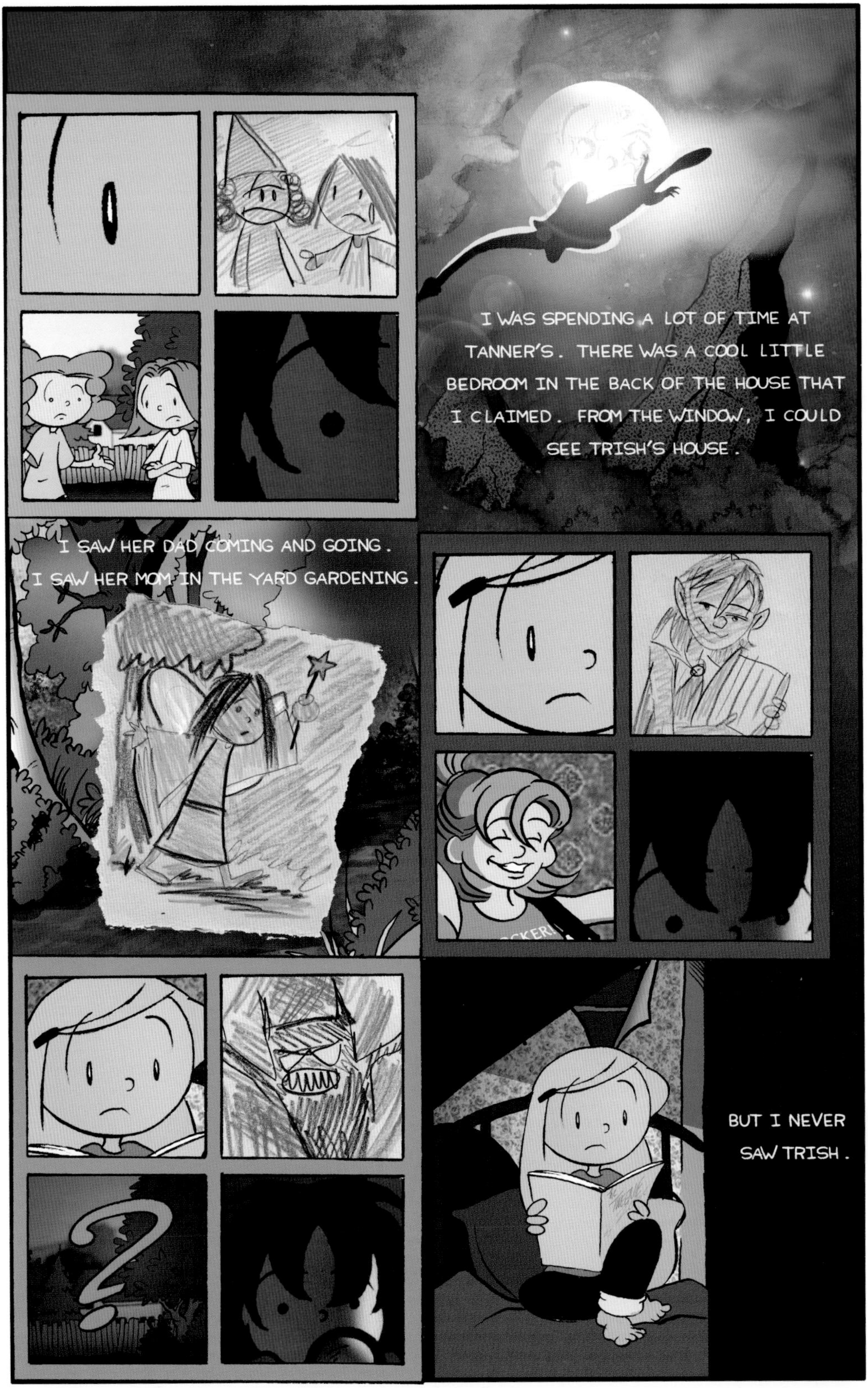
I WAS SPENDING A LOT OF TIME AT TANNER'S. THERE WAS A COOL LITTLE BEDROOM IN THE BACK OF THE HOUSE THAT I CLAIMED. FROM THE WINDOW, I COULD SEE TRISH'S HOUSE.
I SAW HER DAD COMING AND GOING.
I SAW HER MOM IN THE YARD GARDENING.
BUT I NEVER SAW TRISH.

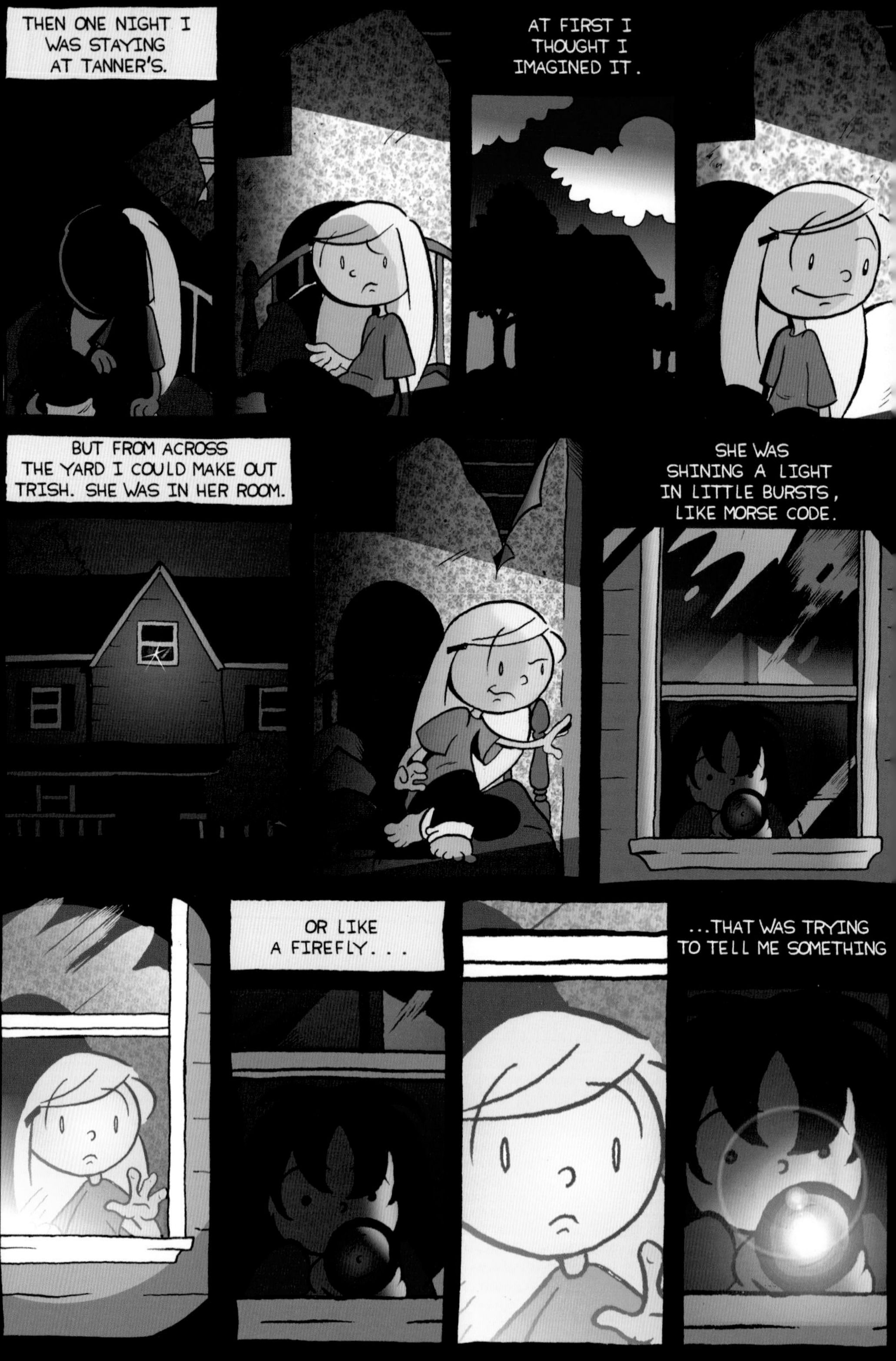
THEN ONE NIGHT I WAS STAYING AT TANNER'S.
AT FIRST I THOUGHT I IMAGINED IT.
BUT FROM ACROSS THE YARD I COULD MAKE OUT TRISH. SHE WAS IN HER ROOM.
SHE WAS SHINING A LIGHT IN LITTLE BURSTS, LIKE MORSE CODE.
OR LIKE A FIREFLY...
...THAT WAS TRYING TO TELL ME SOMETHING

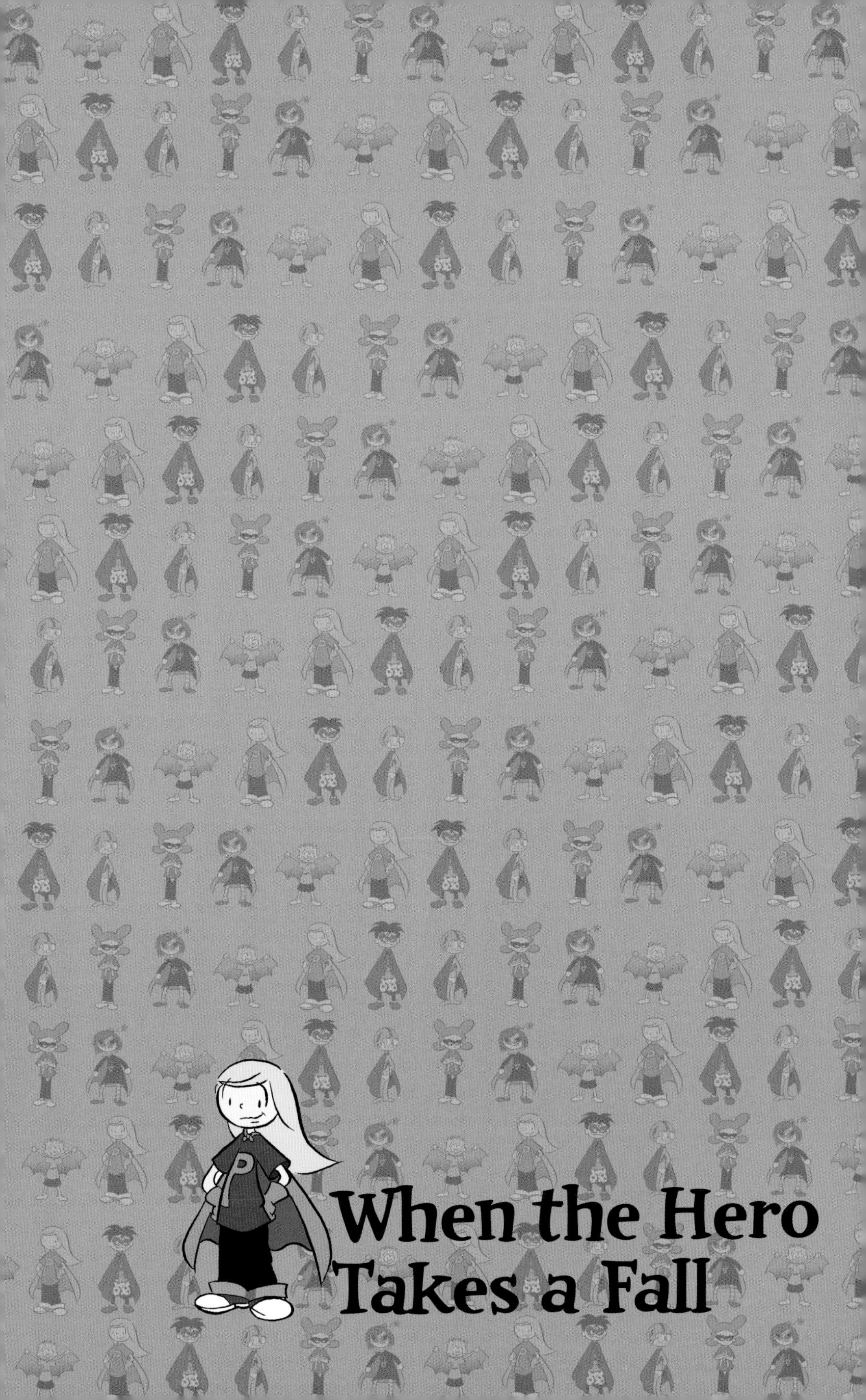

When the Hero Takes a Fall

BEFORE SCHOOL STARTED UP AGAIN, TANNER DECIDED TO LET ME HAVE A SLEEPOVER AT HER HOUSE. ALL THE GIRLS WERE COMING, EVEN TRISHIA. I WAS SUPEREXCITED. THEN, ON THE DAY BEFORE THE PARTY, TANNER SAT ME DOWN.

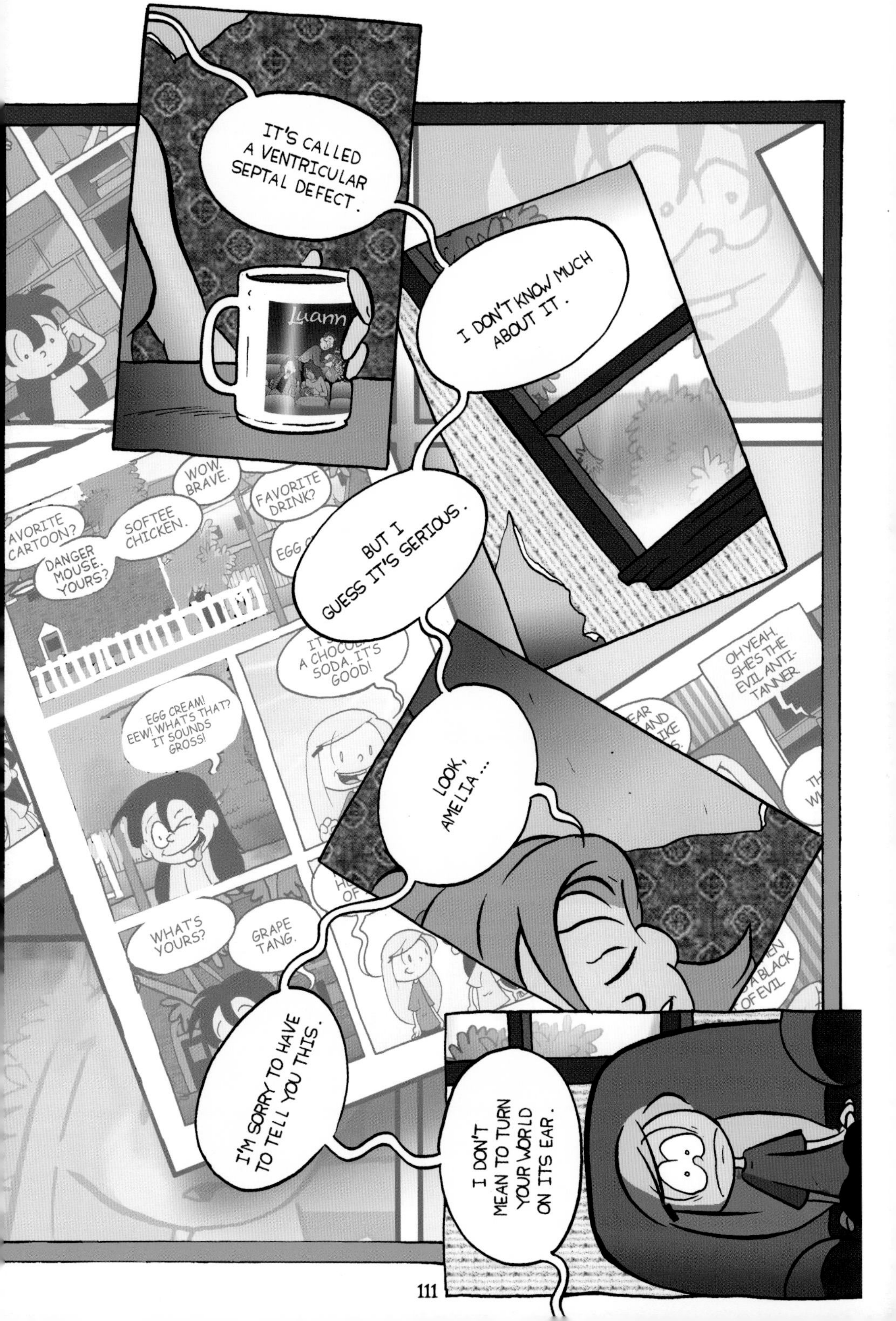
IT'S CALLED A VENTRICULAR SEPTAL DEFECT.
I DON'T KNOW MUCH ABOUT IT.
BUT I GUESS IT'S SERIOUS.
LOOK, AMELIA...
I'M SORRY TO HAVE TO TELL YOU THIS.
I DON'T MEAN TO TURN YOUR WORLD ON ITS EAR.
Luann
WOW. BRAVE.
FAVORITE DRINK?
SOFTEE CHICKEN.
DANGER MOUSE. YOURS?
EGG CREAM! EEW! WHAT'S THAT? IT SOUNDS GROSS!
WHAT'S YOURS?
GRAPE TANG.
OH YEAH. SHE'S THE EVIL ANTI-TANNER.

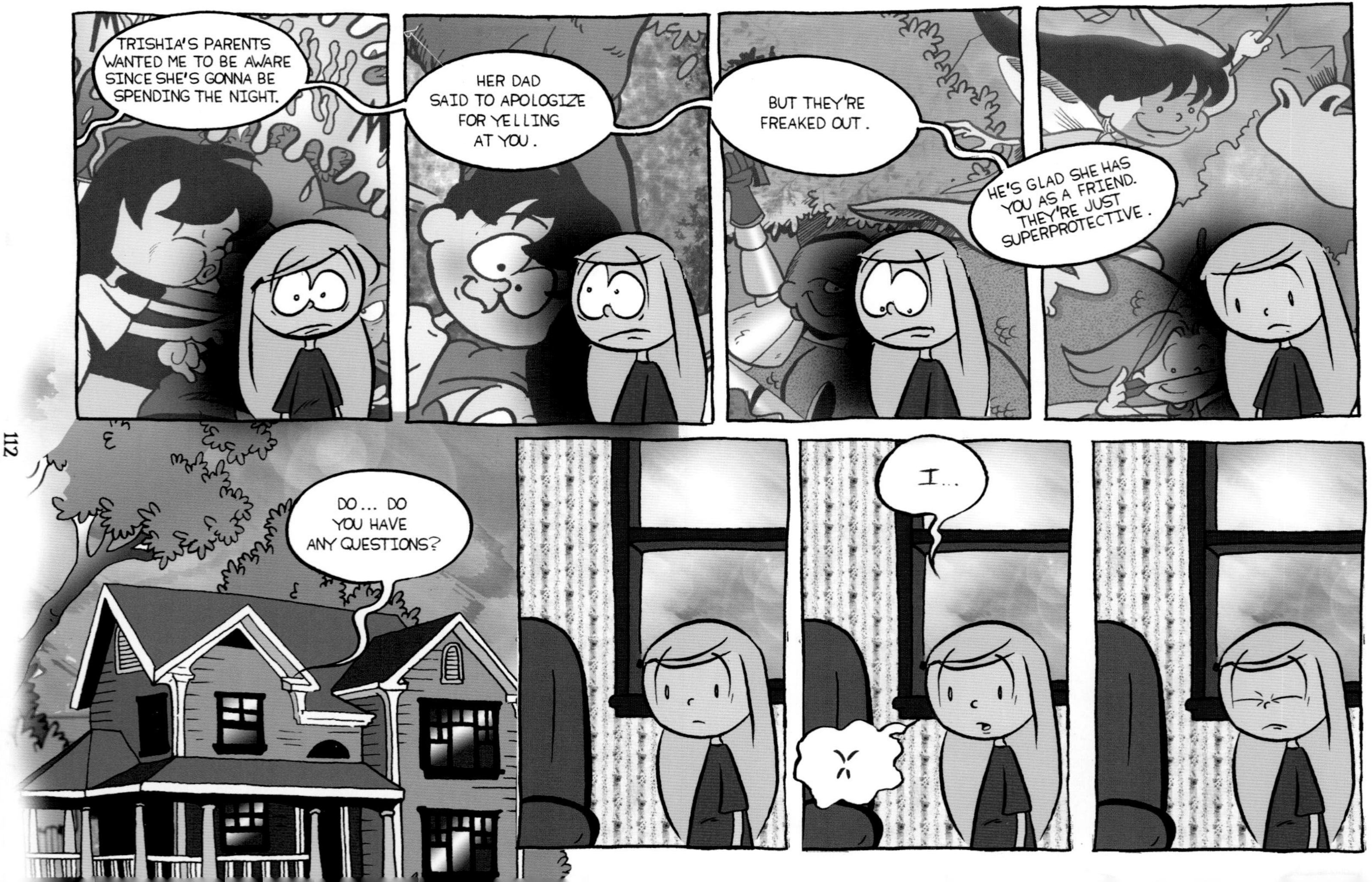
TRISHIA'S PARENTS WANTED ME TO BE AWARE SINCE SHE'S GONNA BE SPENDING THE NIGHT.
HER DAD SAID TO APOLOGIZE FOR YELLING AT YOU.
BUT THEY'RE FREAKED OUT.
HE'S GLAD SHE HAS YOU AS A FRIEND. THEY'RE JUST SUPERPROTECTIVE.
DO... DO YOU HAVE ANY QUESTIONS?
I...

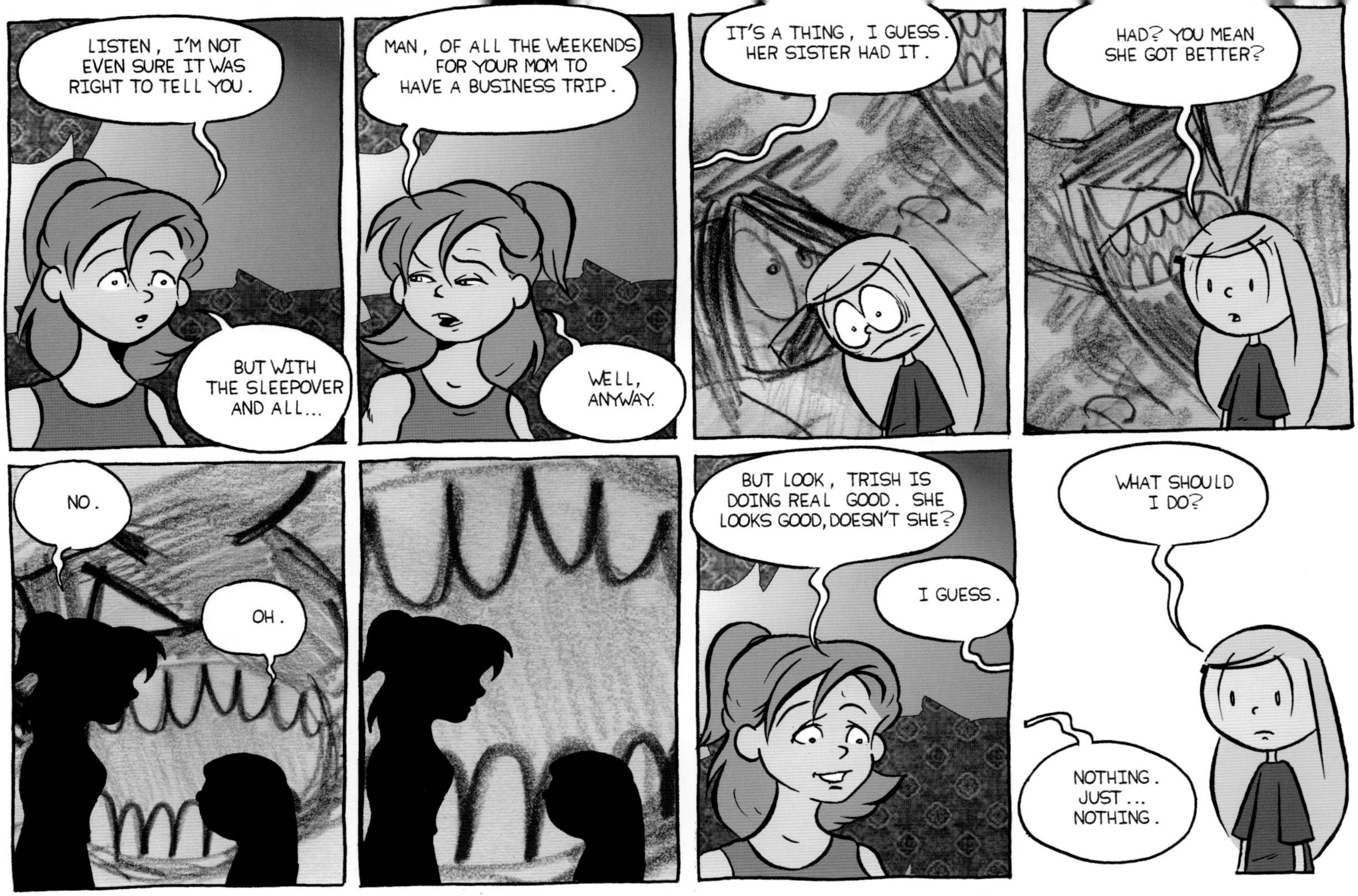
LISTEN, I'M NOT EVEN SURE IT WAS RIGHT TO TELL YOU.
BUT WITH THE SLEEPOVER AND ALL...
MAN, OF ALL THE WEEKENDS FOR YOUR MOM TO HAVE A BUSINESS TRIP.
WELL, ANYWAY.
IT'S A THING, I GUESS. HER SISTER HAD IT.
HAD? YOU MEAN SHE GOT BETTER?
NO.
OH.
BUT LOOK, TRISH IS DOING REAL GOOD. SHE LOOKS GOOD, DOESN'T SHE?
I GUESS.
WHAT SHOULD I DO?
NOTHING. JUST... NOTHING.

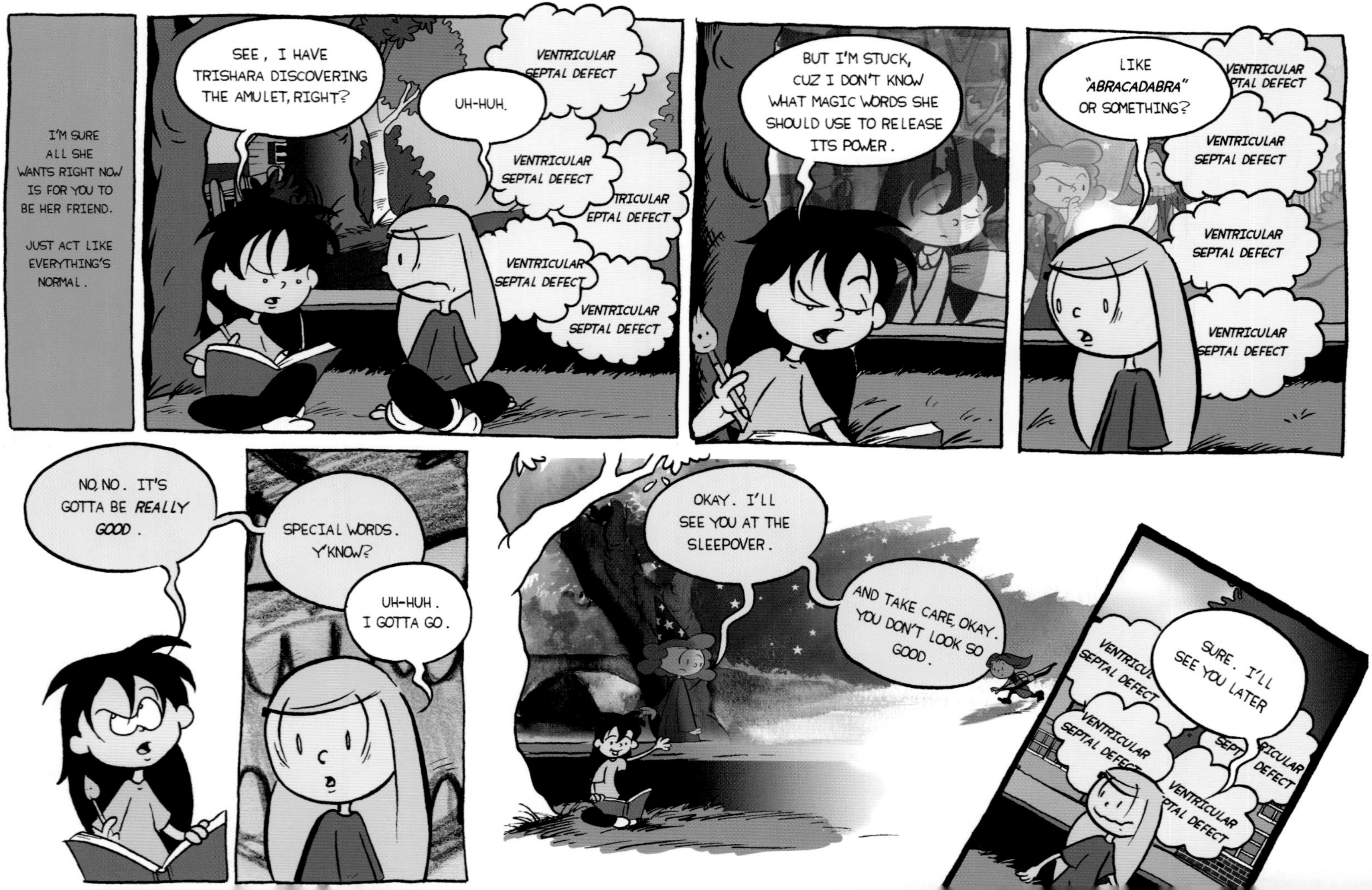
I'M SURE ALL SHE WANTS RIGHT NOW IS FOR YOU TO BE HER FRIEND.
JUST ACT LIKE EVERYTHING'S NORMAL.
SEE, I HAVE TRISHARA DISCOVERING THE AMULET, RIGHT?
VENTRICULAR SEPTAL DEFECT
UH-HUH.
VENTRICULAR SEPTAL DEFECT
TRICULAR EPTAL DEFECT
VENTRICULAR SEPTAL DEFECT
VENTRICULAR SEPTAL DEFECT
BUT I'M STUCK, CUZ I DON'T KNOW WHAT MAGIC WORDS SHE SHOULD USE TO RELEASE ITS POWER.
LIKE "ABRACADABRA" OR SOMETHING?
VENTRICULAR PTAL DEFECT
VENTRICULAR SEPTAL DEFECT
VENTRICULAR SEPTAL DEFECT
VENTRICULAR EPTAL DEFECT
NO, NO. IT'S GOTTA BE REALLY GOOD.
SPECIAL WORDS. Y'KNOW?
UH-HUH. I GOTTA GO.
OKAY. I'LL SEE YOU AT THE SLEEPOVER.
AND TAKE CARE, OKAY. YOU DON'T LOOK SO GOOD.
SURE. I'LL SEE YOU LATER
VENTRICU SEPTAL DEFECT
VENTRICULAR SEPTAL DEFE
SEPT
RICULAR DEFECT
VENTRICULAR PTAL DEFECT

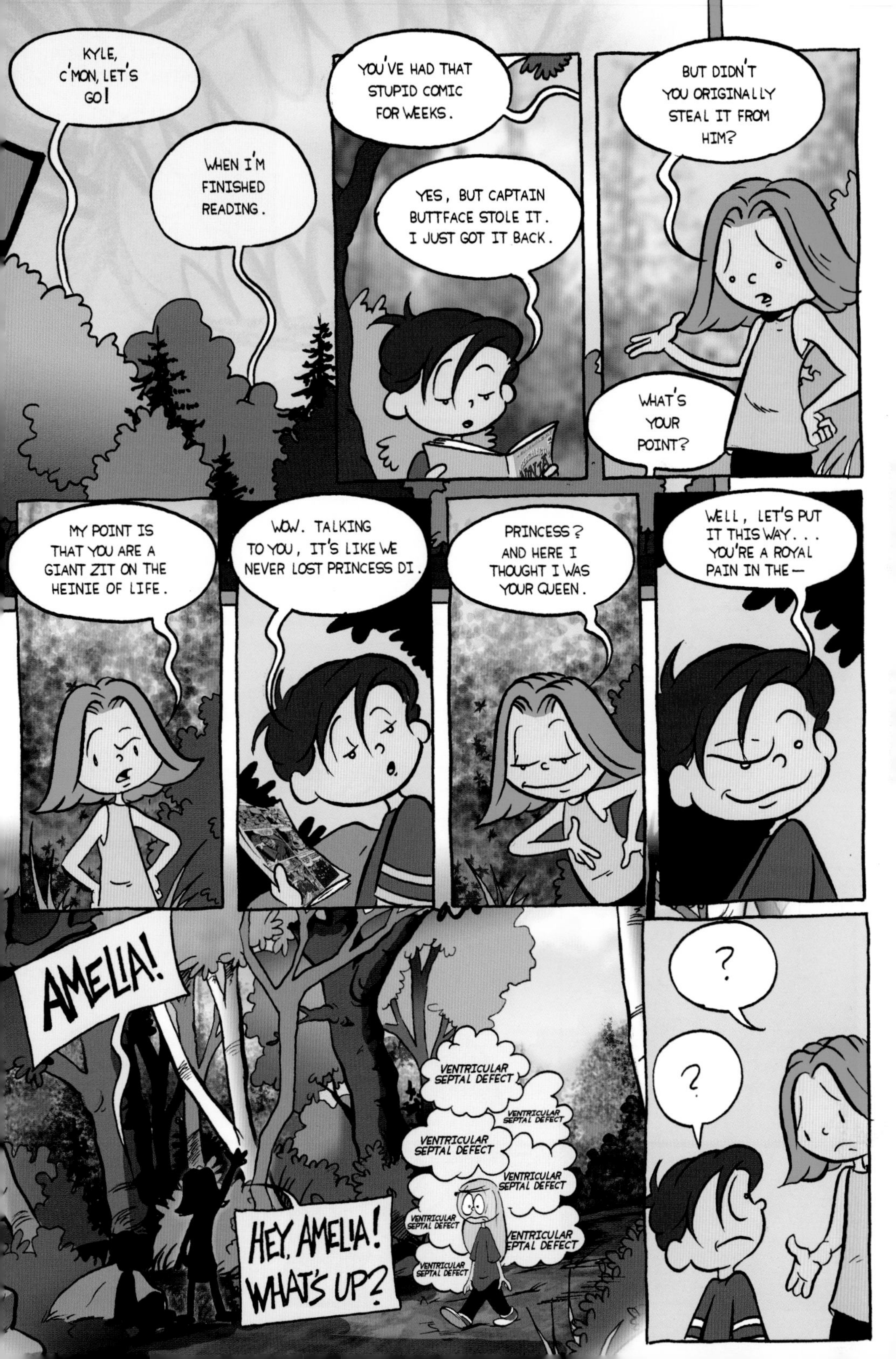
KYLE, C'MON, LET'S GO!
WHEN I'M FINISHED READING.
YOU'VE HAD THAT STUPID COMIC FOR WEEKS.
YES, BUT CAPTAIN BUTTFACE STOLE IT. I JUST GOT IT BACK.
BUT DIDN'T YOU ORIGINALLY STEAL IT FROM HIM?
WHAT'S YOUR POINT?
MY POINT IS THAT YOU ARE A GIANT ZIT ON THE HEINIE OF LIFE.
WOW. TALKING TO YOU, IT'S LIKE WE NEVER LOST PRINCESS DI.
PRINCESS? AND HERE I THOUGHT I WAS YOUR QUEEN.
WELL, LET'S PUT IT THIS WAY . . . YOU'RE A ROYAL PAIN IN THE—
AMELIA!
HEY, AMELIA! WHAT'S UP?
VENTRICULAR SEPTAL DEFECT
VENTRICULAR SEPTAL DEFECT
VENTRICULAR SEPTAL DEFECT
VENTRICULAR SEPTAL DEFECT
VENTRICULAR SEPTAL DEFECT
VENTRICULAR SEPTAL DEFECT
VENTRICULAR SEPTAL DEFECT
?
?

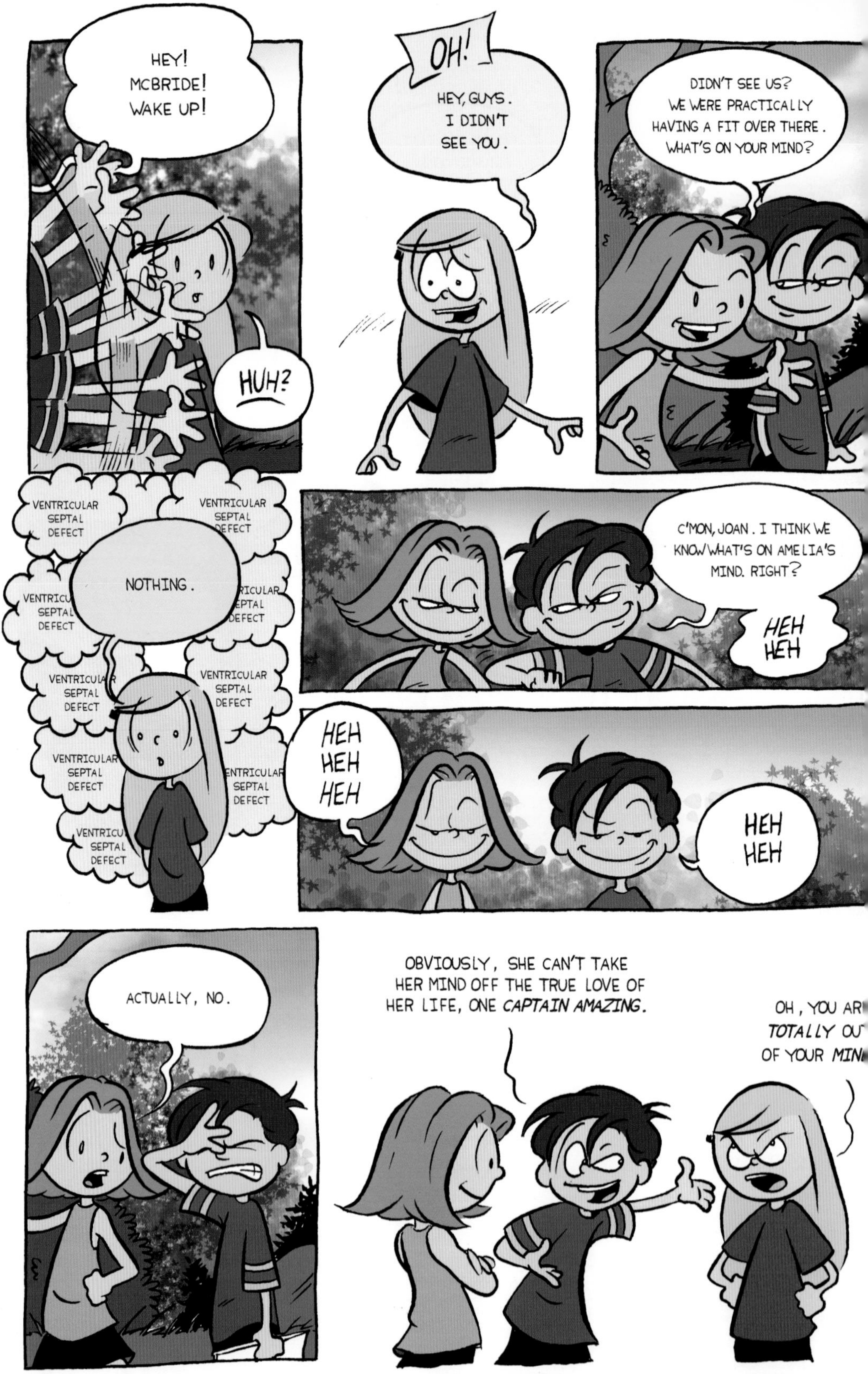
HEY! MCBRIDE! WAKE UP!
HUH?
OH!
HEY, GUYS. I DIDN'T SEE YOU.
DIDN'T SEE US? WE WERE PRACTICALLY HAVING A FIT OVER THERE. WHAT'S ON YOUR MIND?
VENTRICULAR SEPTAL DEFECT
VENTRICULAR SEPTAL DEFECT
NOTHING.
C'MON, JOAN. I THINK WE KNOW WHAT'S ON AMELIA'S MIND. RIGHT?
HEH HEH
HEH HEH HEH
HEH HEH
ACTUALLY, NO.
OBVIOUSLY, SHE CAN'T TAKE HER MIND OFF THE TRUE LOVE OF HER LIFE, ONE *CAPTAIN AMAZING*.
OH, YOU AR *TOTALLY* OU OF YOUR *MIN*

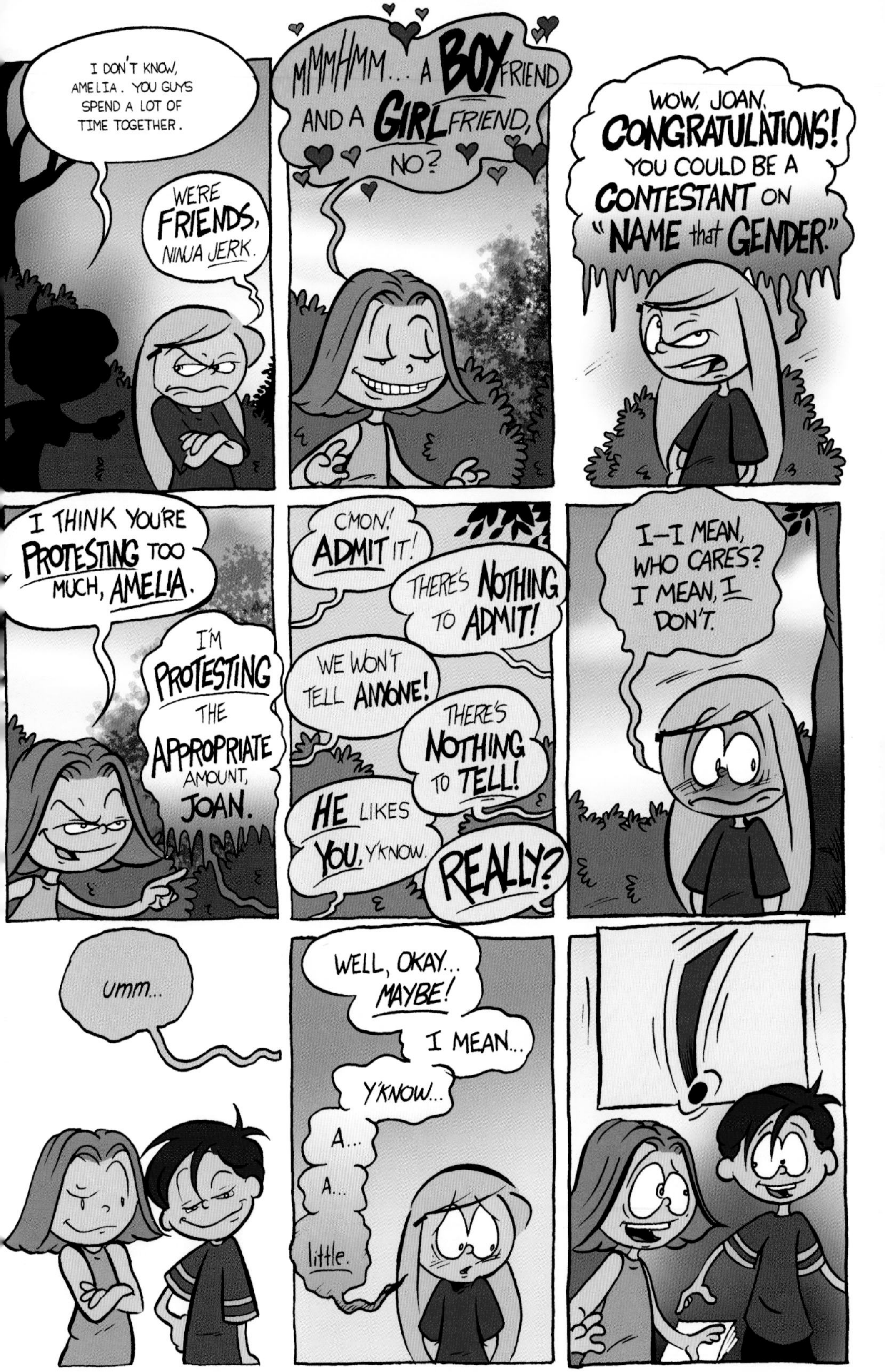
I DON'T KNOW, AMELIA. YOU GUYS SPEND A LOT OF TIME TOGETHER.
WE'RE FRIENDS, NINJA JERK.
MMMHMM... A BOYFRIEND AND A GIRLFRIEND, NO?
WOW, JOAN. CONGRATULATIONS! YOU COULD BE A CONTESTANT ON "NAME that GENDER."
I THINK YOU'RE PROTESTING TOO MUCH, AMELIA.
I'M PROTESTING THE APPROPRIATE AMOUNT, JOAN.
C'MON! ADMIT IT!
THERE'S NOTHING TO ADMIT!
WE WON'T TELL ANYONE!
THERE'S NOTHING TO TELL!
HE LIKES YOU, Y'KNOW.
REALLY?
I-I MEAN, WHO CARES? I MEAN, I DON'T.
umm...
WELL, OKAY... MAYBE!
I MEAN...
Y'KNOW...
A...
A...
little.
!

I CAN'T BELIEVE SHE ADMITTED IT!

WE WERE ONLY JOKING!

DOES SHE KNOW? ARE YOU GONNA TELL HIM? DO YOU THINK HE LIKES YOU BACK? HAVE YOU EVER HELD HANDS? HAVE YOU EVER KISSED?

KISS? ONCE... SORTA.

HOLY COW! DID HE KISS YOU?

NO.

YOU KISSED HIM?!

only to make up for kissing Kyle.

WOW! YOU ARE A TOTAL BIMBO!

I AM NOT A BIMBO!

YES YOU ARE! YOU'RE BETTY BIMBO!

Fine. I'm BETTY BIMBO. Can we PLEASE DROP it?!

SURE, BETTY.

AND IF YOU PROMISE TO BE MY PERSONAL SLAVE FOR ALL ETERNITY, I WON'T EVEN MENTION IT AT THE PARTY TOMORROW.

SURE. WHATEVER. LET'S JUST GET OFF THIS STUPID GREENBELT.

THIS PLACE CREEPS ME OUT.

REALLY?

>SIGH< YES, KYLE, REALLY.

INTERESTING.

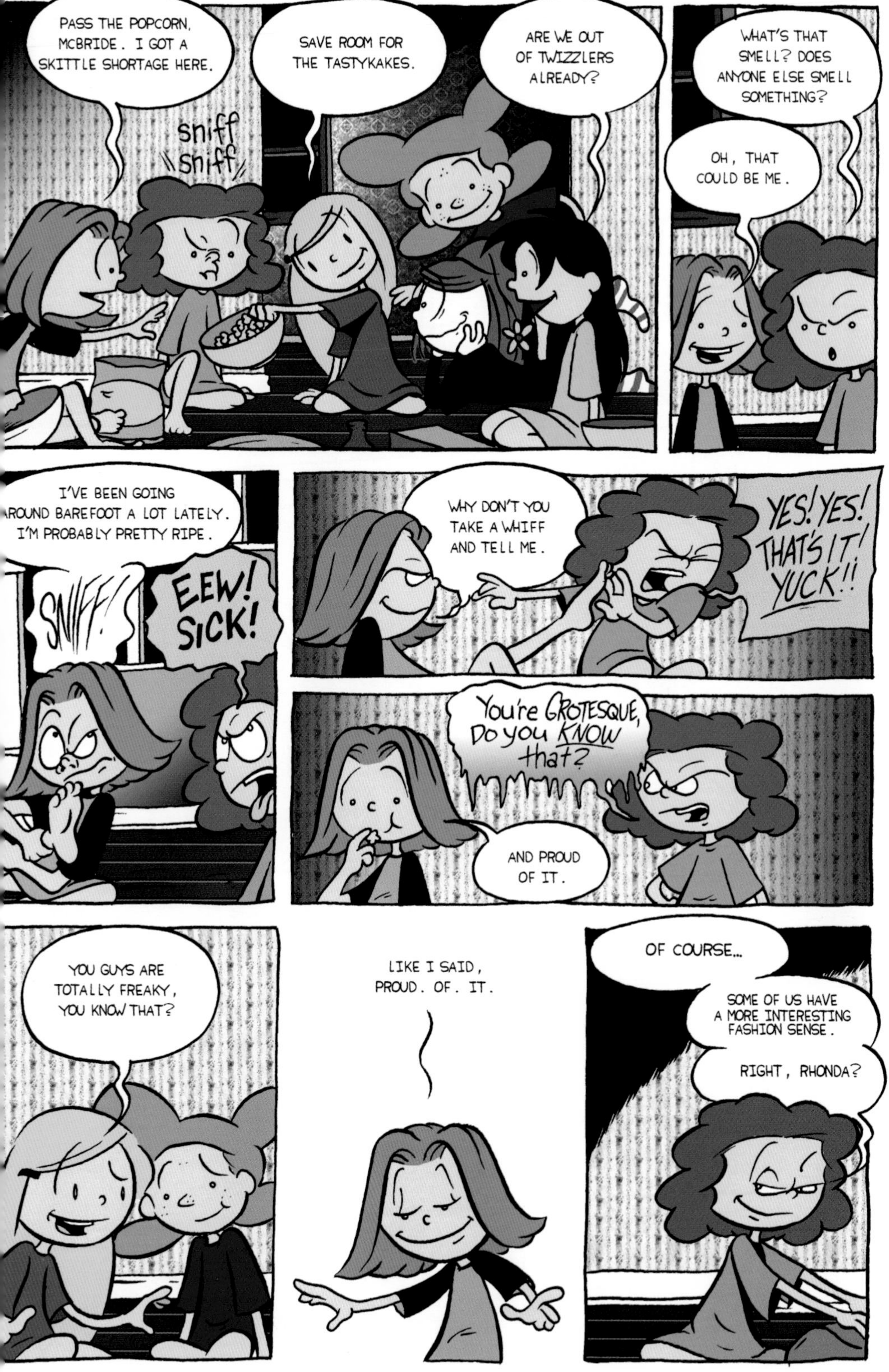
PASS THE POPCORN, MCBRIDE. I GOT A SKITTLE SHORTAGE HERE.
sniff sniff
SAVE ROOM FOR THE TASTYKAKES.
ARE WE OUT OF TWIZZLERS ALREADY?
WHAT'S THAT SMELL? DOES ANYONE ELSE SMELL SOMETHING?
OH, THAT COULD BE ME.
I'VE BEEN GOING AROUND BAREFOOT A LOT LATELY. I'M PROBABLY PRETTY RIPE.
SNIFF!
EEW! SICK!
WHY DON'T YOU TAKE A WHIFF AND TELL ME.
YES! YES! THAT'S IT! YUCK!!
You're GROTESQUE, Do you KNOW that?
AND PROUD OF IT.
YOU GUYS ARE TOTALLY FREAKY, YOU KNOW THAT?
LIKE I SAID, PROUD. OF. IT.
OF COURSE...
SOME OF US HAVE A MORE INTERESTING FASHION SENSE.
RIGHT, RHONDA?

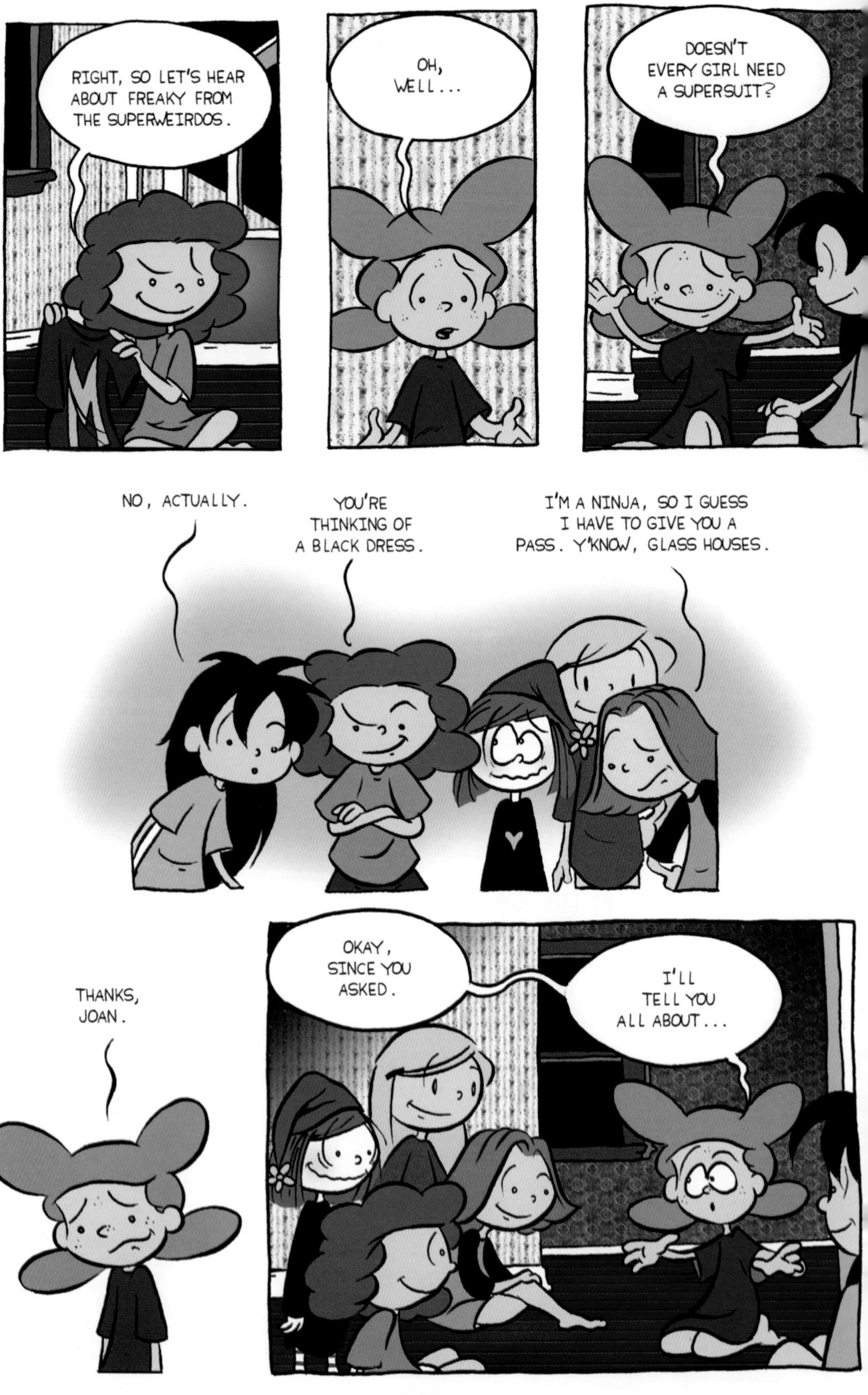
RIGHT, SO LET'S HEAR ABOUT FREAKY FROM THE SUPERWEIRDOS.
OH, WELL...
DOESN'T EVERY GIRL NEED A SUPERSUIT?
NO, ACTUALLY.
YOU'RE THINKING OF A BLACK DRESS.
I'M A NINJA, SO I GUESS I HAVE TO GIVE YOU A PASS. Y'KNOW, GLASS HOUSES.
THANKS, JOAN.
OKAY, SINCE YOU ASKED.
I'LL TELL YOU ALL ABOUT...

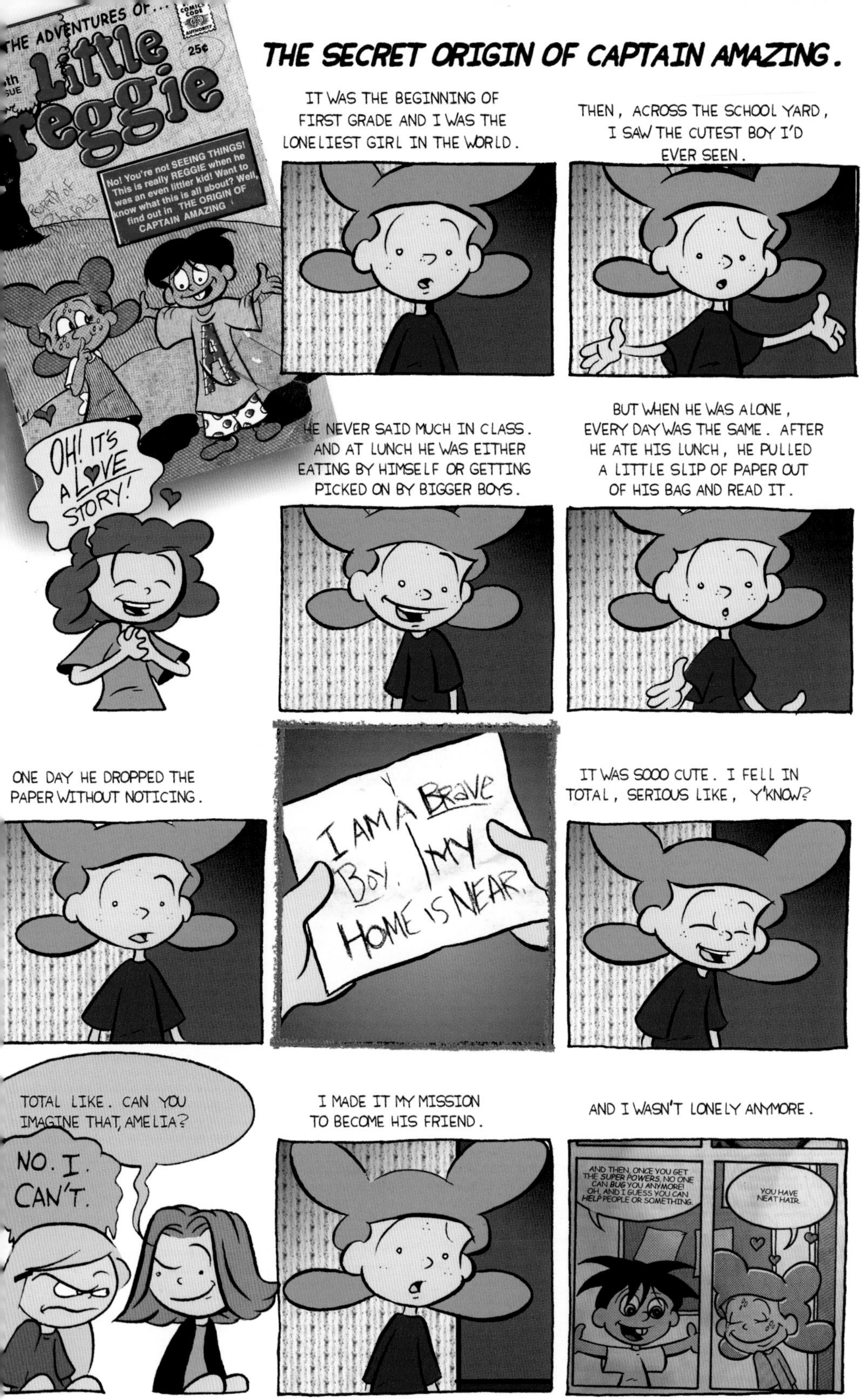
THE SECRET ORIGIN OF CAPTAIN AMAZING.
THE ADVENTURES OF... Little Reggie
COMICS CODE AUTHORITY
25¢
No! You're not SEEING THINGS! This is really REGGIE when he was an even littler kid! Want to know what this is all about? Well, find out in THE ORIGIN OF CAPTAIN AMAZING
OH! IT'S A LOVE STORY!
IT WAS THE BEGINNING OF FIRST GRADE AND I WAS THE LONELIEST GIRL IN THE WORLD.
THEN, ACROSS THE SCHOOL YARD, I SAW THE CUTEST BOY I'D EVER SEEN.
HE NEVER SAID MUCH IN CLASS. AND AT LUNCH HE WAS EITHER EATING BY HIMSELF OR GETTING PICKED ON BY BIGGER BOYS.
BUT WHEN HE WAS ALONE, EVERY DAY WAS THE SAME. AFTER HE ATE HIS LUNCH, HE PULLED A LITTLE SLIP OF PAPER OUT OF HIS BAG AND READ IT.
ONE DAY HE DROPPED THE PAPER WITHOUT NOTICING.
I AM A BRAVE BOY. MY HOME IS NEAR.
IT WAS SOOO CUTE. I FELL IN TOTAL, SERIOUS LIKE, Y'KNOW?
TOTAL LIKE. CAN YOU IMAGINE THAT, AMELIA?
NO. I. CAN'T.
I MADE IT MY MISSION TO BECOME HIS FRIEND.
AND I WASN'T LONELY ANYMORE.
AND THEN, ONCE YOU GET THE SUPER POWERS, NO ONE CAN BUG YOU ANYMORE! OH, AND I GUESS YOU CAN HELP PEOPLE OR SOMETHING.
YOU HAVE NEAT HAIR.

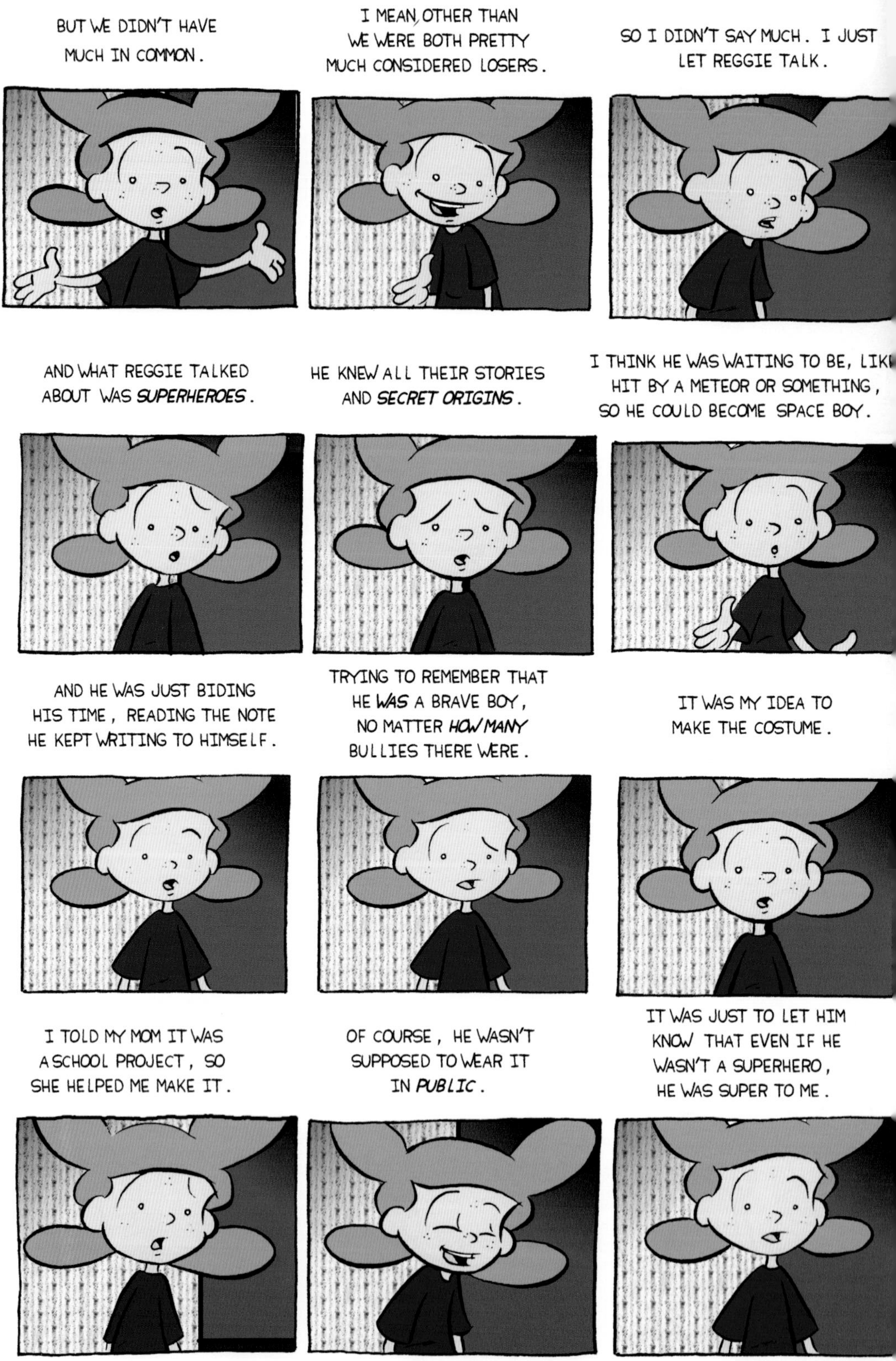

BUT WE DIDN'T HAVE MUCH IN COMMON.
I MEAN, OTHER THAN WE WERE BOTH PRETTY MUCH CONSIDERED LOSERS.
SO I DIDN'T SAY MUCH. I JUST LET REGGIE TALK.
AND WHAT REGGIE TALKED ABOUT WAS *SUPERHEROES*.
HE KNEW ALL THEIR STORIES AND *SECRET ORIGINS*.
I THINK HE WAS WAITING TO BE, LIKE HIT BY A METEOR OR SOMETHING, SO HE COULD BECOME SPACE BOY.
AND HE WAS JUST BIDING HIS TIME, READING THE NOTE HE KEPT WRITING TO HIMSELF.
TRYING TO REMEMBER THAT HE *WAS* A BRAVE BOY, NO MATTER *HOW MANY* BULLIES THERE WERE.
IT WAS MY IDEA TO MAKE THE COSTUME.
I TOLD MY MOM IT WAS A SCHOOL PROJECT, SO SHE HELPED ME MAKE IT.
OF COURSE, HE WASN'T SUPPOSED TO WEAR IT IN *PUBLIC*.
IT WAS JUST TO LET HIM KNOW THAT EVEN IF HE WASN'T A SUPERHERO, HE WAS SUPER TO ME.

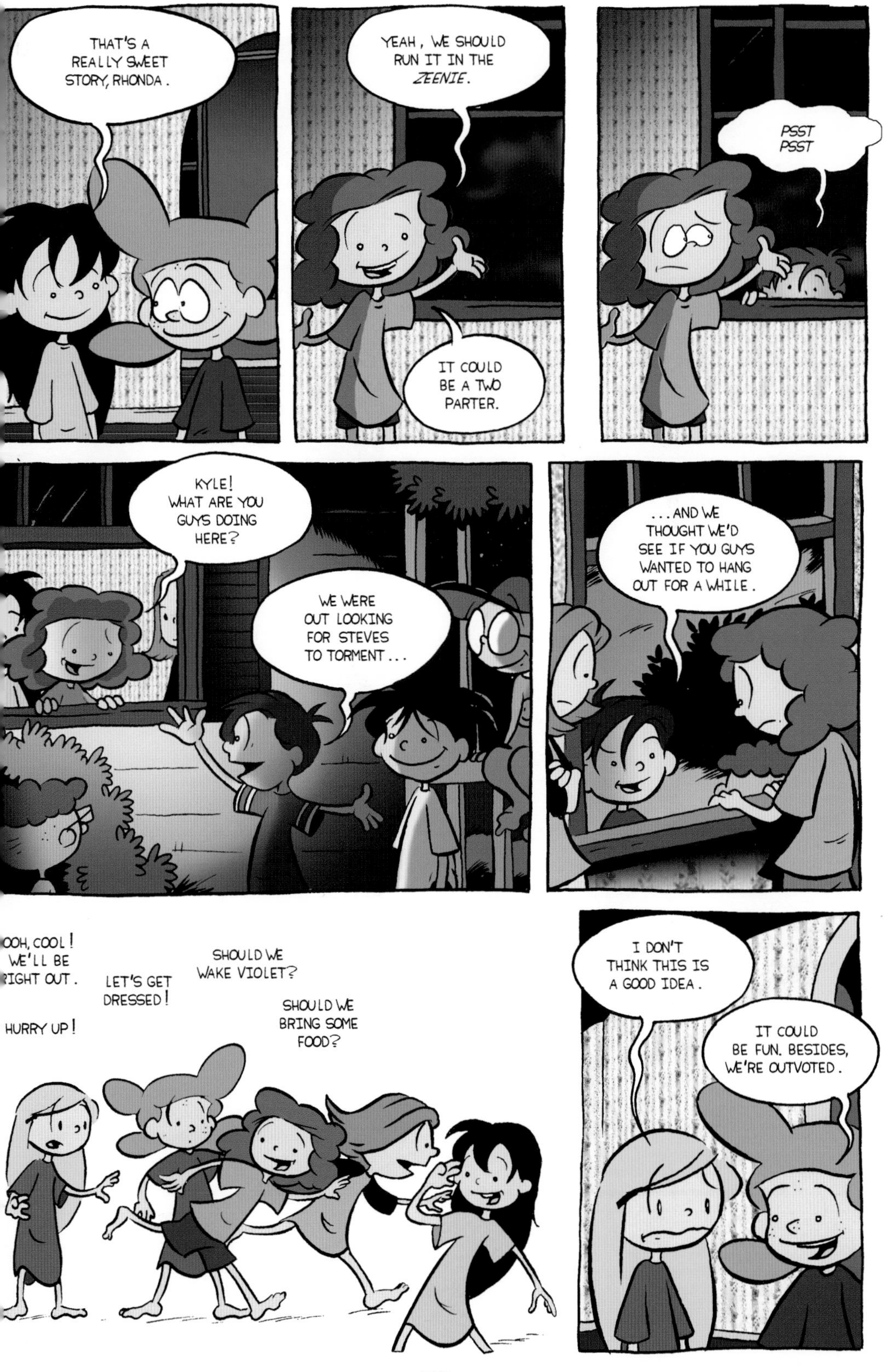
THAT'S A REALLY SWEET STORY, RHONDA.
YEAH, WE SHOULD RUN IT IN THE *ZEENIE*.
IT COULD BE A TWO PARTER.
PSST PSST
KYLE! WHAT ARE YOU GUYS DOING HERE?
WE WERE OUT LOOKING FOR STEVES TO TORMENT...
...AND WE THOUGHT WE'D SEE IF YOU GUYS WANTED TO HANG OUT FOR A WHILE.
OOH, COOL! WE'LL BE RIGHT OUT.
HURRY UP!
LET'S GET DRESSED!
SHOULD WE WAKE VIOLET?
SHOULD WE BRING SOME FOOD?
I DON'T THINK THIS IS A GOOD IDEA.
IT COULD BE FUN. BESIDES, WE'RE OUTVOTED.

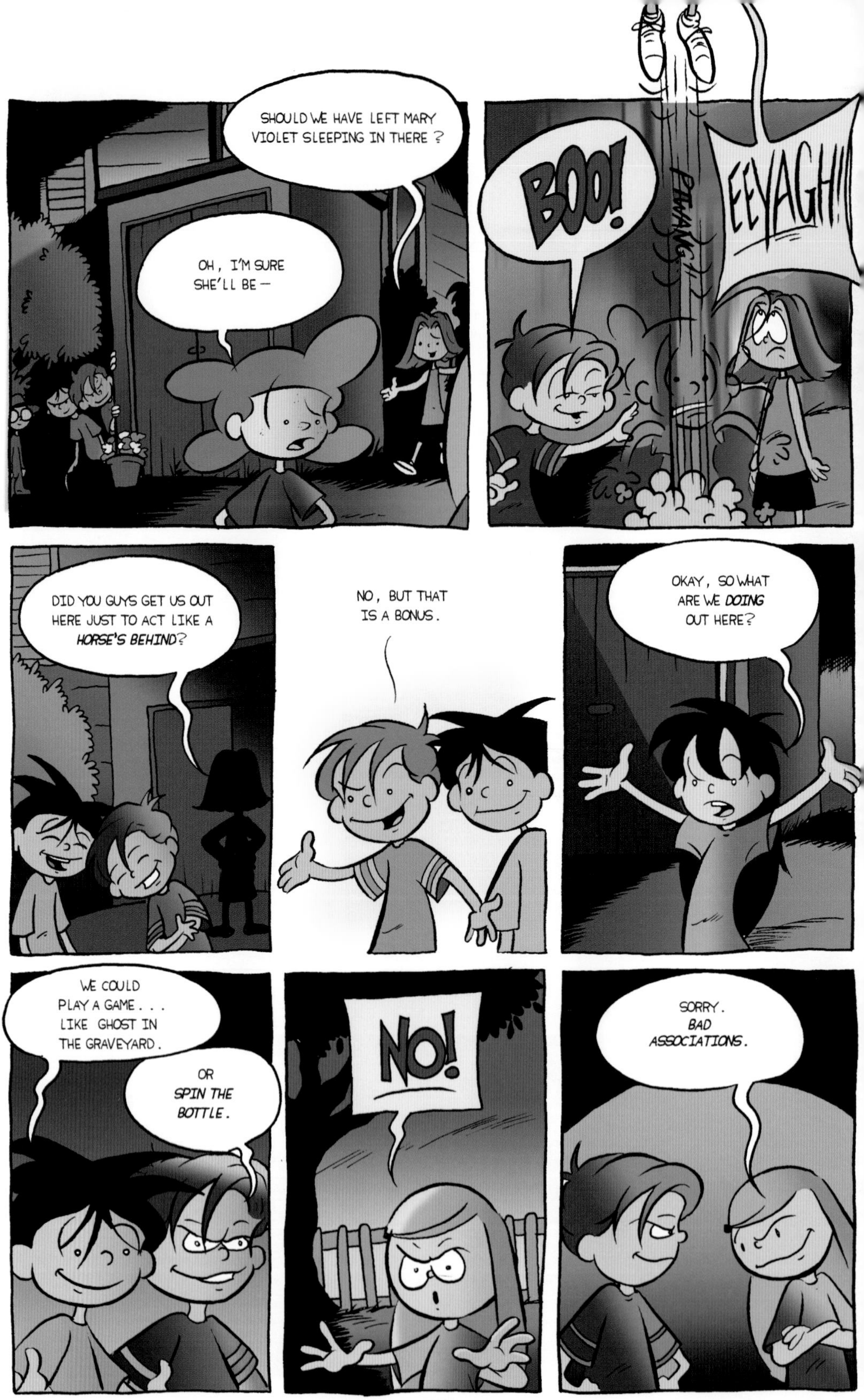
SHOULD WE HAVE LEFT MARY VIOLET SLEEPING IN THERE ?
OH , I'M SURE SHE'LL BE —
BOO!
PTWANG!
EEYAGH!!
DID YOU GUYS GET US OUT HERE JUST TO ACT LIKE A *HORSE'S BEHIND*?
NO , BUT THAT IS A BONUS .
OKAY , SO WHAT ARE WE *DOING* OUT HERE?
WE COULD PLAY A GAME . . . LIKE GHOST IN THE GRAVEYARD .
OR *SPIN THE BOTTLE* .
NO!
SORRY . *BAD ASSOCIATIONS* .

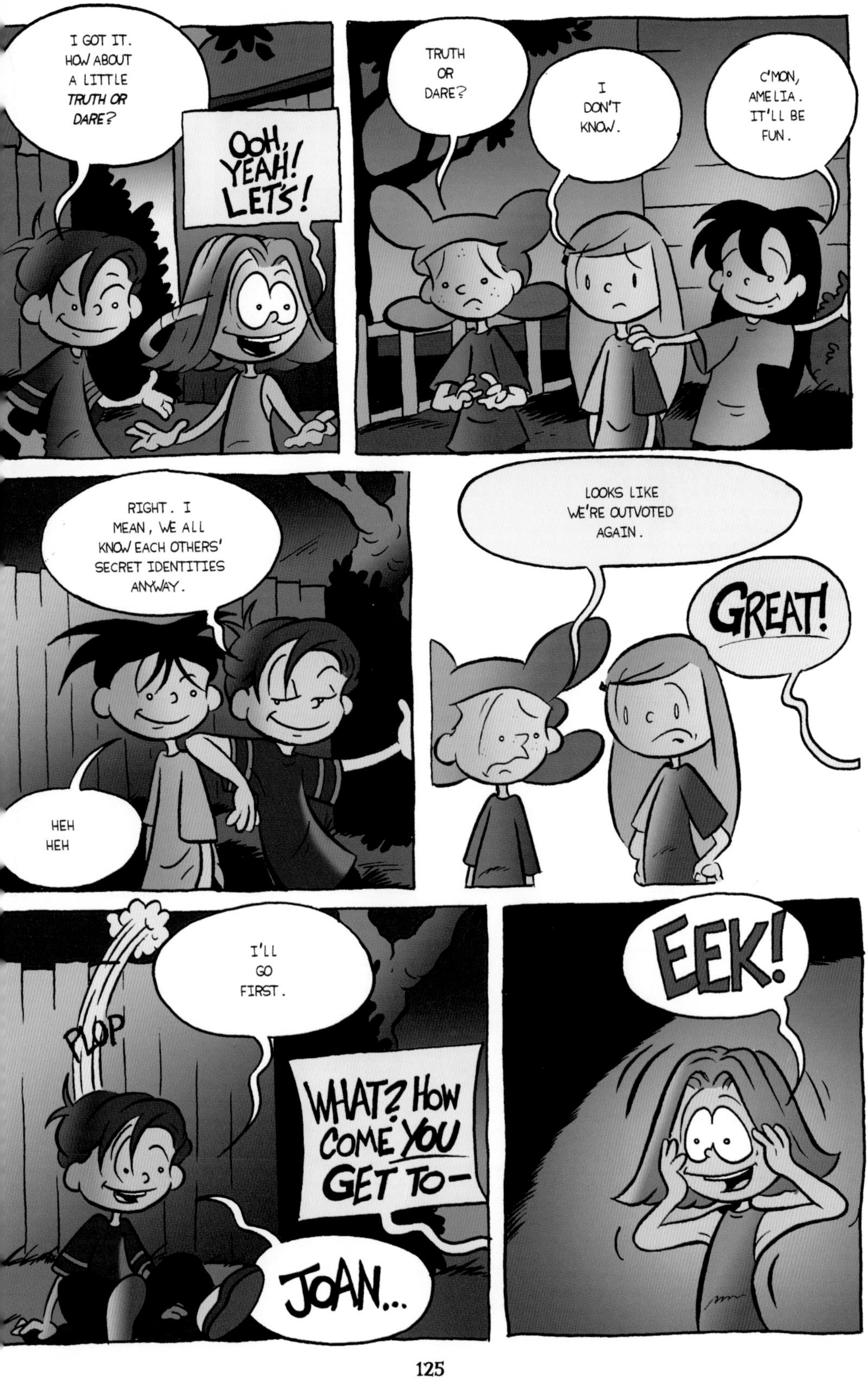
I GOT IT. HOW ABOUT A LITTLE *TRUTH OR DARE?*
OOH, YEAH! LET'S!
TRUTH OR DARE?
I DON'T KNOW.
C'MON, AMELIA. IT'LL BE FUN.
RIGHT. I MEAN, WE ALL KNOW EACH OTHERS' SECRET IDENTITIES ANYWAY.
HEH HEH
LOOKS LIKE WE'RE OUTVOTED AGAIN.
GREAT!
PLOP
I'LL GO FIRST.
WHAT? HOW COME YOU GET TO-
JOAN...
EEK!

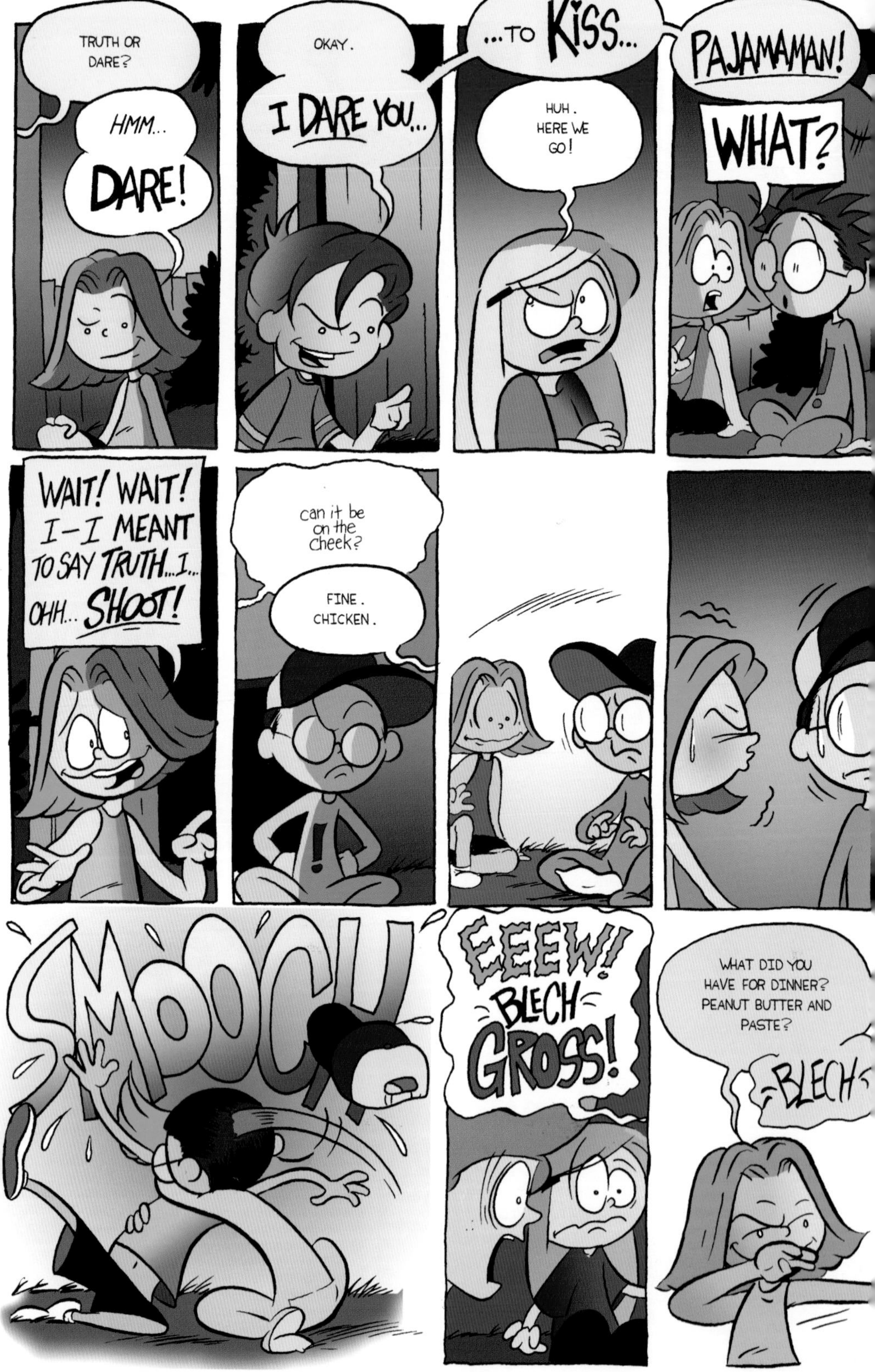
TRUTH OR DARE?
HMM... DARE!
OKAY.
I DARE YOU...
...TO KISS...
HUH. HERE WE GO!
PAJAMAMAN!
WHAT?
WAIT! WAIT! I-I MEANT TO SAY TRUTH...I... OHH... SHOOT!
can it be on the cheek?
FINE. CHICKEN.
SMOOCH
EEEW! BLECH GROSS!
WHAT DID YOU HAVE FOR DINNER? PEANUT BUTTER AND PASTE?
BLECH

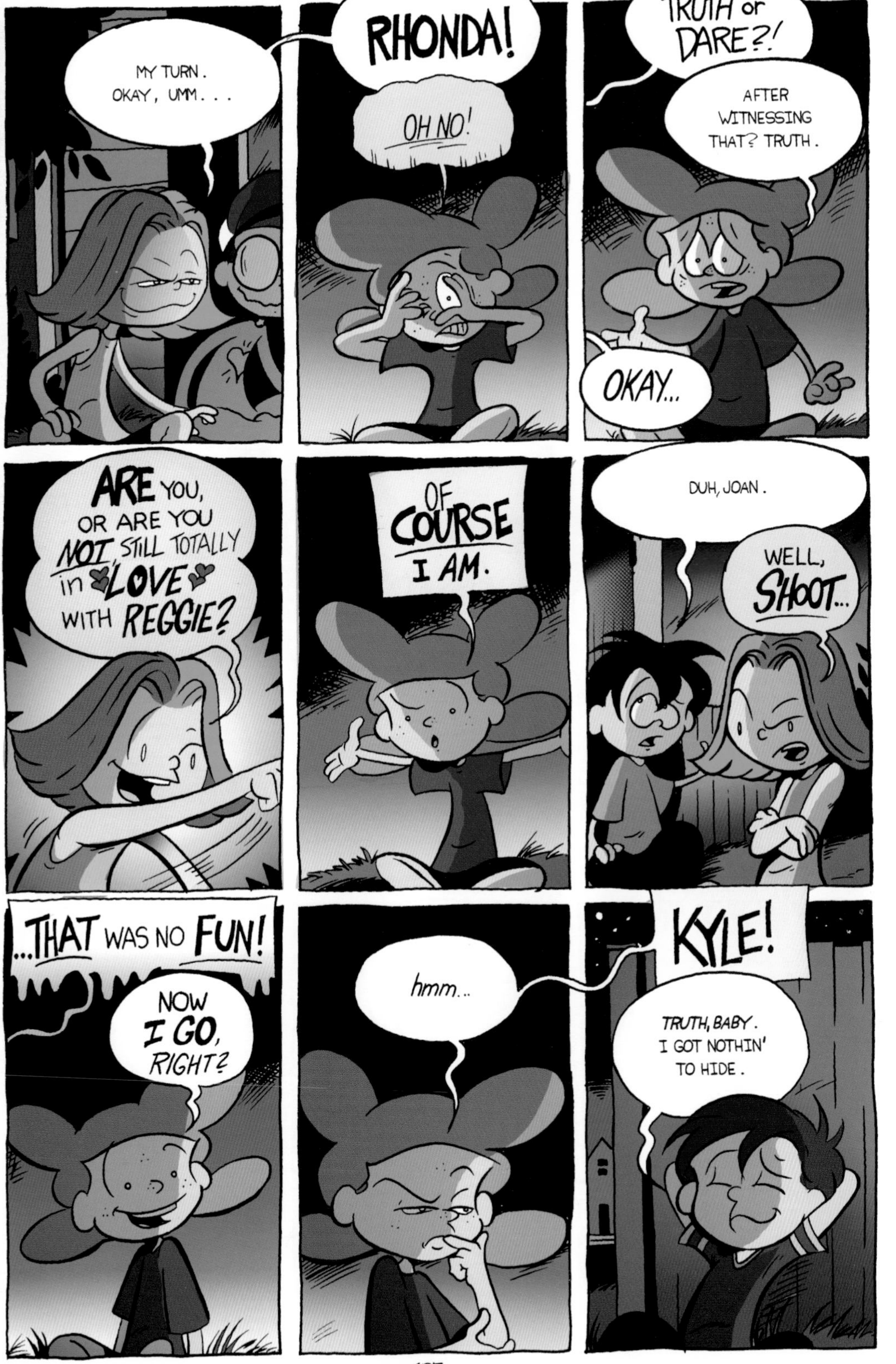
MY TURN. OKAY, UMM...
RHONDA!
OH NO!
TRUTH or DARE?!
AFTER WITNESSING THAT? TRUTH.
OKAY...
ARE YOU, OR ARE YOU NOT, STILL TOTALLY in LOVE WITH REGGIE?
OF COURSE I AM.
DUH, JOAN.
WELL, SHOOT...
...THAT WAS NO FUN!
NOW I GO, RIGHT?
hmm...
KYLE!
TRUTH, BABY. I GOT NOTHIN' TO HIDE.

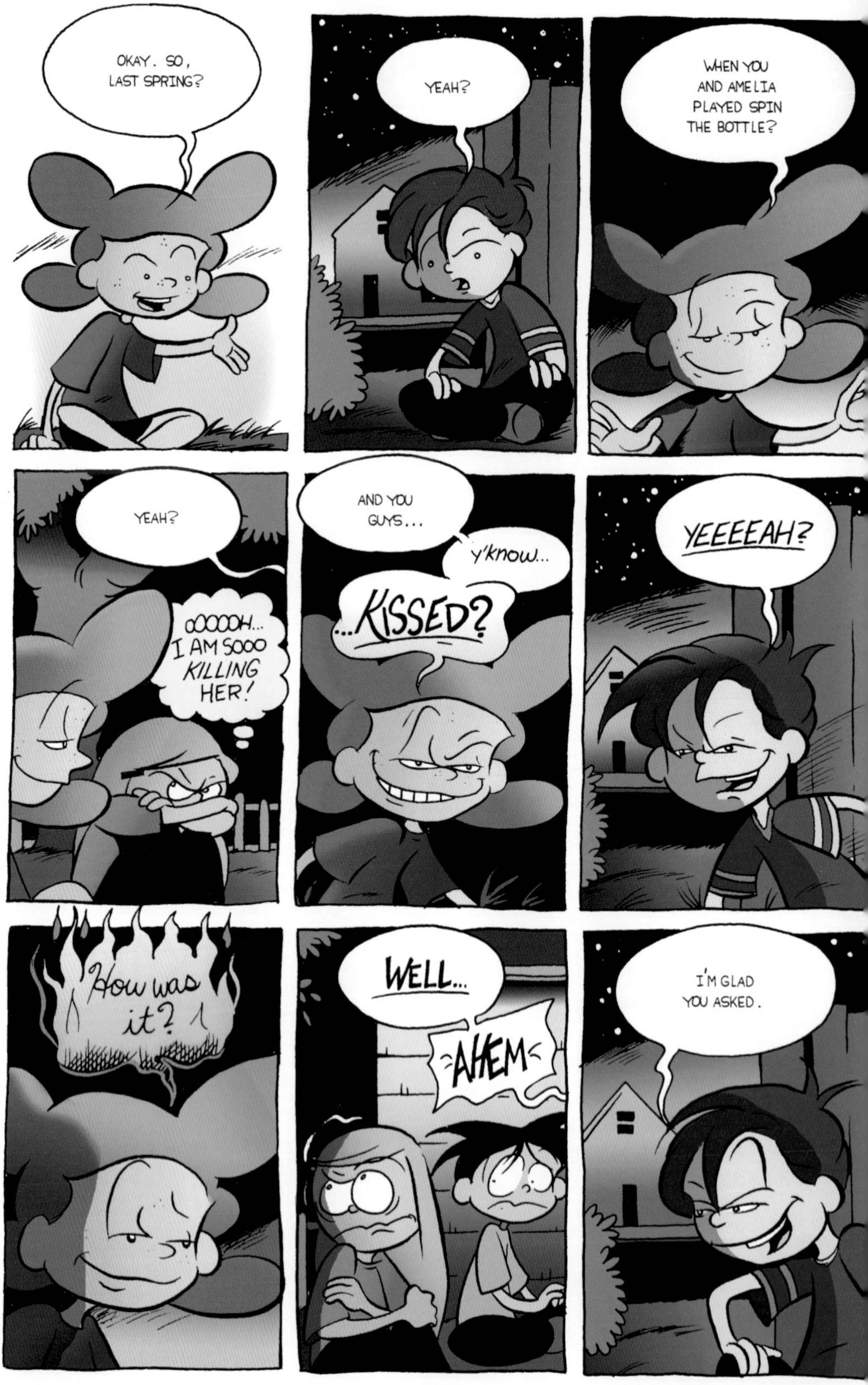
OKAY. SO, LAST SPRING?
YEAH?
WHEN YOU AND AMELIA PLAYED SPIN THE BOTTLE?
YEAH?
OOOOOH... I AM SOOO KILLING HER!
AND YOU GUYS...
Y'KNOW...
...KISSED?
YEEEEAH?
How was it?
WELL...
AHEM
I'M GLAD YOU ASKED.

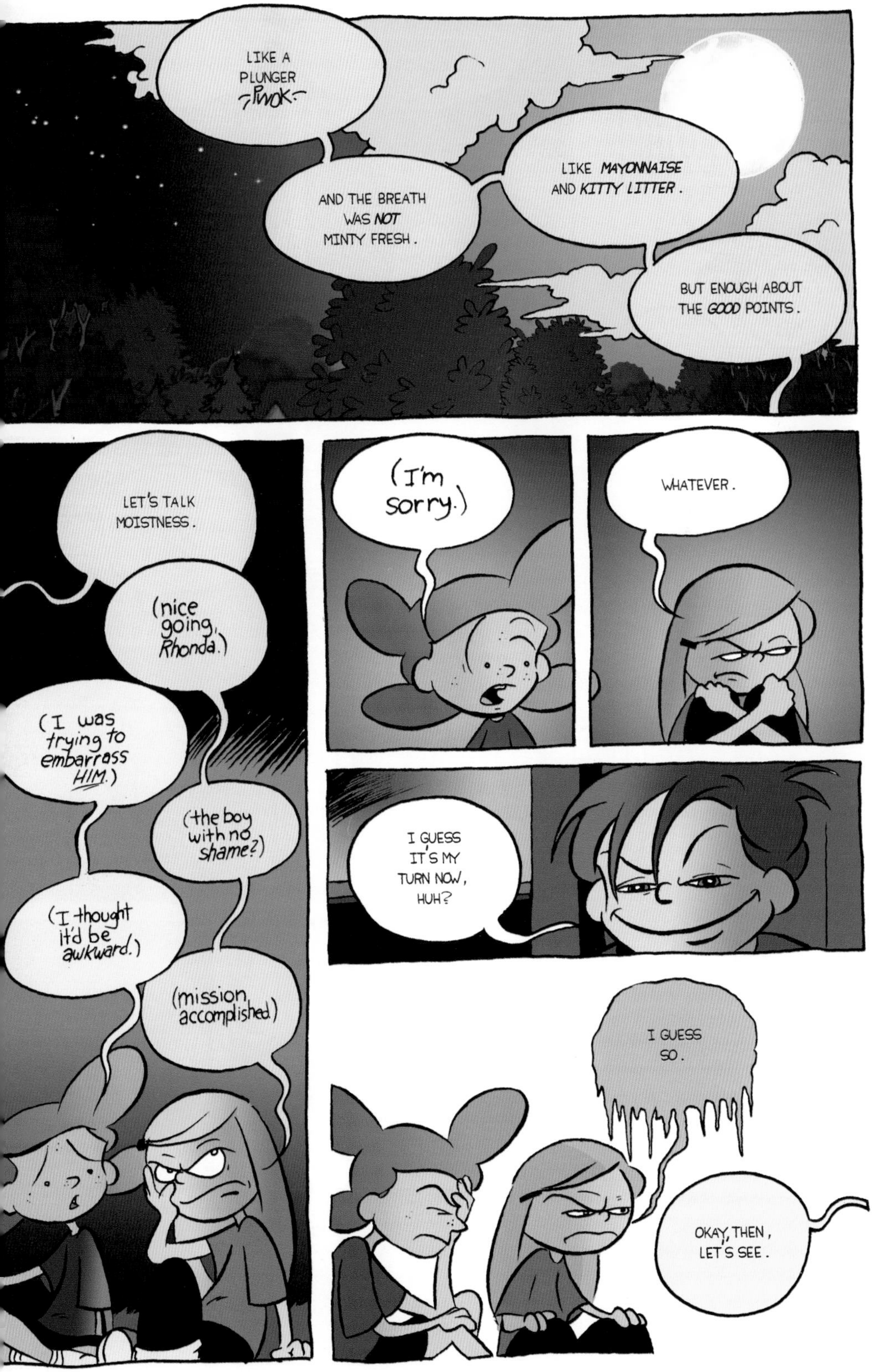

LIKE A PLUNGER
PWOK
AND THE BREATH WAS NOT MINTY FRESH.
LIKE MAYONNAISE AND KITTY LITTER.
BUT ENOUGH ABOUT THE GOOD POINTS.
LET'S TALK MOISTNESS.
(nice going, Rhonda.)
(I was trying to embarrass HIM.)
(the boy with no shame?)
(I thought it'd be awkward.)
(mission accomplished)
(I'm sorry.)
WHATEVER.
I GUESS IT'S MY TURN NOW, HUH?
I GUESS SO.
OKAY, THEN, LET'S SEE.

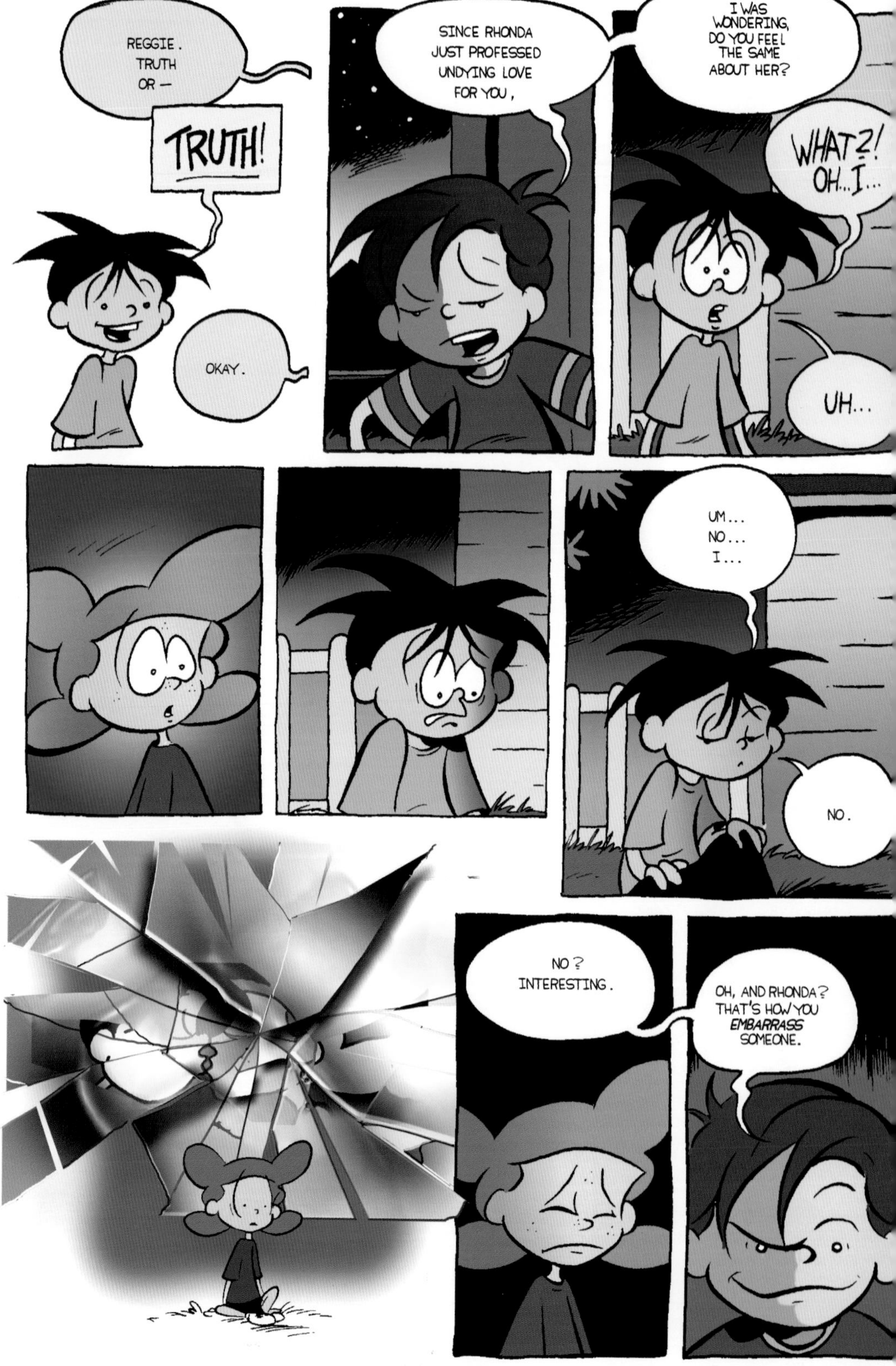
REGGIE. TRUTH OR —
TRUTH!
OKAY.
SINCE RHONDA JUST PROFESSED UNDYING LOVE FOR YOU,
I WAS WONDERING, DO YOU FEEL THE SAME ABOUT HER?
WHAT?! OH...I...
UH...
UM... NO... I...
NO.
NO? INTERESTING.
OH, AND RHONDA? THAT'S HOW YOU EMBARRASS SOMEONE.

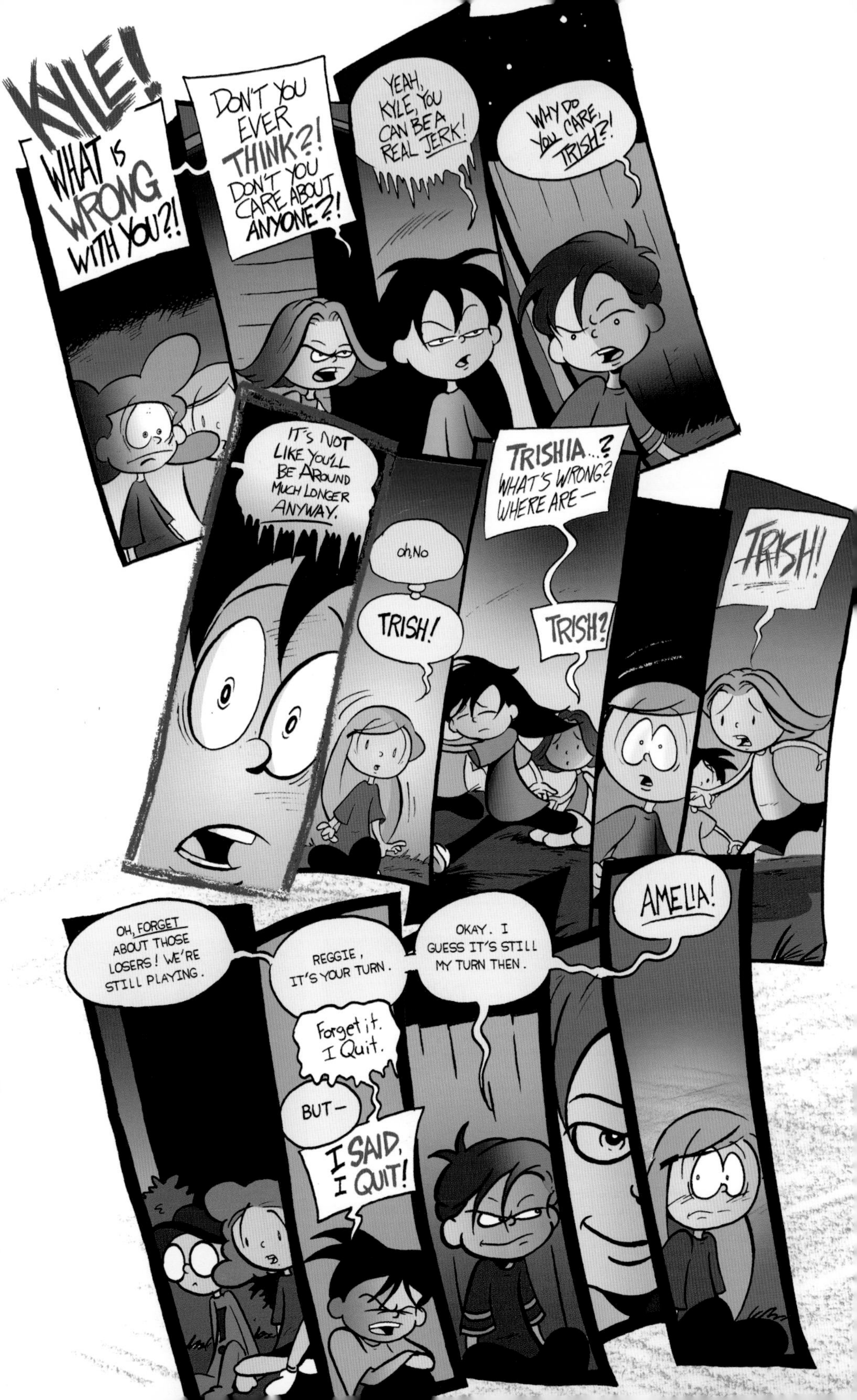
KYLE! WHAT IS WRONG WITH YOU?!
DON'T YOU EVER THINK?! DON'T YOU CARE ABOUT ANYONE?!
YEAH, KYLE, YOU CAN BE A REAL JERK!
WHY DO YOU CARE, TRISH?!
IT'S NOT LIKE YOU'LL BE AROUND MUCH LONGER ANYWAY.
oh, No
TRISH!
TRISHIA...? WHAT'S WRONG? WHERE ARE—
TRISH?
TRISH!
AMELIA!
OH, FORGET ABOUT THOSE LOSERS! WE'RE STILL PLAYING.
REGGIE, IT'S YOUR TURN.
OKAY. I GUESS IT'S STILL MY TURN THEN.
Forget it. I Quit.
BUT—
I SAID, I QUIT!

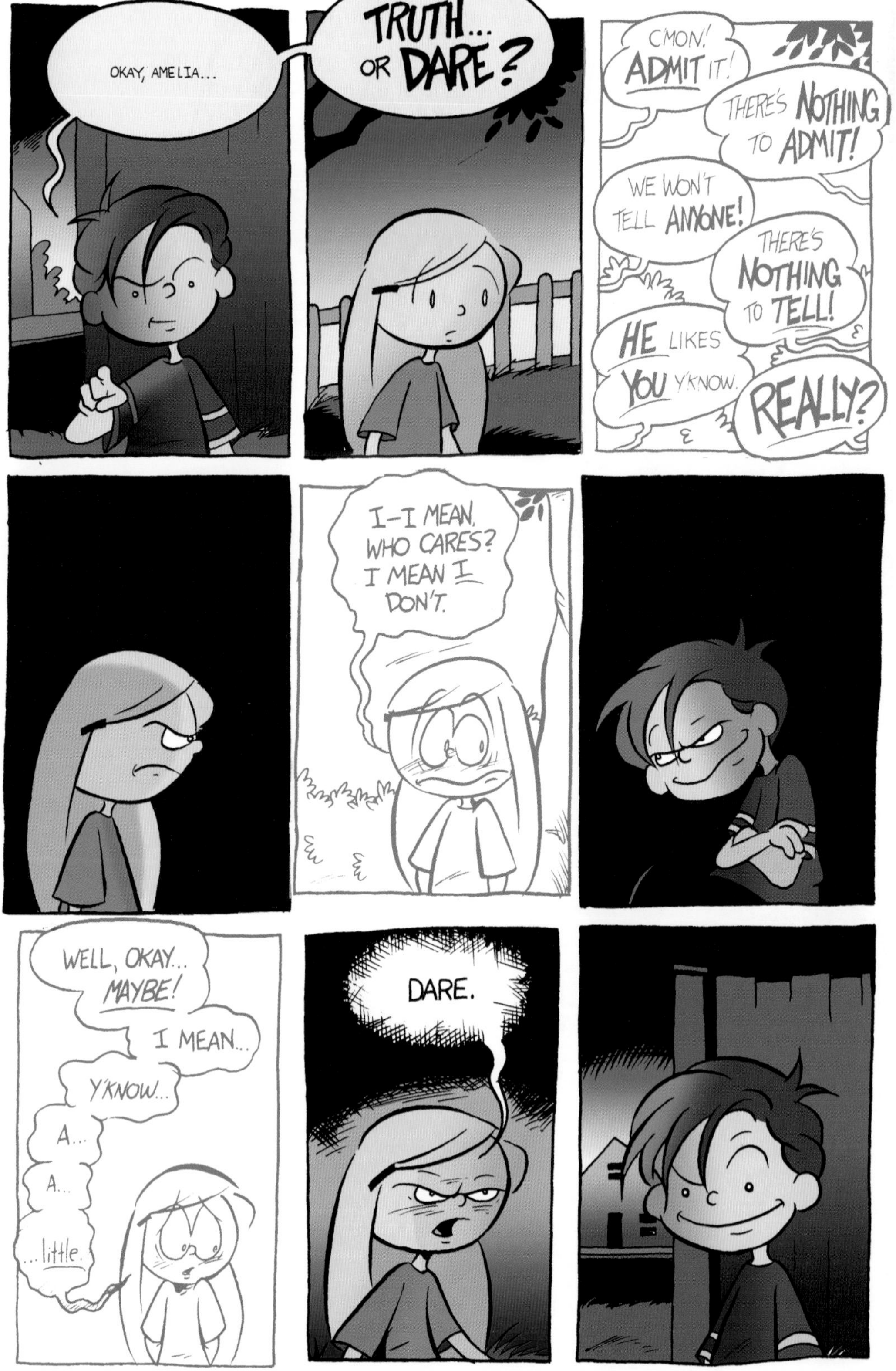
OKAY, AMELIA...
TRUTH... OR DARE?
C'MON! ADMIT IT!
THERE'S NOTHING TO ADMIT!
WE WON'T TELL ANYONE!
THERE'S NOTHING TO TELL!
HE LIKES YOU Y'KNOW.
REALLY?
I-I MEAN, WHO CARES? I MEAN I DON'T.
WELL, OKAY... MAYBE!
I MEAN...
Y'KNOW...
A...
A...
...little.
DARE.

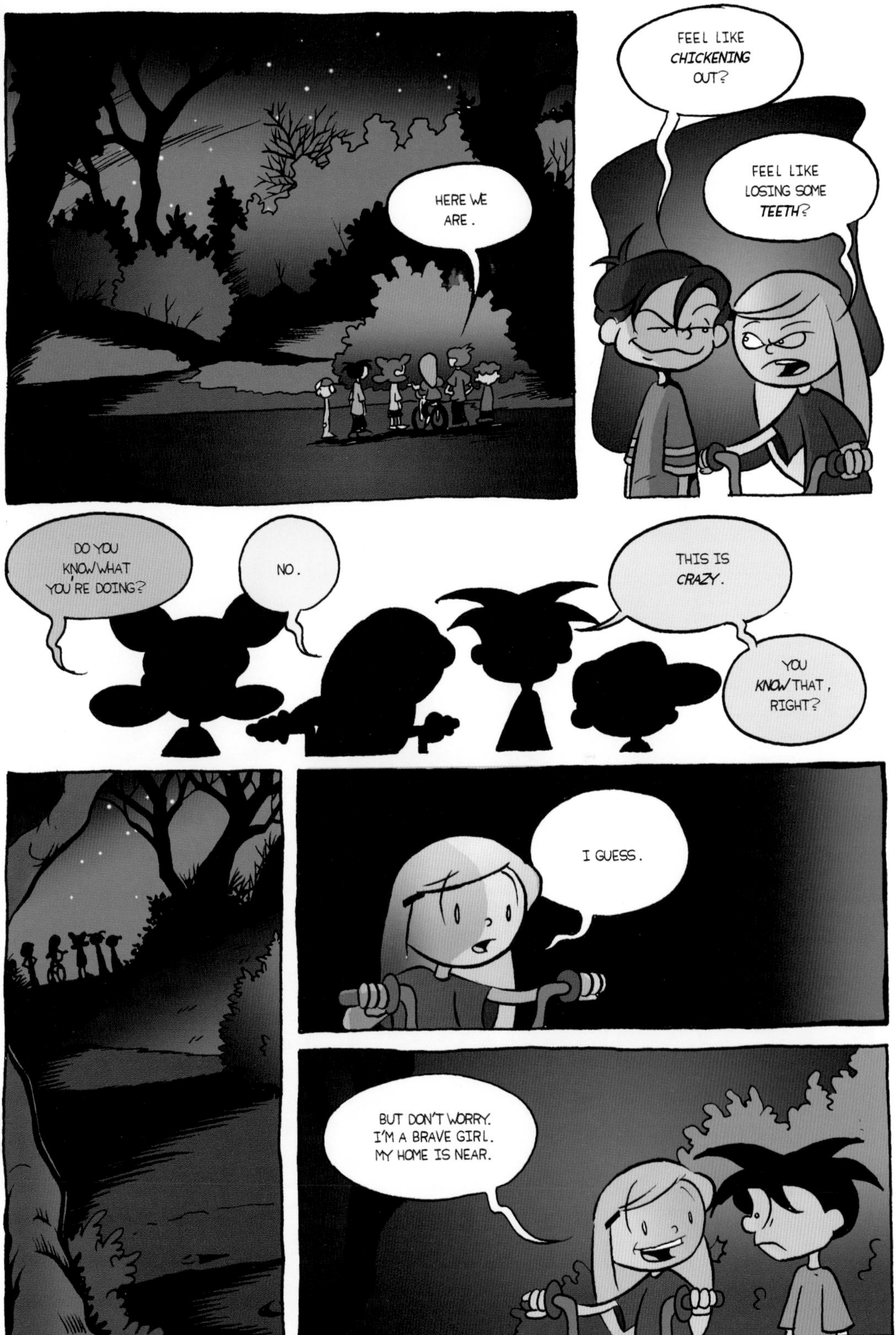
HERE WE ARE.
FEEL LIKE CHICKENING OUT?
FEEL LIKE LOSING SOME TEETH?
DO YOU KNOW WHAT YOU'RE DOING?
NO.
THIS IS CRAZY.
YOU KNOW THAT, RIGHT?
I GUESS.
BUT DON'T WORRY. I'M A BRAVE GIRL. MY HOME IS NEAR.

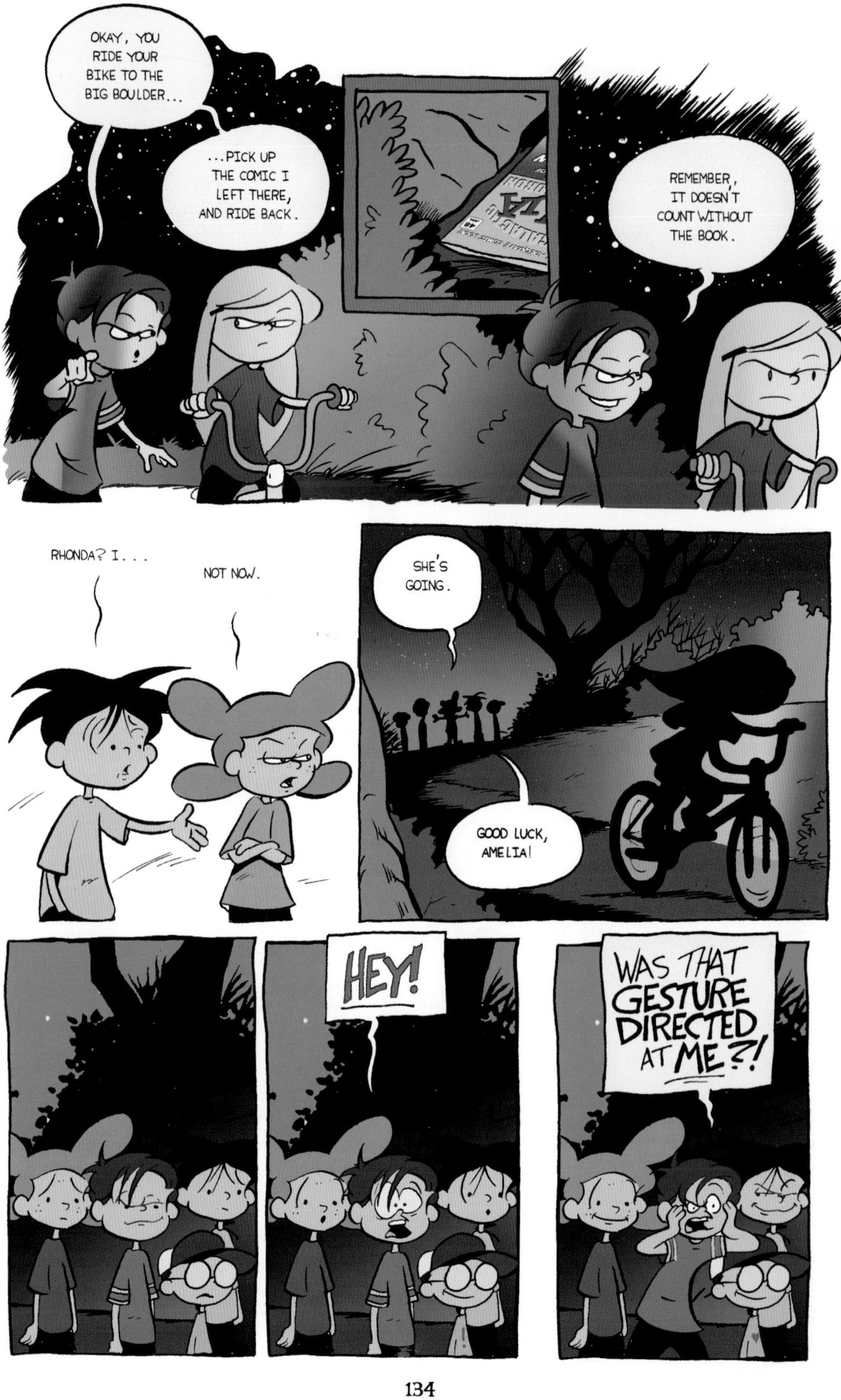
OKAY, YOU RIDE YOUR BIKE TO THE BIG BOULDER...
...PICK UP THE COMIC I LEFT THERE, AND RIDE BACK.
REMEMBER, IT DOESN'T COUNT WITHOUT THE BOOK.
RHONDA? I...
NOT NOW.
SHE'S GOING.
GOOD LUCK, AMELIA!
HEY!
WAS THAT GESTURE DIRECTED AT ME?!

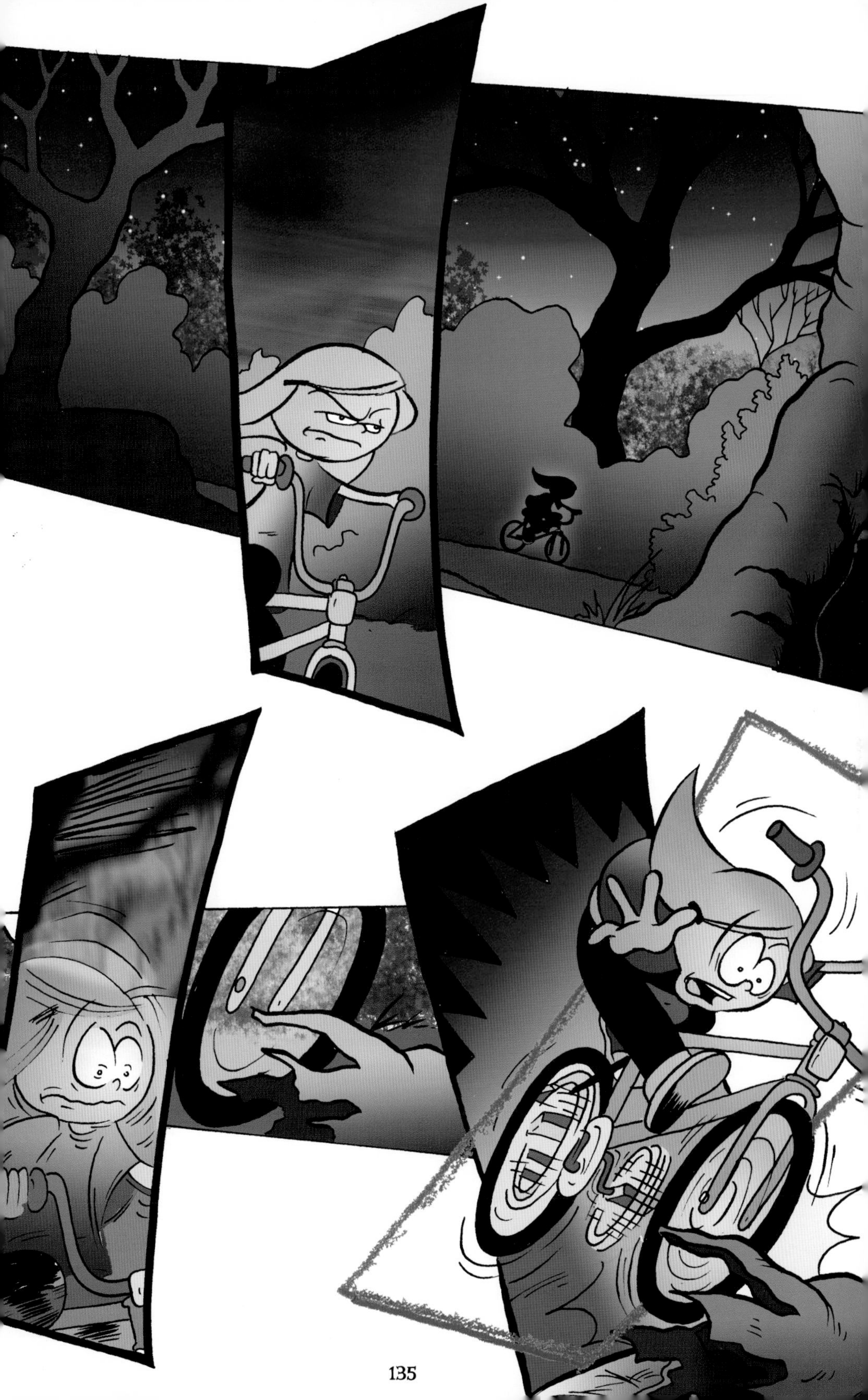

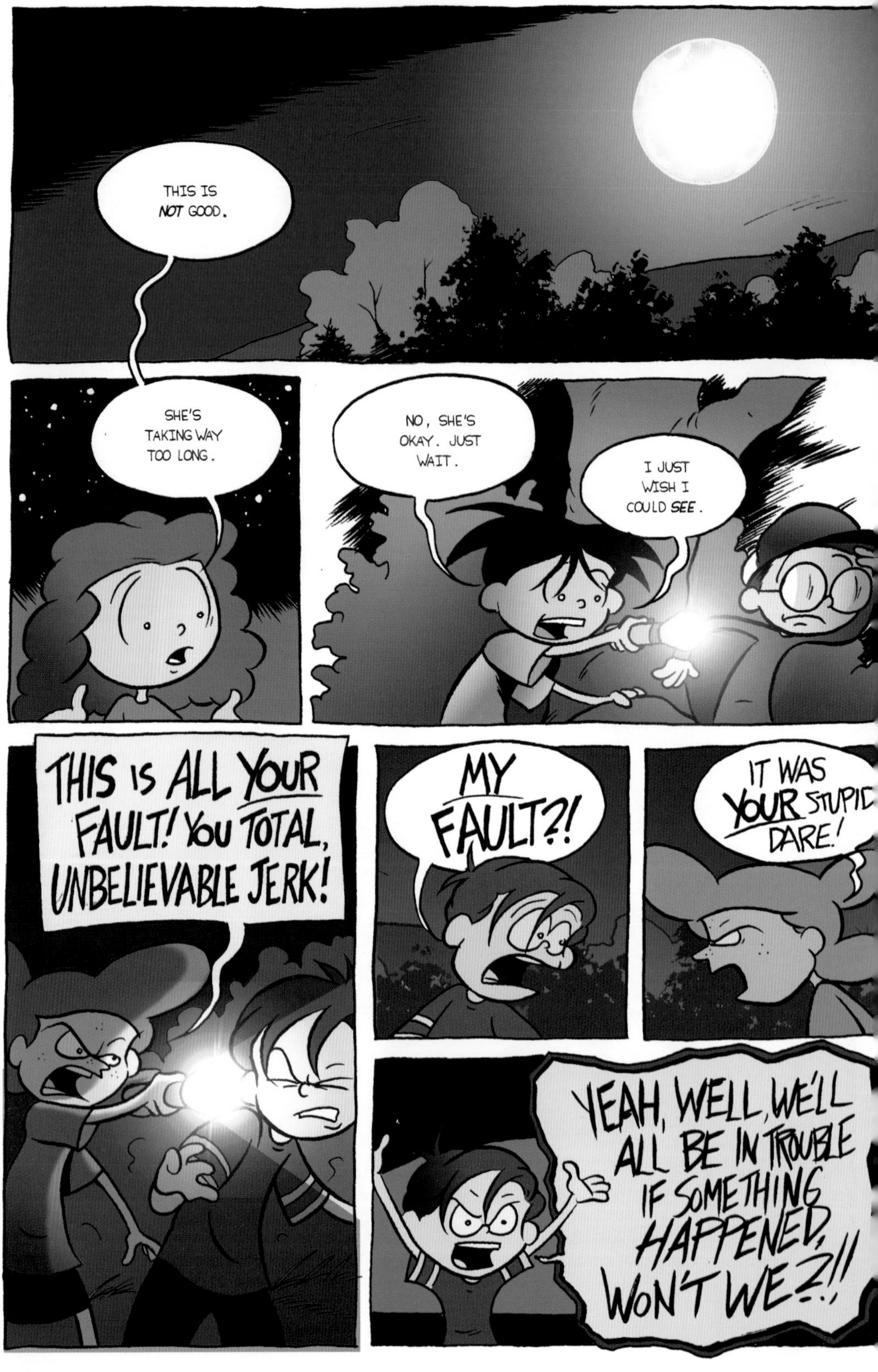
THIS IS NOT GOOD.
SHE'S TAKING WAY TOO LONG.
NO, SHE'S OKAY. JUST WAIT.
I JUST WISH I COULD SEE.
THIS IS ALL YOUR FAULT! YOU TOTAL, UNBELIEVABLE JERK!
MY FAULT?!
IT WAS YOUR STUPID DARE!
YEAH, WELL, WE'LL ALL BE IN TROUBLE IF SOMETHING HAPPENED, WON'T WE?!!

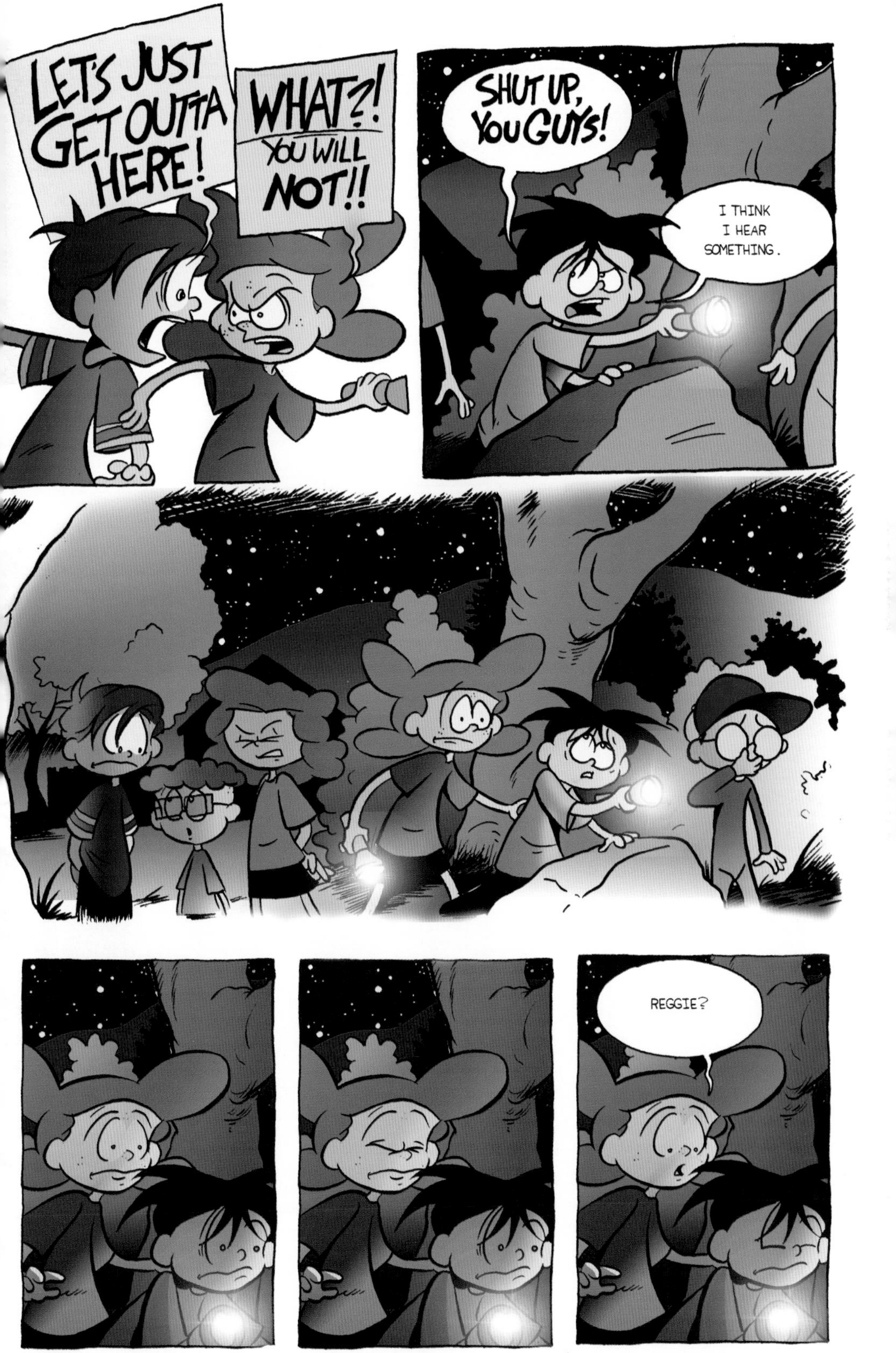
LET'S JUST GET OUTTA HERE!
WHAT?! YOU WILL NOT!!
SHUT UP, YOU GUYS!
I THINK I HEAR SOMETHING.
REGGIE?

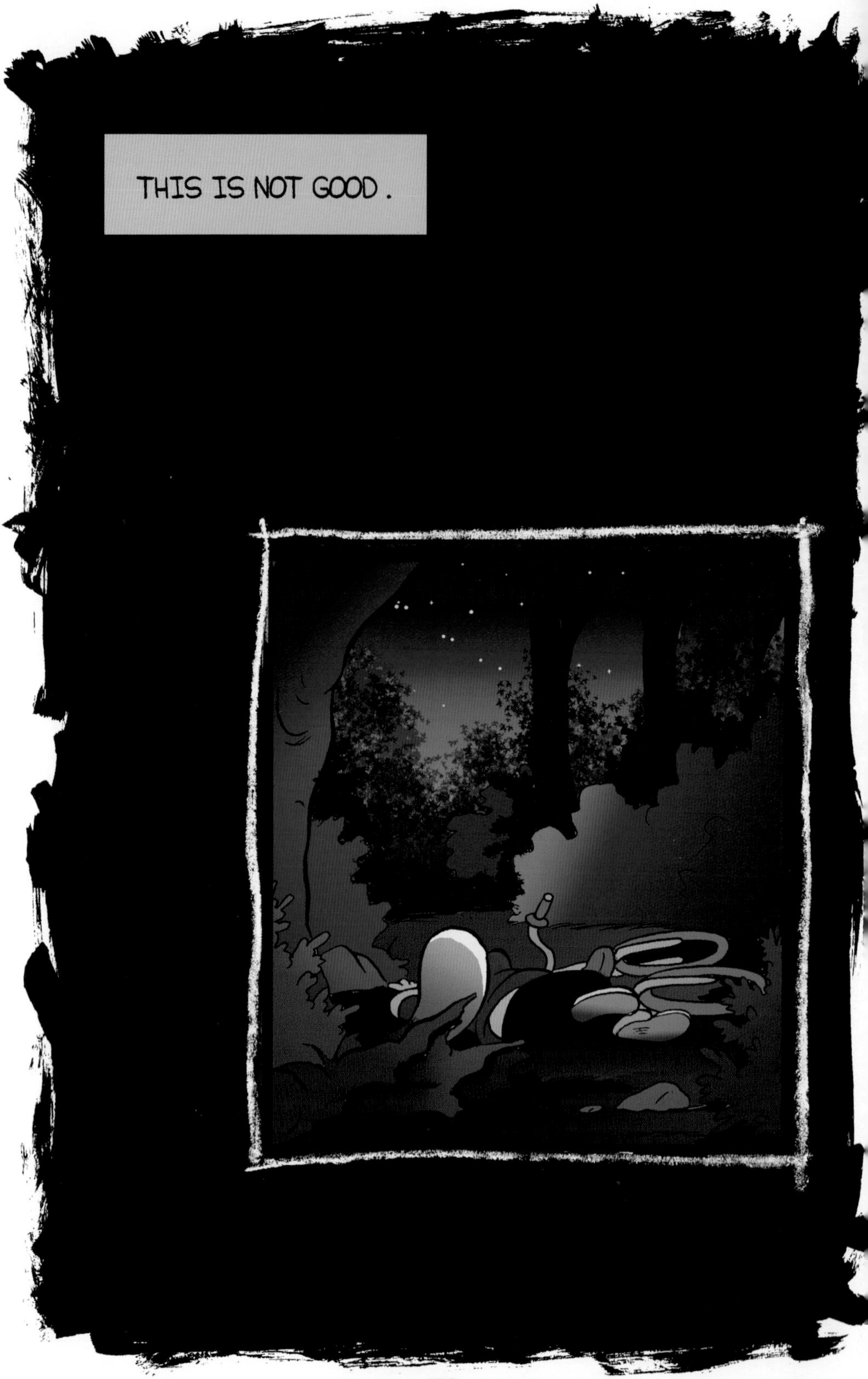
THIS IS NOT GOOD.

Against
Unbelievable
Odds

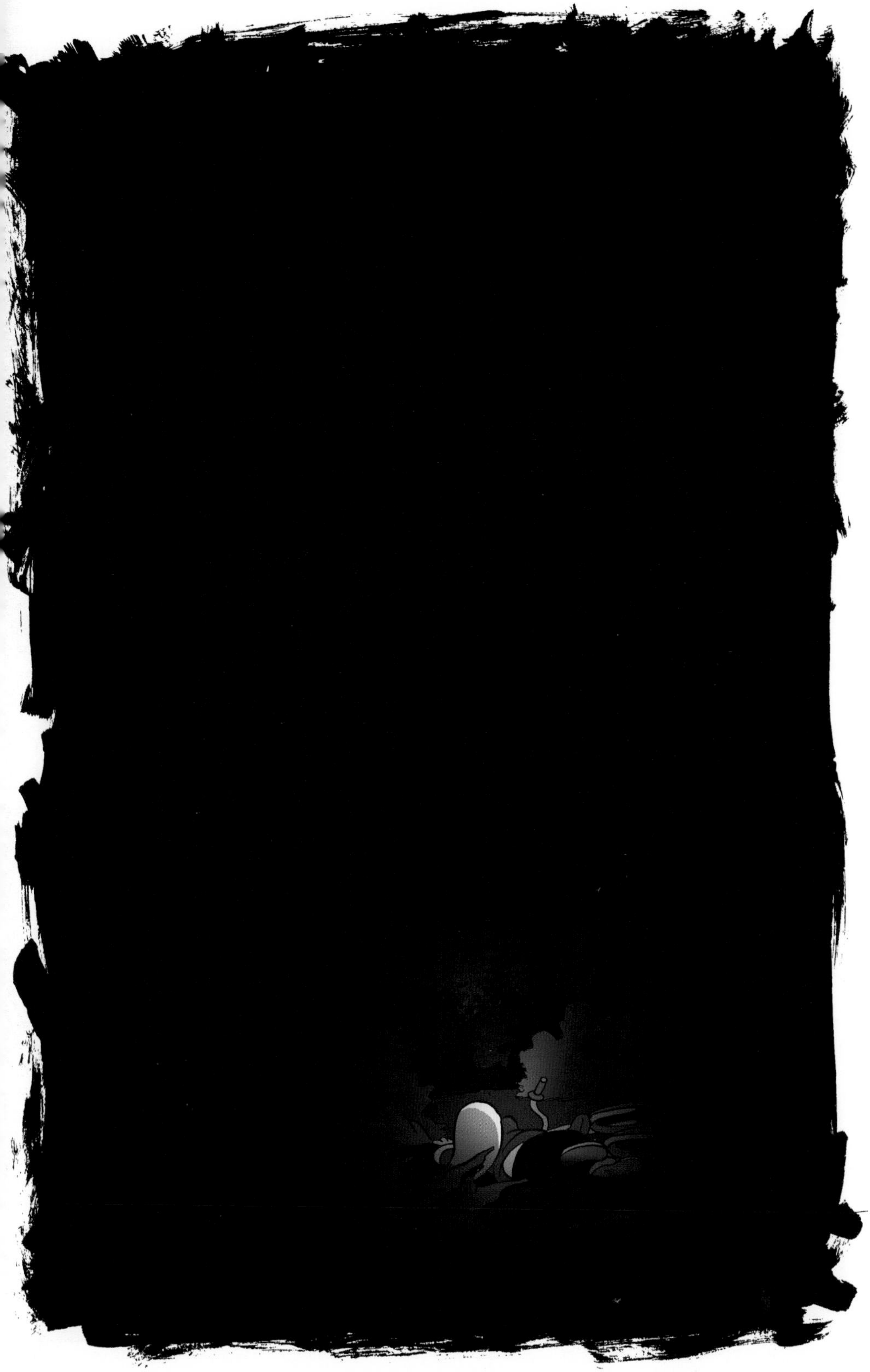

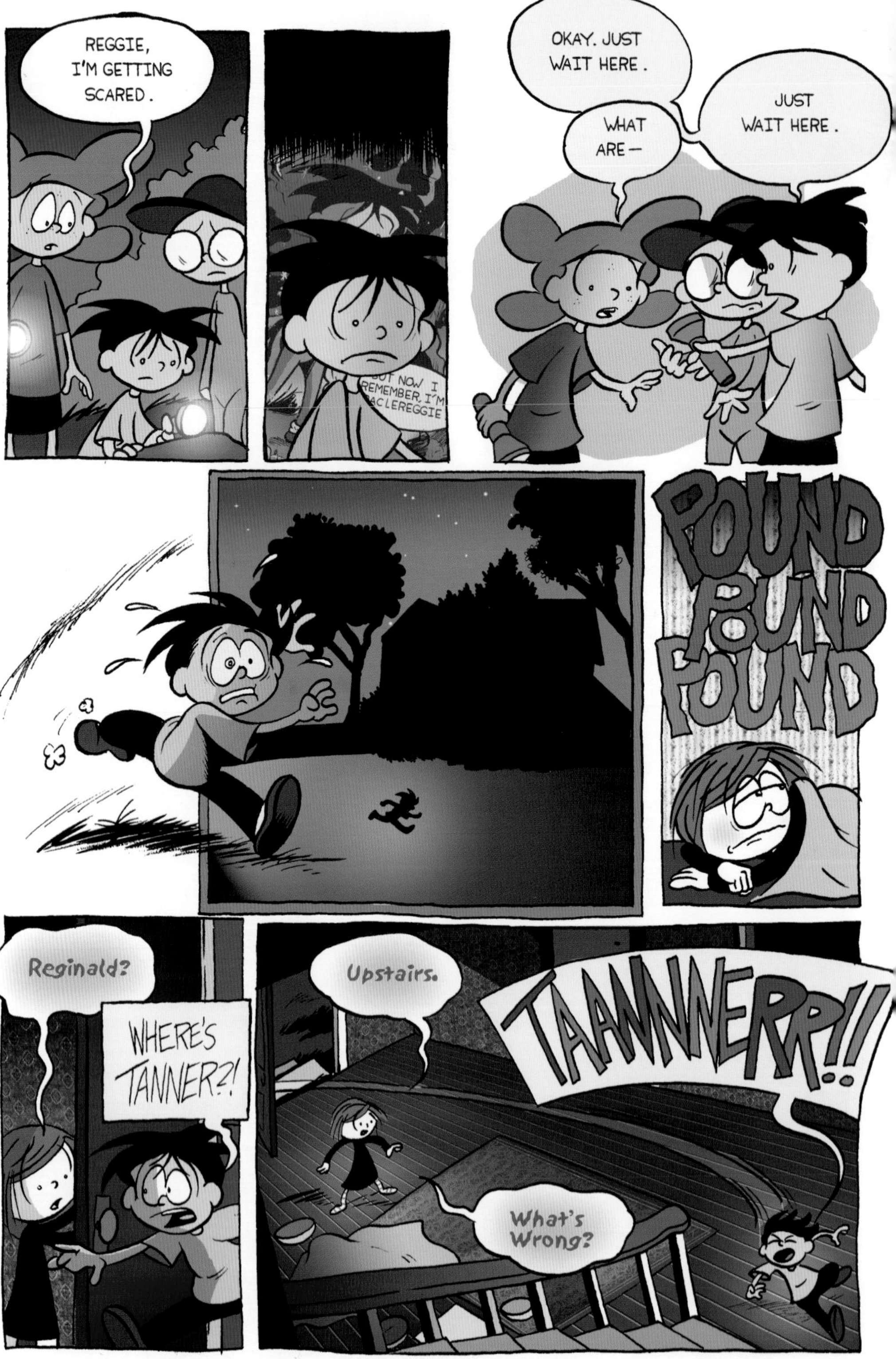
REGGIE, I'M GETTING SCARED.
BUT NOW I REMEMBER, I'M ACLEREGGIE
OKAY. JUST WAIT HERE.
WHAT ARE—
JUST WAIT HERE.
POUND POUND POUND
Reginald?
WHERE'S TANNER?!
Upstairs.
TAANNNERR!!
What's Wrong?

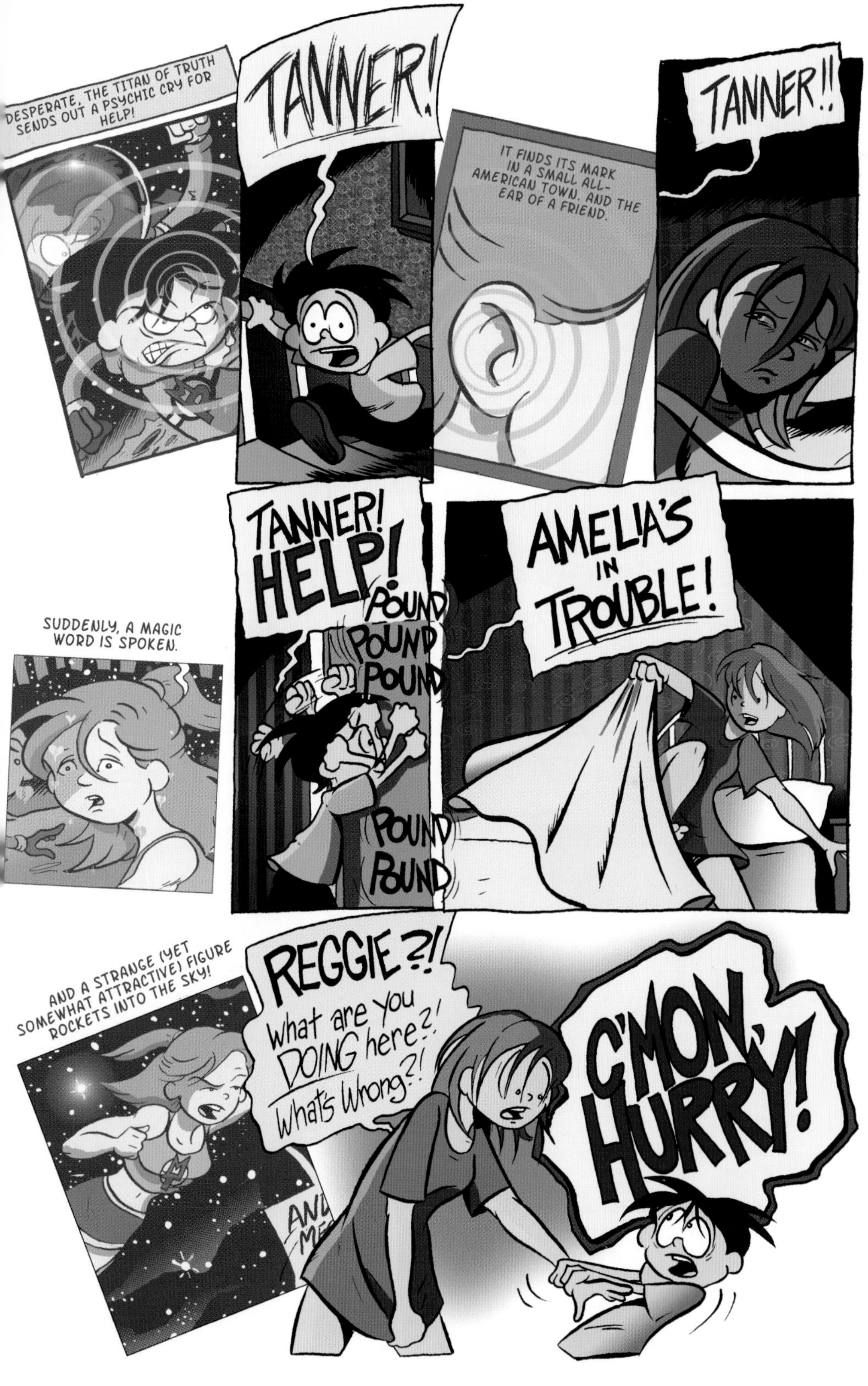

DESPERATE, THE TITAN OF TRUTH SENDS OUT A PSYCHIC CRY FOR HELP!
TANNER!
IT FINDS ITS MARK IN A SMALL ALL-AMERICAN TOWN. AND THE EAR OF A FRIEND.
TANNER!!
SUDDENLY, A MAGIC WORD IS SPOKEN.
TANNER! HELP!
POUND
POUND
POUND
POUND
POUND
AMELIA'S IN TROUBLE!
AND A STRANGE (YET SOMEWHAT ATTRACTIVE) FIGURE ROCKETS INTO THE SKY!
REGGIE?!
What are you DOING here?!
What's Wrong?!
C'MON, HURRY!

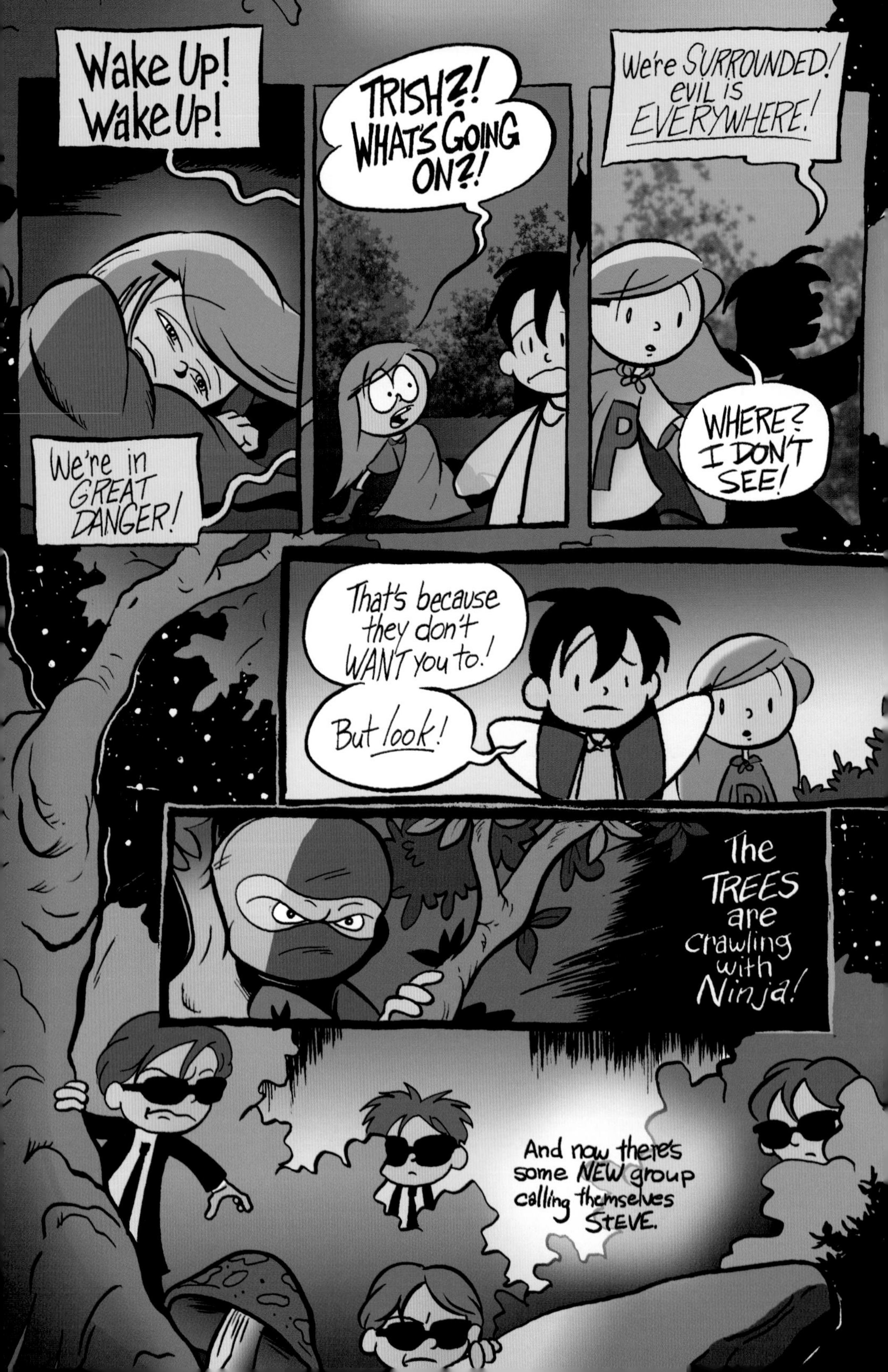
Wake Up! Wake Up!
We're in GREAT DANGER!
TRISH?! WHAT'S GOING ON?!
We're SURROUNDED! evil is EVERYWHERE!
WHERE? I DON'T SEE!
That's because they don't WANT you to!
But look!
The TREES are crawling with Ninja!
And now there's some NEW group calling themselves STEVE.

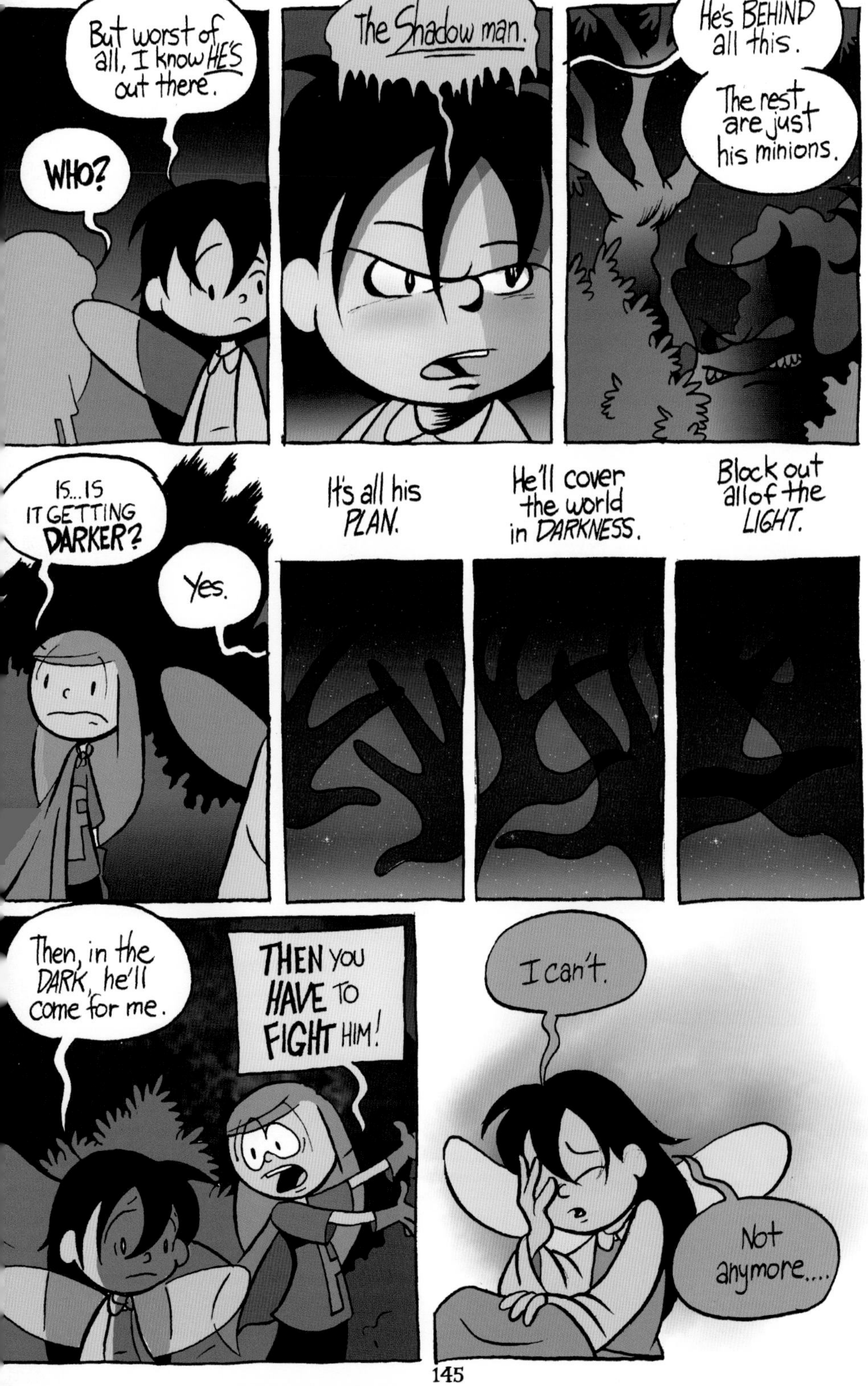
But worst of all, I know HE'S out there.
WHO?
The Shadow man.
He's BEHIND all this.
The rest are just his minions.
IS...IS IT GETTING DARKER?
Yes.
It's all his PLAN.
He'll cover the world in DARKNESS.
Block out all of the LIGHT.
Then, in the DARK, he'll come for me.
THEN YOU HAVE TO FIGHT HIM!
I can't.
Not anymore....

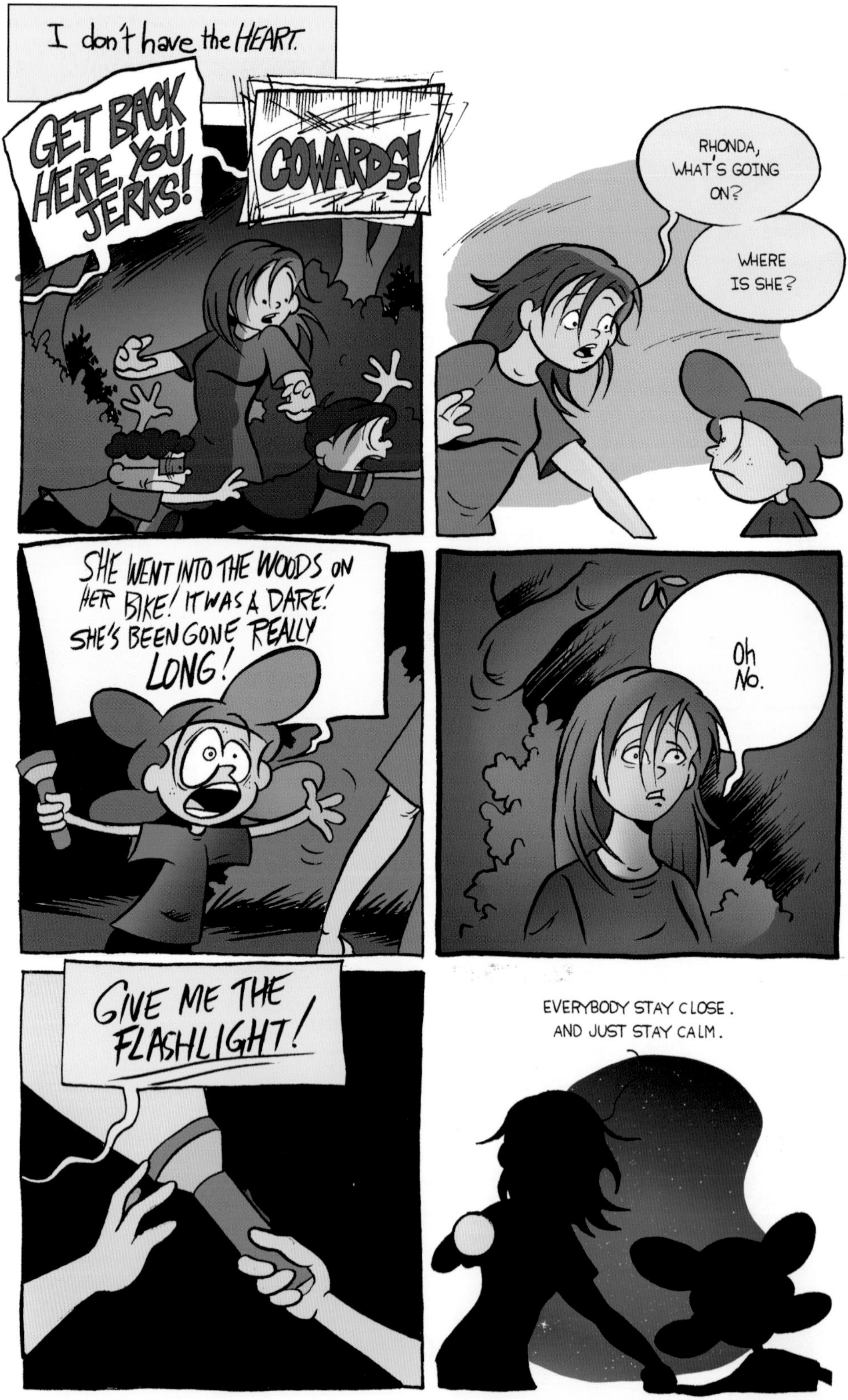
I don't have the HEART.
GET BACK HERE, YOU JERKS!
COWARDS!
RHONDA, WHAT'S GOING ON?
WHERE IS SHE?
SHE WENT INTO THE WOODS ON HER BIKE! IT WAS A DARE! SHE'S BEEN GONE REALLY LONG!
Oh No.
GIVE ME THE FLASHLIGHT!
EVERYBODY STAY CLOSE. AND JUST STAY CALM.

WE'RE GONNA FIND HER.

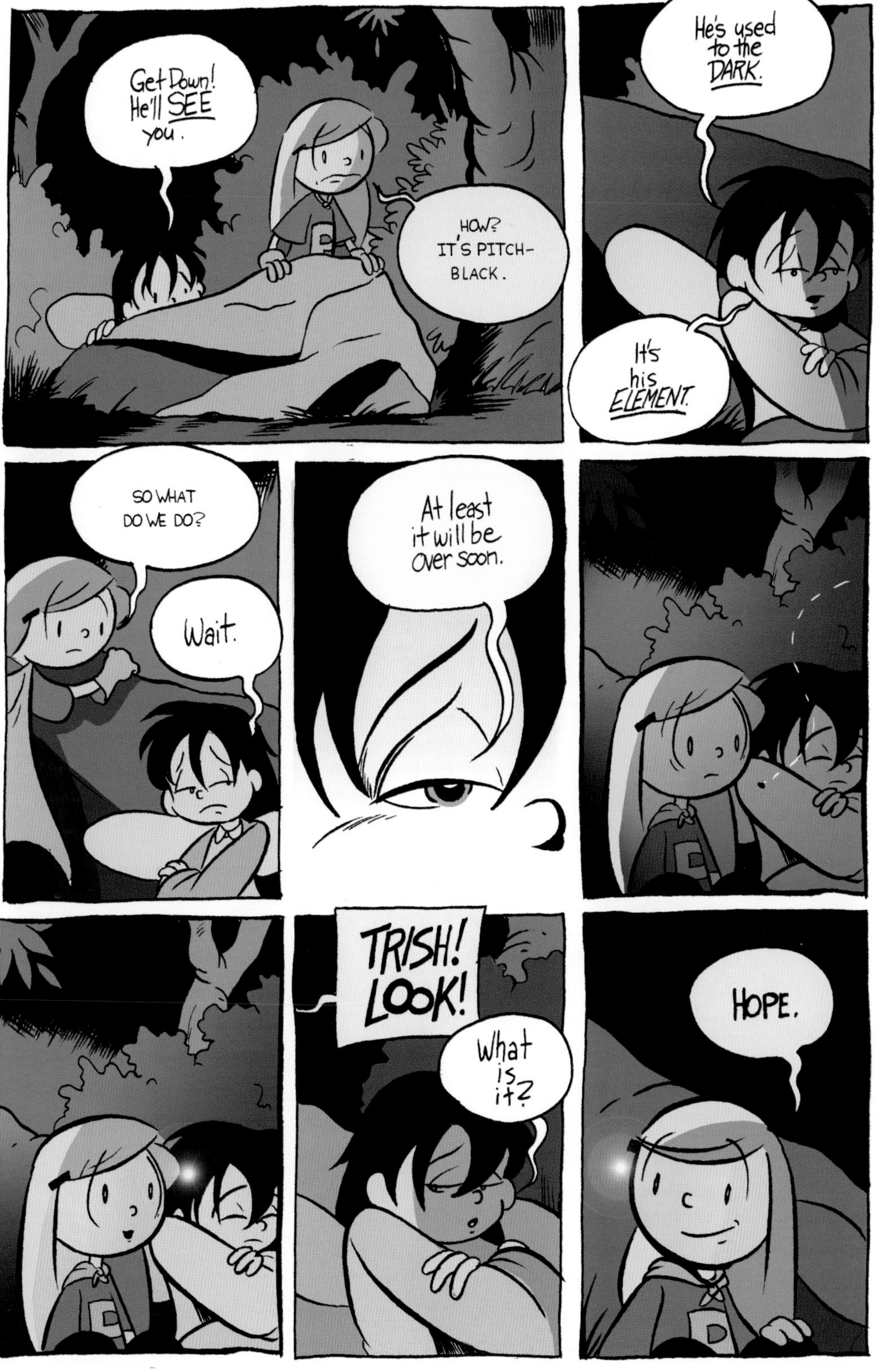
Get Down! He'll SEE you.
HOW? IT'S PITCH-BLACK.
He's used to the DARK.
It's his ELEMENT.
SO WHAT DO WE DO?
Wait.
At least it will be over soon.
TRISH! LOOK!
What is it?
HOPE.

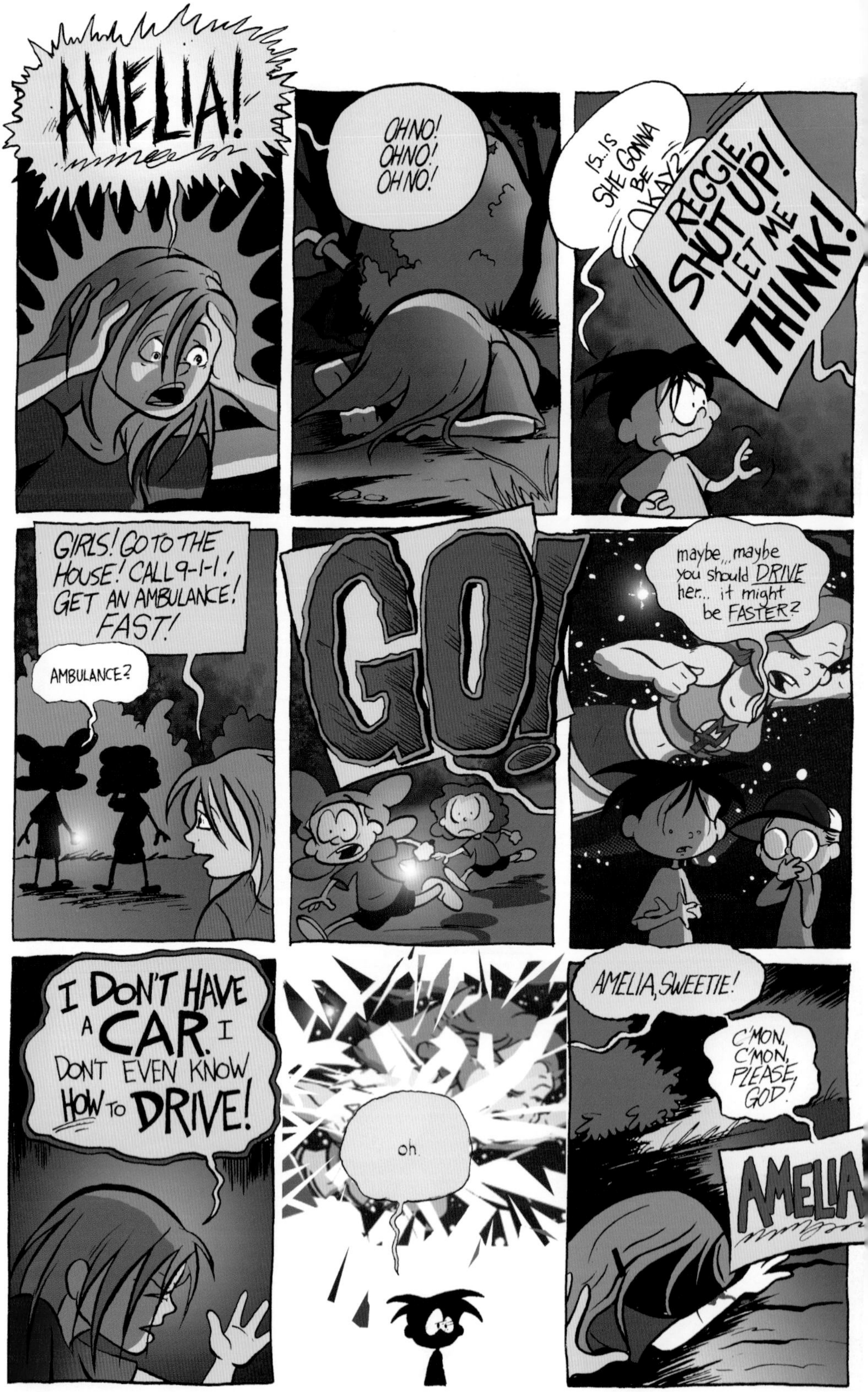
AMELIA!
OH NO! OH NO! OH NO!
IS..IS SHE GONNA BE OKAY?
REGGIE, SHUT UP! LET ME THINK!
GIRLS! GO TO THE HOUSE! CALL 9-1-1! GET AN AMBULANCE! FAST!
AMBULANCE?
GO!
maybe,,,maybe you should DRIVE her... it might be FASTER?
I DON'T HAVE A CAR. I DON'T EVEN KNOW HOW TO DRIVE!
oh.
AMELIA, SWEETIE!
C'MON, C'MON, PLEASE, GOD!
AMELIA

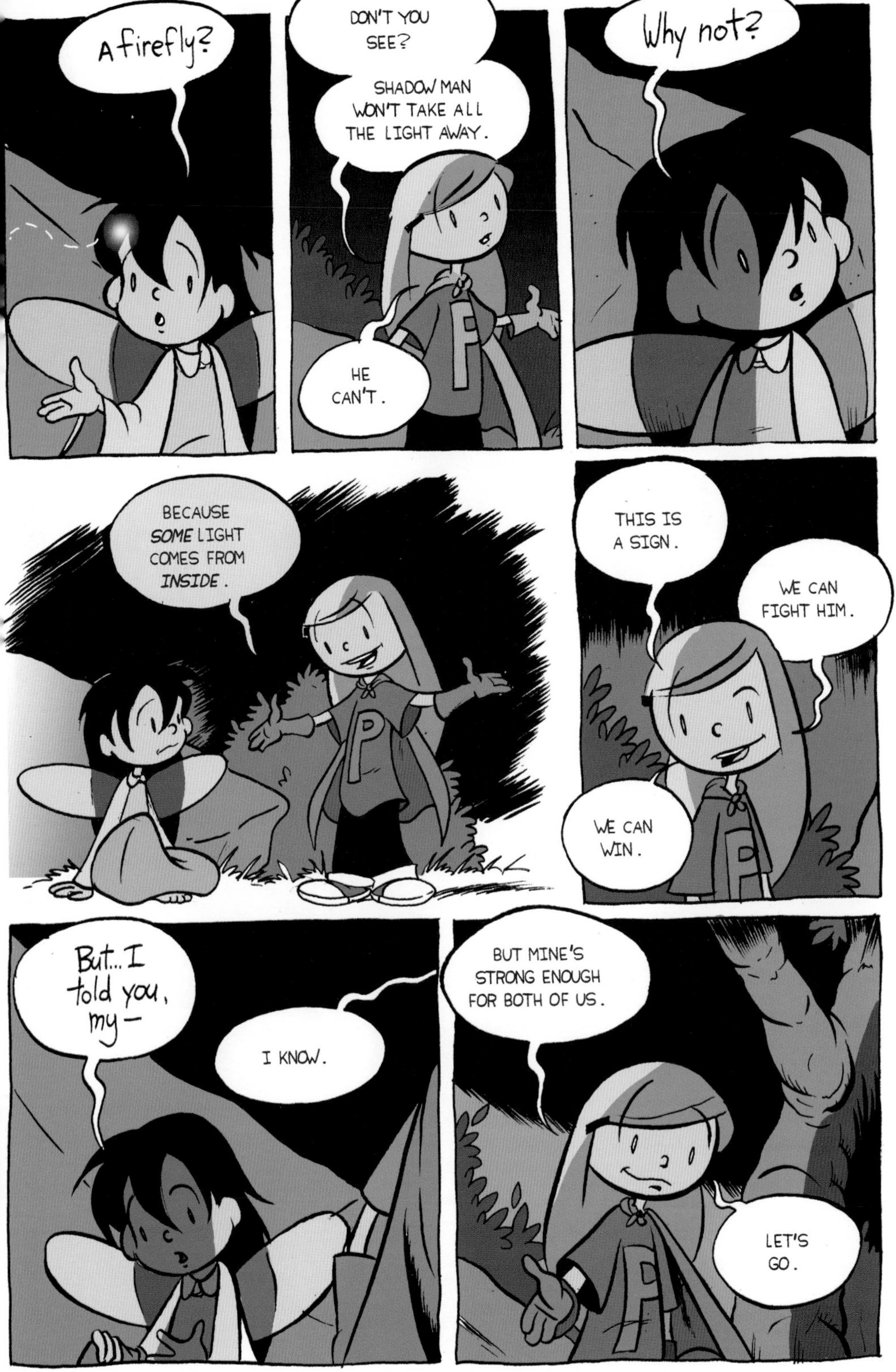

A firefly?
DON'T YOU SEE?
SHADOW MAN WON'T TAKE ALL THE LIGHT AWAY.
HE CAN'T.
Why not?
BECAUSE SOME LIGHT COMES FROM INSIDE.
THIS IS A SIGN.
WE CAN FIGHT HIM.
WE CAN WIN.
But... I told you, my—
I KNOW.
BUT MINE'S STRONG ENOUGH FOR BOTH OF US.
LET'S GO.

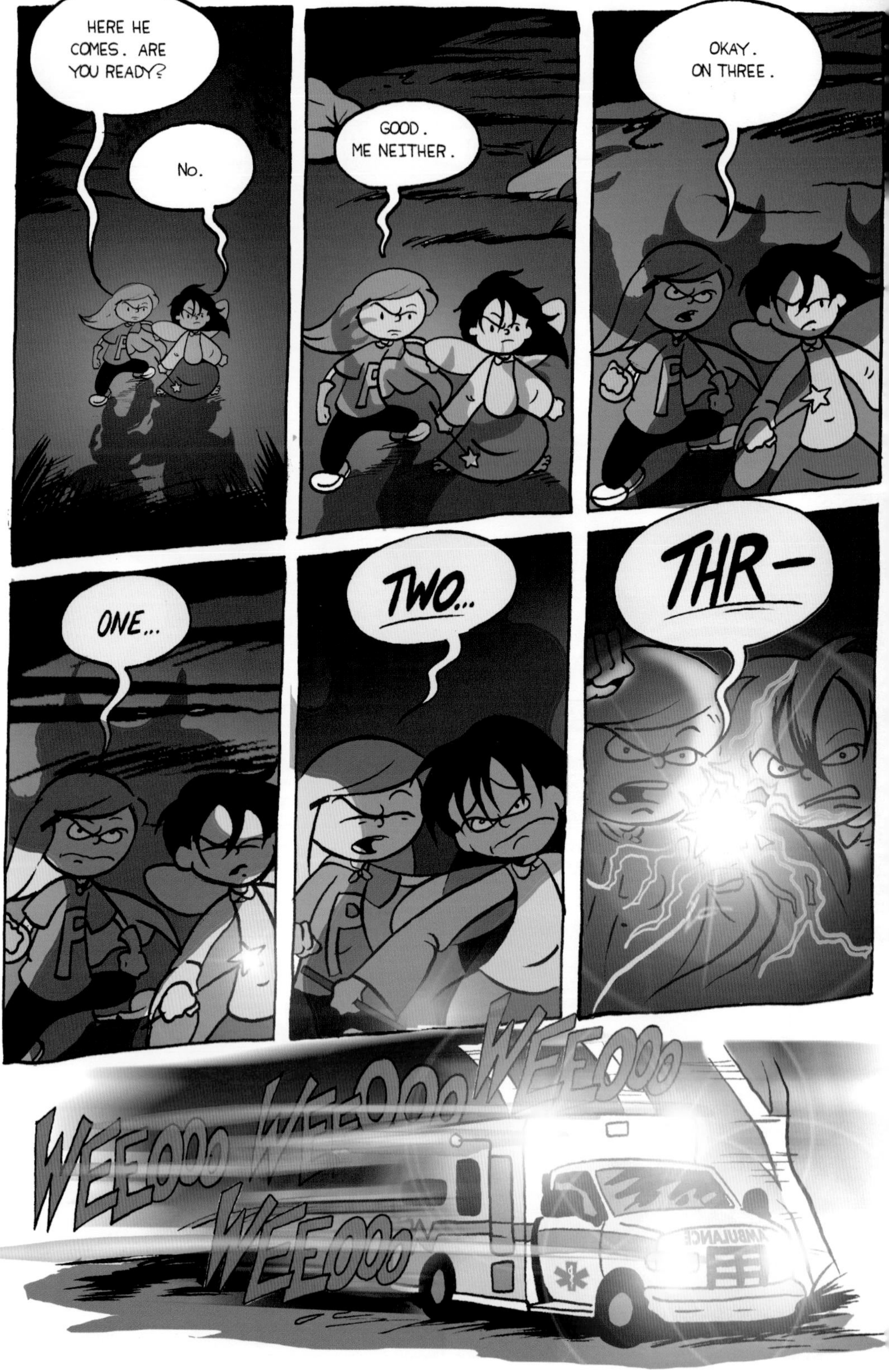
HERE HE COMES. ARE YOU READY?
No.
GOOD. ME NEITHER.
OKAY. ON THREE.
ONE...
TWO...
THR-
WEEOOO
WEEOOO
WEEOOO
WEEOOO
AMBULANCE

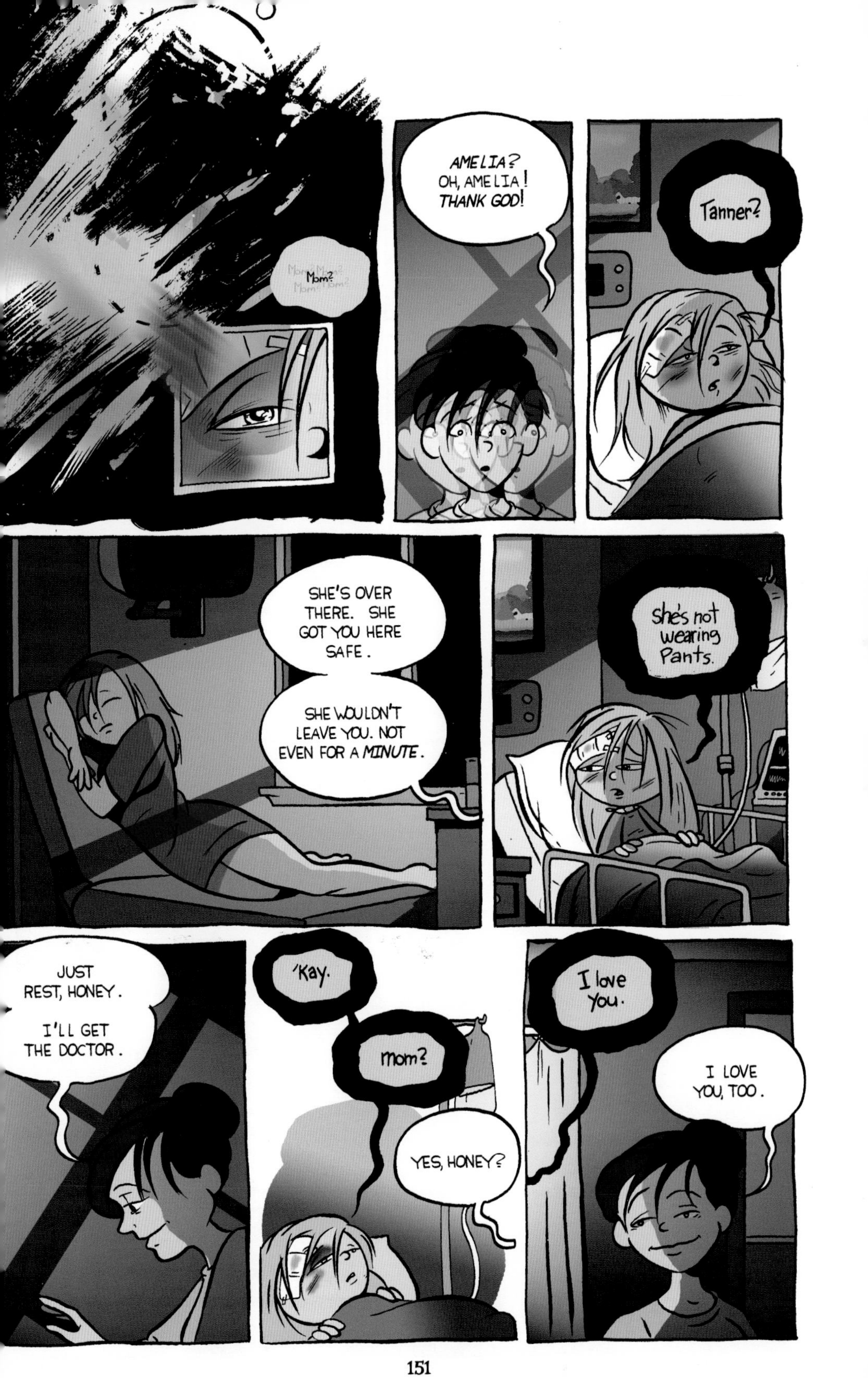
Mom? Mom? Mom?
AMELIA? OH, AMELIA! THANK GOD!
Tanner?
SHE'S OVER THERE. SHE GOT YOU HERE SAFE.
SHE WOULDN'T LEAVE YOU. NOT EVEN FOR A MINUTE.
she's not wearing Pants.
JUST REST, HONEY. I'LL GET THE DOCTOR.
'Kay.
mom?
YES, HONEY?
I love you.
I LOVE YOU, TOO.

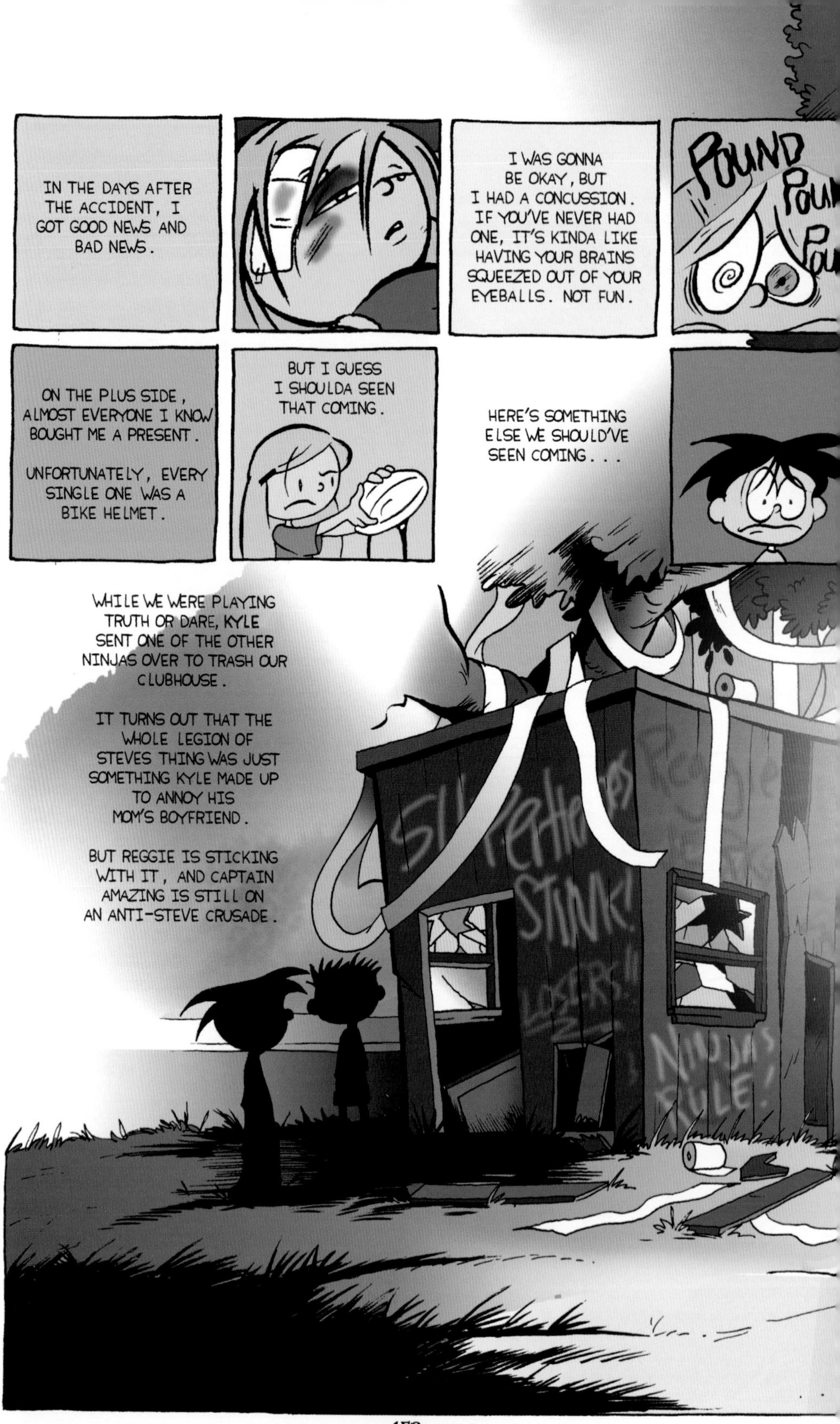
IN THE DAYS AFTER THE ACCIDENT, I GOT GOOD NEWS AND BAD NEWS.
I WAS GONNA BE OKAY, BUT I HAD A CONCUSSION. IF YOU'VE NEVER HAD ONE, IT'S KINDA LIKE HAVING YOUR BRAINS SQUEEZED OUT OF YOUR EYEBALLS. NOT FUN.
POUND
POUND
POUND
ON THE PLUS SIDE, ALMOST EVERYONE I KNOW BOUGHT ME A PRESENT.
UNFORTUNATELY, EVERY SINGLE ONE WAS A BIKE HELMET.
BUT I GUESS I SHOULDA SEEN THAT COMING.
HERE'S SOMETHING ELSE WE SHOULD'VE SEEN COMING . . .
WHILE WE WERE PLAYING TRUTH OR DARE, KYLE SENT ONE OF THE OTHER NINJAS OVER TO TRASH OUR CLUBHOUSE.
IT TURNS OUT THAT THE WHOLE LEGION OF STEVES THING WAS JUST SOMETHING KYLE MADE UP TO ANNOY HIS MOM'S BOYFRIEND.
BUT REGGIE IS STICKING WITH IT, AND CAPTAIN AMAZING IS STILL ON AN ANTI-STEVE CRUSADE.
STINK!
LOSERS!
NINJAS RULE!

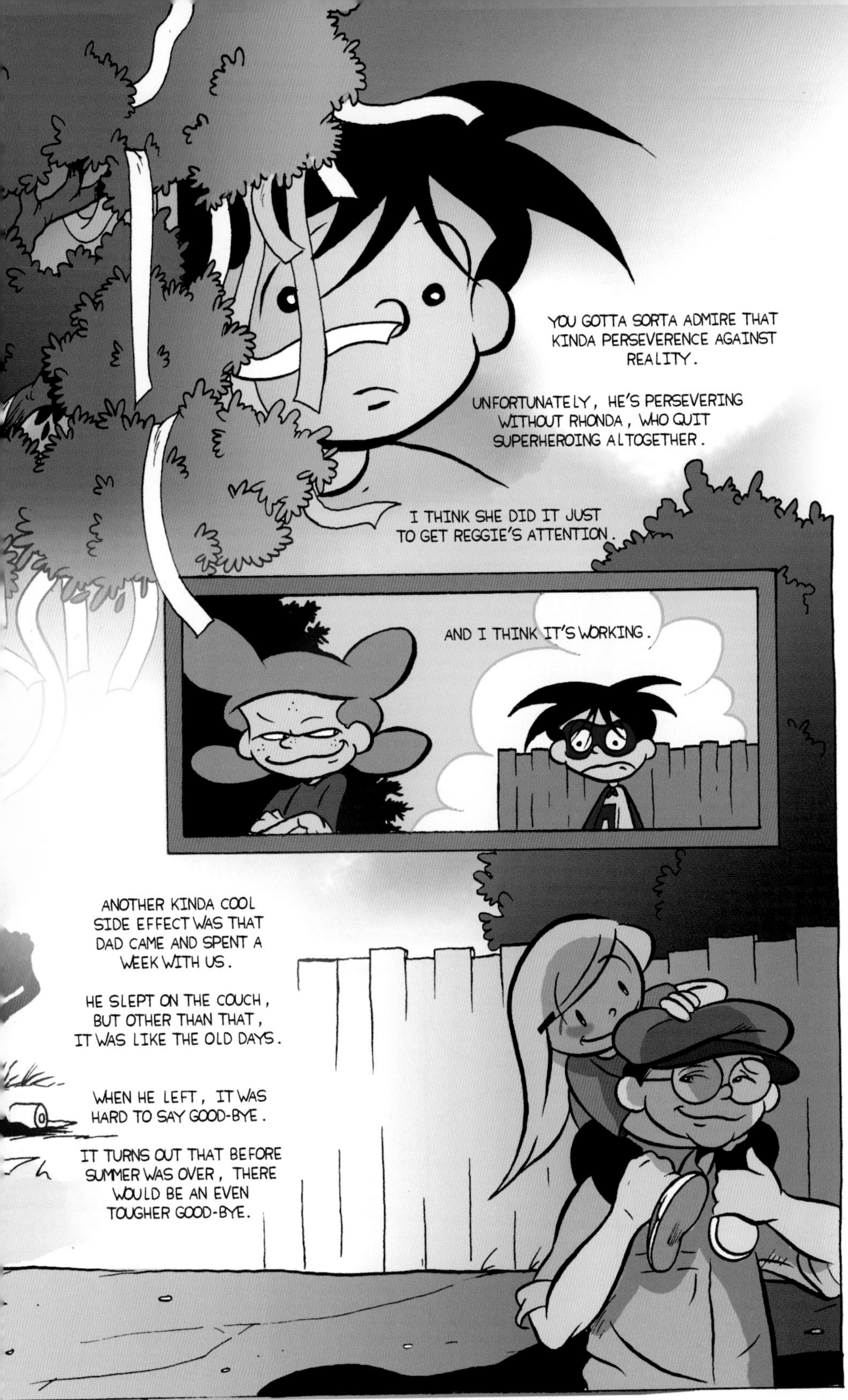

YOU GOTTA SORTA ADMIRE THAT KINDA PERSEVERENCE AGAINST REALITY.
UNFORTUNATELY, HE'S PERSEVERING WITHOUT RHONDA, WHO QUIT SUPERHEROING ALTOGETHER.
I THINK SHE DID IT JUST TO GET REGGIE'S ATTENTION.
AND I THINK IT'S WORKING.
ANOTHER KINDA COOL SIDE EFFECT WAS THAT DAD CAME AND SPENT A WEEK WITH US.
HE SLEPT ON THE COUCH, BUT OTHER THAN THAT, IT WAS LIKE THE OLD DAYS.
WHEN HE LEFT, IT WAS HARD TO SAY GOOD-BYE.
IT TURNS OUT THAT BEFORE SUMMER WAS OVER, THERE WOULD BE AN EVEN TOUGHER GOOD-BYE.

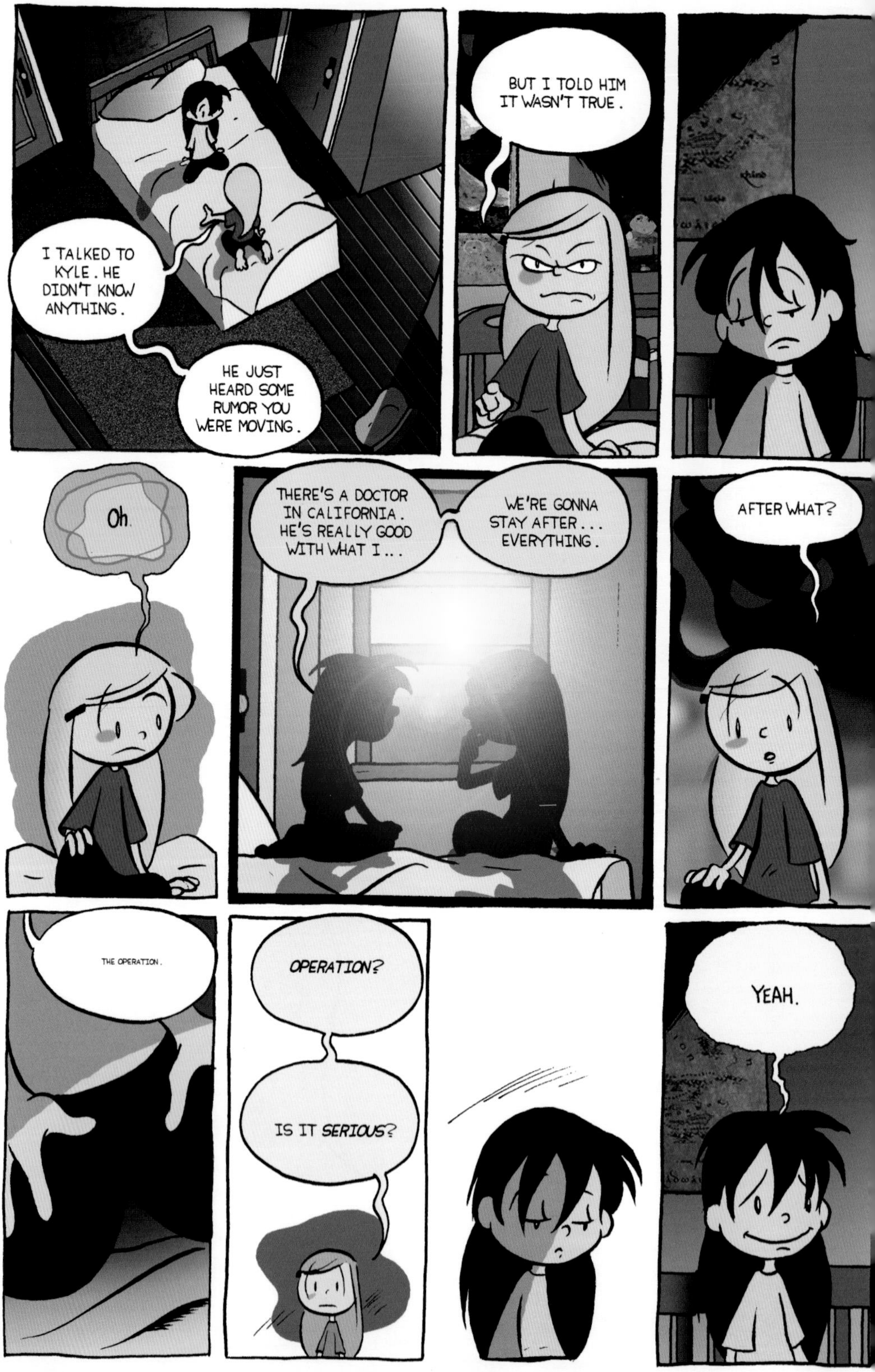
I TALKED TO KYLE. HE DIDN'T KNOW ANYTHING.
HE JUST HEARD SOME RUMOR YOU WERE MOVING.
BUT I TOLD HIM IT WASN'T TRUE.
Oh.
THERE'S A DOCTOR IN CALIFORNIA. HE'S REALLY GOOD WITH WHAT I...
WE'RE GONNA STAY AFTER... EVERYTHING.
AFTER WHAT?
THE OPERATION.
OPERATION?
IS IT SERIOUS?
YEAH.

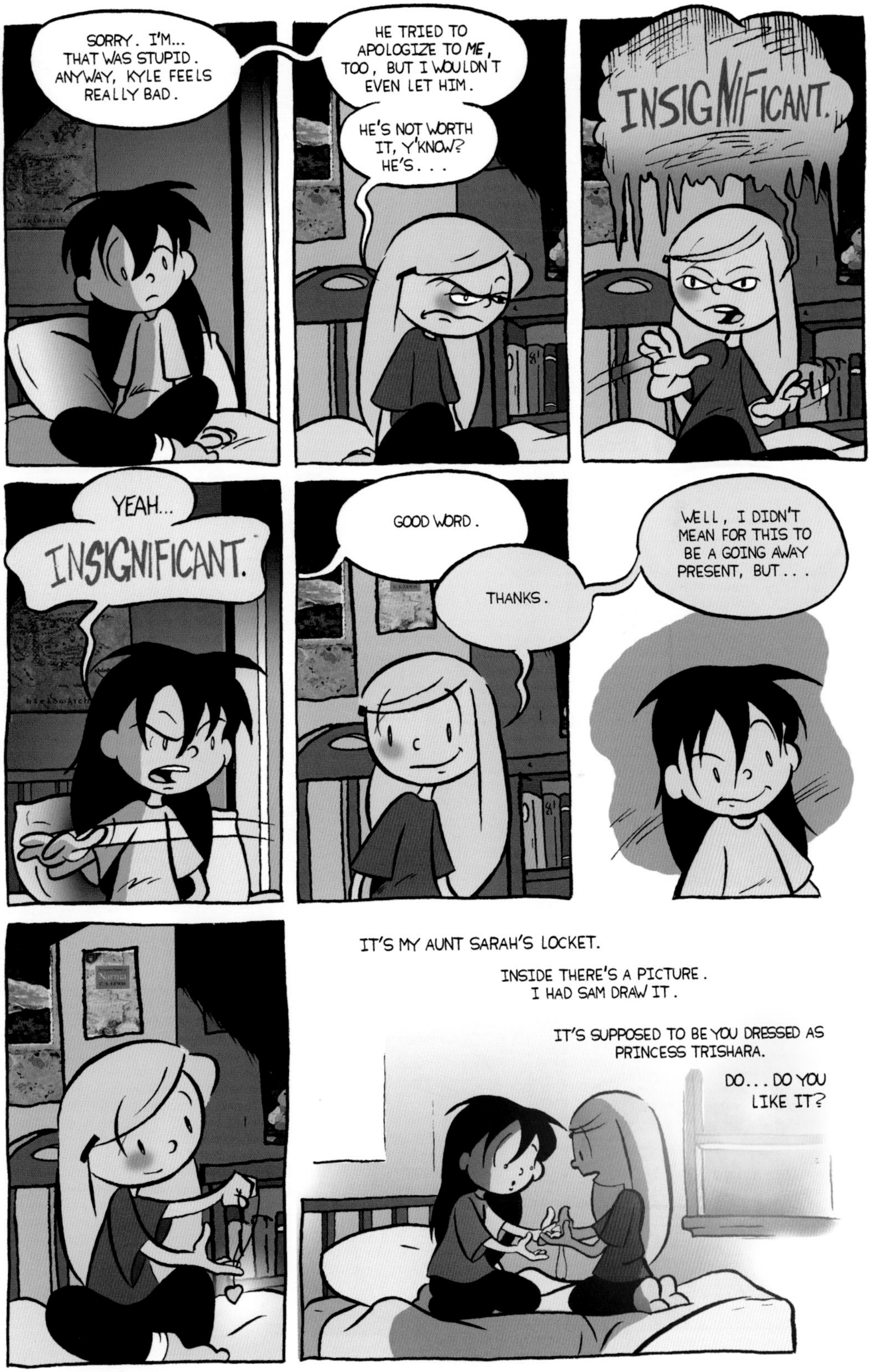
SORRY. I'M... THAT WAS STUPID. ANYWAY, KYLE FEELS REALLY BAD.
HE TRIED TO APOLOGIZE TO ME, TOO, BUT I WOULDN'T EVEN LET HIM.
HE'S NOT WORTH IT, Y'KNOW? HE'S. . .
INSIGNIFICANT.
YEAH... INSIGNIFICANT.
GOOD WORD.
THANKS.
WELL, I DIDN'T MEAN FOR THIS TO BE A GOING AWAY PRESENT, BUT . . .
IT'S MY AUNT SARAH'S LOCKET.
INSIDE THERE'S A PICTURE. I HAD SAM DRAW IT.
IT'S SUPPOSED TO BE YOU DRESSED AS PRINCESS TRISHARA.
DO. . . DO YOU LIKE IT?

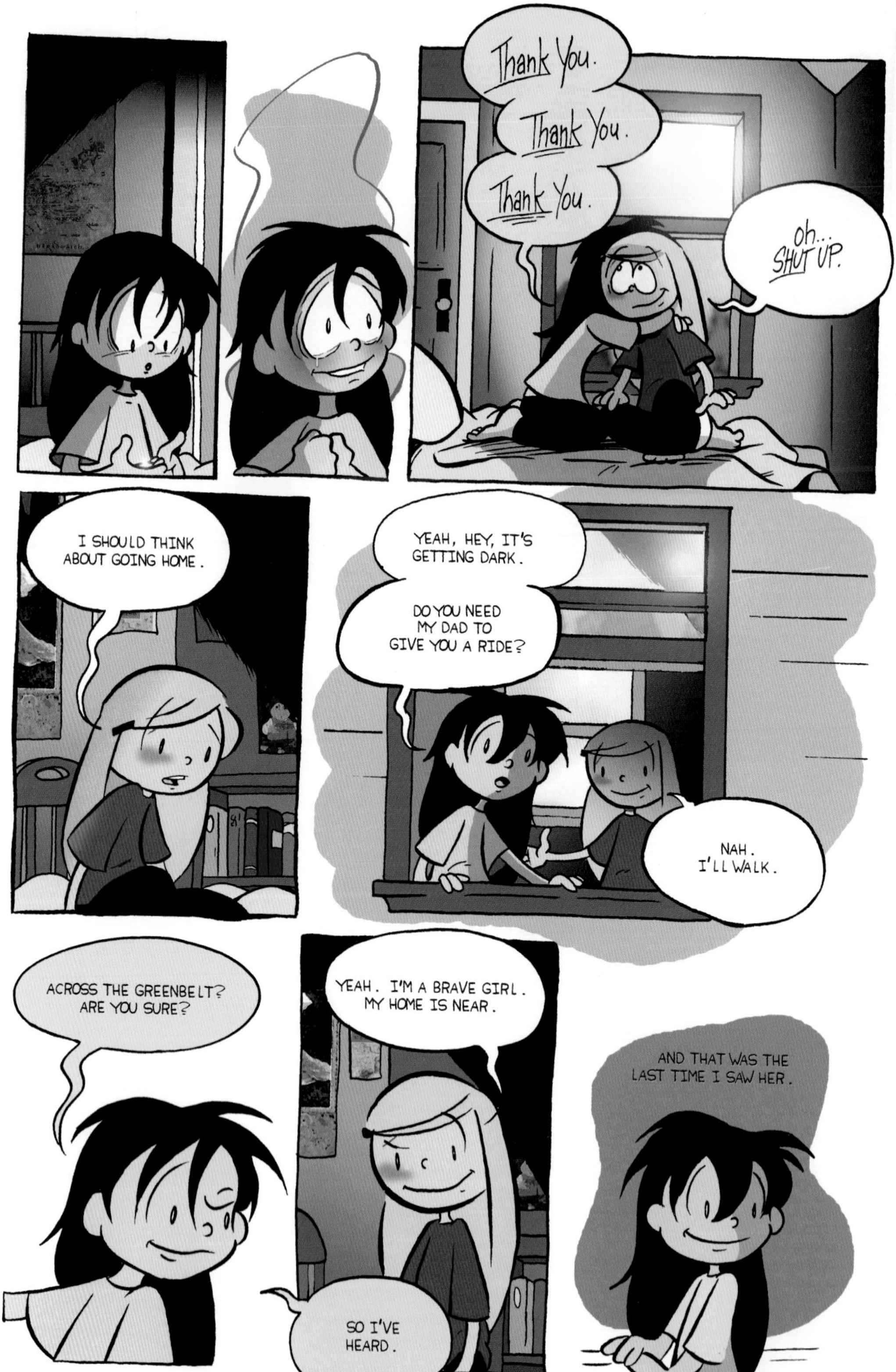
Thank You.
Thank You.
Thank You.
oh... SHUT UP.
I SHOULD THINK ABOUT GOING HOME.
YEAH, HEY, IT'S GETTING DARK.
DO YOU NEED MY DAD TO GIVE YOU A RIDE?
NAH. I'LL WALK.
ACROSS THE GREENBELT? ARE YOU SURE?
YEAH. I'M A BRAVE GIRL. MY HOME IS NEAR.
SO I'VE HEARD.
AND THAT WAS THE LAST TIME I SAW HER.

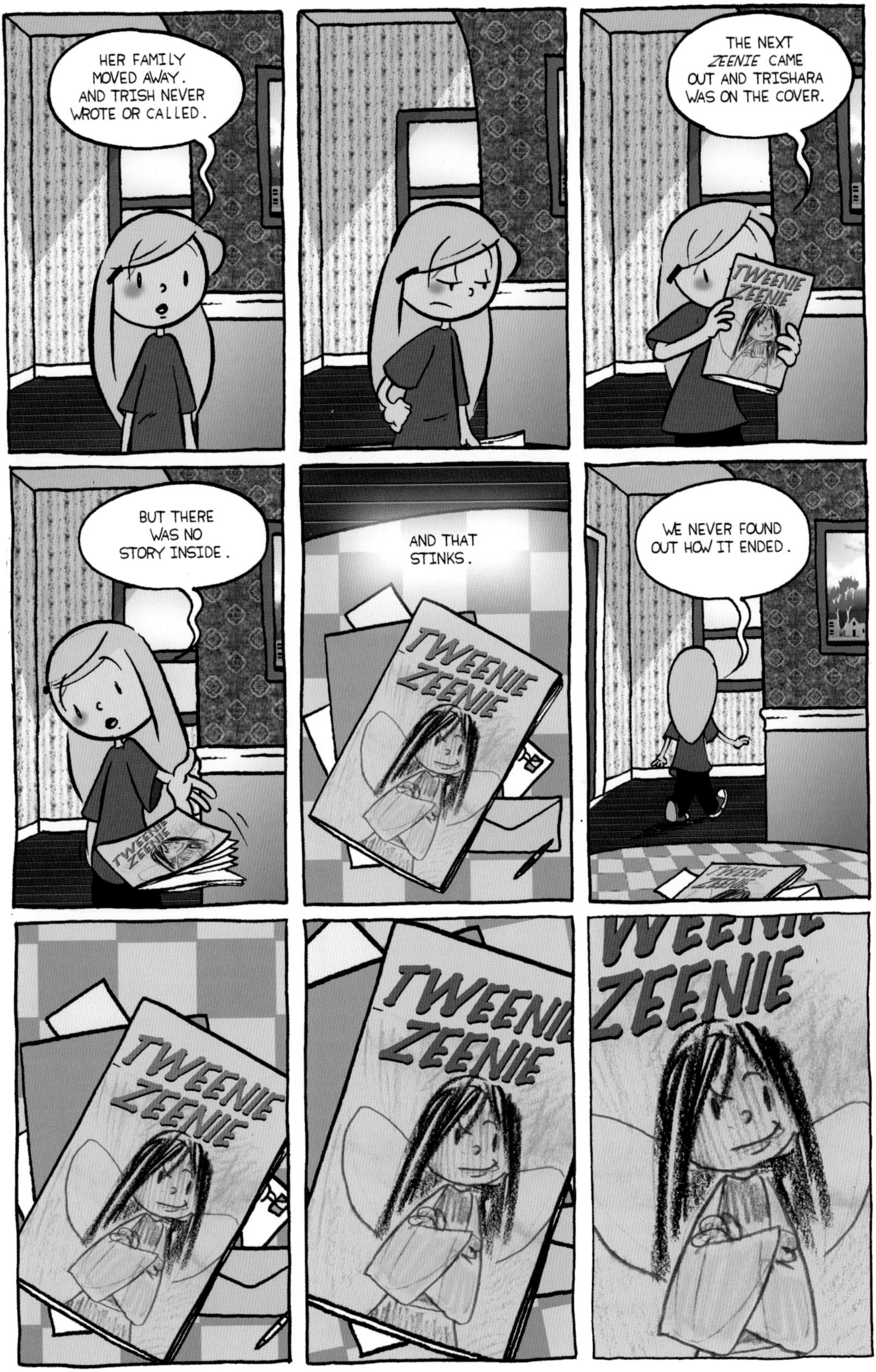
HER FAMILY MOVED AWAY. AND TRISH NEVER WROTE OR CALLED.
THE NEXT *ZEENIE* CAME OUT AND TRISHARA WAS ON THE COVER.
TWEENIE ZEENIE
BUT THERE WAS NO STORY INSIDE.
AND THAT STINKS.
WE NEVER FOUND OUT HOW IT ENDED.
TWEENIE ZEENIE

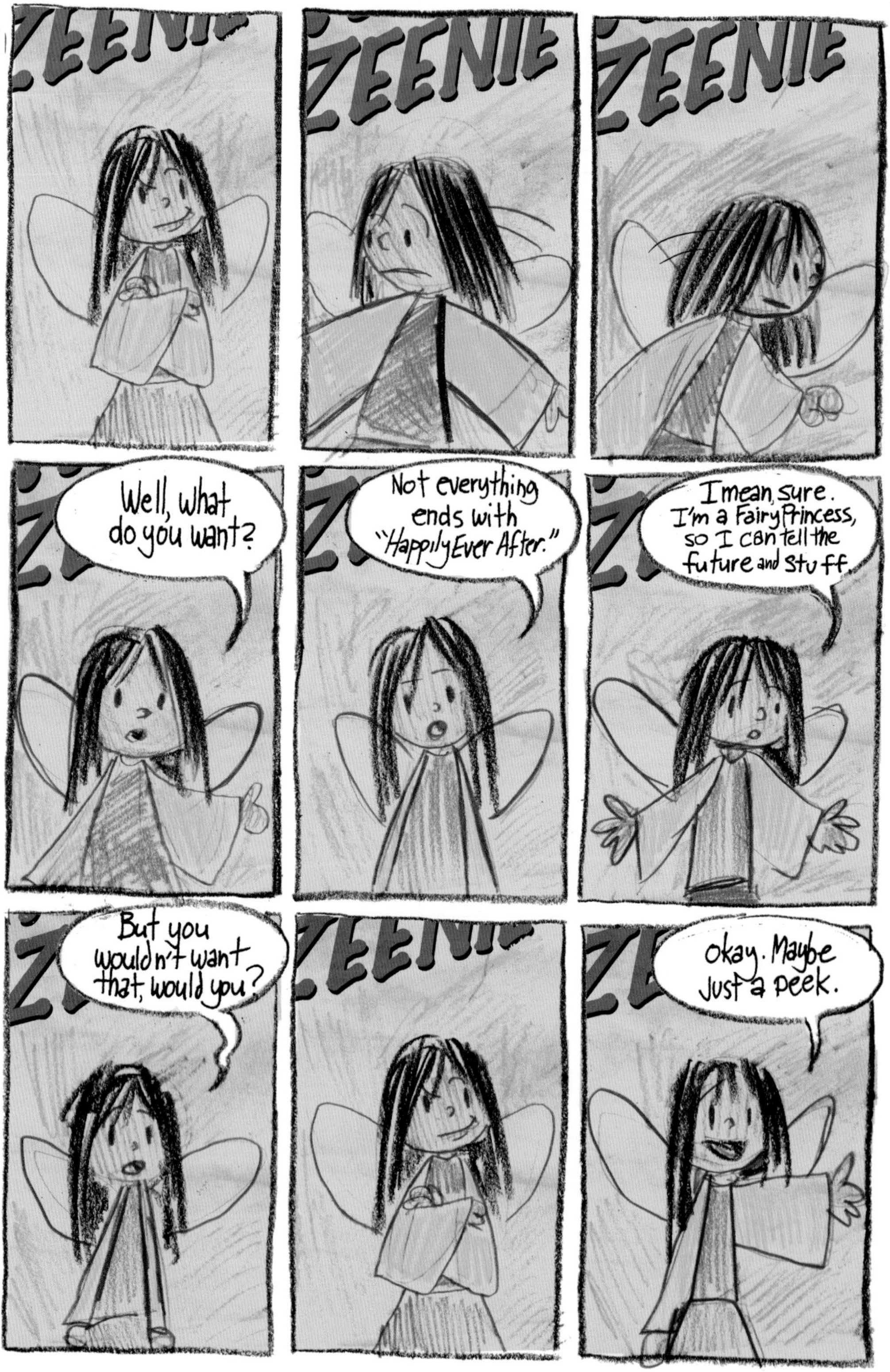
ZEENIE
ZEENIE
ZEENIE
Well, what do you want?
Not everything ends with "Happily Ever After."
I mean, sure. I'm a Fairy Princess, so I can tell the future and stuff.
But you wouldn't want that, would you?
Okay. Maybe just a peek.

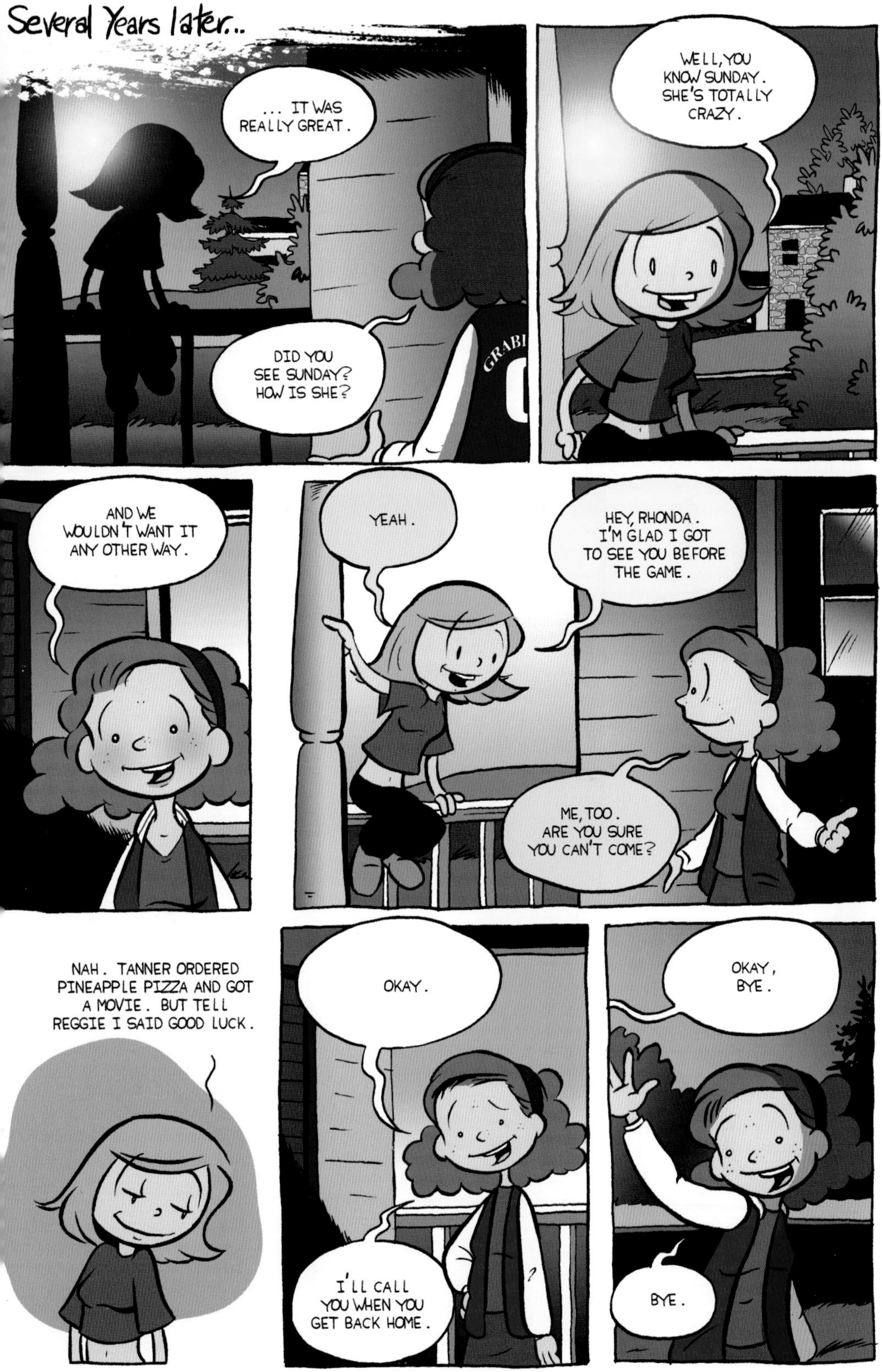
Several Years later...
... IT WAS REALLY GREAT.
DID YOU SEE SUNDAY? HOW IS SHE?
GRABI
WELL, YOU KNOW SUNDAY. SHE'S TOTALLY CRAZY.
AND WE WOULDN'T WANT IT ANY OTHER WAY.
YEAH.
HEY, RHONDA. I'M GLAD I GOT TO SEE YOU BEFORE THE GAME.
ME, TOO. ARE YOU SURE YOU CAN'T COME?
NAH. TANNER ORDERED PINEAPPLE PIZZA AND GOT A MOVIE. BUT TELL REGGIE I SAID GOOD LUCK.
OKAY.
I'LL CALL YOU WHEN YOU GET BACK HOME.
OKAY, BYE.
BYE.

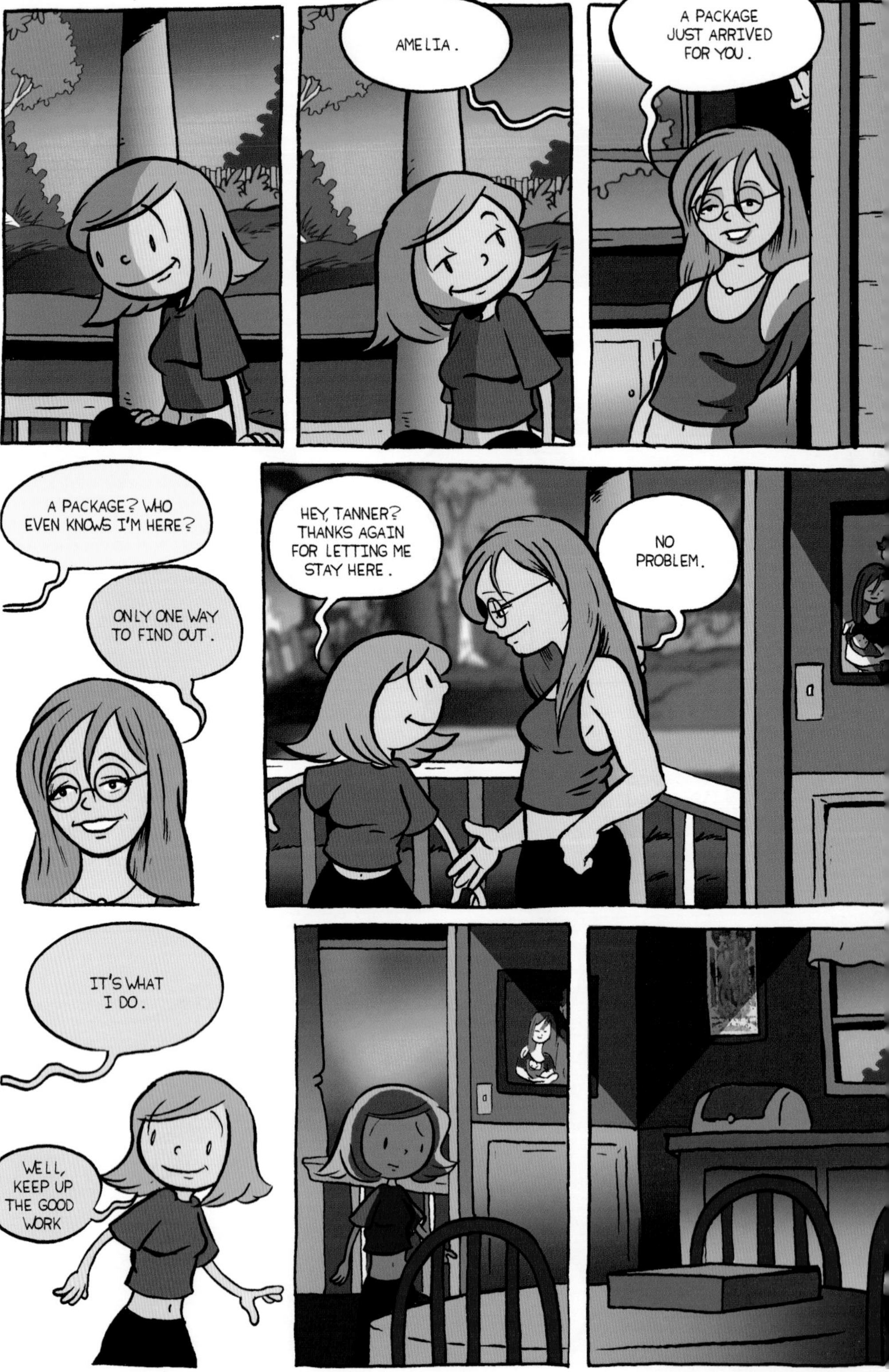
AMELIA.
A PACKAGE JUST ARRIVED FOR YOU.
A PACKAGE? WHO EVEN KNOWS I'M HERE?
ONLY ONE WAY TO FIND OUT.
HEY, TANNER? THANKS AGAIN FOR LETTING ME STAY HERE.
NO PROBLEM.
IT'S WHAT I DO.
WELL, KEEP UP THE GOOD WORK

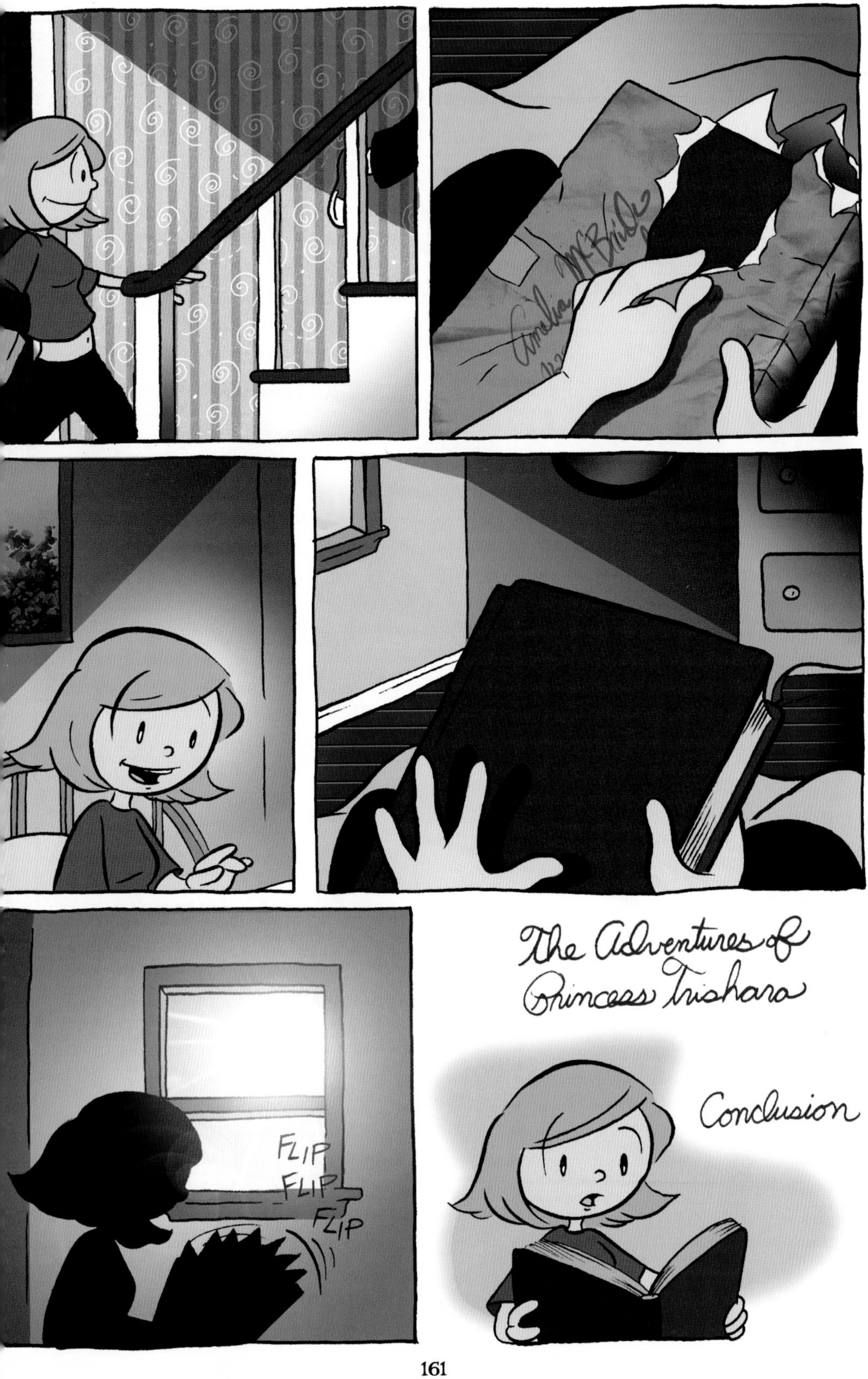
FLIP
FLIP
FLIP
The Adventures of Princess Trishara
Conclusion

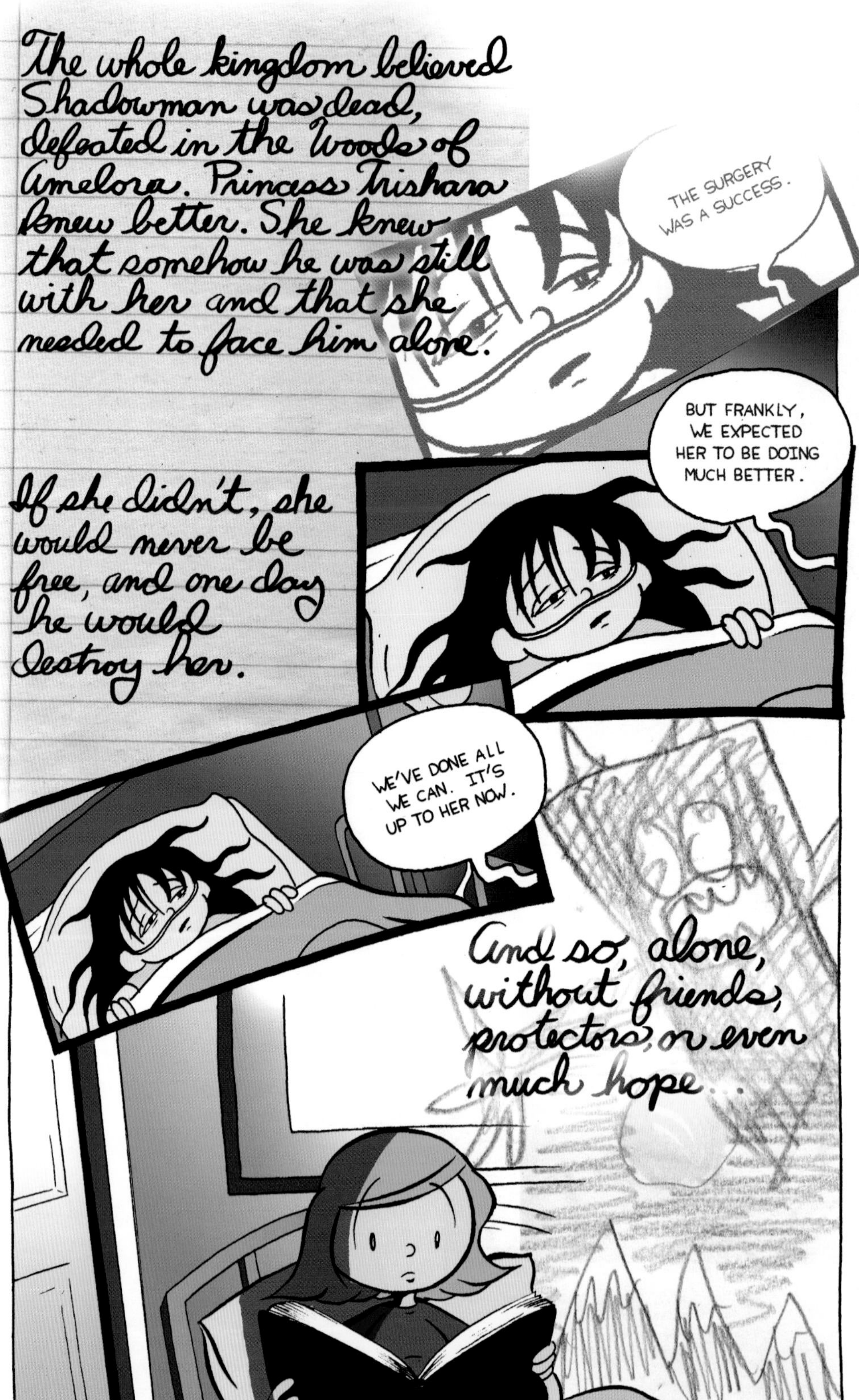
The whole kingdom believed Shadowman was dead, defeated in the Woods of Amelora. Princess Trishara knew better. She knew that somehow he was still with her and that she needed to face him alone.
THE SURGERY WAS A SUCCESS.
BUT FRANKLY, WE EXPECTED HER TO BE DOING MUCH BETTER.
If she didn't, she would never be free, and one day he would destroy her.
WE'VE DONE ALL WE CAN. IT'S UP TO HER NOW.
And so, alone, without friends, protectors, or even much hope...

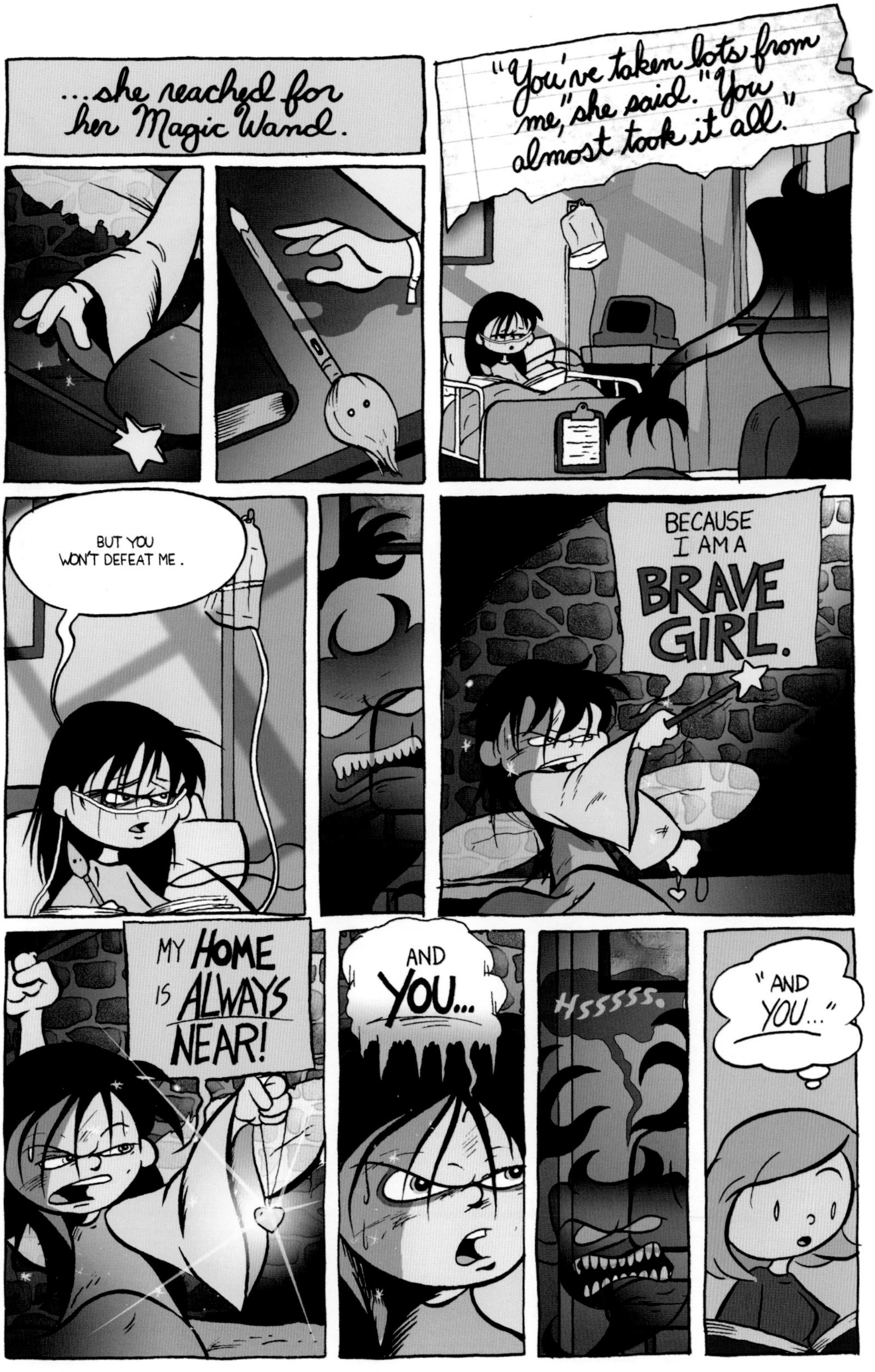
...she reached for her Magic Wand.
"You've taken lots from me," she said. "You almost took it all."
BUT YOU WON'T DEFEAT ME.
BECAUSE I AM A BRAVE GIRL.
MY HOME IS ALWAYS NEAR!
AND YOU...
HSSSSS.
"AND YOU..."

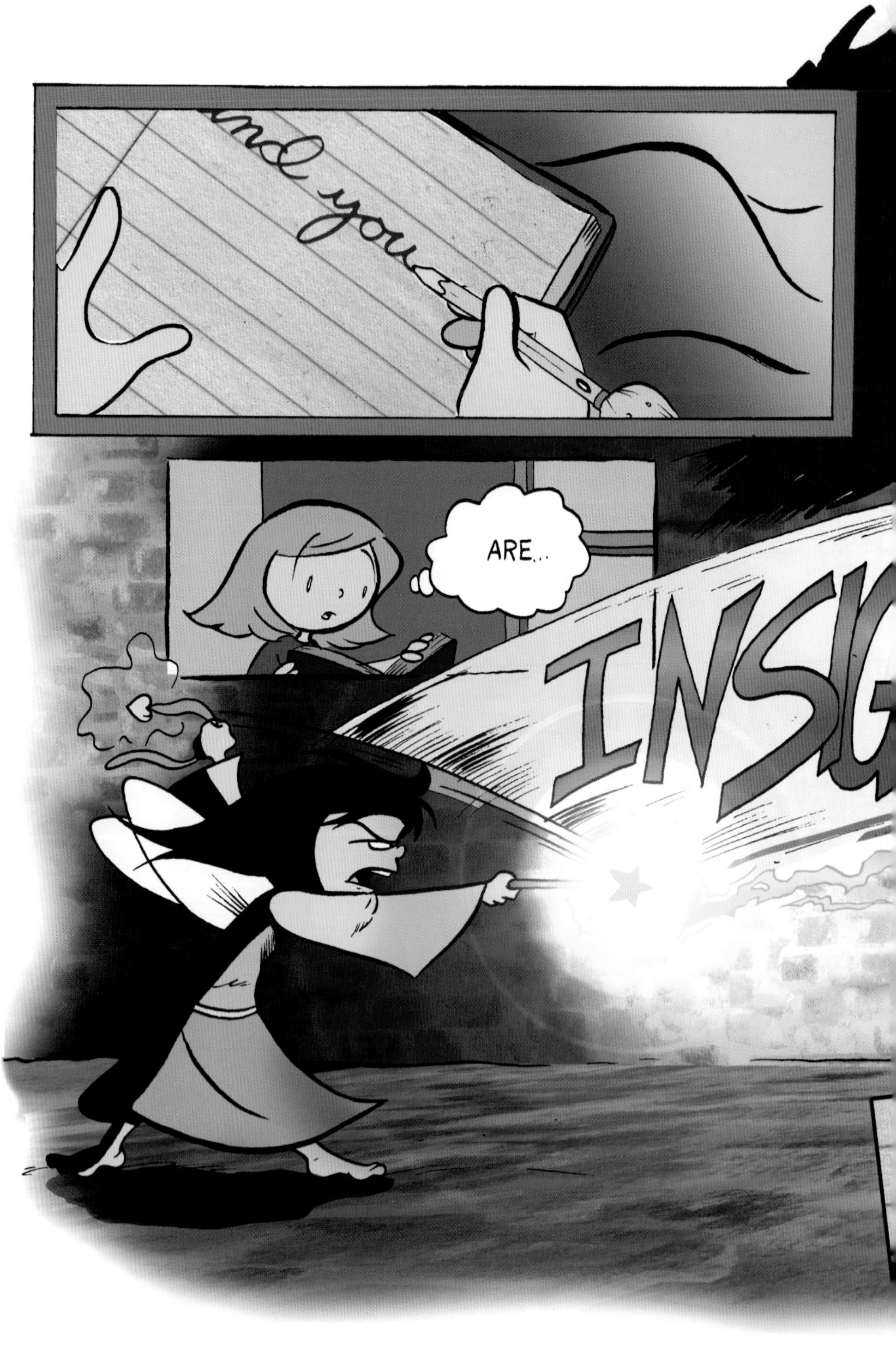
and you
ARE...
INSIG

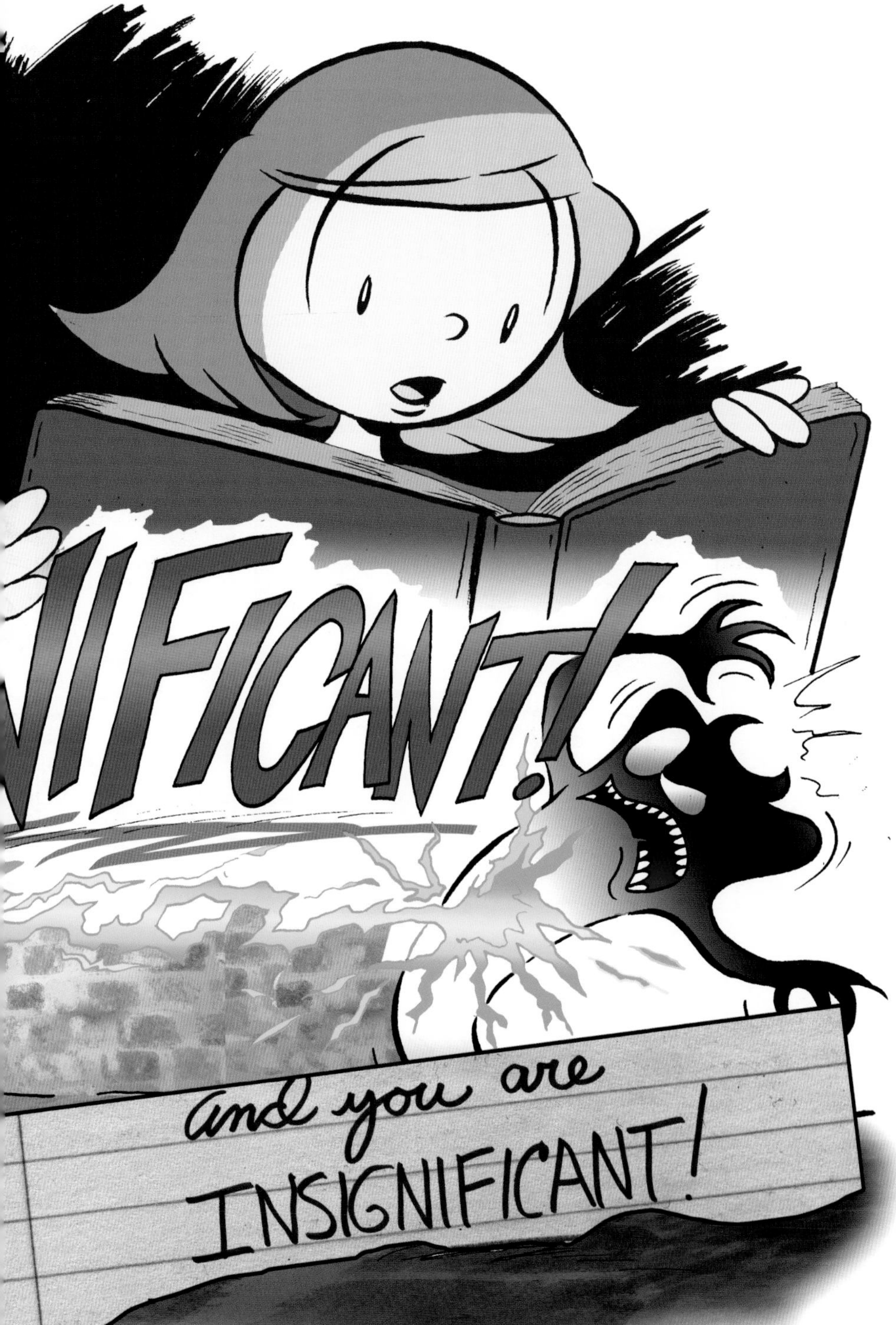
NIFICANT!
and you are
INSIGNIFICANT!

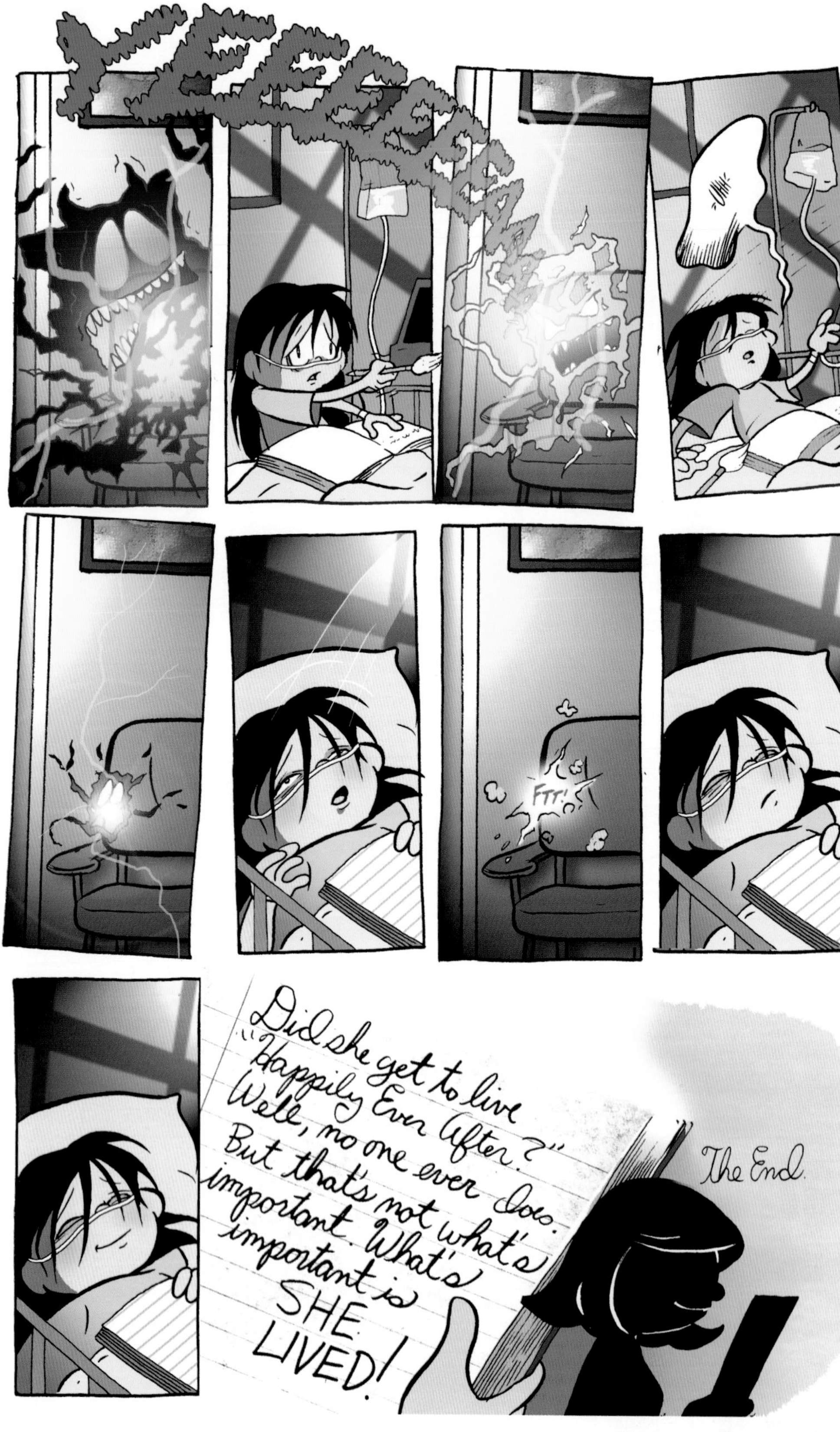
-UHH-
FTT!
Did she get to live "Happily Ever After?"
Well, no one ever does.
But that's not what's important. What's important is SHE LIVED!
The End.

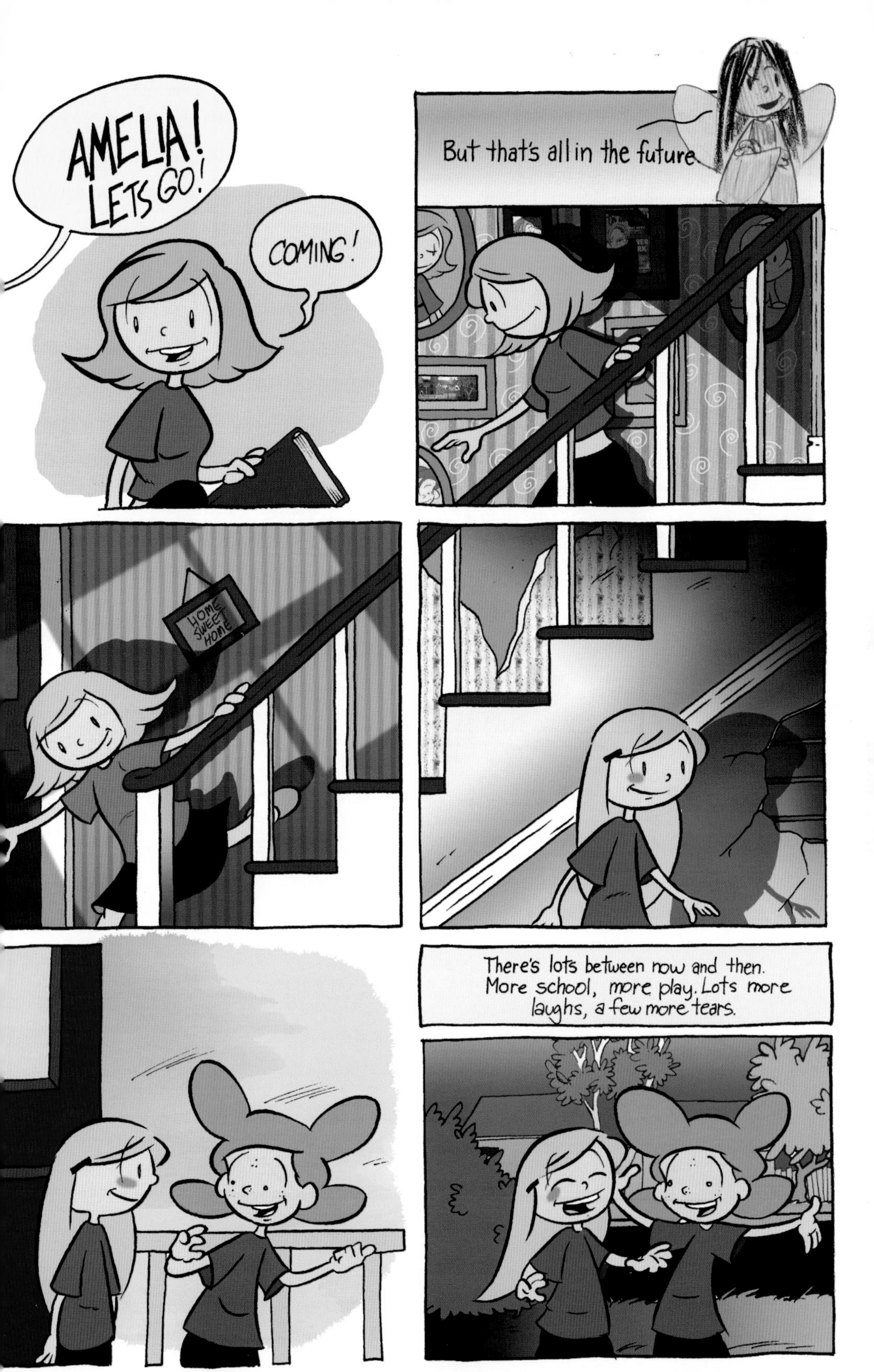
AMELIA! LETS GO!
COMING!
But that's all in the future.
HOME SWEET HOME
There's lots between now and then. More school, more play. Lots more laughs, a few more tears.

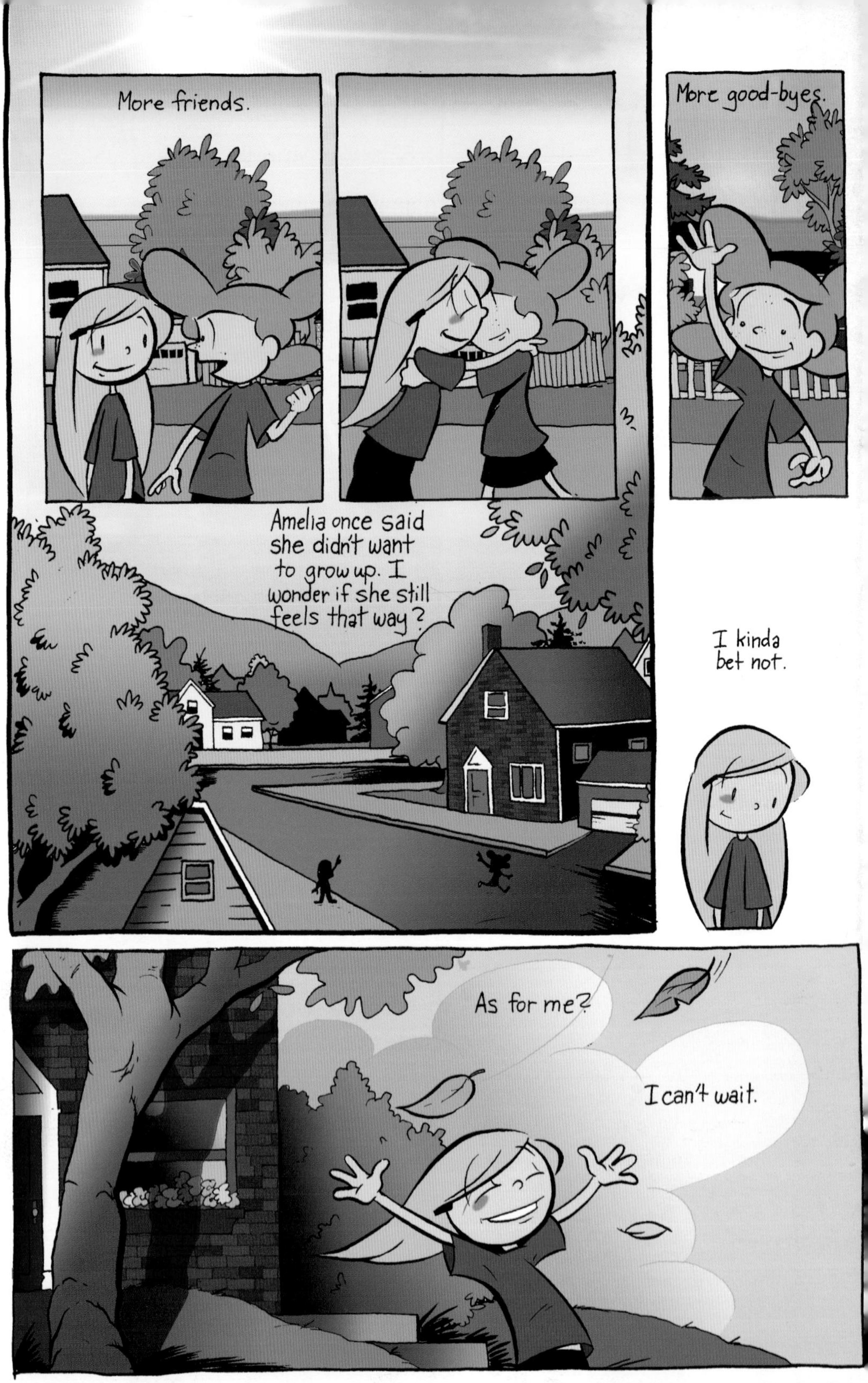
More friends.
More good-byes.
Amelia once said she didn't want to grow up. I wonder if she still feels that way?
I kinda bet not.
As for me?
I can't wait.